Bloodhunters v2: Blue Blood

Xine Fury

Bloodhunters Volume 2: Blue Blood

Contents

Part 1

Part 2

Bonus Story: The Lives of Wisp

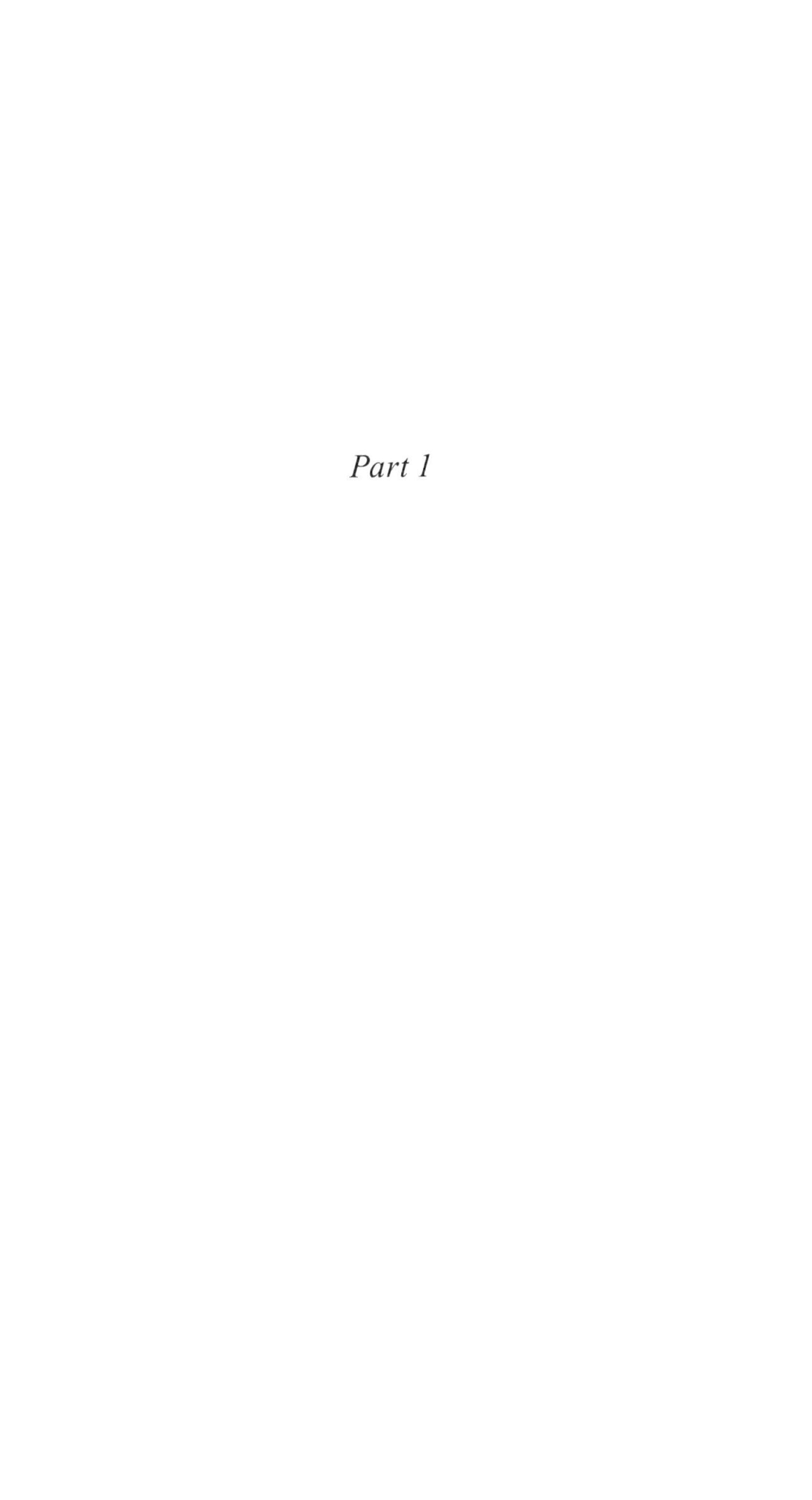

Part 1

01.00 *I Know Who You Are*

ED0012.28.2500

The wind howled around Whisper's helmet, and she felt the chill air even through her insulated flightsuit. She felt exposed out in the open like this, but she couldn't use her stealth abilities. She could only draw in shadows when there were shadows to draw, and out here, in the frigid arctic wastes, there was blinding whiteness as far as the eye could see.

At least it stopped snowing, she thought. The truth was, she probably could have parked closer, but she didn't want anyone on the Bloodwind tracking her location. In retrospect, that had been pointless. She was headed towards the only building on this entire icy continent, and leaving a deep trail along the way. Anyone who tracked her shuttle would have no problem figuring out her destination. In taking the extra precaution, all she'd really done was to ensure she'd be too tired to fight when she got there.

If she got there. That last blizzard had been a doozy, and she could swear that the building just kept getting farther away the longer she walked. Not that she wanted to speed things up. As tough as this walk was, she dreaded what was waiting for her inside.

"I know who you are," the note had said. Then, on the back, "I have a job for you. Meet me alone or I will tell everyone your secret." Underneath that, it listed the planet and the coordinates of the building. Two days earlier, the note literally fell out of the sky. Whisper had been on a mission, when a small silver orb flew up to her, dropped the envelope, and flew away. The drone self-destructed once it was at a safe distance, thereby making the sender untraceable.

Whisper wondered what they could possibly have planned for her. Were they just going to turn her in for the reward? Maybe, but if so, threatening to expose her identity was an odd choice. After all, if they turned her in, her identity would be exposed anyway. But somehow this "job" the note mentioned was even more chilling than the prospect of getting arrested. What if they wanted her to assassinate someone? She'd rather be executed than be forced to kill an innocent person.

No, if that happened, she'd run, and adopt a new identity elsewhere. She'd miss her friends – some more than others – but then, those friendships were doomed anyway. She couldn't hide her identity forever. Someday she'd be found out, and the bonds she'd formed with the Bloodwind crew would be broken.

But maybe she was jumping the gun. There was still a chance she'd be able to get out of this. Maybe she'd be able to defeat this would-be blackmailer at their own game. Maybe they could come to a deal. Maybe the job they offered wouldn't be so evil.

Are you listening to yourself? she thought. *Life doesn't work that way.* Whoever this person was, they weren't hiring Whisper to pick up milk from the grocery store. If they just wanted a bounty hunter, they would have hired someone through the Bounty Hunter Registry. No, if they really had a job for Whisper specifically, then they needed her stealth skills, and that meant they were up to something shady. Something Whisper would most definitely not want to do. But she

would hear them out before she said no. The alternative –
having her identity exposed, finding a new persona, and
losing all her friends – was just too much.

The facility wasn't much farther now. The black
rectangular building stood out like the nose on a polar bear.
As the only sign of civilization in many kilometers, Whisper
didn't even have to look at her GPS. This was the place. She
hesitated for one more moment – was she doing the right
thing? Giving in to a blackmailer? But she wouldn't be able
to sleep until she found out how much they knew, and what
they wanted from her. Taking a deep breath, she continued
her hike.

The afternoon heat felt like it would boil Bloodstone alive.
Her helmet's internal cooling system worked overtime as
she trekked across the dry, cracked dirt. But the sun's heat
was nothing compared to the anger raging through her soul.
She couldn't stand it when other people had control of the
situation, and it infuriated her that she was giving in to this
demand.

She looked at the message again. "Greetings Datan
Taush," it said, followed by a cryptic job offer and a set of
coordinates. She had received the message on her
Bloodstone account. Whoever had sent it, they knew her
deadname, a name she'd abandoned years ago. Bloodstone
had used every trick she had to trace the sender, but
whoever it was, their tech skills were top-notch. She'd even
tried replying to it, but the number was no longer in service.

It better not be the damn Grunthians again, she thought. It had
barely been two weeks since the Grunthians coerced her
into helping them, under the threat of outing her to the
galaxy. Come to think of it, that mission had also ended up
with her trekking through a heat-scorched landscape. They
had promised to leave her alone after that – or at least
implied it – and Bloodstone was going to be furious if they
tried to blackmail her again so soon.

As she walked, she thought about the limits she would go to in order to protect her identity. She liked that fugitives found her mysterious Bloodstone persona intimidating, and she'd been able to use her celebrity status to request higher rates. But she also dreamed of the day when everyone would call her by her true name, Detanna Taush. It was a long-term goal. She just needed to milk Bloodstone's fame a bit longer, so she could save up for a major transition procedure.

On the other hand, she knew her reputation was deeper than the mask. She'd still be able to get plenty of work if the universe learned she was a trans woman. And she'd still be able to demand top dollar. But she refused to let someone else decide when it was the right time. If this person was planning to threaten her into working for free, they were going to be disappointed… or, more likely, disintegrated.

Fueled by anger, Bloodstone stomped toward the lone concrete hut, wishing she'd parked just a little bit closer.

"Come back to us," the voice had said. It was the last thing Yna remembered from her dream. As it faded, she stumbled out of bed and into the restroom. As she passed the mirror, she did a double take. For just a moment, she'd seen two people in the mirror. Her human face and her energy form, superimposed on top of each other. Now wide awake, she studied her reflection. Everything looked normal now. She touched her hand to her face and felt nothing but flesh.

I must have still been dreaming, she thought, turning away from the mirror. But as she turned her head, for just a second, she thought she saw it again.

Raven, Trenyn, and Dervish were eating breakfast in the galley when Yna shuffled in, Panther trotting along behind her. Yna moved like a zombie, her eyes barely open.

"Did you even go to bed?" Dervish asked.

"Bad night," Yna replied. "Weird dreams."

What about? Trenyn asked. They were fascinated by human dreams. Navorans didn't dream the same way humans did. Instead, their sleeping minds went into a receptive mode, where they saw the thoughts of other Navorans all night. They called it the mindweb, and it was one of the reasons Navorans had no concept of privacy. Except that here on the Bloodwind, light years away from their home planet or any other Navorans, Trenyn was out of the mindweb's range. The only thoughts they heard at night were Raven's.

"I don't really remember," Yna said, grabbing some cereal out of a cabinet. "I saw my energy form a lot. I think there were other people like me."

Maybe it means you're lonely, Trenyn proposed. *Subconsciously you wish you had more peers.*

"You've got us," Dervish said, standing up and hugging Yna around the shoulders.

"I just wish I knew where I was from," Yna said. "Or why I can do what I do."

"Don't worry, Yna," Raven said. "We've got some new tests we can run on you. If you want to stop by the medbay later, we'll give you our… undivided…" her voice trailed off as her comm unit chimed. She studied the screen with a perplexed expression.

What's wrong? Trenyn asked, but Raven just shook her head.

"Excuse me," Raven said, and left.

Trenyn's skin yellowed with worry.

The wide, black building had no windows, and the large metal doors were partially blocked by the snow. Whisper couldn't find any other tracks leading to the building, or any evidence that it had recently been entered. She tried opening a door, but it was both locked and rusted shut. She walked around the side of the building, looking for more doors. Every door she found was similarly locked and rusted. She looked up at the roof. The structure was only two stories tall. Climbing on top of a nearby snowdrift, she took out her whip, latched it onto a pipe, and climbed onto the roof.

This is ridiculous, she thought. She already didn't want to do this, and now she had to work for it? The nerve of some blackmailers.

There was very little snow cover on the roof, the majority of which was covered with solar panels. Whisper wandered around, stepping over steam pipes and utility boxes until she found a maintenance hatch. It was locked, but not as securely as the doors below, and Whisper managed to break in with little effort.

Once inside, she found that the building was only one story after all, it just had high ceilings. She climbed down a ladder that led to a catwalk, and got a feel for the layout of the building. It was a massive storage unit. Wooden and metal crates lined every wall, some stacked almost to the ceiling. The lights were on, but she couldn't see or hear anyone else in the building.

Using her Auroran abilities to muffle her footsteps, she walked the length of the catwalk. There was an office in one corner, but she could see the lights were off from here. There were also some restrooms and a few storage closets. But there was one thing that stood out, that seemed out of place in the otherwise pristine storage facility. In the center of the floor, where the building's two largest paths crossed, there was a small folding table with a single chair. She could see a small metal box on top of the table. There was no way that table was supposed to be there, where it would have blocked forklifts and foot traffic.

Whisper considered hiding, to see if her blackmailer came by. But the more she thought about it, the more she just wanted to get this over with. There was no way she hadn't been spotted on the way in, so there was no point in continuing her stealth now. She hopped off the catwalk, onto a crate, another crate, and finally the floor. She walked over to the table and sat down. The metal box turned out to be a speaker, with a single red button. She pressed the button and waited.

"Alterra Sarr," a voice said. It was deep and electronically disguised. Whisper couldn't tell if the speaker was male or female, much less their species.

"I am the bounty hunter known as Whisper," she replied. Even if this person knew her identity, she didn't want to confirm it. Especially if she was being recorded.

"Have it your way," the voice said. "Whisper. I have a job for you."

"Why didn't you go through the Registry?"

"I can't go through legal channels," the voice said. "I need you to retrieve a family heirloom. It was stolen from my family generations ago. In the eyes of the law, it belongs to the family that stole it."

"Why me, though?" Whisper asked. "If you can't hire a bounty hunter, just hire a thief."

"It is guarded in a very secure location," the voice said. "Only someone with your skills could possibly retrieve it."

"Will I be paid?" Not that she actually cared about the money. But she was playing the role of Whisper, not Alterra. If she was being filmed, she wanted it on record that she behaved like a bounty hunter instead of a fugitive.

"You will be paid ten thousand credits," the voice said. "But you won't do it for the money. You'll do it because you know what will happen if you don't."

Whisper thought for a moment. It wasn't such a bad deal. Even if this mysterious employer was lying about their claim to the heirloom, Whisper didn't care. It was one thing to steal a hovercar from someone who lives paycheck to paycheck, thereby totally disrupting their life. But this was just transferring some random object – which only had value because some appraiser arbitrarily deemed it so – from one wealthy person's vault, to another wealthy person's vault. No one would be hurt, no one would starve. Some trillionaire would have one less bauble to brag about.

And if her employer was being honest about the object's origins, so much the better.

"If I do this for you," Whisper said, "How do I know you won't blackmail me again when you want something else?"

"You don't," the voice said. "You have no reason to trust my word, but you have it anyway. After this job, there is nothing else I need from you."

Whisper sighed. She couldn't trust them, but she didn't feel she had a choice. "Where is this heirloom?"

The android looked human, but not so much that anyone would ever be fooled. Its skin was made of peach-colored rubber, and it had very limited facial expressions. It wore a threadbare tuxedo, and it reminded Bloodstone of a life-size ventriloquist's dummy.

"Welcome, friend," it said. "Welcome welcome welllllcome! Won't you have a seat?" The android gestured to the only pieces of furniture in the hut, a small wooden table with two chairs.

Bloodstone sat down. "Why am I here?" she asked.

"Can I get you anything?" the android asked. "Coffee maybe?"

"Sit," Bloodstone demanded, her voice rising. "What do you want?"

The android shrugged and sat down. "As you wish. I apologize for my hospitality. You're here because someone needs a job done, and you're the best."

"Then why not just hire me through the Registry?" Bloodstone asked.

"Because the man we need to catch is above the law. He has more m-m-m-money than he could spend in ten lifetimes. He's paid off IGP agents, judges, and even kings. There is no way he will ever be charged with a crime."

"If he can't be charged, what's the point of me bringing him in?" Bloodstone asked, dreading what she knew was coming. Unlicensed bounty hunters were often just glorified assassins, and Bloodstone wanted no part of that lifestyle.

"Because you won't be bringing him in," the android said. "You will simply bring us his private financial records."

"I won't kill... wait, what?" It wasn't what Bloodstone had been expecting to hear.

"This man is the worrrrst," the android said, slurring the last word. It was obvious that it had been repurposed for this encounter. Whatever its original function had been, it had probably been out of commission for decades before being reactivated. "He owns a planet, and he sells his own citizens for their organs. But he uses layers and layers of false paperwork to keep his reputation clean. But he's also meticulous. He keeps track of everything he does. Find those records, and we can finally prove... prove... prooooove... his crimes, freeze his assets, and bring him to justice."

"And my pay?" Bloodstone asked.

"Ten thousand credits, and we keep your identity a secret," the android said.

Bloodstone nodded. It was good money and good incentive. "If you betray me," she said, "there's no place in the galaxy your employer can hide from me."

"We have no reason to betray you," the android said. "All we want is justice."

"I'll take the job."

Raven read the message one more time. She'd received it once before, but she'd dismissed it as junk mail. This time, however, she read the text more carefully. There were some private details in there, things that no one should know but her. Either she'd been hacked, or this was on the level. And she used so many layers of security, she would have known if she'd been hacked.

The message was from a man named Cyric Vermon, and he claimed to be her half-brother. Raven didn't find that too hard to believe. Her father had been married multiple times, to a variety of women, and he probably hadn't been faithful to any of them. Raven may well have had dozens of half-siblings running around out there.

It was the next part she had trouble accepting. Apparently, Cyric was a member of something called "The Council of Heirs," a group of Lord Vermon's children, all of whom shared claim to the throne of Valos. It was one thing to find out she had family, but quite another to wake up and learn she was royalty. It was a lot to take in, and she had a big decision to make.

Seen as a whole, the security system looked impenetrable. Laser grid, motion detectors, armed guards, fingerprint scanners, pressure plates, and every other cliché anti-theft device that helped trillionaires sleep better at night. But taken one layer at a time, they were nothing Whisper hadn't cracked before. She studied the layout, observed the guards' habits, picked a few pockets, planned her route, and made her move.

Three floors above, seven guards lay unconscious in the study. A tiny red drone undocked from Bloodstone's wrist, and hovered in front of the study entrance, standing guard. Bloodstone scanned the walls, looking for hidden safes. There were three, but two were decoys, filled with explosives to take out any would-be burglars. Bloodstone pulled a painting off the wall and studied the third safe's locks. She would need to hack five separate codes to unlock the door. *Only five? Child's play,* she thought, and got to work.

Lord Mordenn Alistair Primrose the Twelfth was the wealthiest person on the planet Primrose. He knew this because, once he'd purchased the planet, he'd evicted anyone whose wealth even approached his own. Some tycoons wouldn't have stopped there, preferring to eliminate the poor and middle class as well. But not Lord Primrose. He needed those citizens, they were his planet's chief export. These insignificant people lived their humdrum lives unaware that the entire planet was just one big organ farm.

But today, those people were rioting. Lord Primrose woke to learn that sometime during the night, there had been a major break-in. The thief, or more likely a team of thieves, had struck in two places. One of his most precious artifacts, a priceless heirloom his ancestors had stolen from a rival family, was now missing. And his account logs, proof of every illegal transaction he'd made, had been taken from his study. Why hadn't someone woken him up immediately? How had these thieves bypassed all of his security measures?

But it didn't matter now. The damage had been done. Outside his window, far down below, he saw news reporters, IGP vehicles, and what had to be several thousand angry citizens swarming the grounds. On the holographic screen above his dresser, he saw his face all over the news, along with the faces of several judges and IGP officers he'd paid off. He wouldn't be able to buy his way out of it this time.

He went to his nightstand, pulled out an energy pistol, and stared at it. Surrender or go down fighting? Would prison be so bad? Surely they wouldn't put a man of his stature in with the common criminals… would they? But he knew better. He put the barrel of the gun against his temple. He closed his eyes, took a deep breath, and pulled the trigger.

Nothing happened. He flipped the weapon over, and saw that the battery was gone. Frantically, he went through the drawer, looking for another battery. He could hear people inside his house now, coming up the stairs. Somewhere in the distance, he heard his name being shouted over an amplifier. He knew he'd put another battery in the drawer, but it was empty, except for what looked like a business card. The side facing up showed a symbol, a star with an eyeball in the center. Primrose recognized it as the symbol of the Inner Eye.

He picked it up and flipped it over. Scrawled on the back, in atrocious handwriting, it said, "No easy way out. - Love, T."

"So they took him alive?"

"He tried to jump out his window, but he just landed on the second-floor balcony and broke his leg. Now he's awaiting trial."

Thresh laughed. "Good. He won't double-cross us again. But I still have one question. If you could get an agent into his bedroom to steal the batteries, why did you need the bounty hunters?"

"That's my business," Tena said, ending the call. Thresh didn't need to know everything. They were partners on one project, but she had many side projects of her own. She didn't need Thresh getting in the way. In fact, once the cannon was complete, she wouldn't need him at all.

Setting her comm unit aside, Tena smiled at her cleverness. Of course she hadn't needed Bloodstone to retrieve those documents. And she had no use for the bauble she'd had Whisper steal. But by blackmailing them, she'd proven the information she had on them was true. After all, they wouldn't have accepted the jobs if they hadn't needed to protect their identities. Bloodstone's secret was useless to Tena, but who knew what she could do with it in the future?

Whisper's secret, on the other hand, meant a great deal to Tena. Not because of the bounty on Alterra's head, but because Tena now knew Alterra was Auroran. When she'd first read that in her father's private notes, she hadn't believed it. Auroris was an urban legend. A planet whose inhabitants were born to be nature's perfect assassins? It had to be a myth. But only an Auroran could have robbed Primrose's vault so easily.

Tena had many uses for Whisper's innate abilities. But not yet. There was no point in capturing her too early, before Tena had the equipment she needed to make use of her. No sense locking Whisper in a cage for a year, keeping her fed and hiding her from Thresh. All that would do is give her more chances to escape. Now that Tena had managed to lure Whisper into her web once, she knew she could do it again, when she was ready for her.

On New Year's Eve, the Bloodwind joined a plethora of spacecraft in orbit around Earth. Every year, Earth hosted the most spectacular interstellar fireworks show in the galaxy. Using multi-stage rockets filled with thousands of timed-release incendiary units, they were able to create beautiful explosions that ordinarily wouldn't be possible in the vacuum of space.

The IGP had almost canceled the event this year. After all, it was the one-year anniversary of the destruction of EarthStation 1, and celebrating with fireworks seemed a bit tasteless. But the organizers had put a positive spin on it. The display was declared to be in honor of those who had died on that day, and any profits received from this year's event would go to their families. The idea still hadn't gone over so well with some people, but the marketing campaign had been very effective, and those offended were now in the minority.

Everyone was present except for Vik, who was visiting family on Earth. The rest of the crew sat on folding chairs in the Bloodwind's cargo bay, watching through a large window on the ship's rear hatch. Ordinarily they kept this window covered with steel panels, but tonight it showed a breathtaking view of the stars.

Whisper wore a casual outfit, just jeans and a T-shirt, and of course, a cloth mask that hid everything but her eyes. Rather than taking in the view, Whisper kept stealing glances at her friends. They'd been together for a year now. She couldn't have been more lucky, falling in with this group. They were good people, even Vik... in his own way.

But as much as she loved them, she was also afraid of them. She felt guilty that she had to hide who she was, and she wondered which one would be the first to turn her in when her identity finally was discovered. Actually, it wasn't much of a puzzle. Bloodstone and Vik would be at each other's throats over which one got the honor. Bloodstone only cared about the reward money, and Vik would try to kill her in a fit of vengeance.

A full year, and she'd made no progress in proving her innocence. The shapeshifter Vraxx was still on the loose, and now apparently someone else knew her identity as well. She could only hope they were true to their word, and wouldn't try to blackmail her again. Whisper sighed, leaned back in her chair, and closed her eyes.

Yna wore her pajamas, and munched on some popcorn as she watched the display. She thought the explosions were pretty, but she kept getting distracted. She hadn't seen any more ghostly images, at least, not full-on. But every time she walked by a mirror, she thought she saw something out of the corner of her eye. She hadn't told anyone yet, and probably wouldn't. Surely it was just her imagination. It would pass.

At first, Panther ran back and forth in front of the window, trying to chase the flashing lights. But after a few minutes he tired of the game, or maybe he just realized the lights were beyond his reach. He curled up behind Yna's chair and daydreamed about a giant tuna steak.

Dervish wasn't sure why this was supposed to be fun. Explosions made her think of war, and war wasn't fun. As she watched, her comm unit vibrated. The message header flashed on her screen. "We've been looking for you," it said. Dervish gasped. Was it the Grunthians? It had to be. Who else would be looking for her? They'd given her to Lord Vermon as a gift, but with him gone, did they want to give her to someone else? Well, she wasn't going to give in without a fight. She had friends now, and she'd picked up some fighting skills over the last year. If they wanted her, they'd have to come get her.

She opened the message. It read, "We've been trying to reach you about your shuttle's extended warranty." Her eyes widened. It was worse than she'd thought. She didn't even own a shuttle.

Raven and Trenyn stared at the fireworks display, not really "enjoying" it per se, but making their own game of it. With each explosion, they each tried to be the first to identify every chemical on display. They played their game telepathically, so as not to annoy the others. They were interrupted by Dervish tapping Trenyn on the shoulder, trying to show them her comm. Trenyn looked at the message and assured her she was in no danger.

Raven had decided to turn down the position on Valos, at least for now. She had no love of politics, and didn't want to take time away from her scientific pursuits. Besides, she had become used to this group of bounty hunters, some more than others, and she wasn't ready to part with them just yet. At the very least she wanted to continue her studies on Yna, and hopefully find a way to make her condition more tolerable.

Detanna wore her armored flightsuit, but her Bloodstone helmet sat on the floor next to her chair. She looked over at Whisper and noticed that her eyes were closed. "What's on your mind?" she asked.

"I was... thinking about Alterra Sarr," Whisper answered. It wasn't a lie.

Detanna nodded. "I know who you are," she said.

Whisper's eyes popped open, and she turned to look at Detanna. "What?" she asked, her hand subconsciously reaching for her whip, which was actually back in her quarters.

"You're a very kind, special person," Detanna clarified. "The kind who hunts down criminals not for the money, but because she doesn't want them to hurt anyone else. And Alterra represents the greatest danger you've ever seen. A woman who would so callously take that many lives is capable of anything. And you're afraid more people will die if she isn't captured soon."

"Something like that," Whisper said.

"Don't worry," Detanna said. "We'll find her. I promise. We won't rest until she's been brought to justice."

Whisper nodded. They were the most threatening words of encouragement she'd ever heard. Once again, she had to admonish herself. What was she thinking? She should be hiding out on the most remote planet she could find, living her life in solitude. But no, apparently she'd decided to hang out with the one woman in the galaxy most likely to catch her. Not to mention an ex-cop who was out for her blood.

But she knew why she was here. A life in hiding wasn't a life worth living. If she wanted to prove her innocence, she had to be proactive. Her best bet would be to find Vraxx, and this group had a better chance of finding him than anyone else in the galaxy.

She sighed and looked out the window. Controversy aside, it really was a well-done display, with burst after burst of bright colors.

One year down. One year on the run. Would next year be any better? She would have to wait and see.

01.01 Closure

ED.02501.01.01

Vik circled the colossal steel orb, looking for Zhari's name. It was the first anniversary of the destruction of IGP EarthStation 1. It was crowded at the memorial, and many people honored their loved ones by placing flowers on the pedestal below the hovering sphere.

Roughly fourteen thousand names were laser-etched onto the sphere. There were four levels of catwalks surrounding the sphere, so that people could reach out and touch the names of their loved ones. Vik was on the ground level. The names were listed alphabetically, and Zhari Ze-Rastt would be near the bottom.

He could have just stood still, and waited for the slowly rotating sphere to bring her name into view. But Vik had never been a "stand still" kind of guy. Of course, he might have found her name a little faster if he'd walked counter to the sphere's rotation instead of with it, but Vik also wasn't always a "think it through" kind of guy.

So what kind of guy was Vik? Brave, a man of action, a hero at heart. Brash but conservative. Distrustful of new ideas, but fiercely protective of his friends. The kind of man who would accuse a progressive activist of corrupting the galaxy's youth, but would jump in front of an energy blast to save the activist's life.

He found Zhari's name and placed his hand against the cool steel. He held his hand still, just in front of her name, letting the sphere's rotation move the letters across his palm. As the grooves of each engraved letter tickled his palm, he tried his hardest to feel something in his heart. He concentrated on her beautiful face, her sense of humor, her eclectic taste in music, her frenetic personality, her perfect body.

Still nothing. He was sorry that her life had been taken from her so unfairly, but that was true of every name on the sphere. He was beyond angry at Alterra Sarr for taking away what was his. But was Zhari ever anything more to him than a possession? He came here seeking proof that he and Zhari had actually been in love, but he was going to leave empty-handed.

They were engaged. Had he dodged a bullet there? *Vik, No!* He chastised himself for his callousness. Whether or not she and Vik were soulmates, Zhari was a wonderful person, and she deserved way better than this. Still, he tried to imagine the future they would have had together, and came up empty.

He walked away from the memorial. There were other names he'd intended to find, friends who meant as much to him as his fiancée had, but he no longer felt the need to see them. They were just words etched on metal.

As he returned to his shuttle, his comm beeped. He saw who was calling and ignored the call. Zhari's parents. He would talk to them when he got there. As long as he was in town, he'd promised to visit Zhari's family and pick up some things he'd left at their place. Probably just some T-shirts and his guitar.

Technically "in town" in this case was nearly ten thousand kilometers away in Kyoto, but Vik didn't get to Earth very often, so anywhere on the planet felt like a short distance. The comm beeped again during the flight. Vik rolled his eyes and answered. "Vik?" It was Zhari's mother, Zeneva, and she sounded distraught.

"This is Vik. What's wrong?"

"It's Zeva," she wailed. "Someone's taken her." Zeva was Zhari's younger sister. She was only a year younger than Zhari, and would be graduating college soon.

"Have you called the police?"

"Yes, we just filed a report," she said. "But you know how they are. We need you."

Vik did, indeed, know how they were. A kidnapping on Earth would be handled by local police, not the IGP. And Earth police were notorious for putting non-human cases on the back burner. "I'll be there as soon as I can," he told her, then hung up. Vik wasn't sure if he'd ever loved Zhari, but he'd be damned if he'd let her family lose another daughter.

"We took a skytram to the memorial this morning," Zeneva said. "To honor our Zhari. Zeva stayed here. She's studying for exams. When we got back, she was gone. And our tree looked like this." They were on the front porch, and Zeneva indicated the effigy on the front lawn.

Someone had taken a large stuffed cat, put a noose on it, and hung it from a tree branch in their front yard. The stuffed animal – based on an ancient comic strip about a lasagna-loving tabby – had a note pinned to it that read "Pusses go home." It was a common slur for Zhari's catlike species. There were also egg yolks running down the house's windows, and a baseball bat lying on the lawn.

"Was there any sign of forced entry?" Vik asked.

"I don't know, nothing looked broken," Zeneva replied, tears running down her gray-furred, feline face.

"Anything broken or missing inside the home?"

"No. I don't think they ever came inside the house." She had answered some similar questions at the police department downtown earlier. Her husband was still downtown, probably making a pest of himself. Not that it would help.

Vik thought for a moment, then asked, "Is Zeva the type of person who would hide and call the police, or was she more confrontational?" Vik had only met Zeva once, at a family dinner. She was usually off at college when Vik visited.

"She is headstrong. She would have yelled at them to go away. Also," she said, pointing at the baseball bat, "that is hers."

Vik nodded. Some hate group probably just wanted to send a message, maybe thinking they weren't home. But when Zeva came outside, they'd seen an opportunity.

"I'll need to research the local hate groups," Vik said, thinking out loud. "Zeneva, could you ask your neighbors if they saw anything? Talk to everyone you can, and let me know what you find out."

"I will. Please find her," Zeneva begged.

Vik called the local police, but they were no help. Then he looked up an old friend in the IGP, Doctor G'Heesh Eshton. "Esh," as Vik liked to call him, was the scientist in charge of the program that gave Vik his antigravity abilities. Even though Esh was halfway around the world, he was able to access Kyoto's police records faster than the local police department. And being an alien himself, Esh understood all too well how useless the local police would be. He had no qualms about circumventing police protocol if it meant saving a life.

He found what he could and sent Vik the data. Three local gangs were known for committing hate crimes against non-humans. Each had its own gang colors.

Vik checked back in with Zeneva. None of her neighbors had seen anything, but the house across the street caught some video on their doorbell camera. The video wasn't the best quality, but it confirmed the scenario they suspected.

An old beat-up hovercar parked in front of the house. Several guys got out, threw eggs at the house, and set up the effigy.

Zeva stepped out to yell at them, wielding the bat. It looked like they teased her for a bit, she took a few swings, then they rushed her. She managed to kick one in the neck, sending him staggering backward, and she got another one across the knees with her bat. But then they overwhelmed her, dragged her into the car, and sped away.

The gang members wore black leather jackets and red execution hoods. But most importantly, they wore armbands colored red and orange. These were the colors of the Nova Wolves. Vik filed through the data Esh had sent him, locating the addresses of known Nova Wolves hideouts.

Vik wasted no time. He had to borrow Zeneva's hovercar, since he had taken an autotaxi here from the shuttleport. She wanted to come with him, but he wouldn't allow it. As a courtesy, Vik called the local police while en route, to see if the new evidence would light a fire under them. They put him on hold, and he was still on hold when he arrived at his destination. "Useless," Vik spat, getting out of the hovercar. He sent a quick text message to the police chief, just to make sure someone knew where he was.

He was hesitant to leave the hovercar parked here. He was pretty sure he would come back to find the Levatech boosters gone. But Zeva's life was more important than a car. "Sorry, Zeneva," he whispered, as he walked away from the vehicle.

Vik was dressed in civilian clothing. A denim jacket, jeans, and a plain gray T-shirt. He hoped he wouldn't stand out too much in this neighborhood. The denizens of these slums could probably spot a plainclothes cop from a kilometer away, and even though Vik was no longer an IGP officer, he retained that look about him. Yep, he already saw a few suspicious stares from some people sitting on their front stoops.

Still, the locals didn't have to know he was here for the Nova Wolves. There was a pawn shop on the corner, and he walked towards it. Just an undercover cop following up on some stolen goods. Probably happened a lot in this neighborhood.

Upon reaching the pawn shop, he ducked into the alley behind it, and jumped to the roof. From there, he jumped to the higher roof of the building next door. He jumped from roof to roof until he found the building he needed. It was an old apartment building. At some point in the past, it had been ravaged by a fire, taking out everything but the walls and floors. Ironically, even the fire escape had somehow burned away and collapsed into the alley below.

None of the windows had glass. The windows on the first three floors were boarded up, but those on the top two floors were completely open. The building itself was made of fireproof styrogene bricks, a lab-grown product made to withstand pretty much anything. It wasn't used much anymore, because it gave off toxic fumes if the weather got too warm. Good thing it was January.

He landed on the roof, but there was no rooftop stairwell. The fire escape probably once granted roof access. He climbed down the side of the building, using his Levatech implants to cling to the outside wall. He peeked inside a top-floor window, which, like the rest of the building's windows, had no glass. Seeing no signs of life, he climbed through.

He was in a one-bedroom apartment. The floor was a burned-out mess, and it didn't look like it had been used in a while. The carpet, wallpaper, insulation, and furniture were gone. The floors themselves were made of styrogene planks, so they remained strong. Judging by the amount of bird excrement on the floors, the fire had happened years ago. But the building still smelled faintly of charcoal. As he passed the former bathroom, he noted that even the toilet had melted. What happened to this place? Were they experimenting with homemade napalm?

Vik stepped through the open doorway – apparently the doors hadn't been styrogene – and quietly walked down the hall, passing a few more open apartments. At the end of the hallway, he reached a stairwell. *Well, I suppose that's why they don't use the top floors*, Vik thought, looking down the stairless shaft. For obvious reasons, Vik wasn't afraid of heights. He hopped down to the landing, then down to the fourth floor. He used his Levatech to slow his fall, not just to avoid injury, but to keep from being heard.

The fourth floor was just as deserted as the fifth had been, except there were some boxes pushed against some of the walls. He took a quick peek in each of the rooms, just to make sure Zeva wasn't tied up in one of them. He also looked in some of the boxes. They were full of old clothing, some of it bloodstained.

Then Vik listened at the stairwell, making sure the third floor was quiet before jumping down. He jumped to the landing, then froze. From the landing, he could see into the bedroom across the hall. From his angle, he could just see the lower edge of an old mattress on the floor, and a pair of feet on it. He would have to be extra quiet from here on out.

He stared down over the edge of the landing. The shaft went all the way down to the basement. Starting with the level below, there were steel ladders bolted to the walls next to the stairwell doorways, making it possible for the Nova Wolves to get between floors. Vik pondered his next move. If he kept searching floor by floor, he increased the chances of being seen, and then it would be him against dozens of people.

Instead, he needed to decide which floor they were most likely to be keeping Zeva on, and head straight there. If he'd had more time, he'd have waited until the early morning, when he imagined most of the gang would be asleep. But Zeva was on borrowed time as it was, if it wasn't already too late.

Well, they wouldn't want to keep her on the first floor. She might cry out, run out the door, or find another way to attract attention. And he didn't see them carrying her up one of those ladders unless they had to. So the basement seemed most likely. Peering down the shaft, he noted that there were lights on in the basement.

Vik used his implants to cling to the wall. He climbed around the side of the stairwell until he was next to the doorway. Then he started climbing downward. He was tempted to just drop, and slow his fall towards the bottom, but that kind of movement might attract attention. From here, he could hear people talking on the floors below him. For a second he thought he even heard cheering.

Footsteps approached the doorway on the first floor. A green-haired gang member reached for the ladder, intent on climbing to the second floor. When he looked up, he spotted Vik.

Change of plan. Vik let go of the wall and dropped like a stone. The gang member opened his mouth to say something, but in one smooth motion, Vik grabbed him. One hand over the mouth, the other around the waist. Vik pulled the thug off the ladder, and both of them landed softly in front of the basement doorway.

As soon as they landed, Vik let go of the thug, pulled out his stun gun, and shot him. The gang member fell to the floor, unconscious. Now that he was at basement level, Vik could hear a great deal of cheering and hollering, and he ducked to the side of the doorway to peek in.

Beyond the doorway, the basement was one large room. He could see at least twenty gang members watching something, their bodies blocking whatever the event was from Vik's view. At least their backs were to him, so he was able to slip in unnoticed. He jumped to the ceiling and held on for a better view.

In the far corner, Zeva and a gang member faced off in a one-on-one fight. The thug was armed with an AON dagger, while Zeva just had the claws on the tips of her fingers. Both opponents had a few cuts and scratches. Zeva was barefoot, wearing only shorts and a bra. Vik shuddered to think what they'd already put her through so far. The rest of the Nova Wolves formed a human wall around the fight, making sure she couldn't make a run for it. They cheered for their friend and mocked their captive, calling Zeva a wide variety of racial slurs.

Vik drew his gun. How many could he take out before they overwhelmed him? Five? Six? Some of them had guns, too, and theirs probably weren't set on stun. But he couldn't wait much longer. Sooner or later, one of them would turn their head and see Vik hanging from the ceiling. He dropped to the floor and pulled out his comm unit.

He still had his IGP-issued comm, which doubled as an amplifier. He stepped back into the stairwell and hid beside the doorway. Cranking the comm unit's volume up to maximum, he shouted into it, "Attention Nova Wolves! This is the police! The building is surrounded! Come out with your hands up!"

Then he leaped straight up, landing in the fourth-floor doorway. He heard the entire building erupt into movement below him. Gang members filed out of the basement, all trying to climb the ladder at once. Vik ran to the window and jumped onto the roof of the building next door. On the bottom two floors, he could see faces peering between the slats of the boarded-up windows.

A door on the ground level opened slightly, and Vik fired a stun blast through it. He must have hit someone, because he could hear the cacophony of chaos even from up there. He jumped back through the window of the Nova Wolves hideout, and jumped down the stairwell. Maybe while the gang was upstairs watching for cops, he could just grab Zeva and go.

There were two gang members left in the basement, having stayed behind to watch the prisoner. One of them was holding her, while the other held a gun aimed at her head. As soon as Vik entered the basement, he held up his hand and aimed an empty palm at the gun. It flew out of the thug's hand, sailed across the room, and into Vik's grasp. With his other hand, he shot the thug with his stun gun.

The other gang member – the same one who had been fighting Zeva earlier – held her in front of him as a shield. One hand was wrapped around her waist, and the other held the AON dagger to her throat. "Drop the guns, man, or she dies!" he threatened. With her free hand, Zeva reached down and grabbed the gang member's crotch… claws fully extended. Dropping to his knees, he let out a scream so loud they could probably hear it across town.

"Vik!" Zeva squealed, running over to him. She gave him a quick hug. Her fur was damp and smelled like urine. He could feel welts on her back. Vik wasn't looking forward to hearing her describe the ordeal later. But he would listen just the same, both to provide emotional support and to help her file a police statement.

They heard people climbing down the ladder, probably responding to that scream. "You know how to use this?" Vik asked, setting the thug's pistol on stun before handing it to her.

"Top of my firearms class," she answered.

"What's your major, anyway?" Vik asked.

"Criminology with a minor in psychology," she said. "But I'm there on an athletics scholarship. Mixed martial arts." She winked.

Vik admired her upbeat attitude, after all she'd been through. She was so much like her sister. Strong emotions came rushing back to him, feelings he had suppressed for a full year. Suddenly he didn't just miss Zhari, he longed for her, he needed her, he felt empty without her. But there wasn't time for any of that right now.

Nova Wolves started filing through the door, but Vik and Zeva easily picked them off. The ladder made it difficult to rush the basement in greater numbers. Vik's biggest worry at the moment was blocking off the doorway with too many unconscious bodies. "Let them get farther in before dropping them!" Vik shouted, using his power to pull one of the bodies away from the doorway.

"But then they have more time to shoot us!" she shouted back. She did have a point.

After they dispatched twelve or so Nova Wolves, they stopped coming down. Vik and Zeva carefully approached the doorway to the stairwell, listening. Vik stuck his head out, peering upwards. It was too quiet. Had the rest of them evacuated, or was it a trap? They quietly stepped into the stairwell.

Something tumbled down from the first-floor doorway. It was small, about the size of a coin. It bounced across the floor, into the basement doorway, making a clinking sound as it rolled and skipped across the concrete. Vik's instincts kicked in. With one arm he grabbed Zeva around the waist, and with the other he grabbed the nearest unconscious gang member. Holding both of them tightly, he jumped up to the fifth-floor doorway. Just behind him, an explosion rocked the building, filling the basement level with fire.

Vik set the gang member down and walked Zeva over to a window. On the street level below, Nova Wolves fled the building, scattering in all directions. And miracle of miracles, sirens wailed in the distance as police hovercars sped into view.

Vik had Zeva grab him across the shoulders, and he once again leaped from rooftop to rooftop, returning to the car. Against all odds, the Ze-Rastt family automobile was still parked where Vik had left it, untouched. They would file a police report later. For now, he had to get Zeva to her mother.

They made it home. After a tearful reunion with her parents, Zeva showered, changed, and bandaged a few cuts. Then they spent a couple of hours at the police department, after which Vik took the family out for dinner. Zeva was in a surprisingly good mood after such a traumatic day. She talked with great fervor about how she'd been the one to challenge the gang member to a fight, on the promise that they'd set her free if she won. She'd known they'd never honor such a deal, but it had bought her some time.

After dinner they went home, and the Ze-Rastts invited Vik to stay the night. After the parents went to bed, Zeva was too wired to sleep. She and Vik sat up all night. First they talked about the events of the day, Zeva finally recounting the parts she didn't want to say in front of her worried parents. How they had ripped off her shirt. The groping, the whipping. At one point they'd tied her up and took turns peeing on her. If she hadn't suggested the one-on-one fight, she was sure they would have raped or killed her next.

She finally broke down in tears at around midnight. Vik held her close, letting her sob it out. Vik told her how brave she was, and mentioned how much she reminded him of her sister. This sparked a whole new conversation, both of them reminiscing, telling their favorite Zhari stories. Vik eagerly listened to Zeva's anecdotes, laughing at things he'd never known about his late girlfriend. Zeva gave Vik her undivided attention, as he remembered all the little quirks he'd found so endearing.

The way Zhari purred in her sleep. How she couldn't stand to talk to people who were chewing gum. The way she hoarded bottle caps. Her passion for bad movies. The way she could never find anything in her purse. Her collection of coins from other planets. The way her ears perked up when she heard a strange noise.

God, how he'd loved her.

Vik left around dawn, not having slept, but somehow feeling more rested than he had in a while. He promised Zeva he would keep in touch, and he kept his word. They wrote to each other at least once a week, for a little over a year. Right up until the day Vik vanished.

01.02   *A Girl and Her Cat*

ED.02501.02.17

Yna rode through the streets and alleys, enjoying the wind on her face. She held on to Panther's neck as if for dear life, but in truth, she trusted her mount more than anyone she'd ever known. They were perfectly in tune with each other; if she lost her grip even a little, he slowed down until she could get a better purchase.

Panther bounded onto a trash bin, then leaped to a low roof, getting a running start before jumping over the street to another roof on the other side. This wasn't the most efficient route to their destination, but it sure was fun. Yna glanced at the comm on her wrist, which currently displayed a GPS. "More that way," Yna shouted, pointing her finger. Panther veered in the direction she indicated, leaping over another alley. A woman tending a rooftop garden screamed as the huge cat landed in front of her, then pounced over her head and bounded away. "Sorry!" Yna yelled behind her.

They were almost there. Yna went over the instructions in her head. Knock twice, then give the passphrase. "Red meat." She repeated it over and over in her head. She was extremely nervous. This mission would require a bit of acting, which was not her strong suit. But Vik was on standby, ready to come to her aid if she got into trouble. When her mission was complete, he'd alert the IGP and the raid would begin.

Krass Curman was the head of an underground fighting ring. Not for people, but for animals. A wide variety of creatures from dozens of worlds fought here. Unfortunately, animal fighting wasn't illegal in this city – very few things were illegal in this city, which didn't even have a formal police force – but the IGP was hoping to get Curman on his off-world crimes. Some of his animals had been stolen or were illegally imported. Some of the previous owners of these animals had mysteriously disappeared.

Knock knock. The guard laughed when he saw Yna's waifish form on the viewscreen, then did a double take when he saw her cat. What a beaut. The boss was going to love this. And she knew the password, so he let her in and led her down the hall.

Yna followed the burly guard, repulsed by everything she saw around her. He led her past the arena, where a fight was taking place at this very moment. A wolf the size of a pony, with bull-like horns, faced off against a giant red boa constrictor. While neither creature was something Yna would want to encounter in the wild, she felt bad for both animals. She wished she could run down there right now and release them.

Then he led her past the holding pens, and Yna felt even worse. These poor animals sat in bare cages that were way too small. Some of these cages hadn't been cleaned out in a while, and the smell was overwhelming. Some of the animals sported improperly-treated wounds, and many of them cringed in fear as Yna walked by, despite being twice her size.

Yna fought back tears. She couldn't do this. If she was going to be convincing, she had to act like this didn't bother her. She'd been ordered to pose as Panther's owner, presenting him as a fighter. She was to negotiate a contract with Krass Curman, asking him lots of questions, keeping him talking as long as possible while he incriminated himself into her hidden audio transmitter. Then she was to ask for too much money, fail the negotiation, and leave with whatever evidence she could get.

But Krass wasn't going to buy any of her act if she burst into tears at every instance of animal cruelty. She would have to harden her heart, at least temporarily.

"The cat goes in here," the guard said, snapping Yna back to the present. He held open a cage door and pointed into the cell.

"But I don't have a contract yet," Yna said.

"The cat has to stay in here while you talk to the boss," the guard said, annoyed. "You think he's going to let you bring a dangerous animal into his office?"

He had a point. Yna gave Panther a comforting ear scratch and led him into the tiny cell. "I promise I'll be back as soon as I can," she said, looking into his big green eyes.

The guard groaned at her sentiment. "Lady, it's just a cat."

Yna nodded. "Of course," she said, as neutrally as possible. Panther whined as he watched her follow the guard out of the room.

The cell was made of cold steel, with a chain link door. It had an electronic lock. There was just enough room for Panther to lay down, provided he curled into a ball. But he wasn't sleepy at the moment. He sat upright, staring out the door, waiting for Yna's return.

Curman's office was the cleanest room in the building, but that was a low bar. It was filled to the brim with examples of "awful taste but excellent execution." Every element of the decor managed to clash with everything else in the room, in a way that just had to be intentional. No one could fail this hard by accident. This was an eyesore that could have been weaponized.

Everything – from the walls to the floors to the furniture

– was covered in animal skins. Animal heads adorned the walls, some with plaques that proclaimed things like, "Rex The Annihilator – 47 Wins, 1 Loss." The implications made Yna's stomach lurch.

But it wasn't just heads on the wall. A few complete animals sat around the office as well, some of the most tasteless examples of taxidermy Yna could imagine. Yna's choices of seating included a large three-eyed reptile that had been turned into a couch, draped with a tiger pelt, or a bench made out of a six-legged shark covered in panda fur. Both choices made her want to vomit, and she decided to do the interview standing up.

Behind a huge elephant-footed desk, Krass Curman wasn't much prettier to look at than the rest of the room. He was human, but you would have been forgiven for wondering. His pale skin had patches of some skin disease, he had several scars that looked like animal scratches, and his cheeks drooped like a bulldog.

He appeared to be one of those people who think that wearing lots of bling made you desirable, because he wore his body weight in gold rings, necklaces, and animal furs. Despite being three times Yna's age, he kept looking at her in a way that made her uncomfortable, licking the corner of his mouth and calling her "darlin'."

"So this cat a yers, it get in a lot a shcraps?" His accent was a mix of seedy underworld and cartoon drunkard. Yna only understood him because of the time she'd spent living with pirates.

"He's won his share of fights," Yna answered, trying to look nonchalant.

"Ya lookin' ta shell him, darlin'? Or just take in da winnins'?"

"Freelance. I choose when he fights. I want ninety percent of the take on every fight he wins," Yna said, with as much confidence as she could muster.

"Ninety! Besht I can do is fifty, darlin'. An that's only if the cat's got shtar power. Even our shupershtars don't take home ninety."

"Eighty-five," Yna countered.

"Yer not lishenin', shweetie. Look, we usually shtart at thirty-five. I could maybe shee forty. Forty-five if you're..." He looked Yna up in down in a way that made her shiver. "...really nishe to me."

"W-why Mister Curman," Yna said, trying to sound flirty. "You old dog. Tell me, is this how you get all your animals?"

"Nah, mosht of my clients aren't ash pretty as you, darlin'.'"

"So where do they come from?" Yna pressed, trying not to step over the line.

"Here and there," he said. His smile was starting to drop. He liked to ask questions, not answer them.

"Oh, don't be shy," Yna said playfully. "You can tell me. I won't tell anyone. Crime gets me... so hot." She ran her hands over her hips, as sensually as she knew how.

"Doesh it?" He didn't look convinced.

"Oh yes," she continued, hoping she wasn't blowing it. "Where did you steal them? Who did you have to kill? Be specific, the details really get me going."

"Are you for real?" he said, then shook his head. "Guardsh, get in here!"

Two guards appeared in the doorway almost immediately, brandishing tranquilizer dart pistols. It was standard issue here, given that they dealt with so many animals. Animals were meant to kill each other in the arena, not get shot to death between matches. The guards stood at attention, waiting for further orders.

"Who are you working for?" Curman asked.

"N-nobody," Yna answered, "I swear, I'm just curious."

"Guards, get 'er out of here. Shee if she's a bit more honesht when tied up in a shnake pit."

"No!" Yna shouted, raising her hands. They started to

glow blue.

"What the— Trank 'er!" Curman ordered, and the guards fired. Two darts struck her, one in the shoulder, one in the thigh. Yna collapsed to the floor, unconscious. With these doses, she would be out for a while.

From his cage, Panther watched as two guards walked through the pens, carrying Yna's body between them. He growled, a low reverberation like distant thunder. This. Would. Not. Do.

He slammed his head into the gate, using his full strength. Nothing. Again. Nothing. He repeatedly headbutted the cage, but only came away dizzy. Except now the gate rattled differently. He looked around the chain link for what had changed. There. In the top right, part of the mesh had torn away from the corner. Panther attacked this weak point. He clawed at the corner, pulling at the mesh. He headbutted again and again, applying force as close to the corner as possible. What started as a few broken metal strands became an open corner, and the more he pulled, the easier it was to break more strands.

Finally the chain link curled down far enough for him to squeeze through. He looked around at the other cages, seeing sad, malnourished, and injured animals everywhere. He didn't have time to attack all their cages the way he had his own. He needed to find Yna. He looked around until he saw a big red button on the wall, under a shield of protective plastic. It was marked "Emergency Release."

Panther couldn't read, but he'd seen the humanoids press buttons. Pressing buttons did things. And pressing big buttons did big things. He clawed at the plastic cover until it came off, then slammed the button with his paw. Sirens blared, lights flashed, and all the cage doors popped open. Panther immediately ran after Yna, as total chaos erupted behind him.

The guards hadn't gotten too far. They'd been carrying

Yna down towards the arena when the alarms went off. Now they set her down and looked around for the source of the alarm. They spotted Panther and raised their weapons. Just as they were about to fire, animals started pouring out of the hallways above. The guards turned and ran. Panther gently grabbed Yna's arm in his mouth, turning her over a couple of times to find the best place to grab her. Finally he managed to bite her jacket, and pulled her towards an exit.

Yna woke up a few hours later, on the roof of an abandoned restaurant. Panther was curled up next to her, keeping her warm. Curiously, she discovered that she'd been sleeping on top of some blood-spattered animal furs – the same animal furs Curman had been wearing during the interview. She reached over and petted Panther, who opened his eyes and gave her a huge lick. She had no idea how he'd done it, nor could she ask him. But she had no doubt that Panther had saved her life.

The IGP descended on the city, their animal control division rounding up a variety of creatures. Many were returned to their original owners, others were given new homes or donated to zoos. None of the arena's employees survived, having been mauled, gored, poisoned, and torn apart by various animals. They never found the body of Krass Curman.

As far as Yna was concerned, Krass was the most tasteless man she'd ever met. If Panther could speak, he would have begged to differ. In fact, he'd found Krass to be quite delicious.

01.03 *Waterlogged*

ED.02501.03.11

Trenyn flew through the water like a torpedo. They held onto a set of handlebars, welded to a small virtrinium orb. Trenyn used their telekinesis to propel the orb through the water, holding on tight to the handlebars with all four hands. They had tried using a similar method to fly in the air, but had been less successful.

It was believed that their ancestors once sported webbing between their bifurcated forearms. You could still see a bit of a ridge there, running from their inner elbows to the tips of their inner pinky fingers. This feature had probably gone away sometime after they started living on land and developed telekinesis. But fortunately, their gills had remained.

The target was Krimson Garr, professional assassin. A few weeks ago on a planet called Miran, a woman named Liza Vixon hired Garr to murder her husband. Vixon had been caught, and now awaited trial for conspiracy to commit murder. It was Vixon herself who put out the bounty on Garr. According to the laws on Miran, the severity of a punishment was diluted by the number of people sentenced. So if a single person committed a murder, they would be executed. If two people committed a murder together, they each got life in prison. If twenty people conspired to commit a single murder, they might get as little as five years each.

So finding Garr literally meant life or death to Vixon. It wasn't the noblest of causes, but catching a professional killer like Garr would probably save more lives in the future, so it wasn't like Trenyn was just in it for the money. Besides, Trenyn had listened to Vixon's side of the story and found her motivations compelling. Mr. Vixon was the CEO of a company that was destroying Miran's air quality, and Liza wanted to inherit the company so she could make it more eco-friendly.

Okay, that still wasn't an excuse for murder. But it was better than killing her husband for his fortune, or because she wanted to be with someone else, or the myriad of other excuses murderers used.

Miran was shared by two sapient species. The surface was populated by humans, the descendants of Earth colonists who settled in before they even knew about the planet's native citizens. The bottom of the ocean was dotted with a great number of large cities, home to amphibious people known as the Gesh.

While situations like this often end in bloodshed, the peace between the humans and the Gesh had never been troubled. They required vastly different biomes, so there was no fighting over territory. Coastal cities had some degree of integration between the two species, but humans in landlocked territories rarely met a Gesh in their lives.

Trenyn found the planet's history fascinating, and wished they had time to visit a few of the planet's museums instead of tracking down a dangerous killer. But every minute Trenyn wasted was a minute in Garr's favor.

The citizens of Vogra City looked a bit like bipedal crocodiles. They were surprised to see a non-Gesh visitor, and many heads turned as Trenyn swam towards Vogra City Hall. Off-worlders weren't uncommon on the surface, but those who lived underwater rarely got to meet extraterrestrials.

Trenyn approached a building made of coral. To get inside, they swam through a short U-shaped tunnel that acted as an airlock. The inside of the structure was still partially filled with water, which came up to Trenyn's waist. The furniture inside was also made of coral, but integrated with technology.

The room was lit by glowing blue crystals. Silicate orbs projected videos onto waterfall-based screens. Conch shells acted as communication devices. It wasn't more or less advanced than other worlds Trenyn regularly visited, it was just different.

A crocodilian receptionist waved Trenyn forward. She had turquoise scales, similar to the hue of Trenyn's skin. She said something in a guttural language that Trenyn didn't understand. Trenyn responded with telepathy, *Do you happen to understand English?*

The receptionist looked surprised at the mental intrusion but quickly regained her composure. "Some," she said. "What you need?"

Trenyn kept it as simple as possible, using both words and images to convey the message. It took a while, but Trenyn left with the information they needed. The receptionist even printed out a map for Trenyn, on a waterproof sheet of pink vellum.

Garr had indeed been through here. The other Gesh ostracized him for his criminal behavior, so he only came through town when he needed supplies. Gesh law was swift and harsh when it came to Gesh-on-Gesh crime. But since Garr's crimes were against humans, the Gesh considered that a surface world problem. Garr was forbidden from living in Gesh cities, but that was the extent of his punishment.

The city officials didn't know exactly where he lived, but he always came from the same direction. The Myraneid Rift was an underwater chasm, a few kilometers North of Vogra City. The inner walls of the chasm were littered with caves, home to Gesh outcasts as well as many dangerous creatures.

Things were about to get dangerous, so Trenyn took inventory. They wore a wetsuit with lightweight armor plating, and a matching helmet with vision-enhancing goggles. They were armed with a pistol that shot tranquilizer darts, specifically designed to work underwater. Each dart was basically a tiny torpedo, filled with a sedative formulated specifically for Gesh. Unfortunately, the gun only held two shots before it had to be reloaded, and Trenyn only carried six shots total. They went ahead and loaded two shots into the pistol.

In their side pouch, Trenyn also carried a pair of virtrinium-lined manacles. Virtrinium was rare and expensive, and whenever Trenyn managed to get their hands on some, they had a hard time deciding which project took precedence. They had a backlog of tools and weapons they hoped to one day infuse with virtrinium, so that Trenyn could manipulate the devices with their telepathy.

How had Lord Vermon acquired so much of the metal that he'd been able to waste them on cell doors? Were there virtrinium mines on Valos? Trenyn thought it would be amazing to get their hands on that much virtrinium, enough to infuse every item they owned, so they could live the way the rest of the Navorans did. Never lifting a finger, able to accomplish any task with all four hands tied behind their back.

Trenyn realized they were getting distracted. And on some level, they were probably doing it on purpose. Trenyn was not a fighter, and Garr was a trained assassin. So far, every Gesh Trenyn had seen had been twice their body weight, with huge snapping jaws full of sharp teeth. Trenyn wasn't sure they'd win in a fight against a Gesh hatchling, much less a full-grown adult who killed people for a living.

I just have to get him to the surface, Trenyn thought. *After that, he's Vik's problem.* Somewhere far above, Vik waited in a boat. Trenyn had a tracking device in their belt pouch, and Vik would be doing his best to stay above Trenyn. One way or another, Trenyn would coax Garr to the surface, and Vik would take him out. At least, that was the plan. The tranquilizer gun was more for protection than anything.

Trenyn now saw the chasm in the distance. Not much light filtered down this far from the surface, and the rift would be even darker. Trenyn turned up the brightness of their goggles. Arriving at the edge, they peered down into the darkness. It was just as they'd been told. Dozens of caves dotted the sides, too many to check individually. Trenyn would have to find a way to get Garr's attention.

Trenyn decided to try the direct approach. They performed the telepathic equivalent of shouting into the chasm. *Krimson Garr! I know you are down there. I am here to collect the bounty on your head. Come out with your hands behind your head, and I will take you into custody. Resist at your own peril.* When they were done broadcasting the thoughts, Trenyn floated by the edge of the chasm and waited. They held their handlebar contraption in their two left hands. With one of their right hands, they held the tranquilizer gun out in front of them, scanning the chasm for movement.

And then they felt a sudden sharp pain from behind, hitting them so hard they saw stars for a second. The gun and the handlebars both went flying. Trenyn turned around, just in time to get knocked in the stomach. Garr floated in front of Trenyn, and they sized each other up. Garr's magenta scales sported hundreds of scars, many of which looked like shark bites. Trenyn's skin flashed yellow with fear.

Garr bared his razor-sharp teeth, and said something in the Gesh language. Garr understood English but couldn't speak it underwater. Only the guttural tones of the Gesh language, spoken through a separate organ in their throats, could travel far enough to be heard through the water.

Regardless, it sounded like a threat. Trenyn looked around for the tranquilizer pistol, but it was long gone. They spotted the handlebar device and called it over to them. Seeing this, Garr sped toward Trenyn like a torpedo. The handlebars reached Trenyn first and pulled them out of Garr's way.

Come and get me, Trenyn taunted, headed for the surface. Unfortunately, Garr was faster. Trenyn saw that they were going to be overtaken. Holding onto the handlebars with their left hands, Trenyn used their right hands to root through their pouches. The gun was gone, but Trenyn still had four darts. They pulled out two of them.

Ow! Garr's powerful jaws jammed down on Trenyn's left leg. His teeth pierced the armor plating and Trenyn's flesh. They couldn't shake Garr loose; it felt like getting trapped in a vise. Trenyn crouched to get closer to Garr and attempted to jab him with a dart. It glanced off Garr's scales, breaking the needle. They were about to try again with the other dart, but Garr saw it coming and released Trenyn's leg.

Trenyn held the dart threateningly, as Garr prepared to charge again. Then both were distracted as a dark shape approached. It was a creature Trenyn didn't recognize, with a body similar to a shark but with the head of a lamprey. It had probably been attracted by the scent of Trenyn's blood. Garr swam backward several meters, taking great delight in what would happen next. The lamprey-shark thing locked on to Trenyn like it was laser-guided, rushing toward its prey.

Trenyn instinctively held up the handlebars in defense, and wedged them into the creature's round maw. They were just the right width to get stuck behind the creature's second row of teeth. It tried to expel the foreign object, but couldn't. Trenyn was about to retreat from the creature, but then had a thought. They used their telekinesis to move the handlebars toward Garr, creature and all. Trenyn grabbed onto the creature's tailfin.

Garr wasn't quite sure what he was seeing. From his

angle, he hadn't seen Trenyn insert the handlebars. All he could tell was that the arthnak was turning toward him. He was familiar with arthnaks, and he knew that they rarely attacked Gesh due to their tough scales. But after Trenyn's initial telepathic threat, Garr knew his foe had mind powers. Just how powerful was this skinny bounty hunter? Had they ordered the arthnak to attack Garr?

He wasn't afraid, though. Arthnaks were tough, but so was Garr. He swam beneath the creature and bit it on the underbelly, where it was most vulnerable. Latching on tight, he could taste the creature's blood, and it momentarily clouded his mind. Then he felt Trenyn's arms wrap around his waist from behind.

Garr immediately let go of the arthnak, but before he could break free of his opponent's grasp, Trenyn jabbed a tranquilizer dart into his soft, unscaled stomach. Garr angrily tore free of Trenyn's grasp. He turned toward Trenyn. Garr tilted his head to the side, then opened his jaws wide, ready to slam them shut on the sides of this interloper's head. That's when things started to get fuzzy. The lights got dim and fleepy, and the flushnuzz went all guufummuuuu…

Trenyn struggled to hold onto Garr's dead weight. They grappled Garr under his armpit with their left arm, and grabbed the arthnak's tail with the other. Compelling the handlebars to fly upwards, the trio burst through the surface of the ocean, just a few meters from where Vik's rented ship bobbed in the waves. Vik used his Levatech powers to pull Trenyn and Garr onto the ship. Trenyn then worked on dislodging their handlebars from the arthnak's mouth, finally working it free. No sense letting the animal suffer, or leaving such a useful tool behind. The confused arthnak swam away furiously.

"Looks like you have a fish story to tell," Vik said.

Thanks to Garr's capture, Vixon got life in prison instead of the death penalty. As for Garr himself, evidence of past assassinations surfaced, and he was given six life sentences and three death sentences. Due to legal challenges regarding his dual citizenship, he would probably be in prison for many years before one of the death sentences would be carried out. In the meantime, he vowed to break out of prison and track down the bounty hunter who caught him.

"Don't worry about it," Vik told Trenyn. "Take it from a cop. These lowlifes make death threats all the time, but they're all talk. They only go through with it, maybe, a third of the time."

Only… a third? Trenyn asked, turning yellow.

"Look, if he does manage to break out, he probably won't even think about you. He'll probably just fall back into his normal routine."

His normal routine is killing people, Trenyn replied.

"…for money," Vik added. "And you're worthless. To him, I mean."

Trenyn did not feel reassured. They were, however, proud to have taken down this killer solo. The praise they received from Bloodstone and the rest of the crew almost made the danger worth it.

Almost.

01.04   *The Dogs of War*

ED.02501.04.21

It was an actual war zone. What had, this morning, been a serene little town - the kind where everyone knows everyone, and the local sheriff is also the town barber, dentist, and undertaker – was now covered in flames. Bombs exploded left and right, while hovering tanks traded flaming missiles with mortar-wielding grunts. Dog-faced soldiers were blown to pieces as unmanned jeeps indiscriminately launched grenades at anything that moved.

General Lars Pollicle, long-retired war criminal with canine features and a never-say-die attitude, had been rumored to be hiding out with his family here on his birth planet, Galea. Off-worlders often thought of Galea as a planet of cat people, but roughly half the world's citizens were more doglike. The Caniks tended to be more xenophobic than the catlike Meu. Few Caniks left their home continent, much less their planet. But here in the Canik Empire, the second largest landmass on Galea, it was dogs as far as the eye could see.

Bloodstone shook her head. One planet giving rise to both cat and dog people? Unlikely. But there were rumors about this planet's origin. Many believed that their evolution had been guided, though by whom or for what reason was anyone's guess. The universe could be a strange and wondrous place.

It could also be a real bitch. Despite the general's combat training, Bloodstone had expected this to be an easy job. After all, Lars was getting on in years and was trying to live life as inconspicuously as possible. Bloodstone had planned to take Lars without a fight, setting a trap for the old dog instead of chasing him down or facing him in combat. She'd brought two companions on this mission: Whisper, for her stealth skills, and Yna, because she needed more training. That had been a mistake. Bloodstone never would have brought Yna along if she'd known the day would turn out like this.

A nearby explosion rocked the building, and bits of ceiling trickled down around them. The lights flickered, then went out. Bloodstone and Whisper could see in the dark with their helmets, but Yna would have been left blind if she were conscious. Whisper checked up on her, making sure she hadn't bled through her bandages. "She's okay," Whisper reported, and joined Bloodstone at the window. Patting Bloodstone on the shoulder, she asked, "Should we make a run for it?"

"I don't know if we should move Yna in her condition," Bloodstone answered. "And we can't leave her here."

"Well," Whisper said, "if we're going to wait this out, we at least need to find somewhere safer. This building could come down any minute. You watch over Yna, I'll scout around."

"No, Whisper, I'll go—"

"I'm better at not being seen," Whisper interrupted. "And you'll make a better protector. Don't worry, I'll be back soon." She was gone before Bloodstone could raise any further objections. The bounty hunter walked over to the sleeping young woman, double-checking her bandages. It was something to do. She looked around for resources. They were in a library, or what was left of one.

Anger filled Bloodstone's mind. Some of it was directed at the idiots fighting outside, but mostly she was mad at her own arrogance. She'd been so sure Lars would be an easy target, that she hadn't taken nearly enough precautions. To be fair to herself, the plan had nearly worked. Whisper had followed Lars around, keeping her distance, learning his routine. Bloodstone had readied some traps, planning to snare him during his daily run. There was a tunnel Lars jogged through every morning on the way to get coffee, which looked perfect for the trap Bloodstone had in mind. They'd kept Yna in the loop every step of the way, teaching her valuable hunting skills.

"It's up to you to develop your own technique," Bloodstone had told her. "There are many types of bounty hunters. I consider myself a jack-of-all-trades, but I probably focus on technology and traps more than most hunters. Whisper uses stealth all the way, nabbing her prey when they least expect it. Some hunters specialize in disguises, and others just use brute force and intimidation. Some of those techniques work better than others, but they're all valid. Just don't become a carrion hunter, or I'll kill you myself."

They'd shown her how to stay unseen, how to set traps, how to track people from a distance; every skill this mission had required. Everything, except maybe, how to stay downwind. Lars had an excellent sense of smell. He was also paranoid, and way more prepared for a fight than Bloodstone ever would have expected. At the first whiff of an off-worlder, he had holed up in his house and called in the local militia.

But that wasn't the end of it. It turned out that the bounty hunters weren't the only ones who had been tracking Lars. Lieutenant Peke Mallermoot, an old rival from his war days, had been staying in town, waiting for an opportunity to get revenge on the retired general. He'd brought a small army of his own, staying at the ready just outside of town. When

Lars changed up his routine, going into hiding and gathering his troops, Peke assumed he'd been spotted and called in his forces. Things had escalated pretty quickly from there, and the friendly town of Saunder's Bay was now a war zone.

The bounty hunters had barely made it inside before the explosions started. They weren't even sure what had hit Yna, they'd just heard her scream and carried her the rest of the way in. And now, maybe half an hour later, the town was in shambles. Bloodstone pulled a small disc from a pouch on her belt, setting it near Yna's head. It gave off a soft glow, enough to see by without attracting attention from outside. Then she took off her helmet. Doing so had an immediate effect on her demeanor, as it always had. Removing the mask was like shedding an entire persona. Instead of Bloodstone, the hunter with a heart of ice and a weapon for every situation, she was now just Detanna, the trans woman who cared deeply for the safety of her companions. She preferred Detanna, but Bloodstone paid the bills.

With one hand she brushed some soot off of Yna's forehead, then checked her temperature. No fever, that was good. And her breathing seemed normal. Detanna just sat with her for a while, watching her breathe.

There was a loud crash, and two canine soldiers – Detanna didn't know if they were team Lars or team Peke, nor did she care – muscled their way into the room. They pointed their rifles at her, barking orders in a language Detanna didn't understand with her helmet off. But it didn't matter what they were saying, their violent intentions were clear. Detanna managed to dispatch both of them before they even noticed the pistol in her hand. She never completely shed the Bloodstone persona; it was always there when she needed it.

Detanna turned her head as she heard a shout of pain in the opposite direction. A third soldier hung from the ceiling, struggling and grasping at the whip around his neck.

Whisper jumped down from the rafters, dislodging the whip and letting the now-unconscious soldier hit the floor with a loud crunch. "I think it's time we left. I found someplace safer, it's not far."

Helmet back on, Bloodstone carried Yna while Whisper led the way.

They ended up in someone's backyard bunker, designed to withstand the tornadoes that sometimes plagued this area during the summer. The owners had unfortunately perished when a tank shell collapsed their home, or the bunker might already have been occupied. It was a well-built hiding place, fortified but inconspicuous, and well-stocked. A perfect spot to wait out this ridiculous little war.

Yna faded in and out of consciousness, resting comfortably on the bunker's couch. While Bloodstone kept some first aid supplies in her belt pouches, they found a much better stash in the bunker. They sealed Yna's wound with an antiseptic paste, before applying fresh bandages. They even found her something for the pain. Okay, it wasn't the level of care she would have received from Raven and Trenyn, but it would keep her stable until they could get her better treatment.

"You should get some sleep," Bloodstone said. "I'll keep watch."

"I'm not tired," Whisper said. "But you can if you want."

Detanna took off her helmet again. "No, but I suppose there's no harm in getting a little more comfortable." The fighting sounded very far away now. Maybe it would be over soon.

"Agreed," Whisper said, taking off her helmet as well. Underneath, she wore her usual ninja-style mask, revealing only her eyes and a minimal amount of skin.

They sat quietly for a bit, on the floor with their backs against the wall. Yna was sprawled across the couch, the only comfortable piece of furniture in the bunker. There were some folding chairs against the wall, but neither of them felt the urge to retrieve one. Eventually, Detanna broke the silence. "I should have been more careful." She was staring at Yna.

"You couldn't have known," Whisper said.

"He was a general. And I knew that," Detanna said. "Why wouldn't he have an army? Why wouldn't he be prepared?"

They were rhetorical questions, but Whisper answered anyway. "You can't predict things that don't make logical sense. Seriously, this sleepy little town is actually full of soldiers? Even the teenager who sold Lars his coffee this morning? While I was scouting for this place I saw a little kid run by – probably about five? I don't know how fast Caniks age… but she carried a grenade launcher. She blew up a tank, then reloaded it like she'd been practicing for years. You couldn't have seen this coming."

Whisper was right, but Detanna wasn't placated. Every bounty hunter had a shtick, and Bloodstone's wasn't actually technology or traps. It was preparedness. She was always ready for anything, and when something took her by surprise, she blamed herself. "If Yna doesn't recover…" she trailed off.

Whisper scooted over and put an arm around Detanna. "She'll be fine," she said. She wasn't used to seeing Detanna's softer side. Back when she'd first met The Great Bloodstone, The Galaxy's Most Notorious Bounty Hunter™, Whisper never would have suspected there was a heart under all that armor. It was good to see her show some compassion, though the brooding wasn't really what they needed right now.

As if reading her mind, Detanna sat up straighter, reaching for her helmet. "This is a waste of time. I should be out there, looking for Lars. Why don't you stay here and watch over Yna, and I'll go complete the mission."

Whisper grabbed her arm. "Bloods… Detanna. We're safe here. Let them wipe each other out, then we'll pick through the ashes. Don't make a target of yourself over a misplaced sense of guilt."

Detanna let go of the helmet. "You're right. I've just… never been very good at sitting still."

Whisper laughed. "Then don't. We'll find something to do. I'll show you how to meditate. You can teach me how to build a net trap. I think I saw a deck of cards around here somewhere. Or we could even just talk."

They ended up playing cards. Detanna taught Whisper a game called Liar's Bluff, a favorite among space pirates. Whisper had never heard of it before, but her knack for reading facial expressions gave her an edge, and she won more hands than she lost.

"Do you think Lars will survive this war?" Whisper asked, drawing more cards.

"Doesn't matter, he's wanted dead or alive," Detanna answered.

"What if the other army gets to his body first?"

Detanna thought for a minute. "I don't think they're after him for the bounty. Idiots. If they'd used our approach, they could have gotten their revenge *and* a reward. But they'll probably blow him to unidentifiable smithereens. If he doesn't wipe them out first."

"There's a saying on Auroris. 'A war requires two sets of villains.' We believe that for a conflict to even happen, there has to be evil people on both sides."

"That's probably true for most wars," Detanna said. "But sometimes villains attack unprovoked, and good people have to make sure it doesn't happen again. Just look at Alterra Sarr. She ended thousands of lives, probably on Vermon's orders. I'm not saying all the cops on that station were saints, but they didn't start this fight. If Earth went to war with Valos over the explosion of EarthStation 1, I wouldn't blame them, and I definitely wouldn't consider Earth the villain in that scenario."

"Did you tell the IGP that Alterra was sent by Vermon?"

"Of course not," Detanna said. "Until we've caught her and collected the reward, we keep a lid on anything we've learned. Exclusive knowledge gives us the edge in finding her. And besides, if Earth went to war over this, they might cancel the bounty and put the money towards the war efforts. Why waste the money if she's just one of a million soldiers? She's more valuable to us if Earth thinks she was a single terrorist, acting alone."

"Well," Whisper said. "If we do catch her, I hope you at least listen to her side of the story before turning her in."

Detanna looked into Whisper's eyes. "I understand. You want to see the good in everyone. And maybe you're right. But my job is just to bring her in. If there's more to her story, I'm sure it will come out at the trial."

"But…" Whisper started to say. There was no point. They'd had this conversation several times already.

"This is a little unfair, you know," Detanna said, changing the subject. "I've lost four hands in a row. I can't tell if you're bluffing through that mask. I'm going to put my helmet back on."

"No, don't," Whisper said, dealing another hand. "I like you better this way. You're such a stiff when the helmet's on."

"Tell you what," Detanna said, looking at her cards. "If I win this hand, you lose the mask."

"You know I can't do that," Whisper said. "I told you, it's my religion. I can't show my face until I get married."

"Well, that's the point of the game," Detanna said. "You lose the hand, you do something you wouldn't normally want to do. We're not playing for money, so we'll play for dignity. If I lose, I'll… I don't know… sing a pop song or something. Your pick, something really embarrassing."

Whisper looked at her cards. "Okay," she said. "If you win, I will take off the mask. But only because I have an unbeatable hand. And only if I'm allowed to record your singing. You're going to *hate* the song I have in mind."

"Deal," Detanna said, looking at her cards. Neither of them drew any additional cards.

Whisper put her cards down. "Read them and sing," she said confidently.

Detanna looked down at Whisper's cards, then up into her eyes, before flashing an evil smile. "Uh oh," Whisper said. She didn't need her intuition to know she'd lost.

Whisper started to reach for her mask. "Wait," Detanna said. "Look, you don't have to do anything you don't want to do."

"Shush, silly," she said. "I'm trying to swindle you. See, I only promised I would take off the mask. I didn't say for how long, or whether you'd be able to see my face at the time."

She placed one hand over Detanna's eyes. Using her ability to manipulate shadow, she created a small zone of darkness over the bounty hunter's field of vision. With her other hand, she pulled up her mask. "Well played," Detanna said, laughing.

Her left hand still blocking Detanna's vision, Whisper leaned in and kissed her. It was meant to be a joke, a whimsical peck like an animated bunny might plant on his hunter before hopping away in laughter. But once her lips were there, she found it difficult to pull away. There was an energy between them, an unstoppable pull, and Whisper soon found herself kissing more deeply.

And Detanna was kissing back. Soon they were passionately making out, Whisper's free hand exploring every inch of Detanna's body, at least the parts that could be felt through that accursed body armor. Detanna did likewise, appreciating Whisper's form with both hands. The cards were knocked aside, forgotten, as things began to escalate.

Then the entire bunker shook as an explosion sounded right outside. A large chunk of ceiling fell on top of them. Whisper managed to pull her mask back on, but she couldn't reach any of her weapons. Detanna was also pinned, her hands stuck under a heavy steel beam. It felt like one of her wrists was broken.

As they struggled to free themselves, the bunker's outer door blew open. Three dog-faced men came down the stairs, pushing their way through the rubble. "I thought I smelled something in here," the leader said. General Lars Pollicle spoke seventeen languages, and currently chose English because his prey smelled like humans. He'd always had good instincts for that sort of thing.

As the smoke cleared, Detanna recognized the general and struggled that much harder. Her hand found her pistol, but the weight of the steel beam kept her from wiggling it free. Lars stepped around the couch, standing over Detanna and Whisper with a comically large gun and a menacing sneer. "You must be bounty hunters," he said. "Well, bounty THIS." He raised his weapon.

Detanna managed to dislodge her pistol, but it was too late. Lars howled in pain, dropping his oversized gun. A glowing blue hand burst through his stomach. He crumpled to the ground, revealing Yna standing behind him. The other two soldiers looked confused and turned their weapons towards Yna, but by this time Detanna had her pistol ready. The soldiers never knew what hit them.

Yna stepped shakily towards the other bounty hunters and started burning through the girder with her still-glowing hand. Within a few minutes, they were free. As they gathered their things, including the body of General Lars Pollicle, Whisper asked the question that had been on all their minds. "Did he seriously say, 'Bounty this?'"

They all laughed, bandaged their wounds, and returned to their ship.

01.05   The Way of the Jilted Heart

ED.02501.05.30

The clouds drifted across the full moon, and Whisper made her move. The clouds traveled quickly, but she stayed in their shadow, using her Auroran abilities to augment her concealment. Her footsteps were completely silent as she crossed a tiny footbridge that arched over a babbling creek.

She could see the dojo in the distance, surrounded by fields of bamboo and cherry blossom trees. Someone was going for a theme. She reached the door, found it to be unlocked, and peeked inside. Empty. She closed the door behind her, sat cross-legged on a tatami mat in the middle of the room, closed her eyes, and waited.

It was just a few minutes before a voice said, "You don't have to run anymore."

"Who's running? I'm just sitting here," Whisper said, her eyes still shut.

"Come home with me. The law won't find you on Auroris," the man said.

"I'm not going back with you," she said.

"Then why did you follow my instructions?"

That had been two days ago. After visiting a city on Florzis to buy some soda and capture the leader of a drug cartel, Whisper had returned to the Bloodwind to find a note in her pocket. One side just read "Come home" in Auroran. The other side listed the location of this dojo and a meeting time.

Whisper opened her eyes, stood up, and faced him. Andoro Korr, also known as the pirate Crossbones, also known as Alterra Sarr's fiancée. He wore a red ninja suit that looked right out of a video game. It had no sleeves, and his bare arms were adorned with multiple skull tattoos. He wore red gloves that could have been bought at a sporting goods store. A black skull and crossbones adorned his chest, and Whisper noticed the hilts of two swords behind his neck.

"You have brought dishonor on your family," Andoro said.

"Who talks like that?" Whisper answered. "Look around, Korr. This is a movie set. And you're Auroran, not Asian. We don't even have bamboo on Auroris."

"It is a beautiful culture and I honor them by emulating their…"

"Cultural appropriation much?" Whisper interrupted. "They didn't even get the details right. The walls and the floor are from different centuries."

"The spirit of the scene is all that matters. As long as…"

"And what's with your outfit?" Whisper continued. "What, you couldn't decide if you wanted to be a pirate or a ninja for Halloween, so you split the difference?"

"Would you just let me talk?" Andoro blurted angrily.

Whisper stared into his eyes – the only visible part of his face – and said, "Talk. But make it worth my time."

"We were meant to be together, Alterra," he said. "You were promised to me as a child."

"You're fourteen years older than me," she said. "Do you not see how gross that is?" To be fair, Auroran betrothals didn't usually involve such a large age gap. Originally Alterra's sister had been promised to him, but she died as an infant. Due to some quirk in their bylaws, Andoro was promised the next born from the same family, be they male or female. Alterra was born seven years later.

"You're an adult now," he said. "You can still choose to honor the tradition."

"Even if I wanted to be treated like some object to be gifted to another person, I would never choose you. You're a pirate. How many innocent people have you killed? How many women have you—"

"It's not like that," Andoro said. "I left Auroris to find you. Piracy just paid the bills while I searched for you. If I just wanted money, I'd turn you in to the IGP."

"You still killed innocents. On my worst day, I wouldn't resort to that."

"So you didn't actually destroy the IGP space station?"

"Of course not," Alterra said.

"I was surprised to see your face on the news," Andoro said. "I would have preferred not to have seen your face at all until the wedding."

Alterra pulled off her mask and threw it on the floor. "If this offends you, that's your problem, not mine. It's an obsolete tradition and I've never believed in it."

Upon seeing her face, Andoro reacted as if she'd made an obscene gesture. "Our traditions make us who we are," he said.

"No, they make you who your grandparents were. Those rules were toxic then, and they're toxic now. Rejecting them makes me who I am."

"You *will* come home with me," Andoro threatened. "Even if I have to make you."

"I... sort of seeing someone now," Alterra said.

"That's fine," he said, though Alterra was pretty sure she heard his voice hitch as he said it. "Let them have your heart. Your body belongs to me."

"That's gross," Alterra said.

"It is our way," Crossbones said.

He wasn't wrong, and that was what pissed Alterra off

the most. Auroran culture often separated the concepts of love and marriage. Marriages might be based on population needs, or to bring two families together. Aurorans were some of the most open-minded people in the galaxy when it came to sexual attraction, but their cultural traditions treated people like commodities and breeding stock.

"It's a big galaxy, can you seriously not find someone else to marry?" Alterra asked. "Oh wait, of course you can't, how silly of me. No one would get past your fashion sense. An arranged marriage is your only hope."

"I am not allowed to marry anyone else as long as you live," he answered. "It's the rule. But of course, there is a loophole." He reached over his shoulders and drew both swords. Shaped like katanas, the AON blades immediately started to glow red.

"You're serious," Alterra said, drawing her whip.

"I am bringing you back to Auroris. Whether it's for a wedding… or a funeral."

They each assumed a fighting stance. Alterra scanned the room for anything that might help her. A whip against two AON swords was not ideal; she wished she'd brought more weapons. Both of them were masters of the same fighting style, hindering the usual advantage she had in fights. And he was probably stronger than her.

But was he as fast? Alterra feinted forward as if to use her whip. Andoro swept one sword in a wide horizontal arc, but Alterra went to her knees, and the blade went harmlessly over her head. As she dropped, she extended her left leg and went into a seamless leg sweep. She knocked her opponent's legs out from under him, and he landed on his back.

It didn't hurt him much, but it gave Alterra a couple of seconds to press the advantage. More importantly, it had pissed him off. Good. He would make more mistakes if he lost his temper. If she were quick, she could end this before it really began. She flicked her wrist, and the whip wrapped around his right arm. The whip electrified, sending several strong jolts through his body. He didn't like that. Using his left arm, he slashed the whip with his sword, severing it clean and ending the shocks.

Welp, there went her only weapon. But Alterra wasn't out of ideas. Not wanting to get any closer to his swords, she gave him a swift kick in his right shin, then bolted out of the dojo. It took Andoro a few seconds to recover from the shocks, and the shin injury had not been random – he stumbled to get to his feet, and couldn't put all his weight on that leg.

He limped out the door, looking around for his prey. He didn't see her anywhere. He felt a blow to the back of his head, accompanied by a shattering sound. He turned around just in time to get hit in the face by a second terra-cotta roof tile. Alterra stood on the roof of the dojo, hurling tiles like they were throwing stars.

Temporarily blinded, Andoro sheathed his swords so he could use both hands to climb onto the roof. He jumped, grabbed the edge of the roof, and attempted to pull himself up. Just as he was getting to his feet, Alterra kicked him in the face, knocking him back to the ground. Now he was livid. He reached for his swords again, but only found one.

He wiped his eyes, blinked a couple of times, and looked up at the roof. Alterra stood at the ready, wielding his missing sword, the blade already glowing bright red. "Get down here!" he shouted, though in his rage it probably sounded more like "Gedouneer."

Still, she complied, gingerly hopping off the edge and landing on her feet. They stood about four meters apart, face to face, equally armed. "Good," Andoro said, "A fair fight."

"I don't owe you a fair fight," Alterra said, throwing one last roof tile she'd been hiding behind her back. A corner of the tile caught him square in the left eye, possibly blinding it for good.

Andoro bellowed in anger, lunging forward. Their blades

clanged against each other, over and over. Even half blinded, he was the better swordsman. He'd spent many years learning the art. He pressed forward and Alterra fell back, until they were in the midst of the bamboo field. Bamboo stalks went flying as Andoro's wide slashes missed their target.

Alterra's thrusts were more conservative, less showy. She fought more efficiently, but still spent more time parrying attacks than making her own. She studied his style as she blocked his strikes, learning his timing. Andoro was so used to fighting with two swords, he didn't seem to know what to do with his left hand. After each thrust, there was a half-second where he would normally follow up with a second slash, but that hand was unarmed.

She grabbed a bamboo stalk, using it to swing around and change direction. Andoro made a low slash to the left, slicing the stalk she held. Alterra jumped over the blade, and while he was still on the follow-through, Alterra rammed the severed bamboo stalk into his good eye. He stumbled around, blind. Then Alterra slammed him in the throat with the hilt of her sword, knocking him backward. His own sword tumbled from his hand as he hit the ground.

Andoro lay face up, feeling the heat of the AON blade against his throat.

"Yield," Alterra said.

"Finish me," Andoro answered.

"I will not," she said. "Your life belongs to me now, and you will do as I say."

Andoro growled but didn't disagree.

Alterra stood firm. "Any further attacks against me will violate your own skewed sense of honor. I know you believe in that crap even if I don't."

"...Fine," Andoro relented. "I relinquish my claim on you. I will return to Auroris empty-handed. You will not see me again."

"Good. Oh, and Andoro?"

"What?" he snapped.

Alterra winked, not that he could see it. "If you happen to see my Mom, tell her I said hi."

01.06   *When Bloodstone Met Whisper*

ED.02501.06.06

Detanna, Whisper, Yna, and Dervish sat around the table in the galley. It was the only spot on the ship where the entire crew could sit at the same table, so they had grown accustomed to using this room for meetings.

Yna was recounting her most recent mission. "I almost had him. He had thrown down his weapon, his hands were raised. Then this other guy shows up…"

"Carrion hunter?" Detanna asked.

Dervish cocked her head. "What's that again?"

Detanna explained, "A carrion hunter is the lowest class of bounty hunter. Lazy opportunists. They wait until a better hunter catches someone, then they swoop in and steal their prey."

Yna nodded. "That's exactly what happened. He just showed up, shot me with some sort of stun gun, and took off with my guy. By the time I could stand up, they were both gone. Later I checked the registry, and found that someone had already claimed the money."

Dervish asked, "What did he look like? Maybe you can report him or something?"

Detanna was already shaking her head. "Don't even bother. I've been down that road. It always just ends up being your word against theirs, plus it hurts your reputation. If people think you're easy to thwart, other carrion hunters will start following you around. That's why I never reported Whisper."

Whisper cocked her head. "Excuse me?"

Detanna winked. "You know what I'm talking about."

"I told you that was just a misunderstanding."

Yna looked from Detanna to Whisper and back, but neither said anything. "Oh, come on," she pleaded. "We have got to hear this story."

"You brought it up," Whisper prompted, glaring at Detanna.

"Well," Detanna said, "It was about three years ago…"

The media had dubbed them "The Brothers Glymm." Elik and Elim Glymm were identical twins, who used their similar appearance to perform magic shows and con jobs. As far as most people knew, they were one person. Elim always introduced himself as Elik. Only Elik existed in the government's database, and only Elik filed taxes. They dressed the same, used the same slang, and had the same mannerisms.

They even dated the same woman. Lisha Sathers was a highly intelligent government agent, but she never suspected she was seeing two people. Nor did she realize that her boyfriend was only seeing her so he could access government secrets. Sometimes they would both visit her at work, being careful never to be seen at the same time, or get caught on the same camera. They had it down to a science. While one spent time with her, the other would root through files in her office.

The information they gathered not only proved useful for their cons, but also turned out to be valuable to other criminal parties. But that also turned out to be their downfall. Lisha nearly lost her job when some information only she possessed was used to blackmail a celebrity. This prompted her to install a hidden security camera in her office, and it wasn't long before she found the truth.

She confronted Elik, presenting him with video proof that he had been in two places at the same time. Caught dead to rights, Elik introduced her to Elim, and the two proceeded to beat Lisha to death. However, Lisha had considered this possibility. Upon her disappearance, the evidence was sent to her superiors and the media. The world now knew that the Glymms were two people, and both were wanted by the law.

Elim ran through the park, his lungs burning, begging him to stop for breath. But he couldn't afford to lose a second right now. He had to reach Elik, to warn him of who was on their tail. He tried to listen for the footsteps behind him, but he couldn't hear over the pounding of his own shoes on the pavement. Or maybe it was his heart he was hearing.

It was a huge park, with jogging paths, a forest's worth of trees, an outdoor café, and a zoo... which was right up ahead. Elim knew he would drop dead of exhaustion before he made it to his brother. What he needed right now was a place to hide until he could catch his breath. He located the zoo's service entrance and pulled a keycard out of his pocket. He waved the keycard in front of the security scanner, and the service door whooshed open. Lisha hadn't known he'd cloned her keycard. It allowed him to enter any city-owned building.

He slowed down a bit once he got inside, looking for a place to hide. He saw several kiosks that sold lobster hot dogs, glowing candy, and antigravity popcorn. But he didn't want to be trapped in a kiosk with no exit. He ran past several cages. Most were empty, the nocturnal animals having been transferred to larger enclosures for the night. He heard a noise behind him, but couldn't tell how close it was. *Just an animal in its cage,* he hoped.

But he couldn't take that risk. He needed a place to hide,

now. He saw a pit enclosure, climbed over the barrier, and dropped down into the enclosure with a splash. A shallow creek ran along the inside wall, entering through a grate on one side and exiting through the other. Before him was a gently sloping hill, and hippo-sized dark shapes lay here and there in the grass. *I sure hope those are herbivores,* he thought.

Whatever they were, they appeared to be asleep. Elim leaned back against the wall, not wanting to sit in the water, but also not wanting to get closer to the sleeping animals. He also knew it would be next to impossible for anyone to see him from this vantage point, so it was better to rest here than on the more visible embankment.

As soon as he stopped moving, the adrenaline faded, and he crashed hard. He couldn't draw in enough air to meet the demands of his lungs. He hoped that the sound of the river covered the sound of his wheezes, but there wasn't anything he could do about it. He was seeing spots. Finally he sat down anyway, no longer caring about getting his posterior wet.

He closed his eyes. He thought it was just for a second, but it was probably closer to five minutes. When he opened them, a man was standing directly in front of him. Black jumpsuit, blood red armor plating, and a domed helmet. Elim sighed. There was no fighting back. On his best day he wouldn't last two seconds against Bloodstone, and right now Elim couldn't even move his arms.

"You stay right here where I can find you," Bloodstone said, tying him up. "I'll be back after I catch your brother."

Elim blacked out again, just for a few minutes. When he opened his eyes, he was tied to a grate, the water gently flowing past him. Bloodstone was gone. One of those hippo-sized beasts, which turned out to be an orange-striped woolly rhino, lapped up water from the stream.

If the creature considered him a threat, it didn't show it. Elim tested his bonds, a smile spreading across his face.

Bloodstone probably knew about their magic act, but had he considered all the skills that went into that act? It wasn't just pretending to teleport and other twin-related tricks. They were also expert escape artists and contortionists.

He wriggled out of the cable, popped his shoulders back into their sockets, and looked for an exit. He couldn't climb the wall, but there was a maintenance door on one of the side walls. The keycard opened it as well, and he took the service tunnels back to the exit. He left the zoo and headed towards the trees, as fast as his sore legs could manage.

He was running on fumes and needed a plan. Taking refuge in a small wooded area, he took a minute to rest against a tree. He hoped Elik was leading Bloodstone on a really long chase, because there was no way Elim could keep this up all night. He sat for a minute, his still-wet backside crunching against the fallen leaves. He stared straight ahead, calculating his next move.

He couldn't go back to the apartment, it would be watched. He had dropped his comm earlier when the chase began, so he couldn't contact his brother. That alone kept him from thinking straight. Elim felt incomplete without his brother. They had shared the "Elik" name for such a long time, that Elim had no identity of his own. Their scams required identical thinking and identical reactions.

So how was his brother reacting now? If Elik did manage to elude Bloodstone, where would he go? Of course. The storage unit. They owned it under a fake name, so it wouldn't be in public records. Now that the thought occurred to Elim, he knew it would occur to Elik too. They weren't telepathic, but they thought exactly alike. But could he make it there? It was across town. He couldn't get a taxi, the driver might recognize him from the news. He couldn't even use an autotaxi, because they didn't take cash and his bank account was frozen.

He was pondering hijacking a car, when something moved in the distance. A dark shape dropped down from a tree. It was as if the shadows had converged to make a humanoid form. It came closer, all black and shapeless yet strangely feminine. Its footsteps made no noise, despite walking through several layers of dry leaves.

Elim wasn't sure if he was really seeing this, or if the stress of the day had driven him to delusions. Either way, he was frozen in place, too scared and exhausted to run. Whatever this thing was, it could have him. As it came closer, the shadows gave way to detail. It was a woman, dressed head-to-toe in dark gray. She knelt down to his level, and he saw his own frightened face reflected in her mirrored faceplate.

"Can you walk?" she asked, in a hushed tone. Elim couldn't find it in him to speak, so he just nodded. "Then come with me," she said, reaching out her hand. "We're going for a ride."

Whisper took Elim to the police station. They took him off her hands and arranged payment to her BHR account. As she turned to leave, she froze for a moment. Bloodstone, the legendary bounty hunter, stood right there in the lobby, Elim's brother in tow. Part of her was intimidated by his reputation, and part of her wanted to snap a selfie with him. Of course she couldn't see Bloodstone's expression through that helmet, but she was unusually adept at reading body language. He… didn't look pleased.

Selfies would have to wait for another time. Whisper sheepishly stepped around them, shrinking under the master hunter's glare. She wasn't sure what she'd done to earn his ire, but as new to bounty hunting as she was, she knew it must have been her fault. She stepped out the door and vanished into the night.

"So you see, I had no reason to think he was spoken for," Whisper said. Dervish and Yna nodded in agreement.

"So you say," Detanna said playfully. "But how do I know that's what really happened? Maybe you actually found him tied up in the rhino pit."

"Are you calling me a liar?" Whisper teased.

"Why don't we settle this outside?" Detanna said.

"Because then we'd be floating in space," Whisper said.

"Outside the galley," Detanna said. "Training room. Right now."

Dervish and Yna gleefully followed them to the training room, to watch them work out their faux argument through hand-to-hand combat. It was becoming more and more obvious to the crew that something was going on between Detanna and Whisper. The question was whether or not they knew it themselves.

01.07   Snake Oil

ED.02501.07.16

Wake up, hooman. Time for pats. Panther nudged Vik's unconscious form, but he wouldn't budge. The wound smelled strange, and Panther bared his teeth while trying to process the new odor. All around them, skittering could be heard. Prey. But too much prey. In these numbers, prey becomes predator, and Panther wasn't sure he could protect his friends from that big a swarm.

Earlier that day…

Raven was even icier than usual. Bloodstone had assigned her and Vik to search for a serial killer on a planet called Saffron Mesa. She looked forward to the mission, but it was her partner she didn't care for. She had to admit it made sense on paper. They had to work with local police, and that sort of cooperation was Vik's specialty. The killer was known for using various toxins, which played into Raven's expertise in chemistry and medicine. But the two of them did not work well together.

They also took Panther along, on the premise that his superior sense of smell could come in handy. Panther was overjoyed to get off the ship for a while. He didn't get taken on a lot of jobs, because so many took place in cities where the presence of dangerous animals was frowned upon.

But Saffron Mesa, especially the city of Kresno, was just the right combination of rural and cosmopolitan. On the one hand, it had dirt streets lined with rustic wooden huts, and the riding animals outnumbered the hovercars. On the other hand, the citizens were a mix of many species from many planets, and most of them carried high-tech sidearms. It blended ancient cowboy motifs with modern diversity, and was the kind of place where a giant feline companion wouldn't even turn heads.

Laws were loose here, and police presence was minimal, which made it something of a haven for both criminals and bounty hunters. But when a serial killer was involved, the law got serious. The sheriff of Kresno had bypassed the Bounty Hunter Registry and contacted Bloodstone directly. The infamous bounty hunter had caught several criminals in Kresno, and was well regarded by local law enforcement. However, Bloodstone was currently on another job, and therefore delegated the mission to a pair of colleagues.

Vik had gone all-in on the town's theme. He was wearing a brown duster and a Stetson. He'd selected his wardrobe to fit in, but it actually made him look more like a tourist. When they'd first entered the office of Sheriff Buck Allman, he'd given Vik a look that said, *Is my town a joke to you, son?* But at least he'd looked at him. He barely acknowledged Raven at all. Even when she asked him a direct question, the sheriff faced Vik to answer.

This is ridiculous, Raven thought. She tapped Vik on the shoulder. "I'm going to ask a few questions around town," she said. Vik nodded and turned back to Sheriff Allman. They had already formed a rapport, despite first impressions. Vik tended to have that effect on lawmen, especially the macho sexist ones that tended to thrive in towns like this.

Panther followed her out the door. The enormous cat was having a great time. There were so many new smells, so much movement. People riding by on giant lizards, kids kicking metal cans in the street, the scent of fresh manure wafting on the wind… it was like a theme park to the feline. And speaking of smells, he detected the distinct aroma of rat coming from down the street. Completely forgetting about Raven, he set off in search of the source.

"Stupid backwater town, stupid sheriff, stupid dust," Raven mumbled, heading for a store down the street. A wooden sign that read "Chemist" dangled from the eaves, swaying in the wind. Raven held her overcoat tightly closed around her metal body. There was too much dust in the air, which irritated her allergies. More importantly, she feared the dust might find its way into her body's mechanisms. Today she wore the older model, while Trenyn performed some repairs on the newer body. Unfortunately, this body was more susceptible to foreign particles.

Once inside, she relaxed a little. The decor was antiquated, but Raven was in her element. Thousands of bottles and boxes of medicines filled the wooden shelves. Drugs for hundreds of different species, as well as bandages and gauzes and hand-held medical scanners. They stocked elixirs that were illegal on most worlds, and the prices weren't bad either. Raven was tempted to stock up. You never knew when a rare pharmaceutical would come in handy.

The proprietor was a kindly old man with bushy eyebrows. He was much more polite than the sheriff had been. Raven asked him plenty of questions, and he was more than happy to answer. The victims – there had been eight so far – had all been poisoned. However, each of them had been given a different poison, and none of these poisons matched anything in existing databases. One victim's skin had turned purple, another had vomited up their internal organs, and another's skin cells completely lost cohesion. It was as if the killer was inventing new poisons and testing them on people.

"Have any of your customers ordered large quantities of

anything unusual?" Raven asked.

"Sheriff asked me the same thing, but I haven't sold anything out of the ordinary," he said. "We get a lot of different kinds of people here, with a lot of different medical needs. But no unusually large orders, and nothing that struck me as odd." The chemist wore a nametag that said his name was Pappy Snert. Raven wondered if Pappy was his real name or a nickname, but didn't ask.

It occurred to Raven that if these murders were experiments, then the killer might need a range of species to test the different effects. The variety of victims so far bore this theory out. To this killer, everyone was a lab rat. And if these were experimental poisons, then there might be failed experiments as well. Poisons that the victims survived.

"Has anybody come in with unusual symptoms? Something mild, something they got over, but still something you'd never seen before?"

"You might want to ask Doc Plevins down the street," Pappy began, then his eyebrows perked up. "But now that you mention it, a woman came in the other day with an odd skin reaction."

"What was strange about it?" Raven asked.

"She said little spikes had grown out of her skin. All over, like she was human cactus. But they fell off on their own. By the time she got to me, her skin was fine. I gave her an antihistamine to be safe, but she was already feeling much better."

"So you don't have any of the spikes?"

"Oh, she brought one in to show me. Darndest thing I ever saw," Pappy said. "One moment, I'll get it for you." A few minutes later he handed her the spike, in a sealed plastic bag.

Raven examined the spike. It was a few centimeters long, narrow like a needle, and looked like it was made of chitin. She opened the bag. There was a faint odor that Raven couldn't identify. Raven didn't want to have to go back to the Bloodwind just to scan the spike, but she also doubted that this old-fashioned town would have the proper lab equipment. But… if whoever crafted the poison had also tested it on any lab animals, they might be able to find the lab by smell. Raven wondered if the local police possessed any bloodhounds.

She pulled out her comm. "Vik?"

"Yeah," said the voice over the comm unit.

"Can you bring Panther over to the chemist's? I need him to smell something."

"I thought Panther was with you," Vik's voice answered.

"No, I left him at the sheriff's."

"I saw him follow you out the door," Vik said.

"Hawking's balls," Raven cursed, turning off the comm.

Panther continued to wander through the town. The buildings had become more sparse, but the rat smell was getting stronger. Out past the edge of town, a little wooden shack sat next to a pond. Panther could detect a mix of smells through the door. Rats, decay, and harsh chemicals. He wasn't sure if finding a nice big rat was worth the other two smells. But he'd come this far.

He pawed at the door to be let in. No response. He pushed on the door with his head. Though the door looked weak, it didn't budge. Then he started digging in the dirt beside the shack. He managed to get about a meter deep when he hit solid metal and could go no further. Knowing he'd been beaten, he sniffed the air again. Somewhere in the distance, someone was cooking steak. He bounded off, hoping the cook was the sharing sort.

"We need to put a locator chip on that cat," Raven said.

Vik pointed at the street in front of the sheriff's office. "At least he leaves some pretty big tracks." The ground was a mix of loose dirt and sand, and Panther's massive paw prints stood out easily.

"Let's go," Raven said, and they followed the tracks. Some of the prints had already blown away in the wind, but for the most part, the cat had moved in a relatively straight line. They lost the trail a few times but quickly picked it back up again. Within fifteen minutes they found the shack.

"Looks like he made a beeline for this building, then changed direction," Vik said.

"That's odd," Raven said. She pointed to the hole Panther had created. "The shack looks dilapidated on the outside, but the foundation's metal."

"Weird," Vik said. "But maybe they just like the town to look consistent. There's probably several buildings here sturdier than they look."

"I think we should check it out," Raven insisted.

"Tell you what," Vik offered. "I'll check it out, you go look for the cat."

Raven looked concerned. Something about the shack bothered her. "You sure you'll be safe?" she asked.

"You bet your brass ass," he said, slapping her on the posterior.

Raven glared at him.

"What?" Vik asked. "It's not like you felt that."

Suddenly Raven wasn't quite as worried about Vik's safety. "Fine. I'll head straight back here once I find Panther," she said. "Be careful."

As she walked off, Vik shook his head. Why did she always have such a stick up her ass? He walked around the shack, attempting to look in the windows. They were all painted black. Arriving back at the front door, he decided on the direct approach. Vik knocked.

Raven found Panther begging at a family cookout. He wasn't being aggressive, just sitting up proper and giving the hosts his cutest puppy dog eyes. Most of the family cowered under the picnic table, while the patriarch attempted to scare the cat off with a spatula.

"Here, kitty kitty," Raven said, and Panther grudgingly followed her away.

By the time they got back to the shed, Vik wasn't there. "Must have gone inside," Raven said. She turned to Panther. "Can you smell Vik? Is he in the shack?"

Panther seemed to understand the request because he lifted his head and sniffed the air. Then his eyes narrowed. His fur stood on end, and he let out a low, rumbling growl. Raven looked from Panther to the shack. Finally she said, "Screw it, I'm going in."

Raven tried to push open the door, to no avail. Then she pulled and felt a little give. She pulled harder and ended up ripping the door off its hinges. Behind the wooden door was a more modern metal door, with a digital keypad. Raven smirked. Digital keypads were her specialty.

The shack's interior was metal and bare. It was all one room, with a cooking area in one corner and a bed in another. The bed had no bedspread and was covered in a layer of dust. Raven peeked in the fridge and saw dozens of stoppered vials containing various colored liquids. The vials were labeled, but only with numbers.

She closed the fridge, then spotted a panel in the middle of the floor. It looked like a trapdoor, but there was no latch, handle, or keypad. "Probably needs a remote," Raven muttered. Panther tiptoed up to the edge of the panel, sniffed, and growled again. The panel slid open with a low hum. "…Or it has a motion sensor," Raven added.

Beneath the panel, stairs descended into the darkness. Panther bounded down the steps and out of sight. "Wait, Panther!" Raven shouted, then followed. "This is not a good idea," she said as she carefully walked down the staircase.

It was dark, but not too dark for Panther's eyes, and Raven's sunglasses had a night vision mode. The basement was a bizarre mix of science and filth. It was a large open room, with concrete walls covered in moss and black mold. Small pools of water had collected here and there on the concrete floor. Along the walls, various folding tables held lab equipment, both modern and ancient. Some of the tables held glass aquariums, holding a variety of snakes and other venomous animals. Some cages under the tables held giant rats. There were four doorways, one on each wall, all of them open. The rooms beyond were dark, but Raven and Panther could hear squeaks and skittering noises coming from them.

But most notably, on the floor in the middle of the room, Vik lay unconscious. Panther ran up to him and nudged him with his head. He was breathing, but barely. Raven cautiously walked over and examined him. There were two puncture wounds in his arm, like a snake bite. But given the spacing, it would have to be a very large snake. Raven looked around the room for a snake that looked large enough to have delivered the bite, but none of them did.

Then the hatch on the ceiling slid shut, and the stairs lowered into the floor. "Welcome, my new tesst ssubjectss," a silky voice said. A feminine figure stepped out of one of the doors. "You have disscovered my laboratory of venomous delightss. None of you will leave here alive."

Not another drama major, Raven thought. She missed the missions where the bad guys were just murderers and thieves. Lately it seemed like everybody wanted to be a comic book villain.

The woman was humanoid, in that she had two arms, two legs, average human height, and normal human facial features. Except she was covered in green scales, had snakelike slitted eyes, a forked tongue, and a large pair of fangs that could be seen when she spoke. She wore a skimpy party dress that looked out of place in the dingy basement. In her right hand, she held an odd-shaped handgun with two barrels.

"My name iss Venomora," she said. "I sspecialize in—"

"Poisons, venoms, toxins, I get the theme," Raven interrupted. "I don't really care who you are or what ridiculous name you've given yourself. What have you done to my friend?"

"Just thiss," Venomora said, and fired her weapon. Raven reflexively attempted to dodge but was too slow. A pair of darts flew from the weapon, hitting Raven in the upper arm. They pierced her overcoat, but not her artificial body. Venomora and Raven stared at each other for a few seconds, waiting for something to happen.

"Sso, what are you, ssome ssort of android?" Venomora asked.

"Right," Raven bluffed. "Your toxins won't work on me, so you may as well surrender and give me the antidote for my friend."

"Very well," the snake woman said, raising her arms wide. "If you won't ssuccumb to my toxinss, then face my hordess of ratss!"

Raven winced. This woman's theatrics were more painful than her toxins. Venomora stepped backward through the door. The skittering and squeaking from the adjoining rooms got louder, and Raven could hear dozens of small doors opening.

Panther was still trying to wake up Vik. His ears perked up at the sound of approaching vermin, and he growled. Swarms of huge rats – some nearly a meter long - poured out of the four rooms. Panther swatted the first few away and fatally bit a few more.

Raven ran over to Vik and threw him over her shoulder. Rats bit at her legs but couldn't cause any damage. "Panther!" she shouted, and ran for the door Venomora had gone through. Panther followed close behind, rats climbing on his back and biting at his sides. Once they were through the doorway, Raven slammed the door shut and pulled a table in front of it. There were still rats in this room, but they numbered in the dozens, not hundreds.

This room was full of empty animal cages. There was another door on the other side, which led to a hallway, and finally to a large bedroom. Raven and Panther burst into the bedroom just as Venomora pulled an energy rifle out of her wardrobe. She turned to greet her guests. "Welcome to my inner ssanct-OOF," she said, as Raven threw a rat at her. The animal hit her square in the face, knocking her to the floor. Her rifle fell out of her hand and scattered across the floor.

Panther continued biting and swiping the rats that had followed them into the bedroom. Raven set Vik on the bed, then grabbed Venomora by the neck, lifting her to eye level. Raven stared the woman in the eyes and noticed that she was now slightly less snakelike. One of her contacts had popped out, revealing an ordinary human eye underneath. The rat had also knocked a few scales off her cheek, revealing peach-colored skin beneath the green makeup.

Venomora's eyes were bulging, and she struggled to breathe. "If you kill me your friend will die," she gasped.

"If my friend dies, you'll wish I'd killed you," Raven answered. "You're going to give him the antidote, and then I'm going to take you to the police."

"Upstairss," Venomora managed to say, and pointed weakly at a remote control on the dresser. The remote had buttons that controlled the stairs, cage doors, and various lab devices. It could also activate an ultrasonic pulse that drove the rats back to their cages.

"You know you're breaking my arm," Venomora said. She had dropped the snake accent and now spoke in her normal voice.

"Then I guess you'll just have to mix the anti-venom one-handed," Raven replied.

They were back upstairs. Vik lay on the bed, still unconscious. Panther sat nearby, licking his wounds. Venomora hunted through the refrigerator for the right mix of chemicals. "This should do it," she finally said, after mixing three vials together.

Raven watched her carefully. "Remember, if he dies…"

Venomora nodded, then injected Vik with the antidote. While they waited for it to take effect, Venomora attempted to bargain. "Look, it's all good, right? Your friend's going to be fine, and I'll leave the planet and never hurt anyone again. I'll even pay you. More than the reward to turn me in."

"No," Raven said.

Venomora started to cry. "I don't want to go to jail," she sobbed. Raven wasn't sure if it was an act or genuine. Between her hammy theatrics and her heavy makeup, it was hard to read this woman.

"Veno…" Raven began. "I'm sorry, I'm not calling you that. What is your actual name?"

"Veronica," she said quietly.

"Veronica, you killed people and you're going to pay for it," Raven said. "But that doesn't mean your life is over. I have a very good friend who's currently serving time in prison. It's turned her life around. Now she's working with the Galactic Science Council to create a new type of FTL engine that might eliminate the need for warp gates. And she's doing it from behind bars."

Veronica nodded, wiping her eyes. Her makeup was badly smeared now.

"Can I ask you, though? Why all this? Why the makeup? Why the killing?"

Veronica sighed. "The toxins are for my doctoral thesis. I'm studying for my masters in xenotoxicology. That's why I picked this town. A wide mix of non-human species, a lot of people who won't be missed. The makeup is so people don't recognize me. I didn't want to jeopardize my job as a teaching assistant."

It was the dumbest thing Raven had heard all day, a day that included a belching contest between Vik and the sheriff. But she tried not to let her distaste show. "I'll put in a good word for you," Raven said. "I have colleagues on the Science

Council. Maybe you can continue your studies in prison, developing antidotes to rare toxins. Use your mind for something that helps the universe. If nothing else, if they see value in your work, it might keep the death penalty off the table."

Vik was starting to stir. The anti-venom was working. Raven leaned forward to examine him. She still held onto Veronica's wrist with one arm, and she used the other to turn Vik's head towards her. His breathing had been shallow before, but it was now returning to normal.

"Thank you for believing in me," Veronica said. Then she used her free hand to jab Raven in the neck.

"Ow! Son of a…" In her shock, Raven let go of her captive, who made a break for it. Veronica ran out the shack's front door, Panther bounding after her. Raven's hands went to her neck, where she found a small hypodermic needle. She pulled it out and examined it. There was a tiny drop of liquid still in the syringe.

There wasn't time to analyze it. She was already getting dizzy. She ran to the refrigerator, hoping it was the same toxin Veronica had given Vik. She'd watched her mix the antidote, and could replicate the process. If it was a different toxin, she was done for.

It was a surreal experience losing consciousness in the cybernetic bodysuit. Ordinarily, this type of toxin would make your muscles feel weak, but for Raven it felt closer to trying to drive while intoxicated. In a strange turn of events, the flesh was willing, but the spirit was weak. Seeing double, she mixed the chemicals and filled a syringe. But when it came time to inject it, she couldn't quite find her neck. She held the needle towards herself, fighting with all her might to stay conscious a few seconds longer. But she just couldn't control her fingers, and ended up dropping the syringe.

"Here, let me help," Vik said from behind her. He picked up the syringe and injected her. Within a few moments,

Raven's head started to clear. "Where's that woman?" Vik asked, and Raven pointed toward the door. He walked over and looked outside.

Panther had Veronica pinned down with one massive paw. She struggled and pulled, but couldn't budge him. "Good kitty," Raven said, now standing beside Vik.

They turned Veronica in and collected the reward. Raven did not put in a good word for her, nor did she write her in prison. She did, however, find Veronica's thesis notes, and submitted them to the Galactic Science Council. Using Veronica's data, the GSC was able to synthesize antidotes to several toxins previously thought untreatable. Veronica wasn't legally allowed to profit from these antidotes, but in the end, her work did end up saving lives.

01.08 *Hunted*

ED.02501.08.03

"Alterra Sarr," Raven said, addressing Whisper directly.

Whisper jumped. "What? What about her?"

Raven just stared at her.

Whisper glanced around the medbay, looking anywhere she could to avoid Raven's eyes. She pretended to be deeply interested in the text of Raven's medical license hanging on the wall. Trenyn's technical certification hung next to it. Apparently their full name was "Trenyn 31746," which actually was kind of interesting.

"I'm your doctor," Raven said. "You can be honest with me."

Whisper sighed and took off her mask. "How did you know?"

"I'm partly telepathic, remember?" Raven pointed at her white irises. "I can't read your mind, but your emotions are an open book to me. I've seen how you react when Alterra is mentioned. I can tell when people are lying, and you only lie when it involves Alterra."

"Well, I–" Alterra started.

Raven interrupted her. "At first I thought maybe you just knew where she was, and wanted to keep the bounty for yourself. But that didn't sound like you. Then I thought maybe you were protecting her."

"I didn't–" Alterra began.

Raven kept going. "I probably would have figured it out earlier if not for your skin tone. But I recently read up on your species, and when I learned you could alter your pigmentation, a few things clicked into place."

"I… You found books about Aurorans?"

"Yes, but they don't have a lot of hard data. Most of the galaxy thinks your people are a myth. The books are mostly legends and speculation."

"Still, I wouldn't mind reading them sometime. See what they got right." Alterra was still trying to keep things light.

"Alterra. Look at me," Raven said sternly, and Alterra obeyed. Raven stared hard into her eyes. "Did you destroy the IGP space station?"

"Of course not," Alterra said.

Raven studied her face and nodded. "I didn't think so. And if I find any way to prove your innocence, I will."

"Thank you."

"But Alterra." The stern voice was back. "I've noticed how you and Detanna look at each other sometimes. And I'm not the only one. Even Vik commented on it the other day, and he wouldn't notice the antlers on a gliffdeer."

Alterra put her hand over her eyes. "…Great."

"You and Detanna… You're not… sleeping together, are you?"

"No! Well, not… yet…"

Raven sighed. "I'm sure you don't need me to tell you how dangerous it is to get involved with her."

"I know," Alterra said.

"Of all the people in the galaxy, she's probably your worst choice."

"I know, I know," Alterra said. "I'm practically her arch enemy. No… more like her ultimate prize. But…"

"But you're going to pursue this anyway," Raven said.

"I'm not pursuing anything. I'm taking things as they

come. But yes, I think… there's something between us. And yes, I know it's a bad idea."

"You're an adult," Raven said. "You can make your own mistakes. I won't say another word about it."

"And… you won't tell anyone? That I'm Alterra?"

"I don't keep secrets from Trenyn, but I promise you it will go no farther than us."

"What have you got for me?" Whisper asked.

"It's for us, actually," Detanna said. "You and I are teaming up on this one."

"Who's the target?"

"Jakk Venson," Detanna said. "He's a big game hunter. He's visited dozens of planets to bring down bigger and more dangerous animals. He has no regard for local hunting laws and doesn't care whether his prey are endangered. A few weeks ago on Tervus Three, he killed three game wardens when they tried to arrest him."

"Where is he now?"

"He was last spotted on the planet Tropis, near a community called Vinehollow."

"I'll be ready in ten minutes," Whisper said.

Vinehollow was bigger than they expected. A huge tourist trap as well as a hub for all sorts of illegal activity, the treetop city was every bit as crowded as a major metropolis. Beyond the wooden walkways, the jungle stretched as far as the eye could see in every direction. Strange animal calls could be heard from below, though some of them were actually from loudspeakers added for ambiance.

Bloodstone and Whisper stepped off the skytram and into the bustling crowds. There were no landing pads in Vinehollow, so they'd had to park more than two hundred kilometers away in Bayport. The mass of tourists and citizens consisted of people from all sorts of worlds.

The bounty hunters didn't want to be recognized as such, so they'd dressed to blend in. Each wore rugged khaki pants and shirt, and bright purple vests with multiple pockets. Both wore cloth masks and goggles. This wasn't uncommon here, as the insects on Tropis had an annoying habit of flying into faces.

They rented a cabin with two bedrooms and a common room. They had to cross a rope bridge to get to the cabin, which had an all-around deck with an unobstructed view of two dozen similar cabins. Inside, the cabin had gone all-out with the jungle theme. The walls were covered in cane stalks, which didn't even grow on Tropis, but it appealed to the tourists. Pictures of wild animals hung on the walls, and the leopard print bedspreads matched the rugs on the floor.

An old-fashioned television sat on a wooden credenza in the common room. It only had two functioning channels - children's cartoons and tourist information. Next to the TV were a few old board games. Beyond that, there weren't a lot of amenities.

"People stay here for fun?" Whisper asked, as she looked through a brochure.

"Hard to believe, isn't it?" Bloodstone said, flipping back and forth between the two television channels.

"So how do we find Jakk?"

Bloodstone turned off the TV. "If Jakk is here, it's to hunt. We'll need to talk to the rangers, and find out if there's been any illegal poaching." She rooted through her knapsack and handed Whisper a card. "It's illegal to go down to the forest floor unless you have a permit, so I've forged documents for both of us. We're here as investigators from the Tropis Game Preservation Authority."

Whisper looked at her card. "Wilma Spur?"

"You won't tell me your real name, so I had to make one up."

"Sorry," Whisper said. "It's a life I've left behind."

"Well, this is your life now," Bloodstone said. "If you

don't like your old name, you should make a new one."

Whisper thought about that. All this time she'd been operating under the assumption that she would eventually prove her innocence and get her old life back. But maybe it was time to admit that her old life was behind her, and find a new permanent name and face. "Maybe I will," she finally said.

"Well," Bloodstone said, standing up, "Right now, we have some rangers to meet. Come along, Wilma."

Two hours later they sat in a ranger station, interviewing a pair of park officials. "We know he's here, but we haven't been able to catch him," one ranger said.

"He knows when he's being hunted," the second ranger added. "He hides his tracks well. Then he makes fake tracks that lead to the traps he's set."

"What time of day does he typically hunt?" Bloodstone asked.

"Early morning," the first ranger said. "We think he's trying to bag a razorback chetal. They're mostly active at dawn."

"Can you point us toward any of the traps he's set?" Whisper asked.

They gave her a map and marked the locations of traps they'd found.

"Thank you for your help," Bloodstone said, rising. "We'll be back if we have more questions."

"Are you going to keep this quiet?" the second ranger asked. "We can't survive without the tourist credits."

"Of course," Bloodstone said. "The TGPA is nothing if not discreet."

"And make sure you get back to Vinehollow before sundown," the first ranger said. "You don't want to be in this jungle after dark."

It was a simple snare trap. The rangers had already cut the

vine so that no animals would wander into it, but Bloodstone could see how it would have worked. Vine here, tree there, counterweight there, trigger here. Bloodstone was more focused on other signs of Jakk's presence. The man had left no evidence that he'd been here. He'd constructed the trap using only items found nearby. He was a master at using nature against itself.

Well, every low-tech problem had a high-tech solution. Bloodstone pulled out a small motion-activated sensor and embedded it in the tree. If Jakk came by to check the trap, it would fire a tiny tracking device that would – hopefully – embed itself into his clothing. Bloodstone looked at the sky. The sun was starting to go down, but they still had two more traps to inspect. "Let's get a move on," she said.

The next two traps both turned out to be pits with wooden spikes in the bottom. The rangers had uncovered the pits and taken out the spikes. Once again Bloodstone placed some sensors in the trees. It was now fully dark, but Bloodstone and Whisper both had night vision modes built into their goggles. They headed back towards Vinehollow.

They were less than a kilometer from the city when they heard a strange growl. They turned just in time to see a large beast charging toward them. Bloodstone and Whisper each dove to one side then fled in opposite directions. The creature followed Whisper, who scampered up the side of a tree like she was climbing a ladder. She looked below and got a good view of the beast for the first time.

It had four legs, armor plating, sharp horns, and a huge gaping maw full of sharp teeth. If you were to combine the most dangerous parts of a triceratops and a shark into one animal, that creature would also have been afraid of this beast. At first, it growled at Whisper from the base of the tree. Then, to Whisper's horror, it started to climb.

Whisper wasn't sure what to do. She had weapons, but she didn't want to risk hurting the animal. They were here to capture Jakk, not become poachers themselves. She reached for her whip, hoping she could shock the creature without harming it. Then she heard a sizzling sound, and a glowing red ball flew past her tree. The creature saw it too and immediately ran after it. Once it was gone, she saw Bloodstone standing nearby, waving her down.

"Hopefully that flare will keep it occupied for a few minutes," Bloodstone said, as Whisper reached the ground. They continued running toward Vinehollow. At one point they heard something rustling nearby, but it turned out to be a harmless moss hare. They reached the city just before dinner time.

After dinner, Whisper and Bloodstone sat on a bench on their deck, looking up at the stars. For all of Vinehollow's touristy atmosphere, it really was beautiful at night. Some of the jungle's nocturnal predators were drawn to light, and while the city had defenses against these creatures, it was better not to attract their attention at all. So the city had a "no exterior lights" policy after 8 PM.

Without the light pollution, the night sky was absolutely gorgeous, with an infinite number of stars shining like love itself. Granted, they could see the same view out the windows of the Bloodwind, but there was something special about seeing it planetside. Something natural. Spiritual. Romantic. The temperature had fallen since the sun had set, and the two hunters cuddled closely on the bench. Whisper's head lay on Bloodstone's shoulder.

It was Bloodstone who broke the bubble. "We should probably turn in early tonight. We have to get up early tomorrow."

"I suppose you're right," Whisper said. "But I'm going to have to take a quick shower first. I really reek."

They went inside. Bloodstone removed her cloth mask, and even though it wasn't her usual iconic helmet, the last bits of her "Bloodstone" personality seemed to come off with it. Now just Detanna, she felt much more relaxed. But not quite relaxed enough for sleep. She turned on the TV. An animated sponge was talking to a squirrel in a diving suit.

She stared at the TV without really watching it. Her mind raced, random thoughts competing for attention, none of them sticking around for very long. How do you track someone who knows how to avoid leaving tracks? How do we survive future animal attacks without harming the animals? How can Whisper smell so nice and claim she reeks?

At this, Detanna's thoughts became less and less about Jakk and more about Whisper. It really had been nice on the bench outside, and she deeply regretted ending it so soon. In truth, she could have sat out there with her all night. She wondered if Whisper was thinking about her right now too.

As if summoned by the thought, Whisper stepped into the common room. She was wearing her cloth mask and a towel. Her gray skin still glistened from the shower, and Detanna found herself struggling to maintain eye contact.

"Good, you're still up," Whisper said, and sat down on the chintzy couch next to Detanna. "I know you wanted to sleep, but I don't think I could turn my mind off if I tried. Anything you want to do?"

About a dozen ideas ran through Detanna's mind, but none of them were appropriate. "We could try one of those board games," she finally suggested.

"Since you suck at taking hints, let me rephrase the question," Whisper said, standing up. The towel fell to the floor.

"I didn't realize you had so many tentacles," said an animated crab on the TV. Detanna and Whisper burst out laughing.

"Well, that was a mood killer," Detanna said, as she turned off the TV.

"Not for me," Whisper said.

"Me neither," Detanna agreed. "Are you sure…"

"Don't overthink it," Whisper said. She grabbed Detanna by the wrist and pulled her toward one of the bedrooms.

"Life is short. I almost got eaten today, by a creature I can't even name."

"I think it was a hornhusker," Detanna offered.

"Still not exactly bedroom talk," Whisper said, removing Detanna's vest.

"Wait," Detanna said. "Do you like women? Or do you think of me as a man? Because I can't…"

"Hush," Whisper interrupted. "I like *you*."

They turned out the lights and pulled the heavy curtains closed. It was pitch black. Even Whisper's greater-than-average night vision couldn't make out more than vague shapes in the dark. Only then did she feel safe enough to remove her mask. The two kissed deeply and slipped beneath the sheets.

Whisper had never been with a trans person before, and wasn't sure how comfortable Detanna was with her own body. She asked "Is this OK?" several times during the encounter, each time she crossed a new threshold. For some couples this might have been a turn-off, but for them it just made it more exciting. They were learning about each other's bodies, their likes and dislikes. It was like being a teenager again, but without all the awkwardness.

When they were finally spent, they lay next to each other for a couple of hours, just talking. They didn't talk about anything serious, or life-changing, or anything that they would remember the next day. And yet, everything they said felt real, in a way none of their previous conversations ever had.

Eventually Detanna drifted off to sleep. Whisper grabbed her mask and went to the other bedroom. She tried falling asleep, but something was nagging at her. Little feelings of guilt jabbed at her gut. Detanna would not have slept with her if she'd known she was Alterra Sarr. Was she taking advantage of Detanna by seducing her? It was a doomed relationship. Sooner or later the truth would come out. Bloodstone would turn her in, and that would be that.

Worse yet, the element of danger had actually been arousing for her. Knowing that at any moment, the lights could come on and she'd be discovered – it was like making love on the edge of a cliff. The thought of being found out had brought her closer to climax than Detanna's tongue had. *What am I even doing?* she asked herself.

But at the same time, don't I deserve a little happiness? I'm on the run for a crime I didn't commit, unable to show my face in public. It had been a stressful year, and frankly, she deserved a little relief now and then. But why did that relief have to come from taking advantage of a friend?

She really had enjoyed it, and she knew Detanna had too. Her partner had been nervous at first, afraid that Whisper wouldn't find her body attractive. She needn't have worried. Aurorans were bisexual by nature, or possibly pan? Omni? Demi? Whisper really didn't know, because her people didn't have words for sexualities. Aurorans fell in love with a person's soul, not their body. Only then did they worry about how to please each other in the bedroom.

She realized she'd just thought the L word. Is that what this was? She'd found Bloodstone attractive long before she'd ever met her. The legendary Bloodstone, who never failed a hunt, who might have been any species or sex. But over the past year and a half, she'd found herself less attracted to Bloodstone and more attracted to Detanna. Bloodstone was an idea, but Detanna was flesh and blood and plump, kissable lips.

Whisper had developed strong feelings for Detanna. But love? It was hard to say. Her panic over the word overrode her ability to analyze it. Maybe if she weren't on the run, always worried for her life, hiding her face from her friends. If she could love Detanna without having to lie to her. Maybe.

Whisper looked at the clock. The alarm would go off in a couple of hours. She gave up on the hope of getting any sleep tonight. Instead, she sat cross-legged on the bed and meditated until the alarm went off.

* * *

Detanna woke up to the alarm, feeling more well rested than she had been in years. The sun wouldn't be up for another hour, so she took a quick shower before getting dressed. When she came back out to the common room, Whisper was there, eating a bowl of cereal. She kept lifting up the bottom of her cloth mask to shove the spoon in her mouth, so that Detanna wouldn't see the lower half of her face.

Detanna just smiled. Even after what they'd shared last night, Whisper still felt the need to hide her face. Her devotion to Auroran tradition was endearing. As much as Detanna wanted to rip that mask off and give Whisper the kiss of her life, she wasn't even tempted to cross that boundary. Whisper's beliefs were part of who she was, and Detanna wouldn't change a thing about her.

"So what's the plan?" Whisper asked.

"We head out to Jakk's hunting grounds, set some traps of our own, hide, and wait."

When the sun finally rose, Bloodstone and Whisper crouched in separate hiding spots, about a kilometer apart. Bloodstone had selected their positions based on Jakk's previous activity, the routes of dangerous game in the area, and her bounty hunter intuition. Each had set up traps of their own around their hiding spots. Not vine or spike traps like Jakk's, but high-tech devices that used motion sensors and stun guns.

Bloodstone was disappointed to discover that the motion sensors she'd set up the previous night hadn't yielded anything. They had detected plenty of animal activity, but nothing humanoid. Either Jakk hadn't gone back to check his traps, or he had spotted Bloodstone's sensors and circumvented them.

To avoid making noise, the two bounty hunters sent text messages back and forth over their comm units. Around noon, Bloodstone texted, "If he hunts in the early morning, we've missed him."

"Maybe he got the animals he wanted and left the planet," Whisper replied.

"How? He can't land a ship in the jungle, and he can't carry the corpses of protected species through Vinehollow."

"Depends on what trophy he keeps? If he skins them here in the jungle, he could take the pelts back in a suitcase."

"No, I think we're missing something," Bloodstone typed.

"Probably," Whisper typed back.

"Let's try further North. Stay there, I'll come to you." Bloodstone put the comm back in her pocket and stood up, stretching. She took a few steps forward and fell into a pit.

"It's been twenty minutes, where are you?" Whisper texted. "Did you find something?"

She stared at the comm, waiting for a reply, but none came. She stood, looking around for signs of movement. The hairs on the back of her neck stood up, but she wasn't sure why. Then she heard a THONG sound, and her reflexes kicked in. She ducked to the side just as an arrow whizzed by her head. She looked in the direction it had come from and saw nothing.

It was the brightest hour of the day, but the trees still cast plenty of shadows. She faded into the spotty darkness, camouflaging herself as best she could. But she couldn't just stand there. She had to choose between finding Bloodstone or the attacker. What if the attacker had already taken out Bloodstone? She couldn't worry about that right now.

She thought she spotted movement in the distance. Another arrow flew straight at her face. This time she snatched it out of the air. She dissipated her shadows and stood perfectly still, holding the arrow and staring in the direction of the archer. She hoped it was an intimidating pose. She could just make out a mud-covered figure in the distance. It was too far to see his face or other details, but she was an expert at reading body language, and Jakk's showed genuine surprise.

She ran towards Jakk, but he bolted. By the time she reached where he'd been, she couldn't find any signs of him. She searched for footprints, broken blades of grass, anything, but all she saw were hoof and paw prints. She didn't want to chase him too far, because she was more worried about Bloodstone. She turned South, planning to find her partner, when she heard an angry growl.

She spotted the source. It was a razorback chetal. It looked like a green-furred lion with scales on its head and bony spines along its back. It was about twenty meters away. It had its eyes locked on her, and was ready to pounce.

"I really don't have time for this today," Whisper said, drawing her whip. She considered running, but she knew this cat was faster. And it could probably climb trees. Hopefully a good zap from her electric whip would scare it off.

The chetal leaped toward her, easily closing half the gap in one bound. Its second leap would bring it down right on top of her. Whisper was about to let loose her whip when an arrow hit the chetal in the side. Jakk stood halfway out of a hole a few meters away. He climbed out and nocked another arrow.

Whisper ran to the chetal's aid. It lay on its side, bleeding heavily. "Get away from it," Jakk said. "Kill's mine."

Jakk was tall and muscular. He had a handlebar mustache and a shaven head, reminding Whisper of a circus strongman. He wore no shirt, just a large vest, camouflaged pants, gloves, and combat boots. And he was covered in mud from head to toe. He still held the bow on Whisper, ready to fire if she made any sudden moves.

Whisper ignored him, examining the chetal's wound. "I can't save it," Whisper said sadly, as the animal's breathing slowed.

"It was a clean kill," Jakk said. "I don't do sloppy. It didn't suffer."

Whisper turned to face him. "Jakk Venson, I have come to take you to the authorities. Come with me willingly, and you will remain unharmed."

Jakk processed this for a moment, then burst out laughing. "You've bitten off more than you can chew, girlie." He drew back his bowstring.

Whisper flicked her whip, jerking the bow out of his hand. The arrow flew far and wide. Jakk drew a hunting knife and closed the distance between them. He was surprisingly fast for his size, and he grabbed Whisper's wrist before she had the chance to whip again. His grip was so strong it caused her to drop the whip. He tried to stab her with his other hand, but she blocked his thrust. Then she kicked him in the stomach and he let go of her.

Whisper drew her own knife, and they stood face to face, each anticipating the next attack. Jakk went first, just missing her with a jab to the chest. Whisper swirled around him, using her dodge as an opening for her own attack. She just missed his arm, again surprised by his speed. This went on for several seconds, each dodging the other's attacks with no blood drawn. Whisper aimed to incapacitate, going for important tendons and such. As a trained hunter, Jakk went for instant kill attacks, focusing on Whisper's heart and jugular.

Whisper dove between his legs, coming up behind him, hoping to stab him in the back of the knee. But he moved his leg just in time, turning to kick her in the back. She stood, feinted left then thrust right, going for his inner elbow. He anticipated her diversion and grabbed her by the throat with his free hand. Whisper stabbed him in the forearm, and he dropped her.

Ducking one thrust, Whisper dropped to the ground and went into a leg sweep. She made contact, but it was like kicking a statue. During the half-second it took Whisper to recover, Jakk dropped his full weight on her, pinning her to the ground. With one hand he grabbed her knife hand, and with the other, he attempted to stab her in the throat.

Whisper grabbed his arm with her free hand, slowing the descent of his knife, but he was just so strong, and she was exhausted.

Jakk paused. When he had grabbed her throat earlier, her mask had come undone. Recognition dawned on his face. "The biggest game of all," he said. Whisper tried to kick him, knee him, anything, but his body weight was crushing. She spat in his face, but he just laughed.

"You know I'm worth more alive," Whisper said.

"It's not about the money," Jakk said. "It's about the hunUHHNT!" Suddenly he was lifted off of her. A second razorback chetal had its claws in him, and it dragged him away. Whisper quickly climbed the nearest tree, found the darkest spot under the canopy, and drew the shadows in around her. From her vantage point, she watched as the female chetal clawed and bit Jakk into bloody pieces. This animal didn't attack out of hunger, it sought revenge for its mate.

Whisper waited in her tree until the chetal finished dismembering Jakk. Then the animal nuzzled the corpse of her mate, and finally disappeared into the jungle. Whisper waited a bit more, then quietly climbed down, retrieved her whip and fixed her mask, then went to find Bloodstone.

Whisper found Bloodstone half an hour later. She had fallen in with her arms above her head, and the narrowness of the pit had prevented her from reaching any of her tools or her comm unit. She'd tried climbing, but the dirt walls kept crumbling in when jostled, so it was slow going. She was starting to make headway when Whisper showed up.

"Are you hurt?" Whisper asked.

"Only my ego," Bloodstone replied. "Jakk must have known exactly where I'd wait for him, to dig the trap there. When I get my hands on him…"

"About that," Whisper interrupted, and filled her in on what she'd missed.

* * *

They managed to locate Jakk's head and turned it in for a reduced bounty. Back aboard the Bloodwind, Whisper invited Bloodstone into her quarters for a chat.

"So, how was he planning to get the pelts off of Tropis?" Whisper asked.

"I found some Levatech discs in his belt pouch. My guess is he was planning to wait until nightfall, attach the discs, then float the carcasses up into the air. Then he'd pick them up in a shuttle and fly off. Or maybe he was just going to do like you said – skin it, take the parts he needed, and sneak them into a suitcase."

"I'm sorry we couldn't bring him in alive," Whisper said. "But I'm glad he won't hurt any more animals."

"Jakk died by his own doing," Detanna said. "He hunted until he became prey. I'll probably die the same way someday."

Whisper wanted to say something but wasn't sure how to say it. "Last night…" she began.

"Oh, no," Detanna said. "Please don't tell me you have regrets. Because honestly, I've been walking on air, and I was hoping you felt the same way. I know I'm… different… but—"

"Nothing like that," Whisper said. "I'm just afraid of leading you on. Fun is fun, but it can't go anywhere. I just can't be in a serious relationship right now. There's… It's just… complicated."

"It's okay," Detanna said. "I'm fine with whatever pace you want to set. I like spending time with you. I'm just glad to have you in my life."

"Thank you," Whisper said, relieved. "I promise, if it were anyone, it would be you."

Detanna nodded. "So… movie tonight?"

"Maybe later," Whisper said. "Right now, I have a better idea." She turned out the lights.

01.09 *Eroddicka*

ED.02501.09.19

A small white ship hurtled through space. Inside, four passengers whiled the hours away. Raven stood behind the ship's pilot, engaging them in a non-verbal intellectual conversation. Her telepathic conversational partner, Trenyn, used all four hands to work the controls.

In the back of the ship, the other two passengers passed the time by playing cards. "Okay," Vik said, "If I win this hand, you have to take off your shirt."

"I'm not wearing a shirt," Dervish replied. "I'm not wearing anything. I'm just using my shapeshifting ability to make it look like I'm fully dressed."

"Then you'll have to shapeshift to where you look like you're topless," Vik said. "Now show me your cards."

"I didn't do so good," Dervish said, showing Vik her straight flush. "See? None of the numbers match."

"Yep, doesn't beat my pair of threes," Vik gloated. "Take it off."

"What are you two doing back there?" Raven called.

"Just practicing," Vik answered. "We are headed for a casino, you know."

"You won't have time for any gambling," Raven told him. "We're on a mission. Now knock it off."

"So, Raven," Vik asked, getting up and walking over to the cockpit area, "What's the plan when we get there?"

"We're looking for a Marae called Vraxx," Raven said. "He may have framed Alterra Sarr."

"I doubt that," Vik said.

"Nevertheless, we should check out any leads," Raven said. "If he was impersonating Sarr when EarthStation 1 exploded, and we can prove it, it's worth our time."

"How do we find him?" Vik asked.

"He's tall and purple in his usual form. Shouldn't be hard to spot. Eros Roddick employs a large number of shapeshifters, both as escorts and as fighters. We should check out both the fighting arena and the brothel areas. We'll find other shapeshifter employees, and ask them if they've seen him. Ask if Vraxx has ever worked there, and where he might be now. If nothing else, maybe we'll run into one of his friends or relatives. Of course, if we just walk in there asking questions, they'll throw us out. We'll pose as regular customers and try to be inconspicuous."

"So what do we do if we don't find out what we need to know?" Dervish asked.

Raven thought about that for a moment before answering. "Then we go to the top. We ask Roddick himself."

The "Pleasure Planet" was not really a planet, but a colossal space station that wandered throughout the galaxy. Its course never brought it too close to systems where its activities might be considered illegal; in fact, it avoided most of the Galactic Nations members altogether. When, on occasion, it had to pass through, say, Earth's solar system, all illegal activities aboard the station would cease until it was out of the system. This rarely happened, though. The Pleasure Planet mostly traveled in neutral or unclaimed areas of space.

To say it was the galaxy's largest casino would be a huge

understatement, but it was much more than that. It was also a fighting arena, a house of ill repute, not to mention a seller of hard-to-find narcotics. In fact, it would be difficult to name an illegal or immoral activity that wasn't being practiced somewhere on this monstrous artificial world.

The owner of the Pleasure Planet, the infamous Eros Roddick, was both charismatic and smarmy. He was as slick as a used spacecraft salesman, and every bit as honest. The fact that he was a former crime boss was both well-known and unproven. At its zenith, his criminal empire was second only to the Inner Eye. But these days, Roddick was clean, legally speaking. He had long ago ceased criminal activities in the areas where they were illegal. He no longer needed to steal, as he was already immeasurably rich. And if he needed someone murdered, he would simply find a legal way to exterminate them.

For example, when Roddick wanted IGP Chief Cravel Lithclo out of his hair, he simply dug up some dirt on the officer. Lithclo spent the rest of his short life in a maximum security prison, where he was beaten to death by the very inmates he had helped to incarcerate, none of whom were connected to Roddick in any way. And then there was rival crime boss Foros "The Tentacle" Rabeed, who Roddick publicly taunted until Rabeed was practically forced to compete in the Pleasure Dome Arena just to defend his honor. He lost his life to a three-headed clorg, in a perfectly legal bout that was broadcast across the galaxy. And in a gesture of goodwill, all proceeds from the ticket sales went to Rabeed's widow.

The Pleasure Planet employed thousands upon thousands of beings of every species. And that included Marae shapeshifters. Marae didn't have an in-born concept of gender, but the Grunthians raised them for specific duties, which often required them to imprint on a specific sex. The female-imprinted Marae made perfect concubines, as they were adept at fulfilling any client's fantasy. The less-malleable but much stronger male-imprinted Marae were perfect warriors to compete in the arena. As a species, the Marae were easy to control, and fiercely loyal to those that raised them. This made them model slaves, though Roddick would have preferred you use the term "employees."

It wasn't much of a stretch to imagine that one of these Marae might have known Vraxx at one time or another. The vast majority of the galaxy's Marae originated from the same place - the breeding camps on the second moon of Grunthar. The Grunthians bred these creatures specifically to sell to people like Eros Roddick or Teykor Vermon. In fact, it was their most profitable export. So of course some of Roddick's shapeshifters could have known Vraxx at some point. The question, really, was whether or not they would remember him, or if they would have any idea where he might be now.

And that wasn't likely.

After several more hours of Vik asking "Are we there yet?" they finally reached the Pleasure Planet. They found a landing zone for the ship, disembarked, and joined a huge crowd headed for the main entryway. They were scanned for weapons, and any lethal devices found were confiscated. Even the hidden devices in Raven's robotic body were disabled, despite none of them being lethal. There was no penalty for having carried the weapons this far. The management knew that for some people it was second nature to be armed; it didn't mean that they actually intended to kill someone. It was no big deal; they also didn't allow outside food or drinks. And all customers were given claim tickets, so they knew that their weapons would be returned.

After they passed the security station, the four bounty hunters entered the grand hall. This immense room really showed off just how glamorous - and kitschy - the Pleasure Planet was. The floor was covered with a luxurious red carpet with gold trim. Here and there about the room were gold-plated Corinthian columns, stretching all the way up to the ceiling - it had to be a hundred meters, at least. Lining the walls, flanking the many doorways, there were huge golden statues of gods and warriors from various cultures. A giant marquee hung from the ceiling, boldly proclaiming "WELCOME TO THE PLEASURE PLANET," followed by directions to the different areas of the station, as well as showtimes for the various forms of live entertainment. Voices from hidden loudspeakers called out the same information. Scantily-clad women and men of various species circulated the room, helping patrons figure out where they wanted to go and how to spend their money.

The sights, the sounds, the enormity of it all... it was overwhelming. It was even more impressive to realize that there were fourteen other grand halls, each just as immense, scattered throughout the Planet.

"So..." Vik asked, "Where do you want to go first?"

"Whatever's closest," Raven answered. "Let's get this over with."

"Welcome to our escort service, what sort of man would you like to escort you this evening?" The humanoid robot at the door was way too enthusiastic about his job, in Raven's way of thinking.

"I'm not looking for a man," Raven answered.

"Very well, a woman then," the robot cheerfully replied. "I believe you will find our selection to be the finest in the galaxy."

"Actually, we need to speak to your shapeshifters," Raven said.

"Of course! Why settle for one date when you can have someone who changes their appearance to fit your mood? But you understand, of course, that they are a bit pricier."

"I'm not here to rent one of your escorts. I just want to talk to them," Raven said.

"You just want to talk? Well, what you do on your date is none of my business," the robot replied. "But you should know that the price is the same no matter what you do with your companion. And no refunds."

"Just let us into the chambers, so we can talk to them," said Raven. Seeing the robot's frown, Raven tried a different tactic. "I have to see your selection before I decide which one I want to spend my evening with, don't I?"

"Very good, then," the robot exclaimed, thankful to get this difficult customer out of his plastic hair. "You may come in and talk to the escorts. But only for fifteen minutes. And no touching!" A door opened next to the robot, and the four bounty hunters went inside.

They found themselves in a large open room, filled with alluring lingerie-clad women from all manner of worlds. Some lounged on huge plush pillows; others just stood around or leaned against the wall. Some played board games with each other, or sat cross-legged on the floor in storytelling groups, or just stood around talking. All in all, it looked like a gigantic slumber party.

"Nice room," said Vik. "I think I'll stay here, while you guys check out the rest of the Planet."

"You'll do no such thing," said Raven. "So... which ones are the shapeshifters. Dervish? Can you pick them out?"

"Um... not really," Dervish answered.

Occasionally, a customer would enter the room, look about for a bit, and then point to a woman. The pair would then leave for a more secluded back room. One heavyset, blue-skinned man strutted proudly into the bordello and made a strange gesture with his many fingers. A small group of women who had been lounging in the back stood up and waved him over to them. The customer went to them and pointed to the nearest one. She walked over to him and changed her shape to match that of his species. He said something to her in his native tongue, and she altered her shape again slightly. Her skin lightened to a pale blue, her bosom enlarged, and her eyes changed color. At the patron's request, she performed a few more minor tweaks to her appearance, until he finally nodded with satisfaction. Then they left together.

Those must be them, Trenyn told the other three bounty hunters. Raven led them towards the group of shapeshifters. When they were about halfway there, a voluptuous blond-furred Galean woman grabbed Raven by the arm.

"You don't want them," the sex worker told Raven, their faces only centimeters from each other. "Sure, they can look like anything you want, but that doesn't make them good lovers. They lack imagination. If you take me instead, I'll give you a night that you will remember for years." The catlike woman put her hands on Raven's shoulders, leaned in close, and nuzzled Raven's cheek with her own.

Raven, in a state of wide-eyed shock, took a few seconds to react. She pushed the escort away, harder than she meant to, yelling "Sorry no thank you!" Every head in the room turned to them.

The robot who had granted them entry came running into the room. "That's it! You're out of here! Guards!" The bounty hunters were led out of the bordello at gunpoint. Once they were in the hallway again, the guards let them loose to go about their business.

"Sorry," Raven said. "But at least they didn't throw us out of the Pleasure Planet entirely. I suppose we should try the fighting arena now."

You enjoyed that, Trenyn told her.

Raven cocked her head. "What? Pushing that woman? No! It was a knee-jerk reaction, I shouldn't have been so viol—"

I mean the nuzzling, Trenyn answered. *I sensed your arousal.*

Raven looked indignant. "I assure you, I did not," she said icily. "And that was very intrusive."

I wasn't trying to sense it, Trenyn explained. The two of them were so in tune, and Raven so rarely experienced strong feelings, that Trenyn usually sensed it when she did.

"Still," Raven said. "Don't… bring it up in front of Vik."

Sorry, Trenyn said, but Raven was lost in thought.

Raven didn't think about her sexuality often. About a year and a half ago, she had kissed a woman and concluded she was asexual. Now she wondered if she had decided too hastily. Maybe she only found very specific people attractive. And was it even just women?

"Wait a minute," Vik said, interrupting her thoughts. "Where's Dervish?"

The three hunters looked around in confusion. Raven asked, "Wasn't she thrown out with us?"

To be honest, I don't know, Trenyn answered. *I just assumed she was behind us.*

Vik smiled. "She must have made herself look like a hooker so she could stay behind and talk to the other Marae!"

"She's smarter than we give her credit for," Raven said. "And please don't say 'hooker.' Do you want to wait for her or go on to the arena?"

I'll wait here for Dervish, Trenyn suggested. *You two check out the arena and we'll catch up with you later.*

"You two here to compete?" This doorman was nothing like the one at the brothel. This was a massive Grunthian with bulging muscles and no sense of humor.

"Actually," Raven began, "according to tonight's event schedule, you have some Marae fighting tonight. We wanted to ask them a few questions."

"We don't allow reporters in the locker rooms," came the gruff reply.

"We're not reporters," Raven said. "We just—"

"Lady," the Grunthian interrupted, "There's only two doors to this arena. One's for spectators, the other's for fighters."

"Fine," Raven said. "Sign us up." Vik stared at her, his mouth open. "What," Raven said to him, "you thought this was going to be easy?"

Raven, this is Trenyn. Can you hear me? Personal communications devices didn't work within the Pleasure Planet. This was partly because of interference from WPMP, Roddick's broadcasting station. But the Planet also had comm blockers to prevent people from cheating at the poker tables, to curb any possible espionage, and to keep customers from having their damn ringtones go off during a show.

Fortunately, telepathy worked just fine. Trenyn's mental projections didn't work at extremely long distances, although they were better at communicating with Raven than with anyone else. This time she was just within range. *Yes,* came Raven's reply. *Did you find Dervish?*

Affirmative. She's here with me now. She managed to talk to several Marae. She also made two hundred credits... Not how you think. But she didn't learn anything useful. A couple of the Marae sex workers did know Vraxx at one time, but they have no idea where he is now. We're on our way to the arena. Are you there now?

It's a bit complicated, Raven replied. *But we're working on it. Come to the arena, and buy tickets for the fights. Try and sit as close to the front as possible.*

We'll be there, Trenyn answered.

"Laaaaaaaaadiiiiiiiiiiiiiieeeeeeeees and Gentlemen! Welcome to the Pleasure Planet Arena!" The announcer bowed, as cheers erupted from all over the massive stadium. "Tonight, for your enjoyment, we will have fights more exciting than you will ever see again in your lifetime! Humanoid against beast, humanoid against machine, and even humanoid against humanoid! We will have humiliation matches and death bouts! You will see fighters from twenty-six different species, with skills and abilities beyond your imagination! And it all starts... Right now!"

Do you see Raven anywhere? Trenyn asked. Dervish looked

around and shook her head. The crowd was way too large, and the seating areas were dark. Trenyn and Dervish had managed to get some great seats, due partly to Dervish's recent earnings. They were only six rows from the front, with a great view of the action.

I'll try to talk to her again, Trenyn mentally told Dervish. *Raven, where are you? We're here in the stadium.*

Busy right now, came the reply. *Just enjoy the fights. You'll see us eventually.*

The first fight was between five Grunthians and a Vikarian maultiger. The Grunthians were armed only with spike-knuckled maces. The maultiger, on the other hand, had fangs half a meter long, and its body was covered with sharp quills. The match took fifteen minutes, and the arena was drenched in blood afterward. The survivors? Two Grunthians, both seriously wounded.

The next match was just as bloody, and involved a couple of Glorkans, a Morthian snow-ape, and a zondarg. The match after that wasn't bloody at all, but very brutal - a sapient robot versus a human cyborg. Both used highly advanced technological weaponry, but thanks to extensive electromagnetic shielding, the cyborg won without a scratch.

Dervish couldn't stand to watch these matches. She kept her face planted on Trenyn's shoulder during the bloody parts. Trenyn, however, viewed the whole thing with scientific curiosity. The matches were pointlessly brutal, but many papers could have been written about the psychological status of the contestants... and the audience. They were also learning a lot about alien anatomy; in fact, an entire Glorkan digestive system lay on the arena floor at that very moment.

Another fight was about to begin. A hush fell over the crowd, and the announcer bellowed, "The next match will pit three teams of two in a three-way last-team-standing anything-goes fight to the finish! Introducing the red team..." Spotlights played all over the arena before settling on two beings entering the arena through a red door. "Thorn and Kiruusk, two of the most celebrated warriors from the planet Vhelra!" The pair of fighters had yellow scales and were clad in white spiked armor. Thorn was armed with a hooked spear, and Kiruusk wielded a barbed sword. Both contestants looked very menacing.

"And for the yellow team, we have two Marae shapeshifters - Skark and Thaloon!" Trenyn and Dervish both perked up with this announcement. The light centered on the two shapeshifters, both of whom were in vaguely humanoid forms but with long reptilian heads and dark gray skin.

"And now the blue team..." The lights played over the arena, keeping the audience in suspense. "One's a former cop, the other's a cyborg, let's hear it for Vik and Raven!" The lights centered on the two bounty hunters, who stood confidently near the blue door. Vik held a stun baton. Raven was armed with a spiked mace.

What the hell do you think you're doing? Trenyn telepathically asked Raven.

It was the only way they would let me get near them, Raven answered, looking up into the audience but unable to pick Trenyn out.

"And now," the announcer bellowed, "Begin!"

The Vhelran gladiators wasted no time rushing their opponents. Thorn, holding his spear straight out like a lance, ran straight towards Vik, who leaped to the side. Raven, meanwhile, had to contend with the Marae known as Thaloon, who had turned into a spiked reptile. Across the arena, the other Marae, Skark, engaged the Vhelran Kiruusk in a heated battle.

The Marae-reptile took a swipe at Raven, ripping her shirt and leaving a shallow groove in the chest plate of her her cybernetic body. Raven used her mace as a shield to deflect the creature's attacks. She didn't want to counter-attack, because she was afraid of killing the Marae before she had a chance to speak to him.

Vik had no such compunctions about harming his Vhelran foe. The problem was, his baton wasn't sufficient to penetrate his opponent's armor. So Vik continued to use his superior speed and agility to dodge attacks while waiting for an opening. It didn't look as if any such openings would be forthcoming.

On the other side of the playing field, the Vhelran warrior Kiruusk quickly slaughtered his Marae opponent. Skark had fought well, but his shapeshifting abilities proved to be no match for a true Vhelran gladiator. The victorious Kiruusk immediately chose his next targets - Raven and Thaloon. Seeing this mad warrior rushing towards her with his jagged sword, Raven knocked her Marae opponent to the side with a powerful fist, so she could concentrate on this new enemy. She wasn't quick enough, however. With one quick slice of the Vhelran's sword, her severed left arm skidded across the floor.

Raven was stunned. *He must be using a virtrinium blade!* she thought. Testing a theory and saving her life at the same time, she quickly brought up her mace and blocked his next swing. Yep, all the weapons were virtrinium. Nothing but the best in Roddick's arena. This was good because it meant that her mace could probably damage his armor. Of course, that would only work if she actually had the chance to swing her mace, and Kiruusk wasn't allowing her to do that. He was obviously an experienced fighter, and he wasn't letting her get a move in edgewise.

Meanwhile, Vik continued to dodge, duck, and run from Thorn. Occasionally Vik would use his Levatech to push his opponent away, but it was like pushing a brick wall. Vik was bleeding from several minor wounds and was starting to lose his stamina. If an opportunity didn't present itself soon, he was done for.

He hadn't long to wait. Suddenly and inexplicably, Thorn dropped his spear. "Dropped" might not have been the right word, though. It looked more like the spear had been wrenched from his hand. Not one to look a gift horse in the mouth, Vik took advantage of his opponent's momentary confusion, pulled the weapon into his hand, and drove it through Thorn's knee.

Raven had a similar experience. Kiruusk had cornered her, and she was unable to avoid his final sword thrust to her face. But at the last moment, his blade was deflected to the side and penetrated the wall next to her head. As Kiruusk tried to pull his sword out of the wall, Raven took her mace and pounded her opponent's back, knocking him to the ground. Then Raven took one final swing, hitting him across the back of the legs. She heard a nauseating crunch as his bones shattered.

Thanks, Trenyn, Raven telepathically told her best friend. She had immediately known who had helped her out. Trenyn's telekinetic abilities were poor for their species, but they had no trouble manipulating anything made of virtrinium.

Raven and Vik were the only ones left standing. The only other competitor still in the fight, the Marae called Thaloon, was only just now recovering from Raven's punch. Raven ducked down beside the Marae and held her mace to his throat. He was too injured to change shape or defend himself. She told him, "Please, I don't want to kill you. If I let you live, will you answer some questions?"

"All right," answered the shapeshifter.

Raven tossed her mace to the ground. She then grabbed Vik's hand, and they raised their arms in victory. There was a small outcry from the audience demanding death and blood, but the rules did allow victors to show mercy to their defeated challengers. Especially when the loser was a Marae, which were considered valuable assets.

After the match, Raven and Vik met with Thaloon in the locker room. He took them to the Marae living quarters, where the bounty hunters managed to speak with more than a dozen shapeshifters. There were no leads. Once again, a couple of them were former acquaintances of Vraxx, but they had no idea where he might be now. Disappointed, they left the Marae quarters and met back up with Trenyn and Dervish. Trenyn helped Raven re-attach her arm while they discussed their next course of action.

"Well, one thing left to try," Raven told them.

"Who wishes to see the great and powerful Eros Roddick?" There was no visible doorman, just a speaker box on the door.

"I'm Raven, and this is Vik, Trenyn, and Dervish. We just want to ask him a few questions."

"Are you reporters or cops?"

"Neither," Raven answered. "We're bounty hunters. We thought he might know something about a case we're working on."

"The master does not have time for such matters. Go away."

"But," Vik said, holding up a large flat box, "we brought a pizza."

The voice immediately became friendly. "Come in, come in!" it said, and the door opened.

Roddick's "office" was a large lavish lounge room, with soft expensive furniture and gaudy decorations. There was a waterfall pouring down one entire wall, flowing into a large pool, in which swam several bathing beauties. In one corner there was a zebra-striped bed shaped like a champagne glass, large enough to comfortably support fifteen humans and their pets. And it probably had. Roddick himself reclined on an oversized beanbag chair, flanked by a pair of beautiful women, barely legal and barely dressed.

Roddick wore gold-plated boots, purple bell-bottomed pants, an open purple shirt, several gold medallions, some oversized rings on every finger, gigantic rhinestone sunglasses, and a purple hat with a feather in it. It was a bold look, and on anyone else, it would have looked like a Halloween costume. But on Roddick it seemed perfectly appropriate.

The bounty hunters sat opposite him, on a large fuzzy sofa, helping the crime lord eat his pizza. "I'm surprised you let us in," Raven said.

"I was hungry and bored," Roddick answered. "Ordinarily I would have had you killed for intercepting my room service, but I thought I might as well hear what you had to say."

"Alterra Sarr," Raven began, "is being sought for the destruction of the IGP Earth space station."

"I know that," Roddick said. "I had to deal with undercover IGP agents for six months afterwards. They were convinced she was hiding out here."

"There's a chance the crime was actually committed by a Marae named Vraxx. He's the former bodyguard of Teykor Vermon. Whether or not this shapeshifter was Alterra all along, or whether he framed her, we don't know." Actually Raven knew for certain that Alterra was innocent, but saying so might have invited questions she didn't want to answer.

"I still don't see how this is my problem," Roddick said.

"We're looking for Vraxx. We thought he might be employed here. Or if not, maybe you would know where he is now. Maybe you would have connections with his current employer."

"Sounds like you want me to do your work for you," Roddick said. "It would take a lot of research on my part to help you. Why should I?"

"Because we were responsible for the death of Teykor Vermon, one of your greatest rivals," Raven answered coldly.

Roddick's eyes opened wide. "That was you?" Raven nodded. Roddick thought for a few minutes, then told them,

"Okay then. I'll give you any information I can find. But you have to do a job for me, to work it off."

Is it illegal? Trenyn asked.

Roddick smiled, revealing several gold teeth. "Perfectly harmless, you have my word. Just a delivery. Something that's out of my reach right now."

"Deal," Raven said.

The small white craft once again hurtled through the vastness of space. The bounty hunters had just finished dropping off a package on the planet Korcha. Vik piloted the ship, while Trenyn performed more repairs on Raven's artificial body. Dervish watched Trenyn work, looking distressed.

Dervish sighed. "I wish I could help those Marae. The way all of you helped me."

"Maybe someday you can," Raven said.

"They didn't seem too unhappy to me," Vik said.

"That's because they don't know any better," Dervish said. "All they know is the jobs they were groomed for. If I could explain to them that there's more to life…"

"So let me get this straight," Vik interrupted. "You want to convince them that they're unhappy, and then save them from it?"

"It's not like that…" Dervish began.

"Don't waste your breath," Raven said. "He won't get it."

"Hey now," Vik said. "I'm not an idiot. I know the Marae are being exploited. And that's terrible. But with all the other problems in the universe, I wouldn't put too much work into saving people who haven't even asked to be saved. Just saying."

"I suppose you're right," Dervish said.

"You know it," Vik said with a smug grin.

"I was talking to Raven," Dervish said.

Raven decided to change the subject. "And you're sure," she asked Dervish, "that no one saw you drop off the package?"

"I don't think so," Dervish answered. "I mean, I just set it on the doorstep and left. I didn't even ring the doorbell. Even if someone saw me, I was in disguise so it shouldn't matter."

I'm still not sure I like this, Trenyn told them. *We don't know what was in it. It could have been a bomb. We might have just killed an innocent person.*

"I scanned it for explosives," Raven said. Everyone looked at her. "What? He said we couldn't look in the package, he didn't say we couldn't scan it. I didn't find anything harmful. No explosives, no metal, no narcotics, and nothing to indicate it could be a virus."

"Well, Roddick said it wasn't anything illegal," Vik said. "I don't trust him, but what's done is done."

Down on the planet Korcha, a little girl opened a parcel that she had found on her doorstep. She was just learning to read, and she found that the package was addressed to her. "Mommy!" she called. "Come look! I got a present!" She opened the box and found a blue stuffed lion inside. There was also a card, which read "Happy Birthday! Love, Dad."

The little girl knew only vaguely about her real father. She had heard her mother talk about him with her new boyfriend, and such discussions usually turned into fights. The girl had heard words like "alimony" and "custody" and "restraining order" thrown around, but she didn't know what any of that meant. All the little girl knew for sure was that right now, her father was out there somewhere, and he loved her.

In exchange for the delivery, Roddick managed to dig up an entire dossier on Vraxx. Unfortunately, it wasn't very informative or helpful. There simply wasn't that much to tell. Vraxx was raised at the Grunthian breeding camp. He was given to Teykor Vermon as a peace offering. Vraxx operated as Vermon's bodyguard for many years. He was last seen on Valos about a week before the IGP space station was destroyed. He hadn't been seen since.

Except, of course, by Whisper, onboard Vermon's space station. If the dossier did nothing else, at least it proved that Alterra hadn't been Vraxx all along. Raven already knew this, of course, being a close friend of Alterra's. But it was nice to have the evidence. Too bad it didn't clear Alterra's name entirely.

And so ended the mission. Vraxx's trail had grown cold. There was nothing to do now but wait, and hope that Vraxx would make a mistake and show himself. Until then they would put Vraxx on the back burner, and pursue other bounties. Successful bounty hunters shared certain qualities, such as strength and cunning. But there was one trait they needed above all else.

Patience.

<h1 style="text-align:center">01.10 Gal Pals</h1>

ED.002501.10.15

"Bark! Bark! Bark!" bellowed the bulldog, looking up from the base of the tree.

"Oh, you want bark? Here's some bark," replied the squirrel, pulling out a saw. A few seconds later a tree branch fell on the dog's head. Little sparrows flitted around in circles as a bump rose from the top of his head.

Dervish and Yna laughed out loud. They had never seen this cartoon before, and they found the slapstick hilarious. Panther was curled up on Yna's bed, and the two women leaned back on him like he was a beanbag chair.

"These are great!" Dervish said when the cartoon was over. "Are there any more?"

"Wait 'til you see the ones with the bunny," Yna said, queueing up another episode. Panther stirred and made a mewling sound, and Yna paused the cartoon. "One minute, I think he needs to go." Yna took Panther out of her quarters and walked with him to the restroom down the hall. When the crew first acquired the Bloodwind, some of the facilities were sized for Grunthians. Most of the toilets had since been resized, but they'd left a few unaltered for Panther. The big cat was surprisingly trainable.

On the way back to her quarters, Yna spotted Bloodstone

coming down the hall. She told Yna good morning and handed her a metal card. Mission time.

Less than an hour later, a small white shuttle descended toward planet Snud. "I want to hear it again," Yna said, sitting in the pilot's seat. Dervish stuck the metal card into the slot under the viewscreen, and the mission data appeared. There were several folders full of relevant files, with an audio briefing in the main directory. Dervish tapped the audio file, and let it play while she browsed the other folders.

"His name is Dregan Flize," Bloodstone's voice said. "At least, that's how people refer to him. No one knows his real name, or what he looks like. He runs a slave trafficking ring. He kidnaps young women and sells them at underground auctions. The two of you will pose as college students on spring break. You will allow yourselves to get kidnapped, learn whatever you can, and escape. With your abilities, it shouldn't be much of a problem."

Dervish smiled nervously, hoping Bloodstone's confidence in her wasn't misplaced. The recording continued. "Each of you will be given subdermal tracking devices, contact lens cameras, and implanted communicators. Yna, I don't know if this tech will survive your abilities, so try not to get separated from each other. Dervish, you'll want to be careful that you don't lose any implants while shapeshifting. We will be watching and tracking you the entire time. If we lose contact, use your best judgment, but your safety comes first. Good luck."

Dervish changed her shape to look more like her idea of a partying college student. Yna wore a short skirt, a blond wig, and makeup. They each wore a purple flower in their hair. While Dervish was used to impersonating a variety of people, to Yna it felt like she was going to a costume party. She had no memory of her childhood, but she'd spent her teenage years on pirate ships. Due to the destructiveness of her energy form, she usually dressed in cheap clothing, and her hair never grew down to her shoulders. This was the first time in her life she'd worn makeup.

It was always spring break somewhere on Snud. They received visitors all year long, from colleges all over the galaxy. The planet hosted one huge, continuous beach party, which gradually shifted location to follow the spring season. The local law enforcement stayed on the verge of exhaustion just keeping the partiers from hurting themselves. Many students hid their vacation plans from their families, which made their disappearances that much harder to track. It was a kidnapper's paradise.

As they walked along a pier, Dervish stared open-mouthed at the swarms of teens and young adults. Some wore swimsuits, others party attire, and a few wore nothing at all – but no one batted an eye. Restaurants and bars lined the pier, all filled to seating capacity. "That's a lot of people," Dervish said.

Yna nodded uncomfortably. She wanted this mission to be over. "So how do we get the kidnappers to notice us?"

"You'll need to get out of the crowds," Bloodstone said through the communicator in her ear.

"Are you not seeing this? This planet is nothing but crowd," Yna responded.

"Figure out where the kids go to be alone," Bloodstone said. "Make out spots and such. Ask around. One of the victims was taken from the laundry room of her hotel. Another was taken from a parking lot."

"It's still going to be like winning the lottery," Yna said.

"Not necessarily," Bloodstone said. "Those flowers I had you put in your hair? Those are purple stellarbells. They don't grow on this planet, but some of the victims were seen wearing them. I have a theory that one of the traffickers hands them out to women who fit their criteria, to mark them for their accomplices. If you've been spotted wearing them, you're probably already being watched, and they're just waiting to catch you alone."

"You might have mentioned that in the briefing," Dervish said.

"Sorry, I was in a hurry. Any other questions?"

"Do the police know about the flower thing?" Yna asked.

"I don't think so. It's just a hunch on my part."

Yna rolled her eyes. Bloodstone often withheld evidence from the police. Partly because she felt the police were incompetent, but mostly because she wanted to collect the bounty herself. It was a common point of contention between Bloodstone and Whisper. To be fair, though, the police on this planet probably wouldn't have known what to do with this information. They would have just posted some signs telling guests not to accept flowers from strangers, and the traffickers would have picked a different method of tracking their victims.

Pushing their way through the crowds, Yna and Dervish spotted signs that pointed to a parking lot. When they got there, it wasn't devoid of people, but at least it had some breathing room. Parked hovercars filled every space. Some were occupied by couples in the throes of passion. Some people sat on the roofs of their vehicles, drinking and talking.

They walked to the far edge of the parking lot and sat on the curb, just talking, trying to fit in. "So why is it called Snud, anyway?" Dervish asked Yna.

Bloodstone's voice answered in her ear. "A few years ago they had a contest to rename the planet. The runner-up was Partytown McPlanetface."

"I keep forgetting you're listening to all this," Dervish said.

"You'll at least turn it off when I go to the bathroom, right?" Yna asked.

"Not a good idea," Bloodstone answered. "Restrooms are prime kidnap spots. But I promise you I've heard worse."

After a while, they got up and went to a new location. They

found a semi-private deck on the roof of a restaurant and chatted there for a bit while eating lunch. Then they found a secluded spot under a dock. Later they sat and talked behind a restaurant. It had actually been a pretty good day, if they didn't think about why they were really there.

At dinner, they spotted another woman wearing a purple stellarbell in her hair. Leaving their half-eaten meals behind, they followed her until she disappeared into the crowd. They kept searching for her but came up empty. In a crowd this large, it was a miracle if you saw the same person twice in one day.

"I got a screenshot of her face from your contact lens," Bloodstone told them. "It's a little blurry, but if she turns up missing later, I should be able to identify her."

At around midnight, they decided to call it quits for the day. They made their way back to their hotel room, determined to resume their efforts in the morning. It had been an exhausting day, and they both fell asleep just minutes after climbing into bed.

Yna awoke in confusion. She was face down, someone was sitting on her back, and she could feel them binding her wrists. Something was tied over her head, a pillowcase maybe, or a burlap sack. She tried to scream but realized her mouth was taped shut. She struggled and received a punch to the kidney in response. Panicked and furious, Yna had to fight her instincts to keep from using her energy powers. She felt herself being picked up and carried away.

"Stay calm," said Bloodstone's voice, quietly in her ear. "I'm tracking you. Wherever they take you, I will come for you."

She was shoved into a cloth… container? It felt too big to be a suitcase, too square to be a sack. She felt another struggling body land on top of her. Then they were buried under a mountain of cloth. Yna heard the wheels squeak as her cloth prison moved down the hallway, and she realized they were in a laundry cart.

Even in the middle of the night, the hallways were noisy. It was no wonder no one heard the previous victims' attempts to attract attention. She felt the cart pass right by crowds of late-night partiers. Yna listened carefully as the cart was pushed into an elevator, descended to the first floor, moved through another hallway, taken out a door, and loaded into a truck. Once the truck was in transit, the captors unburied them and pulled them out of the laundry cart. Then they pulled the sacks off of their heads.

"If you want to live, you're going to do what we say," said a male voice. It was dark in the back of the truck, and Yna was still disoriented. She was lying on the floor next to Dervish.

"Obedient girls live long, happy lives," said a second voice. "But give us a hard time? They'll never even find your body."

"Nod and look scared," Bloodstone said in her ear. Yna nodded. Looking scared wasn't an issue. "Now stare at them. I want to see their faces." Yna looked at her captors, even though she could only see their silhouettes. Apparently Dervish could still hear Bloodstone as well, because she did the same. "Still too dark," Bloodstone said. "But I'll run a voice analysis."

"Your old lives are over," said the first kidnapper. "This is a one-way street. Accept it. Embrace it. Fight back? Dead. Try to escape? Dead."

During the ride, the captors continued to threaten them. They laid out some ground rules, but most of them amounted to "always follow orders." The real reprogramming would begin when they reached headquarters. The van drove on for more than an hour. Since it hovered, Yna couldn't tell whether they were driving over roads, sand, or even water. She was glad Bloodstone was tracking them, because she had no idea where they were.

Finally it came to a stop, and the captors put the bags back over their heads. "Come on," said the first guy. Each kidnapper grabbed a prisoner, pulled her to her feet, and marched her out of the van. They heard several other male voices around them. One whistled appreciatively. Yna felt a hand grope her thigh, and came very close to switching on her power. She wondered if Dervish was similarly fighting the urge to change into something monstrous. Yna took great joy in the mental image of Dervish growing spikes and fangs, and ripping their captors to pieces.

They heard an electronic whine as something moved around them. "Tracking devices," one guy said.

"Figures," another said. "Must have overprotective parents. I'll take care of it."

"If we lose contact, I promise I will find you," Bloodstone said in their ears, speaking quickly. "But if you think you're in danger, use your powers and escape. You're more important than—"

Dervish and Yna both winced as they felt an electric shock. Then they heard the scanner move around them again. "All clean," their captor said. They could no longer hear Bloodstone in their ears.

They were loaded onto a shuttle, and taken somewhere else. By the time they reached their destination, Yna and Dervish weren't even sure if they were on the same planet. It hadn't felt like they'd been through a warp gate, but it was hard to be sure.

The shuttle landed, and they were marched down some metal stairs. It was colder here. Definitely not spring weather. Yna thought she could hear waves in the distance, so maybe they were still on Snud. Then a door closed behind them, and she could only hear the sound of women crying.

They were taken into a room, their bags removed and hands untied. The room was no bigger than Yna's quarters back on the Bloodwind, but this one had sleeping for twelve. There were four sets of bunk beds, each three beds tall, with barely any walking space in between. Ten of the beds were currently occupied, the other prisoners either sitting or lying on their beds. The guards told the two newcomers to change clothes, then they left, locking the door behind them.

The other women were wearing simple white shirts and one-size-fits-all pajama pants. Similar outfits were on the two empty beds. "You had better put those on," one of the other prisoners told them. "They'll be back soon, and they'll hurt you if you don't comply."

Dervish sat down on one of the beds, eyeing the clothing. "What do you think?" she asked.

"I'm about vacationed out," Yna said. She walked over to the door and ignited her hand. She burned through the lock, then called Dervish over.

While Yna introduced herself to the other prisoners and explained their plan, Dervish changed her form until she looked like one of the guards. Then she poked her head out into the hallway. Waving to another guard, she called out, "Excuse me, I'm having trouble with this lock, can you help?"

The other guard walked over, entered the room, and examined the lock. "How in the world—" he started to say. Then Dervish turned one arm into a tentacle, wrapped it around the guard's neck, and choked him until he was unconscious. Yna grabbed his gun and handed it to another prisoner.

Dervish went back out into the hallway, looking for more guards. Poking her head around the next corner, she waved to a guard and called him over.

This went on for some time.

"Got it," Bloodstone said.

"You have their location?" Raven asked. She stood at a nearby console, attempting to reestablish the connection with Yna or Dervish. So far she'd had no luck.

"I hacked their air traffic control satellites," Bloodstone

said. "Starting from their last known location, a single transport ship flew to the other side of the planet and landed on an oil derrick in the middle of the ocean."

"I'll come with you," Raven said.

"I'll get the shuttle ready," Bloodstone said. "And bring Panther."

It wasn't actually an oil derrick, just made to look like one. As the shuttle landed on the pad, Bloodstone noticed it was crowded with armed women dressed in white. As Bloodstone, Raven, and Panther stepped down the exit ramp, they raised their hands and made it clear which side they were on.

"I'm here to bring your captors to justice," Bloodstone said. "...and to retrieve my friends. Have you seen a shapeshifter and a woman who can turn into energy?" They nodded and pointed them in the right direction. As soon as they were inside, Panther picked up Yna's scent and bounded down the hall. Bloodstone and Raven struggled to keep up, passing dozens of dead or unconscious guards along the way. Some had been shot, some beaten, and others were tied up.

Finally they reached a large office. Six older men, dressed in business attire, were tied up against the walls. In the center of the room, a seventh man lay spread eagle on the floor. Dervish held him down, restraining him with tentacles. Yna stood above him, kicking him repeatedly in the crotch. Panther nearly knocked Yna over as he bounded up to lick her face.

"Dregan Flize, I presume?" Bloodstone asked. The man on the floor turned his head and groaned what might have been an affirmative. "I have come to collect the reward on your head." Looking at the other men, she added, "And the police are on their way for the rest of you."

Police and other emergency services arrived to make arrests and to take the former captives home. Dregan Flize was sentenced to life in prison, and his operation was dismantled for good. The slave ring had kept detailed records, and even more women would be recovered in the following months.

When Dervish and Yna got back to the Bloodwind, they continued right where they'd left off. "You'll love this one," Yna said, getting comfortable against Panther. "The rabbit goes on vacation."

"Oh, don't use the V word," Dervish said, and they both laughed. From that point forward, they decided that the word "vacation" meant cartoons and popcorn. Let others waste their money on tourist traps, they had everything they needed right here.

01.11 LifePurge

ED.002501.11.26

Trasa was known as the City of a Trillion Lights, but right now the only illumination came from the fires. Explosions rocked the city, and building after building collapsed. From the shuttle Bloodstone could see a fiery line of destruction, starting from the power plant, moving through downtown, and headed toward the suburbs. Evacuations were in progress, but the roads were bumper-to-bumper. Many of the cars were now abandoned as people fled on foot.

"Put us in front of the target," Bloodstone ordered, and Raven guided the ship toward the source of the carnage. "Vik, get us down there." Vik grabbed Bloodstone around the waist, and they jumped out the open hatch. As they rapidly approached the ground, Vik used his Levatech to slow their fall. Vik wasn't used to carrying this much weight, and they landed hard, but neither was injured.

Bloodstone and Vik readied their weapons. No stun pistols this time. Their target needed to be destroyed, not captured. Bloodstone carried a Z119-XL Nova Rifle, which fired rapid energy bursts as well as magnetic explosive rounds. Vik carried an IGP TS-379B Tankstopper Rifle, which fired focused armor-piercing beams and had a built-in grenade launcher. Both wore heavier armor than usual, and used vision enhancements in their helmets to see through the smoke and fire.

"Split up," Bloodstone ordered. "You go high, I go low." Now less encumbered, Vik jumped to the roof of a nearby building and made his way toward their target. As Bloodstone ran along the sidewalk, she looked up and saw a beam of light emanate from their foe. It fired upwards, at the retreating landing shuttle. The beam pierced the left engine, and the shuttle went down, disappearing behind the skyline.

"Raven? Can you hear me? Are you okay?" There was no answer over the comm. Back burner. Right now they had a robot to stop.

The robot was actually three separate pieces of technology. The body was that of a humanoid Warbot MK-79. Two arms, two legs, heavily armored torso, and loads of integrated weaponry. The head was a spherical sensor drone, model 404-NF. It could see in any light, detect life forms on nearby planets, or count the cilia on a microscopic organism. It already knew Bloodstone and Vik were here, no doubt about it.

The third component was the most deadly. A computer program called "Lifepurge.exe," designed as the ultimate exterminator. This program could be installed on any machine, and it would adapt to make full tactical use of the machine's capabilities. It was created to wipe out a specific swarm of disease-carrying insects, but the programmers had hoped to eventually use it to fight cancerous cells.

But for some unknown reason, someone had installed the program onto the sensor drone. Awakened with a need to destroy, the drone paired itself with the nearest source of weaponry, the Warbot. Now it walked the streets of downtown, destroying everything in sight. There was no telling how many lives had already been lost.

"Shouldn't we have bombed this thing from a distance?" Vik said over the comm, firing a grenade at the robot and dodging its return fire.

"Sure, bring that up now," Bloodstone said, firing her own rounds. It was a good idea, but the Bloodwind didn't actually have any bombs. Bounty hunters generally tried to recover their targets in a recognizable condition, and heavy explosives weren't the best way to do that. At this very moment, Trenyn was aboard the Bloodwind, assembling some missiles. But that would take a while, and lives were being lost now.

The planet had no army, instead relying on military drones that could be deployed from a satellite. The first thing Lifepurge had done upon awakening was to destroy these satellites using surface-to-space weapons. Off-world armies had been summoned, but they were still at least an hour away. The Bloodwind had already been in the vicinity when the planet issued the emergency bounty.

This bounty didn't pay nearly enough. Bloodstone had already lost a shuttle to this warbot, and possibly a crew member. But she had to put that out of her mind. Raven was tough, and a quick thinker. She would have bailed before the shuttle crashed. Bloodstone had her own life to protect right now.

She found herself missing Whisper. Her stealth skills would have come in handy right now. Knowing her, she'd find a way to sneak up behind the warbot and pull out its battery pack or something. But Whisper was off on another, probably safer mission, along with Yna and Panther. And as much as Bloodstone missed her skills, she was glad Whisper was somewhere less dangerous.

Bloodstone hid behind a concrete outcropping, the remains of the torn-up sidewalk. Nearby explosions shook her off her feet. She peeked out from behind the concrete, and zoomed in on the warbot with her long-range scope. The bot immediately rotated its head to look straight at her, and fired a missile. Bloodstone dove into a nearby hole, as the missile exploded above her.

The hole turned out to be a spot where the road had collapsed, opening up into the sewer. Bloodstone recognized this tunnel as the one where she'd caught a fugitive named A'Tral, nearly two years ago. She'd ended up letting him go after hearing about the crisis on EarthStation 1. Her prey had asked her how she'd known which tunnels to trap. Little did he know she'd put traps in all the tunnels. This sewer was a common escape route for fugitives. The trap that had caught A'Tral hadn't even been set for him specifically.

What was so special about this sewer? It was spacious, laid out in an easy-to-navigate grid pattern, with enough side tunnels to evade the cops. It ran the entire length of the city, from the prison to the spaceports, and the tunnels were labeled with street names so you always knew where you were. It was also under several meters of steel and concrete, making it difficult for above-ground sensors to detect anyone below.

"Huh," Bloodstone said, focusing on that last point.

"I've hit it several times, but I don't think I've hurt it," Vik said. He kept his distance from the warbot, making sure never to stay in one place too long. He didn't receive an answer. "Bloodstone? Can you hear me?" Still no answer. Great. If Bloodstone was down, Vik wasn't going to last long. The only reason they'd lasted this long was because the warbot's attention was divided between two targets.

But Vik wasn't about to give up. He knew he didn't need to defeat the warbot, just keep it from killing civilians long enough for the military to get here.

"How's it going?" said Dervish's voice over the comm unit.

"Peachy," Vik replied, dodging a collapsing building. "Is this a social call, or…"

"Trenyn has a missile almost ready," Dervish said. "But the targeting system needs something to follow. We need you to stick a tracer on the robot, so the missile can home in on it."

"Oh, is that all," Vik said, wondering how he was going to get that close to the thing.

"That's all!" Dervish replied cheerily, oblivious to Vik's sarcasm. "Just let me know when it's on there, and we'll fire. Bye!"

Vik rooted through his side pouch for a tracer. Nearly everyone on the team kept a couple in their pockets at all times. He pulled out one of the small discs and turned it over. It was magnetized, so all he needed to do was get within throwing range of the warbot. But the only way to close the gap without being blown to pieces was to have someone else distract it. And he was alone.

Vik hid behind a mound of rubble, his mind racing to construct a plan. He noted a broken sign nearby, which identified the rubble as the TrumbleSide Sportsplex. Suddenly he remembered an old blastball play from college. *Could work,* he thought. He pulled a flashlight out of his pouch and switched it on.

He burst from his hiding spot, jumping over the rubble and making a run for the warbot. He ran in a zigzag pattern, holding the flashlight in one hand, set to strobe mode. Hoping the flashing light would distract the robot, Vik fired a couple of grenades – not at the warbot, but off to the sides. Thinking the explosions came from additional attackers, the warbot's attention was divided between the explosions and the flashing light.

As Vik got closer, he threw the flashlight to his left, using his Levatech power to augment the throw. It went far, and the warbot wasted a couple of seconds firing at it. Then Vik leaped toward the warbot, tracer ready. He was almost within throwing range...

...and then the warbot fired a missile at him. Vik just managed to deflect the missile with his Levatech power, knocking it into a nearby office building. The explosion still knocked Vik to the ground and partially buried him under rubble. Vik looked up and saw the warbot preparing to finish him off. But then he noticed something else. A few meters behind the robot, a manhole cover had slid aside. A red rifle protruded from the manhole. Just as the warbot was about to fire, Bloodstone's Nova Rifle fired a pair of magnetic rounds at the back of the warbot's knees.

The explosion severed the robot's legs. It struggled to its side, trying to identify the attacker. It scanned the area the rounds had come from, but Bloodstone had already dropped back down into the sewer. The warbot put so much priority on the scan that it didn't notice Vik land nearby. Vik threw the tracer, which attached itself to the warbot's back. As Vik leaped away, he shouted into his comm, "Now, Dervish!"

A few seconds later, a missile broke through the clouds, on a direct route to the warbot. As the missile neared its target, the warbot detected the danger, drew a bead on it, and fired. It was a direct hit, and missile components blew apart in all directions. Trenyn had counted on this, however.

The outer casing now gone, the remaining missile – now basically just a metal rod - continued its course. Meanwhile, the expelled chaff burst into bright, sparkling lights, confusing the warbot's sensors. It was a boring missile. Not to say it was uninteresting, but rather it was designed to bore through a target's armor and release the payload inside. The corkscrew-like tip spun and penetrated the robot, straight through the torso, hitting Vik's tracer like a bulls-eye. A napalm-like chemical ignited inside the robot, burning it from the inside out. In seconds it was just a hunk of melted slag.

The head, however, had other ideas. The round drone ejected itself from the body and hovered away. It had no weapons, but that was just a temporary setback. It just needed to find something armed and mobile, like a tank or a fighter plane. Then it could pair with the vehicle and continue its extermination mission. It scanned the environment, detecting nothing but wreckage. Finally it located a shuttle and zipped away to investigate.

Vik watched it fly off, but couldn't get off a shot in time. He saw Bloodstone climbing out of the manhole and went over to help. Vik told her about the drone, and they limped in the direction he'd seen it go.

The drone arrived at the shuttle and scanned it. Unfortunately, it was too damaged to fly, and didn't carry any armaments. But as the drone performed the scans, it detected something more interesting. Just a few meters from the shuttle, a new robot body lay in the rubble. Having arms again would open up a world of possibilities. It whooshed over to the body and attempted to connect to its software.

"I don't think so," Raven said. Getting to her feet, she pulled out her weapon and fired. Her sidearm wasn't as fancy or destructive as Bloodstone's or Vik's rifles. It was just a simple electromagnetic disruptor. But it was more than enough to fry the drone's circuits, erasing all traces of the Lifepurge.exe program. The metal ball dropped out of the sky, harmless and inert.

By the time the military arrived, there wasn't much for them to do besides organize rescue efforts. The bounty hunters were paid for stopping Lifepurge, and were even reimbursed for the damage to their shuttle. The remains of the warbot and scanner drone were taken to a government lab, and a full investigation would be forthcoming. They never discovered who installed the software on the drone.

"I'd call that a successful test, wouldn't you?" Tena asked. She was wearing a red sequined party dress, even though she wasn't planning on leaving the lab today.

"All you did was destroy a random city," Thresh answered in a gruff voice. He studied her with his white eyes, trying to figure out her endgame. There was nothing wrong with the occasional massacre, but it was risky to cause this much destruction. He didn't want to get caught for something so minor as destroying a city, when they had much bigger plans on the horizon.

"Next time it won't be random," Tena replied, laughing.

She continued laughing just long enough to make Thresh uncomfortable. He knew she was a loon, but he needed her. He had great plans for her lunacy, plans he couldn't accomplish alone. The others on the Council would never approve of their project, but he and Tena were about to take care of that.

The Council was due for a shake-up. Then there would be a demonstration. And after that? The rest of the galaxy would tremble at their might.

01.12 The Fall

ED.002501.12.13

"We're wasting our time," Whisper said. "She won't be here."

"How can you be so sure?" Vik asked.

"Call it hunter's instinct," she replied. Of course, she couldn't tell him the real reason they wouldn't find Alterra Sarr today. There had been an increase in Alterra sightings over the last few months, and Whisper honestly couldn't say why. Either her alter-ego had achieved Elvis levels of cult status, or the shapeshifter Vraxx was having a bit of fun.

Vik and Whisper walked down the streets of Suiak, one of the largest cities on the planet Galea. The city's architecture reminded Vik of his hometown of Detroit, back on Earth. The people, however, did not. The catlike Galeans gave Vik strange looks as they walked past.

"Alterra must have stood out like a sore thumb here," Whisper said. With her helmet on, she could well have been Galean herself, and thus didn't garner as much attention as Vik. "I wonder how well they tell humans apart," she mused. "Maybe they just saw a human woman with dark hair, and assumed it was Alterra."

"Zhari never had any problem recognizing humans," Vik

said. "Heck, when it came to picking faces out of a crowd, she was better than me."

It belatedly dawned on Whisper that this was the homeworld of Vik's late fiancée. "Oh," she said. "I'm sorry, this must be hard for you."

"Being on Galea?" Vik asked. "A bit. I never visited it with her. We'd always planned to. I looked forward to having her show me around."

They walked in silence for a few minutes. Whisper felt like she should be giving him some words of comfort, but everything she thought of sounded trite and hollow. It occurred to her that Vik never seemed to care about anyone else's feelings, but she still felt guilty at her inability to express her sympathy.

And then there was the fact that Vik blamed Alterra for Zhari's death. Whisper felt like such a fraud, walking beside Vik as if they were friends, knowing how he felt about her true identity. Her helmet's mirrored faceplate was a thin barrier keeping Vik from the truth. In the back of Whisper's mind, she longed to take off the helmet and accept the consequences. Maybe she could convince him, maybe she couldn't. But it would be better to die as herself than to live as an impostor.

Just a little longer, she told herself. If they caught Vraxx today, then hopefully she'd be able to prove her innocence. Not that she expected Vraxx to cooperate, but with the right interrogation techniques, maybe she could trick him into confessing his role in the destruction of the space station.

"We're here," Vik said, shaking Whisper out of her thoughts. The sign above the door read, "Suiak City Police Department." Vik held the door open for Whisper, and they approached the front desk.

"May I help you?" a buxom Galean woman asked from behind the desk.

The woman was extremely attractive, and Whisper expected Vik to have trouble maintaining eye contact. She'd seen him ogle women before, but today Vik was all business. "My name is Vik Lambert, IGP liaison, and this is Whisper, a bounty hunter. We have an appointment with your head detective."

"Of course," she said. "I have you down. Please have a seat on the bench over there, next to the... *hookers*." She lowered her voice on the last word, almost hissing it.

"Sex workers," Vik corrected her, and they went to sit down. Whisper cocked her head. This didn't sound like Vik.

They sat on a plastic bench next to a pair of scantily-clad Galean women. Vik didn't even glance at them, except for a quick nod of acknowledgment. Whisper might have thought he just wasn't interested in Galean anatomy, except of course she knew he was. Was Vik becoming less of a jerk, or did being on Zhari's home planet just bring out the best in him?

They didn't have to wait very long. A detective with golden fur came out to greet them, then led them back into his office. His name was Tuvall Lee-Norrd, but everyone called him Leo, and he insisted Vik and Whisper do the same. They all sat down, said a few pleasantries, and got down to business.

"How do you know it was Alterra Sarr?" Vik asked. "Could it have just been a similar-looking human woman?"

"I thought the same thing," Leo said. "But one of the witnesses got a picture. Here." He pulled up an image on his tablet. It was a little blurry, but it was obviously Alterra. Or at least, someone trying very hard to look like her.

"Why did you call us?" Whisper asked.

"If I'd made this public, my city would be swarming with off-world bounty hunters right now," Leo replied. "Not only would it cause a panic, but it would probably scare Alterra off. But I've heard of your group. You're the best. I was hoping to meet Bloodstone, though. Any chance you could get me his autograph?"

"I'll see what I can do," Vik said. "But for now, I'd like to talk to some of these witnesses."

By the end of the day, they had spoken to four witnesses but had been unable to reach the other two. Alterra had been spotted at a shopping mall, a subway station, and a fast food restaurant called BurgerMouse. In all three sightings, it seemed as if Alterra wanted to be seen, and made no effort to hide her identity.

"I'm surprised there weren't more witnesses," Vik said, now seated at a table in BurgerMouse. He gestured at the dining Galeans around them, noting how some of them kept glancing at him. "Especially since she was probably the only human in the crowd. All of these are public places, and yet she was only seen by a couple of people at each location."

"It supports my Vraxx theory," Whisper said.

"You're still on that?" Vik asked.

"It makes sense, Vik," Whisper said. "Vraxx disguises himself as a random Galean. Maybe he puts a hood or something over his head so people don't see the change itself. He waits until only one or two people are looking in his direction, then he morphs into Alterra and throws back the hood. Then he puts up the hood and quickly changes back before more people see him."

"She wasn't wearing a hood in the picture Leo showed us," Vik said. "And why would Vraxx draw attention to himself only to hide again?"

"To make sure people keep looking for Alterra," Whisper said, obviously frustrated. "He can't show himself to too many people, or they'll swarm him and turn him in. But if he shows himself to a few people at a time, they'll know she's still out there. A lot of bounty hunters have given up the chase by now. They think she's gone too deep underground, or maybe even dead. But Vraxx is out there taunting us, making sure we never stop hunting her."

"Whisper," Vik said, his voice taking on a condescending

tone, "I'm sorry, I just don't buy the conspiracy angle. It's like Bloodstone said, if Alterra's a shapeshifter, then she was a shapeshifter all along. No one's trying to frame her. Human or Marae, she blew up the station."

"Vik," Whisper began, her voice rising.

Vik held up his hand and continued. "But let's pretend you're right. Vermon's dead. He's been dead for two years. Why would Vraxx still be following his orders? If it's all part of some grand conspiracy, wouldn't that have ended with Vermon's death?"

"Marae slaves are conditioned to be loyal," Whisper said. "You remember what Dervish was like. This might be all Vraxx knows how to do. He might spend the rest of his life following Vermon's final order."

"I just find that far-fetched," Vik said. "And it doesn't matter anyway. I intend to catch Alterra Sarr, regardless of her species. The justice system can sort it out after that."

Whisper took a deep breath and changed the subject. "Want to go check out that subway station?"

"Let's," Vik replied, and they stood up.

They split up at the subway station, with Vik looking over security camera footage and Whisper thoroughly examining the area where Alterra had been spotted. It was nearly midnight by the time they admitted defeat. Tomorrow they would check out the mall and try to contact the other two witnesses. They took a cab back to their hotel.

The door to their suite was unlocked and stood slightly ajar. Vik and Whisper looked at each other, then drew their weapons. Vik kicked open the door. Someone had ransacked their suite, but they were gone now. Their suitcases were open, the contents strewn all over their bedrooms. Nothing appeared to be missing.

"Is there a camera in the hallway?" Whisper asked, rooting through her things.

"On it," Vik said, headed to the door. Before he got two

steps, both of their comm units buzzed simultaneously. It was an automated message. Someone was attempting to break into their shuttle.

"Let's go," Whisper said.

The shuttle was parked in a designated area on the roof of the hotel. While Whisper took the stairs up the three remaining flights to the roof, Vik climbed out the window onto the fire escape, then jumped the rest of the way to the top. He reached the shuttle first, just as it was taking off. He leaped toward it, using his Levatech ability to hold onto the side. Then he worked his way over to the side door and typed a code into the keypad. The door slid open, and Vik slipped inside.

"Alterra Sarr," Vik said, as he stepped into the cockpit. He aimed his energy pistol at the back of the pilot's helmet. "Put your hands up and don't make any sudden movements."

Except it wasn't Sarr. When the pilot turned around, Vik saw it was a Galean he didn't recognize. Male, orange fur with black stripes, probably in his mid-thirties.

"Aw, man, you're not the one I wanted," the pilot said.

Vik's shoulders slumped with disappointment, but he kept his weapon aimed at the pilot. "Who are you?" he asked.

"None of your business," the pilot said, turning back to the control panel. "Now go away or I'll crash us both."

"You're not the one in control here," Vik said with exasperation. Who did this guy think he was?

"There she is…" the pilot said, pulling up the video feed on one of the shuttle's viewscreens. The view was from one of the exterior cameras, mounted underneath the shuttle.

Vik gasped. The feed showed Whisper, who was currently underneath the shuttle, holding onto the left rear landing strut.

"Stay right there and keep her steady," Vik ordered the

pilot. He stepped backward and turned toward the side door.

"Nah," the pilot said, and violently veered the shuttle into a hard right spin.

This was not one of my better ideas, Whisper thought, hanging from the landing strut. She had reached the rooftop just as the shuttle was leaving. Reacting more on instinct than common sense, she'd whipped the landing strut and climbed her whip to reach the shuttle. But after that, she'd been at a loss for where to go next. No hatches were in reach, and there weren't enough handholds to climb around to the shuttle doors. The wind threatened to blow her off at any moment, and she held on tight, her elbow locked around the strut's framework.

If the thief decided to take it into space, she was done for. It really depended on why they'd stolen the shuttle. If it was just a run-of-the-mill shuttlejacker, they might take it to a chop shop elsewhere in town. Whisper hoped this was the case, because then it would be a relatively short flight. But given how their hotel room had been ransacked, it felt more like they'd been targeted. And Whisper wasn't sure what to expect if that were the case.

Suddenly the ship jerked hard to the right, and it was all Whisper could do to hold on. Then it went left, right, and left again, each jerk nearly jostling her loose. What was going on up there? Whisper tried to reposition her arms for a better grip, when another quick jerk threw her off completely.

Whisper watched the shuttle get smaller and smaller as she fell.

Vik tried to open the door, intent on jumping out after Whisper. With his Levatech abilities, he knew he'd be able to slow his own fall, and hoped he'd be able to save her as well. Unfortunately, the doors were now locked. "Open it!" Vik ordered, turning back to the pilot.

"Make me," the pilot said, sounding like a truculent twelve-year-old.

"Open it or I'll shoot," Vik said.

"I've locked out the controls," the pilot said, smiling. "Shoot me and it'll take you at least five minutes to get back in. Your friend will be road pizza by then."

Vik glanced at the emergency escape hatch above the pilot's seat. "Get out of my way," Vik said, approaching the pilot.

"You'll have to go through me first," the pilot said.

"What is your problem?" Vik asked, confused by the pilot's erratic responses. Rather than wait for an answer, Vik punched the pilot in the face. The pilot stood up and tried to punch him back, but Vik dodged and countered. Then the pilot lunged at Vik and the two wrestled on the shuttle floor.

Skyscrapers soared past Whisper. She turned over so that she was facing the ground, held out her arms, and did her best to control her direction. Maneuvering herself until she was just a couple of meters from an apartment building, she whipped a balcony railing. Her whip was stretchy, but the sudden stop still nearly pulled her arm out of the socket, and she lost her grip on the whip's handle.

She tried to grab the next balcony's railing, but her fingers hit the railing too hard, and she slipped away. She finally landed on a third balcony, two floors below the one she'd whipped, spraining her ankle in the process. Even with the pain in her ankle and shoulder, she considered herself very lucky.

She struggled to her feet, leaned on the railing, and watched the shuttle flying off in the distance. She wasn't sure what was happening inside, but the shuttle jerked around erratically, and was headed straight for one of the city's tallest buildings.

* * *

The pilot was no weakling, but his fighting skills couldn't compare to Vik's IGP training. Most of the pilot's blows failed to connect, while Vik knew just where to strike to inflict maximum pain without causing permanent damage. Soon the pilot collapsed in a punch-drunk haze. Vik sat in the pilot seat, but the controls were still locked out. Touching anything just prompted the computer to ask for a password. Vik glanced at the pilot. How had this punk known how to do that?

A large building loomed closer and closer on the viewscreen. Vik knew he'd never regain control in time. He popped the emergency escape hatch open and climbed halfway out. He was about to jump the rest of the way, but several thoughts rushed through his mind at once. Could he also save the pilot in time? How many people would die when the shuttle hit the building? Was there another way?

This isn't going to work, Vik thought, climbing the rest of the way out of the shuttle. Using his Levatech abilities, he kept one hand secured to the shuttle, and he aimed the other at the building. He hoped that his powers were strong enough to repel the shuttle before it hit. If he could at least slow down the impact, it would cause less damage. He would probably die in the process, but it might save a few lives inside the building. *At least I'll die a hero,* he thought.

The shuttle jerked back and forth as it swiftly approached the building. Vik concentrated as hard as he could, which was difficult with all the doubts clouding his mind. As the shuttle got closer and closer, it gradually slowed and became less erratic. *Am I really doing this?* Vik thought.

No, he was not. Vik looked back into the escape hatch and saw that the shuttle thief was back in the pilot's seat, groggily turning the shuttle away from the building. The Galean looked up, spotted Vik, and attempted to lock out the controls again. But before he had the chance, Vik reached into the hatch and used his abilities to pull off the pilot's helmet. Then he repelled the helmet with as much force as he could muster, hitting the pilot in the head and knocking him out.

Vik climbed back into the shuttle and landed it safely. The thief was just starting to wake up again when they touched ground. "Who are you?" Vik demanded, his gun once again trained on the thief. "How did you access the shuttle codes? Who are you working for?"

"Sssshe didn't wannnt you, ssshe wanted herrrr," the thief slurred.

"Who, Whisper?" Vik asked. "Who wanted her?"

"Teeeee…" the thief began. Then his eyes opened wide with shock, and he dropped dead.

The thief was identified as a professional burglar named Jevek Feen-Kirtt, or "Jett" to his friends. A medical examination determined that he'd been under the influence of Nepeta-C, a recreational drug that causes irrational behavior in some Galeans. But that wasn't what killed him. His death was caused by an electric shock to the heart, induced by an implant. They also found the remnants of transmitters embedded in Jevek's eyes and ears. Someone had monitored everything he'd seen and heard, and then killed him to keep him from talking. Unfortunately, there was no way to trace where the tech had come from.

"He also had a holographic device on him," Vik said. Whisper currently sat in the Bloodwind's medbay, while Raven tended to her injuries. Vik had just received an update from Detective Leo, and now he excitedly relayed the information to Whisper. "That's how he made Alterra appear. Leo watched the security footage again, and Jevek was present every time there was an Alterra sighting. The real Alterra has probably never set foot on Galea."

"I still don't get it," Whisper said. "What was the point of any of this?"

"I think he wanted you," Vik said. "My guess is, whoever hired him was trying to draw you there so they could capture you. Think. Are there any bounties on your head?"

A rather large one, Whisper thought, but instead she answered, "Not that I know of."

"Do you have any enemies?"

"In this job?" Whisper asked. "I'd be shocked if I didn't."

"Well… be careful," Vik said. "I think someone's after you."

Whisper sighed. What else was new? But it was one thing for someone to come after Alterra, quite another for someone to look for Whisper. Unless, of course, they knew her secret. Just who were these people?

She would find out soon enough.

Part 2

02.00 Carrion

ED.02502.01.02

It was a beautiful day, warm with balmy winds. It was also snowing. The atmospheric anomalies that created such diverse weather patterns were just part of the reason that Frella was such a successful resort world. The planet featured many exotic vacation spots, and its quaint architecture and antiquated machinery only added to the ambiance. The planet was so rich in unique, natural beauty, that technological progress would only have left it marred like a poorly cut jewel.

At this moment, four hunters and a lion-sized cat sat around a table at the Happy Godar Inn. Raven, Trenyn, and Dervish had stayed behind on the Bloodwind, which was still in orbit over Frella. It had been two years since the destruction of EarthStation 1. While Alterra Sarr was no longer the constant subject of media attention, the reward fund was still out there, just waiting for someone to bring her in. It was still the largest reward ever offered for a single fugitive, and Alterra sightings were still reported rather frequently. Which is what brought them to the Inn today.

Bounty hunting was frowned upon by the Frellans, and the only way the locals had allowed their presence was with pre-approval from the police. As part of their compliance, Bloodstone had placed Vik in charge of this mission. Now, sitting across the table from Bloodstone, Vik wondered if he was ready for such a responsibility. He tried not to look toward the cold gaze that he knew must be coming from behind that red faceplate.

Vik was being tested. He knew that the more experienced hunter would want to hear his suggestions on where their quarry might be hiding. In truth, Vik had no idea what to do next. He slowly peered around the bar, examining the clientèle. This place, while a bit backward, wasn't nearly as seedy as the taverns this job usually required he visit. Actually, it was quite nice. The building appeared to have been made almost entirely of wood, which was a rare sight these days. The walls sported an array of decorative kalme leaves and glitti flowers, adding to the establishment's tropical theme.

Studying the other customers, Vik noticed few, if any, of the low-life criminal types he was used to seeing when on a case. The only patrons of this bar seemed to be rich vacationers. Groups of wealthy businessmen and their nymphlike companions laughed and sipped at odd-colored liquids. Romantic couples stared into each other's eyes, each convinced that the other was the entire universe. A tipsy Vhelran sang karaoke to a group of his friends. A few customers glanced over at the bounty hunters apprehensively.

Vik wondered if coming here might have been a dead end. He looked at his teammates. Yna and Whisper were engaged in a lighthearted conversation. Vik glanced back at Bloodstone and quickly looked away again. She was still staring at him.

Bloodstone was actually looking past Vik, trying to find a server. When one of them looked her way, she gestured and the server came over. "Hi! What can I get for you today?" There was a hint of nervousness in her voice. Obviously, she recognized the galaxy's most infamous bounty hunter.

A few of them ordered alcoholic drinks. Vik ordered club soda. "Not drinking?" Bloodstone asked him.

"Nah, I want this one to go perfectly," Vik replied. "I don't want to miss my big chance at catching Alterra just because I was buzzed."

"Suit yourself," Bloodstone said. "But don't get your hopes up. There are sightings like this all the time, and there's no reason to believe this one is more credible than the last. And even if she's here, we're not just going to run into her at an inn. We'll be here for a few days. That's why we got those rooms upstairs."

"Speaking of those rooms," Whisper said as she rose from her seat, "I'm going to go upstairs for a bath."

It was a quaint room, overpriced for its size, but it had a nice view. Whisper disrobed and drew a bath. She loved a good, hot soak, but rarely had the opportunity. The freighter was built for efficiency, not comfort, and therefore only had showers. She probably could have convinced Raven and Trenyn to engineer something up for her, but it never seemed like a priority.

Before stepping into the tub, she double-checked the lock on the door to her room, and also locked the door to the bathroom. As a final precaution, she wedged a sample shampoo bottle under the door, hoping it would make it more difficult to open. Only then did she feel safe enough to do what she was about to do. She stepped into the claw-footed metal tub, reclining into a comfortable position.

Alterra let every one of her muscles relax, and she shifted her skin color back to her lightest, cream-colored complexion. Her eyes lightened until they were ice blue. It wasn't taxing to maintain the darker tone – it wasn't like she was constantly clenching a muscle or having to concentrate on her pigmentation – but it was still a relief to change back now and then. It was like stretching after being crammed in a small space for several hours.

* * *

Back downstairs, the waitress walked over and delivered their drinks. Bloodstone then flipped open a small panel on the underside of her helmet, and pulled out a long flexible straw. She put the end of the straw in her drink and sipped it. After a few sips, she said, "Now Vik, not to overstep your authority on this mission, but you might start by asking a few questions. Nobody here looks like the type who would know anything, but—" She stopped talking when a light on her wrist computer lit up. Bloodstone stood up and yelled, "Everyone get out! Now!"

Multiple explosions rocked the inn, and the ceiling came crashing down.

Alterra had been nearly asleep in the bath when she noticed something odd. There was a smoke detector on the ceiling, directly above her. *That's an odd place to put...* but before she could finish the thought, she heard a loud noise. The room shook, the bathwater splashing violently. The ceiling started to collapse. She drew her knees up to her chest and covered her head with her hands. A large chunk of wood fell into the tub where her feet had just been. Then she screamed and held on as the bathtub crashed through the floor.

Half of the building had collapsed into a pile of wood and stone rubble. Many patrons had survived by hiding under tables, and were now digging themselves out of the mess. Others were not as lucky. Bloodstone pulled herself out from under a pile of broken boards, and then helped her teammates do the same. Bloodstone looked around for the source of the explosions. Outside of the inn, through what used to be the northern wall of the building, people of many species ran around trying to help the injured or get to safety. But four people only stood there, in the middle of the street, staring straight at the bounty hunters. One of them, a greenish-blue-skinned reptilian man, pointed at Bloodstone and shouted "Over there!"

Another of the four mysterious newcomers, a human woman with short black hair, shouted to Bloodstone. "Glad we got your attention! We know Alterra Sarr is in the building! So back off, she's ours!" She gestured toward another of her group, a large Grunthian who carried an impressive arsenal of explosives and other weapons. The Grunthian raised a huge cannon and pointed it toward the inn.

The last of the mystery group, a male of indeterminate species because his suit completely covered his body, took a few steps forward and announced, "Bloodstone, this doesn't involve you! Just walk away so we can dig her out and collect our bounty."

Bloodstone raised her hands to show she wasn't armed. She now recognized the rival hunters. She tried to keep up-to-date on the competition. The woman's name was Astral, the Grunthian was Broot, the reptilian was Gekko, and the suited creature was known as Xox. They weren't exactly big names in the hunting business, but it seemed significant that they were working as a group. Granted, Alterra's reward was big enough to share, or Bloodstone wouldn't have teamed up with her crew.

By this time most of the surviving patrons had evacuated the inn. Bloodstone looked at the Grunthian for a moment, her gaze locked firmly on the explosives that adorned the creature's body. Inside her helmet, a targeting computer zeroed in on a single grenade. She twitched one of her fingers, and a small dart shot out from the underside of her belt, piercing the explosive sphere strapped to Broot's body.

Bloodstone shouted "Get down!" while diving away from Broot. Her teammates dropped to the ground as another explosion sent flaming debris flying in all directions. Bloodstone recovered first, and saw to her dismay that Broot had been the only casualty. The other three rival hunters had each taken refuge in their own ways, and were even now taking aim with their various weapons.

Panther growled, ready to pounce. Yna transformed into her energy form. Vik drew his stun pistol and fired at their opponents.

The remaining rivals, however, had a few surprises of their own. Gekko rapidly climbed up the building on the opposite side of the street, firing his energy pistol from a safer vantage point. Xox removed his gloves, and his hands came apart and formed tentacles that stretched toward Bloodstone's group. Astral hid behind a barricade of rubble and collapsed. Soon an energy form, much like Yna in appearance, rose from her unconscious body.

Bloodstone barked out orders like a drill sergeant. "Vik! You follow the lizard man! Yna, take the energy woman! Panther! Sic the tentacle guy!" Bloodstone ducked behind some rubble, then fired a few shots at Astral. The blasts flew harmlessly through her. Then she fired a few shots at Xox, but his suit seemed to be impervious to energy weapons.

Xox now had Panther entangled in a writhing mass of vine-like appendages. Yna and Astral wrestled in the air, each unaffected by the other's abilities. Bloodstone held back and vanished behind a pile of girders and floorboards. She would try to get behind Xox and take him out with an AON knife.

Under the debris, Alterra emerged from the overturned bathtub. She was covered in small cuts and bruises, but nothing was broken. She spotted a corpse nearby, an inn patron who had been killed by the collapse. While it seemed in bad taste to do so, she took the victim's clothing and put it on. She needed it more. The clothes were too large and ripped in several places, but it was better than being naked.

She heard weapons fire in the distance, and a million thoughts raced through her mind. *Find a weapon. Find a safe place to hide. At least find a mask.*

Then she felt a hand on her shoulder. "So they were right, you are here," a familiar voice said. Whisper turned around to find herself facing the muzzle of Bloodstone's pistol. "Don't try anything," the bounty hunter said. "Looks like today's my lucky day."

Two very similar energy beings fought each other in the air. Punching, kicking, clawing, and choking, the luminescent duo waged a very frustrating battle. Neither combatant seemed to be able to hurt the other. At one point Yna got her opponent in a chokehold, a fruitless endeavor since Astral had no need to breathe. Unable to speak in this form, an exasperated Yna thought, *Just die already!*

You first! her opponent replied. The retort wasn't audible, but nevertheless Yna heard it perfectly.

The combatants simultaneously realized that they could communicate with each other telepathically. Yna released her hold, and the surprised pair hung there in the air, regarding each other. After a few seconds Yna mentally asked Astral, *Who are you? Are we the same species?*

I don't know, came Astral's reply. *I've never met anyone like myself. I've always been able to project my spirit from my body. But I see with you it works differently, your spirit engulfs your body.*

Yna thought, *My spirit? I always thought... I never knew what to think. You think this is my spirit?*

I believe mine is a manifestation of my mental energy, replied Astral. *I know nothing about you. But we seem to be similar. Tell me, what can you do besides fly? Can you pass through walls, or possess other bodies? Can you mentally project energy blasts? Are you able to go underwater? Can you levitate other objects? Can you—*

Slow down! Yna interrupted. *Are these all things you've learned how to do?* Her newfound comrade nodded. Yna continued, *I don't know... most of those are things I've never tried... I know I can't go through walls, maybe because unlike you, my body is still in here... nor can I go underwater, it tends to knock out my power...*

Good to know, Astral replied. Without warning, a blast of electric blue flame erupted from Astral's forehead, hitting

Yna square in the chest. It didn't hurt, but it knocked her backward, slamming her into the water tower on the rooftop behind her. The tower ruptured, and water gushed over Yna. She fell onto the roof, unconscious.

Nothing personal, Astral thought, *just business.*

Bloodstone and Alterra Sarr faced each other. Alterra's eyes darted around the area, looking for ways to escape. She knew she only had one chance to get away and preserve her identity. Bloodstone hadn't made the connection that Alterra and Whisper were one and the same. If she could just get out of Bloodstone's sight long enough to escape, she could return to the Bloodwind as Whisper and no one would ever know.

But that meant beating Bloodstone, who currently held a gun to her face. If she were to draw on her Auroran training and abilities, she could probably do it. But that would also let Bloodstone know she was Whisper. Bloodstone was an expert at analyzing combat tactics, and would recognize Whisper's fighting style right away.

So she would have to beat Bloodstone using only IGP fighting techniques, because that's what Bloodstone would expect her to know. And she'd have to do it while wearing oversized pants that kept trying to fall down.

"Wait," she said. "I didn't do it. It was an impostor, I never blew up that space station. I was framed by Teykor Vermon."

"Tell it to your lawyer," Bloodstone replied. "I still get paid if the court finds you innocent. I promised a friend that I would bring you in unharmed. Please don't make me break that promise."

Alterra nodded and held out her hands. Bloodstone reached inside a belt pouch for her cuffs, never taking her eyes off her quarry. Then, just for a second, Bloodstone's attention was diverted as she saw Yna fly into a water tower.

That was all the time Alterra needed. In a single motion, she kicked the gun out of Bloodstone's hand and punched her in the gut. She had hoped to find some shadows somewhere in which to hide, but she knew that she couldn't use her Auroran abilities if there was any possibility that Bloodstone was watching. To buy herself a few seconds, Alterra attempted to give her opponent a roundhouse kick to the chin, but Bloodstone had already recovered and caught her leg in mid-kick. Throwing her to the ground, Bloodstone said, "So, you do want to do this the hard way. I'm game."

Vik, having jumped to the top of the building, had extreme difficulty tracking his lizard-like enemy. The strange reptilian kept popping up, taking a few shots at Vik, and scuttling off to another hiding place before the ex-officer could react. Gekko was extremely quick and seemed to be able to climb any surface with ease.

"Nya, nya," the creature taunted, then scurried down the side of the building. Vik ran to the edge and peered over, but the pest had already disappeared. Then he intuitively ducked as two shots went off behind him. Gekko had gone around the corner and come back up another side of the building. Vik leaped high into the air, firing at the other hunter from above, and then landed softly on the other side of the rooftop. Unfortunately, Gekko was long gone by the time Vik landed, having slithered into a ventilation shaft.

Vik poked his head into the vent, but there was no sign of Gekko. Vik pondered for a moment. *Think! Think!* he told himself. Bloodstone often admonished him for his brashness, and he was determined to impress her for once. He'd noticed that Gekko wore a temperature regulating backpack. That probably meant he was cold-blooded. Was there any way to exploit this?

Still peering into the vent, Vik heard a noise behind him. He turned around just in time to dodge a blast from Gekko's pistol. Vik fired back, but he missed. Gekko's next shot hit him in the leg, and he staggered toward the edge of the building. Gekko ran forward and kicked Vik in the chest, sending him tumbling off the roof.

Panther was not having fun with his new playmate. Xox continued to entwine him in his long tendrils, choking the air and the strength right out of him. The more tentacles Panther pulled off, the more wrapped around him. He tried clawing the vine-like appendages, but they were too thick. As Xox pulled Panther closer to him, the cat had an idea. He went limp, and let himself get pulled over to Xox. When he got within arm's length, Panther quickly sprang to life clawed open Xox's suit. The viny monster screamed in surprise, and Panther continued to claw and rip through the material, finally batting off Xox's helmet.

Without the suit to keep himself together, Xox fell to the ground as a mass of tentacles. His head consisted of a single eyestalk, protruding from a mound of twitching, writhing coils. The horrific thing undulated toward Panther, who wisely kept his distance. The cat knew that he could easily outrun this creature, but he backed away carefully to keep an eye on it. Panther looked around to see if his friends were around, but found himself alone. He sniffed the air, then bounded away.

Alterra fought a losing battle. So far, there had been no opportunities to escape. Bloodstone was well versed in IGP hand-to-hand training, and seemed to know her every move before she made it. After several long minutes of fending off Bloodstone's attacks, Alterra was defeated. Bloodstone knocked the wind out of her, secured her arms in a tight hold, and bound her wrists and ankles with cuffs before she could recover.

Looking down at her struggling prey, Bloodstone almost seemed disappointed, like she'd been hoping for a bigger fight. Vik's voice came over her comm. "Yna's down! I think my leg is broken!"

Bloodstone tapped a key on her wrist computer, and a tiny syringe popped out of the cuff. "Sleep," Bloodstone said, injecting Alterra with a serum. Bloodstone pulled out another set of binder cuffs and secured Alterra to a metal post. Then she attached a small tracking device to Alterra's shirt. Even with these precautions, Bloodstone was reluctant to leave Alterra, even for a moment. But she couldn't abandon her crew.

Vik had landed on a balcony two floors below the roof. His leg was indeed broken. Bloodstone called the Bloodwind and had Raven come down in a landing shuttle. He told Vik to stay put, then checked on Yna. She was just starting to wake up when Bloodstone found her, next to the ruptured water tower. "Are you going to be okay by yourself?" Bloodstone asked. "I need to find Whisper."

Yna assured her that she'd be fine. Panther caught up to Bloodstone back at ground level. "Where's Whisper?" Bloodstone asked. "Can you smell her?" After all this time, Bloodstone still didn't know how much the cat understood. Panther led Bloodstone back to a clearing in the rubble, where the bounty hunter had fought Alterra.

"No, I need..." Bloodstone began, then did a double take. Alterra was gone.

02.01 *Wisp*

ED.02502.01.02

Alterra dreamed that she was in a courtroom, being sentenced to death. Vik was the presiding judge, while Bloodstone was the prosecuting attorney. A cauldron of lava was suspended above her head, tiny drips of which occasionally spilled out, burning holes in her clothing. Bloodstone grilled her relentlessly, exposing every lie she had ever told, some going all the way back to her childhood. While Bloodstone barked out accusations, Vik's finger hovered ominously above a large red button, helpfully labeled "Death."

After Bloodstone had listed about a thousand crimes, she took off her helmet, revealing her beautiful face. As usual, her entire demeanor seemed to change when she did this, like she was a different person. But Detanna was still just as angry. "And worst of all," she was saying, "You led me on. You made me think you loved me, when all the while you were hiding this from me. You made me think we had a future together."

"I've heard enough!" Judge Vik shouted. "Alterra Sarr, you have been found guilty of mass murder, lying to your friends, and betraying a loved one. Your sentence will be carried out immediately!" He pressed the button and the cauldron began to tip, spilling hot red lava over the edge. Alterra watched in horror as the deluge of burning death poured down towards her face...

It wasn't much of a consolation when she woke to find she was strapped to a bed. *Here we go again,* she thought, trying to focus her eyes. Though she was still shaking from the dream, she had the presence of mind to assess the situation. She was still wearing the civilian clothes she'd donned after the explosion. Whoever had her knew she was Alterra. Which meant they were either bounty hunters or law enforcement.

But this room didn't feel like law enforcement. The room was dark, but not too dark for her Auroran eyes. It looked like a hospital room, or maybe a laboratory. Medical equipment adorned the walls, various machines that looked like they were made to examine all sorts of species from the inside out.

She was still fair-skinned. She briefly wondered if she would be better off shifting to a darker tone. No. Her captors knew who they had, and wouldn't be fooled by skin color. Besides, they probably didn't know of her Auroran heritage, something she could exploit later.

She examined the straps holding her down. *Hmm. Thorough.* Metal bracers bound each wrist, with short chains keeping her hands to her sides. Her ankles were similarly bound. But there were also seven thick straps crossing her body at regular intervals. The straps looked like they were made of strong rubber. This would be overkill for an ordinary prisoner, so her captors obviously considered her dangerous.

She attempted to pull her hands out of the bracers. They were tight, but she thought she might be able to do it if she could clench her hands enough. It might require breaking her thumbs, though. It wouldn't be the first time. As she wriggled her wrists, something beeped. A red light turned on somewhere behind her head. She couldn't see the light itself, but it reflected off the walls. It quickly went back off.

She struggled again, and again there was a beep and a light. Like a warning. She was strangely reminded of the tilt sensor on a pinball game.

The door slid open. Two figures entered. One was tall and feminine, the other was short with a large head. They didn't turn the lights on, but Alterra could make out most of their features. The woman looked human. She was thin, with dark hair, and rather severe facial features. She had sharp protrusions on her elbows, and Alterra couldn't tell if they were part of her body or her clothing. Her eyes were white like Raven's. Alterra realized that she saw other facial similarities as well.

Her shorter companion was of a species Alterra didn't recognize. He was bald, with cracked skin that reminded her of dried-out desert mud. He held a tablet computer, which he glanced at every few seconds.

The woman spoke in a silky voice, but her tone was more authoritarian. "Don't worry, we're not turning you in. We have other uses for you," she said. "But, we don't need you awake. Doctor?" The diminutive doctor gave Alterra an injection, and everything faded to black once again.

"You're not turning her in? I thought you wanted her for revenge, for her role in the death of your father. What, are you going to torture her instead?"

"She's going to be our master donor," Tena said.

"Alterra Sarr? A cop? I thought you wanted a skilled assassin."

"Doctor X, what do you know of the Auro-Chi?"

The scientist rolled his eyes. His name didn't even start with an X. But Tena had long ago stopped trying to learn how to pronounce his name, and Doctor Yxyllthyll was afraid to contradict her again. He still had a scar from the last time. "Just the urban legends. I don't believe they exist. It's modern cryptozoology. A mysterious race of people who are born to be assassins. Until one day, the entire race just vanished."

"They're real, and Alterra is one," Tena replied.

"What makes you think that?"

"Because my father said so. He tried to recruit her a few years ago. She refused, then became his worst enemy. So he framed her for the IGP explosion. And then she helped kill him."

"I'm going to need more proof than that. I've worked with your father, and he was prone to megalomania and had a persecution complex. I wouldn't put it past him to imagine..." He trailed off when he saw Tena's expression. Sheepishly, he said, "I... I... I'd like to take a sample of her DNA for examination."

"You'll do more than that. You're going to use her DNA to create an army of assassins, loyal to me. The Inner Eye will be more powerful than ever before." Some little girls wanted a pony, but Tena had always wanted an army of loyal assassins. From the time she was big enough to access the gene lab without a stepstool, she'd attempted to perfect the cloning process. Of course, the first thing she'd tried to clone was herself, as she considered herself the pinnacle of evolution. But for some reason, Vermon genes didn't take well to cloning.

She'd experimented with other humanoid species, but found that raising the clones was a frustratingly slow process. Tena was a lot of things, but patient wasn't one of them. She wanted that army while she was still young enough to have fun with it. She researched ways of speeding up growth without sacrificing training, and implanting artificial memories that would inspire absolute loyalty. It was a tall order, but once she'd learned of Doctor X's skills, everything started falling into place.

"Yes, mistress," Doctor X said, and began preparations.

Tena's lab was a good distance from Valos, floating in free space. Tena liked to keep her secrets far from where her meddling siblings could stumble across them. But there was another reason for the distance. The nature of the technology meant that it couldn't be near an inhabited planet, lest disasters happen.

The space station resembled a spoked wheel. The outer ring held the labs, the landing bay, sleeping quarters, and everything else needed for long-term scientific experiments. The spokes were access halls that led to a giant metal ball in the center of the station. This large, round room held only one thing.

"Here it is, the Chronal Accelerator." Doctor X was pleased with his creation, waving his short arms proudly. There actually wasn't much to look at. From inside, it still just looked like a round, mostly empty room. Tena didn't look impressed, but then, she rarely did.

"Explain the process again," she asked skeptically.

"When activated, time speeds up in this room. We can control the speed. This will allow us to bring Alterra's clones to adulthood."

Tena frowned. "But won't that make them mindless, feral creatures? I need my clones trained from birth. Trained to be living weapons, and loyal only to me."

"Trust me," he said.

A few hours later, Doctor X held up a vial of yellowish liquid. "It's ready to be grown Come, let me show you how quickly I can age it."

He led Tena back to the station's central chamber, which now contained a large glass sphere full of amber liquid. He placed the vial into an opening and pressed a few buttons. "I am now transferring the tissue into the artificial womb," X told her, even though she already understood the process. Then he led her out of the central chamber, back to the control room, and continued to narrate the process.

"In a matter of minutes, we will age the fetus nine months." He turned a knob. As they watched from the safety of the control room, time sped up in the central chamber. Before their eyes, the microscopic zygote grew into a visible fetus, floating in the artificial embryonic fluid. He had to slow time back down a couple of times to make a few adjustments, and to attach a nutritive tube to the fetus.

In just under two hours, they had a newborn baby. Doctor X was ecstatic. "Congratulations, it's a girl!"

Tena rolled her eyes. "It's an exact copy of Alterra's DNA. Aren't they all going to be girls?"

"You have no sense of humor," X chuffed. "Now comes the fun part. Follow me." They went back to the central chamber, where the doctor opened a drawer and pulled out a small bodysuit, covered in wires and tubes.

"And that is…"

"This… is everything you need to simulate an entire childhood." He pulled the baby out of the embryonic tank, and carefully fit her into the tiny bodysuit. He placed her in a padded bed, making sure all the tubes were attached correctly. "This suit will provide her body with nutrients, and extract wastes. The suit is self-cleaning inside, so she won't get bedsores. It will stretch as she grows. It will stimulate her muscles to make her strong."

He attached a visor to the infant's face. "She will see only what we want her to see. The suit provides haptic feedback so that everything feels real. Her childhood will be packed with education and training. She will be a master of martial arts, weapons, and technology. She will live a more enriched life in that bed than most people who have everything. Then, when she's about twenty, we'll unhook her and see what we've created."

"And how long will that take?"

"I'm going to slow down the process so that if something goes wrong, I have time to fix it. She'll grow a year every twelve hours. So in ten days, you'll have yourself an assassin."

"Ten days for one assassin?" Tena griped, as if that were

unfathomably slow.

"If this first one is successful, we will work on automating the process," Doctor X said. "For the next batch, we'll grow five at a time, and maybe shave off a couple of days to boot. Eventually we should be able to cut it down to five days, perhaps growing more than a hundred at once."

Tena nodded. "Let's get started."

"First things first," X said. "What do you want to name her?"

A cloud passed over Tena's face, and her head felt fuzzy for a second. Her next thought felt as if it originated from somewhere other than her brain, like a voice whispering in her ear. "She's an offspring of Whisper, let's call her... Wisp." Her mental block cleared up as soon as the words were out of her mouth. She nodded her head and smiled with confidence. "Yes, that's it. 'Wisteria Sevona Parx,' or 'Wisp' for short."

"Wisp it is," Doctor X noted on his computer, not even bothering to wonder where Tena came up with that name.

"I found your tracking device," Raven said. "It looks like Alterra's headed for the Velchon system."

"You know what to do," Bloodstone said.

Raven locked in a course for the nearest warp gate. Yna and Panther had stayed behind on Frella. They were still hoping to find Whisper among the wreckage or elsewhere in town. The rest of the crew took the Bloodwind to follow the tracking device Bloodstone had placed on Alterra earlier.

Of course, Raven knew that both groups were looking for the same person. She wasn't sure if Alterra had fled on her own, or had been abducted by some other bounty hunter. Either way, she was determined to find her. She only hoped this didn't end with Bloodstone capturing Alterra and turning her in.

Raven wasn't sure what she would do if it came to that.

* * *

"Aren't we overloading her with information?" Tena asked, watching the blur of images on the viewscreen.

The doctor shook his head. "From her point of view, time is flowing normally. She experiences life at the same rate we do, it's just that time is flowing faster in there."

It had been a full day since they'd hooked the infant up to the machine. In Wisp's virtual world, she was now two years old. She was already reading and writing and could speak five languages. She was just starting to learn martial arts.

The bodysuit had grown with her, but it was time to switch it out for a new one. Doctor X slowed time back down and remotely sedated the child. Then they entered the Chronal Chamber and put her into a larger bodysuit. They would have to do this at least once a day until she was fully grown.

Now ready to continue, they left the Chronal Chamber and sped up time again.

The Bloodwind was on a wild goose chase. Every time they thought they'd found Alterra's location, the signal vanished. Whenever they found it again, it was near a different planet. In the past twenty-four hours they'd gone through four different warp gates, and Bloodstone was starting to wonder if it was all a trick.

But they didn't have any better leads, so they continued the search.

It was Wisp's fourth birthday. She led a happy, if busy life. Her parents were martial arts experts, and they'd started her early, teaching her how to fight as soon as she could walk. Wisp's parents were also geniuses, and they taught her all about science, mathematics, and chemistry. Wisp's parents were supportive, loving, and disciplined.

Today Wisp's parents threw her a party, and all her school friends were there. She received a ton of presents, which were nice even though Wisp wasn't very materialistic. She had cake and ice cream, there were games, singing, and even a clown. It was probably the best day of her life. Or it was until about three o'clock, when the assassins arrived.

There were two of them, knocking on the door like they were just neighbors or something. One was dressed in black, with a red vest and a domed helmet. The other was a woman dressed in gray.

In front of Wisp, her parents, and the entire party, the one in the black outfit said, "I am Bloodstone, and this is Whisper. We're bounty hunters. We have been hired to kill you." Bloodstone pointed at Wisp's parents. Then, in unison, the bounty hunters pulled out their guns and fired. Wisp's parents were dead before they had time to react. Then the bounty hunters picked up the bodies and dragged them out of the house.

Wisp found herself unable to move throughout the entire scene. It was as if she was in a dream, where her feet were rooted to the floor, and her arms felt like they were trapped in molasses. When the door finally slammed shut, Wisp managed to scream. All the children around her were wailing, but Wisp barely perceived it. Instead, she ran to the door and opened it, screaming for her parents. When she got outside, the assassins were already gone.

Outside the time chamber, Tena watched the scene Wisp had experienced, very pleased. Of course, she wasn't viewing it at the same time that Wisp had lived it, because the scene would have happened too quickly in the Chronal Chamber. When Tena was done viewing the recorded memory, she went back to watching the girl's growth progression. It was amazing, watching this person grow before her eyes.

Usually it was a very gradual thing, but sometimes there were growth spurts where she seemed to shoot up another inch in just minutes.

"That scene was badly written," Doctor X said.

"Not to a four-year-old," Tena replied.

"So this is your plan?" X asked. "Use her to assassinate Bloodstone and Whisper? Whisper's just down the hall. If you want her dead, I can just inject her with poison."

"It will be a test of her skills," Tena said. "And if she's successful, we'll motivate the next batch to take out other targets. Each batch can be specifically bred for our needs at the time."

Another day wasted. Bloodstone was positive someone was playing with them. If it was Alterra, then she obviously knew about the tracking device. But why was she leading them around the galaxy instead of just ditching the device?

But then, that's exactly what she'd done, Bloodstone realized. At the next warp gate, Bloodstone hacked their records to see what ships had been through recently. She did the same at the following warp gate. She had a hunch, but it would take a little more time and data to prove her theory.

Wisp was now six, and lived with her Aunt Tena. In the two years since her adoption, Tena had saved Wisp's life three times. Once from a burning house, then from a rabid dog, and finally from a kidnapper. There was no one in the world Wisp loved more than Tena, and she would do anything for her. Anything.

Bingo. While Raven continued to pilot the ship, following the pings from that damned tracking device, Bloodstone compared star charts and shipping routes. She finally matched the tracking device's route to that of an automated delivery ship. Hacking into the ship's parent company, Contemporal Shipping Inc, Bloodstone was able to find a list of future scheduled deliveries. When it reached its next stop, the Bloodwind would be there first.

Bloodstone held no illusions that Alterra would be on the ship. But it would be foolish not to at least check it out.

"She's waking up, Doctor." The voice sounded like Aunt Tena, but deeper. Wisp, feeling groggy and disoriented, tried to open her eyes but couldn't see anything.

Everything around her felt different. The air was cool against her cheeks, but in a way she'd never felt before. It all felt surreal... but at the same time, it felt more real than her real life. She started to have a panic attack.

Another voice spoke. This one didn't sound human. "Don't worry, she won't remember any of this. Even if she does, she'll think it was a dream." A pair of hands touched her arm. She would have flinched, but she was paralyzed. It was as if her body was drugged, but not her mind.

"I thought she wasn't supposed to wake up during these transfers."

"Auroran physiology is unique. I'll increase the dosage." Wisp felt a prick in her neck. Almost immediately she calmed down. The world slipped away.

When she woke up again, she was in her bed and everything was back to normal.

The delivery ship landed at a spaceport on Arbon. As the androids unloaded the cargo, Bloodstone boarded the ship and looked for any passengers. The ship was empty, and Bloodstone found the tracking device wedged in one corner. That solved that mystery. But where was Alterra, and what had happened to Whisper?

Back to the drawing board. The only idea Bloodstone had left was to look at the delivery history, and see if she could figure out at which stop the tracking device had been placed aboard the ship. Unfortunately, the ship had made several stops each day, so it would take a while to check out all the leads.

* * *

Wisp was eleven years old when she had an awakening. Strange memories flooded her mind. Nothing felt real. A red light blinked at the periphery of her vision no matter where she looked. The air felt cool against her face. It felt just like that dream she'd had a couple of years ago.

She couldn't move. Something was restraining her. It felt like sleep paralysis, except it was daytime and she was wide awake. She looked down at her hands, and she could see them in front of her, but she could plainly feel that they were still at her side.

She wanted to run and tell Aunt Tena, but something told her not to. Instead, she closed her eyes and withdrew into herself. She willed herself to feel every inch of her body. Her *real* body. She kept her eyes closed, no longer trusting them.

She wiggled her fingers. She moved her hand around her thigh until she felt a strap. She followed the strap until she found a buckle. She removed the buckle, and immediately felt less restricted. One at a time, she found more restraints and removed them. There was something stuck to her eyes, like weird goggles. She removed them and blinked a few times, finally seeing the real world for this first time.

She couldn't believe what she saw. Had she been abducted by aliens? She pulled off several tubes, wires, and restraints, then jumped down from the bizarre chair she'd been strapped into. She looked down at herself. She was wearing what looked like some sort of wetsuit.

There was a computer nearby. She wanted to know where she was, so maybe the information was in there. There was no password because the entire station was supposedly secure. She rapidly looked through all the project details, using computer skills she had learned during her artificial childhood.

Clone. Army of assassins. Donor to remain imprisoned on-site for future DNA farming. While mere seconds passed in the rest of the universe, Wisp spent hours studying the station data. Tena was not her aunt. Tena was a monster.

Wisp knew what she had to do.

Tena didn't like sleeping at the station, but it was a six-hour flight back to Valos, and she didn't want to be too far from the project. "Tena! Tena!" Someone was shaking her. She groggily opened her eyes and found herself staring at Doctor X.

"We have to leave, now!" he said.

"Whu?"

"Now, or we both die!" He pulled on her arm.

Tena snapped awake and got to her feet. "What's going on?"

"No time!" he said, and ran off. Tena followed him, still not sure what was happening.

They reached the docking ports, but one of the ships was gone. "Where's my ship?" Tena asked.

"Later, we have seconds!" Doctor X boarded the other ship, and Tena followed. A minute later they were in space, watching the space station disintegrate from a safe distance.

"What. Happened." Tena asked, giving the doctor a deadly look.

"I'm still trying to figure that out," X said, going through data on his tablet. "It looks like someone overloaded the Chronal Accelerator."

"Alterra must have gotten out. But how?"

"I couldn't tell you," X said. "As far as I can tell, she set the Accelerator to maximum speed, and took your shuttle. The Accelerator aged millions of years in minutes. The results were so drastic it took the rest of the station with it."

"And Wisp?"

"She would have aged into dust within the first few seconds. I'm sorry. By the time I knew we had a problem, it was too late."

Tena was furious. If she hadn't needed X for her other projects, she would have eviscerated him right there. As it was, he still ended up with a few scars.

Meanwhile, far away, a small ship sped away from the Valos system. Wisp made plans to return Alterra to her ship. "Are you sure you don't want to come with us?" Alterra asked.

"No thank you," Wisp answered. "I have my own plans."

Alterra darkened her skin again. At their next stop, she acquired some clothing and a new mask. Then she contacted the Bloodwind and set up a rendezvous point.

Bloodstone was ecstatic to see Whisper again. The crew pressed her for information, but of course Whisper couldn't tell them the whole story. Still, she stuck as close to the truth as she could. She told them she'd been kidnapped by one of Vermon's offspring, but that she eventually escaped. She didn't tell them anything about Wisp.

02.02   The Council of Heirs

ED.02502.01.15

In a grand chamber of the largest palace on Valos, the Council of Heirs met to discuss the future of their planet's government. The eight offspring were seated around a large circular table. Two chairs remained empty, including the largest one. In Arthurian legend, the round table represented equality. It meant that no knight was more important than any other in the group. But the Valos council's table only served to postpone bloodshed. None of the eight could seize power without a majority vote, which was unlikely. Any perceived attempt to take power by force would provoke immediate retaliation. This is why the late Lord Vermon's luxurious chair remained unoccupied - sitting as equals kept the peace. Barely.

All were the children of Teykor Vermon, but no two had the same mother. While each of them inherited their father's white irises - and a bit of the psychic talent that went with it - they bore few other similarities to each other. During his long life, Lord Vermon had sired many children with a variety of women of several species. Some of those offspring had suffered ill fates, very recently. This bickering council consisted of the only heirs currently living on Valos, who were old enough to be given command. Their current topic of debate was the fate of the Inner Eye, Lord Vermon's secret criminal organization.

Cyric was a politician at heart. Tall and fit, square-jawed, with a fair complexion and a large vocabulary, he had the kind of face that made people instantly love him, and a voice that could soothe a zondarg. He always chose his words with great care, even now as he shouted at his half-siblings. He had always been morally opposed to Lord Vermon's criminal ties, and now he implored the others to shut down the Inner Eye and allow Valos to form a legitimate government. He played to their interests; instead of focusing on morality, he explained why exporting trade goods would be more profitable in the long run, and how they would all live longer without the IGP breathing down their necks. But his opponents saw right through his pandering.

Seated to Cyric's right, Lemondrop sided with her charismatic brother. She had golden hair and golden skin to match, with bright purple freckles on her cheeks that always made her look ten years younger than she was. She believed in peace above all else, and while she wasn't as eloquent as Cyric when it came to compelling speeches, she was every bit as strong in her convictions. She believed that breaking up the Inner Eye was the key to saving Valos from itself, and ending all the violence their crimes had caused.

On Cyric's other side sat Venus, a rough-looking woman with no hair and a large scar on her left cheek. While she was technically on the anti-crime side, her intentions weren't nearly as noble as Cyric's or Lemondrop's. She had no regrets about her life of shady dealings, and she cared nothing about peace or morality or making the universe a better place. She simply felt that they'd made enough profit from the Inner Eye, and it was time to quit while they were ahead. The longer they kept it going the more they risked getting busted and losing everything.

Sitting directly across from Cyric was Threshkel, who was every bit as ambitious but diametrically opposed to everything Cyric believed. Intelligent but sleazy, Threshkel was built like a tank but spoke like a snake oil salesman. He argued with subtle wit and a friendly tone, but it was obvious that murder was in his eyes. His many facial tattoos added extra menace to his death stare, which made Cyric feel uneasy despite his immunity to Threshkel's fear-inducing psychic talent. Thresh not only wanted to keep the Inner Eye running, he wanted to expand it, even going as far as to conquer other worlds. He saw himself as the future emperor of a vast intergalactic empire, and he didn't appreciate his cowardly half-siblings standing in his way.

To his left sat Tena, looking like a supermodel's corpse with her flawless pale skin and bright red lipstick. There was a crazed look in her eyes. She was amazed at how badly the others were missing the point. Tena felt that she was the only one at this table who had truly loved their father. The others fed on Lord Vermon's empire like Galean shark-spiders eating their way out of the womb, each only caring about their own hunger. Did none of them care what father would have wanted? She was filled with fire and was ready to rip apart any planet that stood in her way. She supported Thresh's plans to expand the Inner Eye, but mostly because it was the quickest path to her own destiny – deadly, torturous revenge on everyone who had ever opposed her father.

Threshkel's other ally was Vernach, a disgusting slob of a man with skin as oily as his hair. He only half listened to everyone's arguments, paying more attention to the bag of sriracha-flavored ham chips he was munching on. Vernach didn't care about politics, empires, or revenge. He just wanted money. The Inner Eye had always done a great job of delivering the goods, and he saw no reason to dismantle it now.

Filling the last two seats were Sekka and Nazdak, neither saying a word. Nazdak, a skinny man with a head for math and no spine to speak of, paid close attention to every word. He even took notes. He nodded in agreement several times, sometimes to Cyric and sometimes to Threshkel. But they all knew Nazdak wouldn't come out in full support of either side until there looked to be a clear winner. For now, he would throw a bone to each side now and then, just enough so that when someone did take control, he could claim he'd supported them all along.

Sekka was the youngest at the table, just barely old enough to be included on this council. She barely even acknowledged the others in the room, paying more attention to the pink squirrel in her lap. Long ago she'd found that by locking eyes with an animal, she could influence its behavior. Right now she had it pantomiming the others in the room, shaking its tiny fists in mock rage. It worked better with some animals than others, but squirrels were especially susceptible. Sekka cared more about animals than people, and it didn't matter to her what her half-siblings decided. As long as they kept the zoos open, she didn't care whether the income came from the Inner Eye or legitimate trade. She figured they'd make the right choice in the end.

"Only a coward would close up shop right now," Thresh said. "Inner Eye profits have never been better."

"Don't you get it, Thresh?" Cyric said. "It's not just about going to prison or being wanted by the IGP. If we're caught breaking Galactic Law, we could start a war!"

"Bring it on," Threshkel answered. "I like the odds. The Grunthians would back us up, as would the Frash, the Entorans, and the Neptunians. If we decimate the Earth, we'll never have to worry about the IGP again."

"T-t-technically 'decimate' would just eliminate one-tenth of the population..." Nazdak offered meekly. He tried not to make too much eye contact with either of them, and spent most of the meeting crunching numbers in the back of his mind. People scared him. Numbers made him feel safe. He had a cybernetic eye implant that gave him a direct feed of the Galactic Stock Exchange, so that a live ticker tape appeared at the bottom of his field of vision.

"Shut it, Naz," Tena snapped. "Thresh has a point. Daddy

had the right idea in taking out the IGP station. But he didn't go far enough. We should finish what he started!"

"Can you two hear yourselves?" Cyric was incredulous. "Our father put so much work into this planet. When he arrived, this world was a prison, just an oubliette for other planets to dump their problem citizens. But under Lord Vermon's leadership, the prisoners won their independence, learned to grow crops, mine for ore, and develop their own technology." When he spoke, you could almost hear patriotic music playing in the background.

"Not to mention building this beautiful city," Lemondrop added, spreading her arms wide and speaking in that melodious voice of hers. She was so passionate about everything and had a knack for making others feel her emotions. Even when doing something as simple as ordering coffee, her voice was full of poetry and raw emotion. "This is a vibrant world full of lovely people and unique natural wonders. Our oceans are crystal clear, our deserts sparkle like diamonds, and our air smells like honeysuckle. The Gilded Cascade is the largest natural waterfall in the galaxy. Why would you want all of this torn apart by war?"

"Well said," Cyric told her. "I'm warning you, Thresh. Your empire is a pipe dream. If you continue this line of thinking, I will block you every step of the way. Do you still think the Grunthians will ally with you when they learn you've been selling weapons to the Ruthwakans? Will the Frash still come to your aid when they find out it was Iena who assassinated their Chancellor? Will the Entorans—"

"Don't push me, Cyric, you may not like what happens next." The threat was blatant, but Thresh could have been reading a bedtime story to a baby koala as far as his voice was concerned. "Our empire will expand with or without your approval. The question is whether you'll be around to see it."

"I'm not afraid of you, Thresh," Cyric answered, then sighed. "But I'm also not your enemy. I implore you, just think on it. This planet is rich in resources begging for export. The virtrinium mines alone could sustain our economy for a thousand years. We don't have to resort to conquest or illicit activity. We can still live like kings without having to get our hands dirty. If we go straight, everyone will benefit. You, me, the entire galaxy."

Tena stood up, patting Thresh on the shoulder. "It appears we are at an impasse," she said. "I propose we meet again in one month to vote on the issue. Use that time to consider our proposals, and we will... consider yours." Her tone made it quite clear she had no intention of considering anything.

Cyric planned to use that month winning over Sekka and Nazdak, maybe even Vernach if he could prove to him that exports pay more than crime. Threshkel's plans were a bit darker. If things went well, Cyric and Lemondrop wouldn't even be around for the next meeting. With them gone, Venus would be easy to win over, and Sekka and Nazdak would naturally fall in line. And once he had control of the council, he might even take out a few more of his half-siblings just to get a larger piece of the pie.

After the meeting, Tena boarded a hovering limo and brooded in the backseat while the autopilot drove her back to her tower. She fumed at the thought of Cyric tearing down her father's work. She thought of Alterra Sarr, still wanted by the IGP after Lord Vermon framed her. This made Tena smile. She could end Alterra's life at any time simply by telling the right people that the bounty hunter Whisper was actually Alterra. At the moment, Tena and Doctor X were the only ones on Valos who knew.

More than two years ago, Whisper had pulled double duty as both a cop and a bounty hunter. She'd tried so hard to prove Lord Vermon's many violations of galactic law, but he'd always been one step ahead of her. He'd thought that crippling the IGP and framing Alterra would kill two birds with one stone, but in the end, it had just led to his own death.

Alterra needed to die, no question. But if Tena told the universe how to find her, then they might capture her alive. And in the process, Alterra might even somehow prove her innocence. Besides, Tena wanted to be there for Alterra's last breath. She wanted to tear the woman to pieces, slowly and painfully. Then she wanted to stomp Alterra's corpse into mincemeat, and mail it to her family with a little card that said, "Sorry for your loss." If Alterra had family. The thought of family derailed Tena's train of thought.

Tena's mother, Mirana, had been a Stoneswoman from the lost tribes of Valos. The Stonefolk were once believed to have died out long before Valos was charted. But after Vermon's rebellion and subsequent exploration of the planet, several tribes were discovered on an island off the Northern continent. And they were dying. A bizarre infestation of red locusts had wiped out most of the plant life on the island, leading to famine. But Lord Vermon saved them. Vermon's detractors said it was just a publicity stunt, and a few even accused him of sending the locusts in the first place. But Tena didn't believe that. As far as she was concerned, her mother would have died if not for her father's intervention, and she was proud to be her father's daughter.

Tena's people eventually died out anyway, including her mother. They slowly perished due to diseases the prisoners had brought to Valos. It wasn't anyone's fault, except maybe the jailers who decided to use Valos as a prison in the first place. Tena often wondered if Valos would still have been chosen if the IGP had known there was a native population of sapient beings. She suspected they actually did know and went ahead with it anyway. But she would deal with the IGP eventually. Her thoughts were interrupted again as they arrived at the lab. She stormed through the automatic door and stomped straight to her office.

Tena pulled off her sleek red gloves and studied her hands. The only visible signs of her mother's DNA – other than her unusually pale skin – were on her hands, feet, and elbows. Small, chitinous spikes protruded from her knuckles, barely visible but sharp as razors. A similar ridge ran down the sides of each hand, from the tip of the pinky to her wrist, a solid line except for small breaks at the joints. Her fingernails were made of the same material, making them much stronger than ordinary nails. She had to use special equipment to trim them into the clawlike points she preferred. Her toenails were similar, and she had an additional spike running straight down from each heel. These were the only ones that really annoyed her. Her ancestors had probably used their heel spikes for traction on unstable ground, but to Tena it just meant she had to have her stiletto heels custom made.

Her most significant biological peculiarities were internal. Her bones were much stronger than that of most species, as unbreakable as steel. Her veins and arteries were embedded in small grooves set in the bones, making it extremely difficult to suffer a hit that would lead to major blood loss. If a sword were to pierce her skin, even if it cut all the way to the bone, it would only sever her rapidly-clotting capillaries. She was also incapable of being incapacitated by pain. She was aware of injuries, but the sensation was more annoying than painful, and not enough to keep her from fighting back.

Her ancestors had used these gifts to cut down trees and forge tunnels in caves. They were a peaceful society, vegetarians who only killed in self-defense. But Tena had learned she could behead someone with a chop of her hand, cave in a face with a single punch, or disembowel a foe with one good kick. You didn't waste talents like that on agriculture. The thought of using her fists on Alterra made her smile. *Soon,* she thought.

The Loving Care Orphanage stood overlooking Lake Vasta, about twenty kilometers South of the Valos Capital City. It was a beautiful building. A perfectly round structure with a transparent purple dome, it allowed the tenants to have an unobstructed view of the natural world around them, while keeping them safe from the more harmful aspects of nature. Two hovering limos approached the building from different directions. Cyric and Lemondrop each exited their respective transports, greeting each other warmly. Then they turned toward the domed building.

It was not a publicity stunt. The press didn't even know they were here. Cyric and Lemondrop had both been raised as orphans, despite their royal parentage. After all these years, they still made a point of visiting the orphanage as often as possible. They wanted to educate the children and give them hope for the future. Before going in, they walked toward the railing. On this side of the building, Lake Vasta ran right up along the side of the dome. From inside the orphanage, the children could see under the water, and learn about aquatic life. It was as beautiful as it was educational. As Cyric looked over the railing, he saw something odd reflected in the water. He glanced up at the sky, his mouth gaping in horror. Before Lemondrop had a chance to ask him what was wrong, he pushed her over the ledge.

A meteor about the size of a hoverbike crashed into the orphanage. Everyone inside was killed instantly, along with Cyric. It left a huge crater that would one day be seen as just an extension of the lake. Rescue bots recovered Lemondrop a few hours after the explosion. She was badly injured, but thanks to Cyric's quick reflexes, she would live. She was brought to Golden Mercy Hospital where she would probably remain for months, assuming no other "accidents" occurred. Scientists and government officials debated for weeks regarding the failure of the planet's defense grid. In the end, Thresh had several prominent meteorologists removed from their posts, and assured the public that no such random acts of nature would ever happen again.

Lying in her hospital bed, unable to move while her bones knit, Lemondrop lived in constant fear. She hadn't thought

Thresh would go so far to seize power, but she had been naive. And now she was completely helpless, unable to move her limbs, unable to speak with her broken jaw, still slipping in and out of consciousness after a month. Surely Thresh wouldn't finish her off so soon after Cyric's death. It would look too suspicious. But then, all it would take was the wrong dose of medicine, or a malfunctioning piece of hospital equipment. Such accidents were rare, but then, so were meteor strikes. But even to the extent that she could communicate, she wouldn't let on that she knew Thresh had been responsible for the meteor. That knowledge would bring about her termination that much faster.

It got to the point that she went into panic mode every time a nurse walked into the room. She winced at every injection, convinced it was going to be poison. The staff saw the fear in her eyes, heard her moans of objection, and saw the way she pulled at her restraints at every routine procedure. Eventually they had to keep her sedated more and more often, because her attempted thrashings threatened to prolong the healing process. Her Vermon heritage already made her immune to some medical treatments, preventing them from cloning her new limbs or using accelerated bone regeneration techniques. So it was vital she not do anything else to slow down her healing.

One day she opened her eyes to see a bubbly, smiling nurse. "You're awake? Wonderful! You have a visitor!" She moved her eyes toward the doorway and was horrified to see Tena standing there. *Don't look scared,* Lemondrop thought. If Tena saw the fear Lemondrop felt, all the cards would be on the table. She had to look happy to see Tena. No, too far. Tena wouldn't believe that. But complacent, at least. Bored, even.

"I'm sorry about what happened to your brother," Tena said, at least attempting to look sincere.

He was just as much your brother as mine, Lemondrop thought angrily. But of course it wasn't true. Family isn't just blood, it's love. And Tena wasn't capable of love. Tears welled up in

Lemondrop's eyes at the thought of Cyric.

"I know, I know," Tena said, seeing the tears. "But the pain will pass. Now listen, I want you to know that Thresh and I are sparing no expense in making sure you get the best medical care possible. In fact, we're planning to move you to a more private facility, where I can keep a close eye on you personally. The doctors are trying to talk me out of it - they think it'll be dangerous to move you until you're more healed. But personally I think it's important you start getting higher quality care as soon as possible, don't you think?" Tena's wide smile was nightmare-inducing.

To be fair, Tena actually kept her word. Lemondrop was transported without incident, to a room in Tena's own tower, where she was watched over by Tena's personal doctor. Of course, Tena wasn't being magnanimous; she only kept Lemondrop alive to avert suspicion. At least in the tower, Tena could keep an eye on her and make sure she never spoke to anyone. Tena gave Doctor X strict orders to keep Lemondrop stable, but maybe be less generous with the painkillers than Golden Mercy Hospital had been. After all, a little pain is good for the soul.

02.03 Homecoming

ED.02502.02.20

Raven sat in the back of an automated hovercab. It was a long ride from the shuttleport, a ride that always brought back painful memories. To distract herself, she pulled out her tablet and read the news. Her custom feed mostly showed science news and medical breakthroughs, but one general news article did stand out.

Rennick Vermon, also known as the criminal Mindwipe, had been murdered in prison. Raven had never met him, but he was technically family. Raven was pretty sure she had a multitude of half-siblings. Her late father had really gotten around. Raven wondered if she should feel sad that a family member had passed away, but all she could think was, *One less rapist in the galaxy.* Was that cold-hearted? She wasn't sure. Rennick was a monster, but you were still supposed to love your family, flaws and all. Or so she'd been told.

Ugh, she thought, putting the tablet away. She didn't need moral dilemmas today. Going home was bad enough without preemptively giving herself guilt feelings. Rennick wasn't family, he was just a criminal who happened to share a bit of Raven's genetic code. And the universe was a safer place without him in it. Period.

Raven hadn't been home in months. She'd only returned to Earth four times since becoming a bounty hunter, and each time she'd only stayed long enough to pick up some tech from her labs. Going home only brought back bad memories. And it wasn't like she had friends or family to visit. There was only Trenyn, the one being she respected above all others, and they already lived with her on the Bloodwind.

It was Trenyn who had helped her regain her mobility. Before that, they'd been her hands, working closely with her to develop new technology. And before that, they'd helped each other study as they worked for their advanced degrees. And before that, Trenyn had saved Raven from herself.

Watching the roads go by in the back of the hovercab, Raven zoned out, remembering the day she'd met Trenyn. The memory was as clear in her mind now as it had been the day it happened. Her mother was dead. Her limbs were gone. Her father was a criminal, but no one would believe her. The other students kept calling her a freak because of her eyes. She had no one to talk to, no one to help her.

She was stuck in an uncomfortable hoverchair gifted to her by charity. It was controlled by a joystick she operated with her chin. In her mind, she had thousands of ideas for improving the chair, ways to make it safer, more comfortable, and more user-friendly. But that would mean working with others, and no one seemed to be able to keep up with her. She just wasn't capable of expressing her ideas in a way other people understood.

It's not that the other students were unintelligent. Just to be admitted to this university, you had to be a genius. Her fellow students were the best Earth had to offer. And yet, it was like she spoke another language.

She got tired of all the stares in the hallway. She was sick of needing a paid companion to follow her around and help her in the restroom. The idea of living like this for the rest of her life was exhausting. One day she decided that she just couldn't do it anymore.

There was a lake near the campus. She'd just gotten out of advanced astrophysics, where someone a few rows behind her had thrown wadded-up paper at the back of her head the entire hour. She could hear them giggling and calling her several impolite names. As she rode her cart towards the lake, the voices of her classmates echoed through her head. This was her life, now and forever. She would never be more than a freak for others to gawk at.

She sat there for ten minutes. A few other students lounged by the lake but got up when the next class started. Raven stayed where she was. She was now all alone. No witnesses. No one to stop her. They would probably think it was an accident. The freak couldn't even control her own hoverchair. No one would come to her funeral. At most, her name would be listed on the "In Memoriam" page of the university yearbook.

She spent a few more minutes talking herself in and out of it. Finally, unable to climb out of her desperation, she drove the hoverchair onto the pier. Moving at top speed, which was barely more than the average person's walking pace, she hovered inexorably toward the far end of the pier. No more hesitations, no more second thoughts. She flew off the end of the pier and splashed into the lake.

The hoverchair wasn't designed for water use, and it sank like a stone. Strapped into the chair, Raven couldn't have saved herself now if she'd wanted to.

And that's when she started having second thoughts. *What am I, nuts?* She thought. A myriad of possible futures flashed through her mind. Ones in which she won the Nobel Prize, or became president, or cured a disease. Faces appeared too, images of historical scientists who had overcome physical challenges to change the world. Suddenly it felt like she was dishonoring them by taking the easy way out.

Not that she still had a choice in the matter. She'd been underwater for nearly a minute now, and she wasn't sure how much longer she could hold her breath. In a panic, she thought *Help! Help!*

To her surprise, she heard back, *I hear you! Where are you?*

I'm in the lake! She replied. *Hurry!*

Seconds later she saw someone swimming towards her. She didn't recognize their species, but she felt an instant connection with them. They thought back and forth to each other at a rapid pace. By the time Trenyn carried her out of the water, Raven already knew them better than anyone else on the planet. This newly-arrived foreign exchange student immediately became Raven's best friend, and from then on they were inseparable.

Raven snapped back to the present. The hovercab had pulled up to her house. She stepped out and approached the door. It wasn't closed all the way. She hesitated, considering every possibility from teenage pranksters to squatters to contract killers. She briefly considered calling the police, but that only reminded her of the night her mother died. The police were useless and probably worked for the Inner Eye anyway.

Besides, if someone was inside, Raven was probably a bigger threat than the cops anyway. In the past two years, she had successfully captured multiple armed fugitives. And even a couple of multiple-armed fugitives. Would Bloodstone call the cops after seeing an open door? Would Whisper? Somehow Raven doubted it. She went inside.

Nothing looked disturbed. She walked through the entire house, calling out "hello" a few times, and found nothing. She was alone, nothing had been stolen or broken, and it didn't look like anyone had been living here. Still, that was odd.

She decided to let it go. She had a reason for being here, and the sooner she was done, the sooner she could get out of this house and stop being bombarded with bad memories. She went straight to the lab and started boxing up equipment.

Every time she came home for lab equipment, she considered hiring some movers to help. But she preferred the solitude, and besides, she could lift a lot more than any movers could. And as long as her body was charged, she didn't get tired. Hired help would just end up getting in her way.

After a few hours, the front lawn was filled with boxes. She would have to rent a truck to carry it all back to the shuttleport, but she would wait until she was done to make that call. She took a break for lunch.

She stood in the kitchen, eating a plain turkey sandwich with mayo on white bread. A charging cord led from her suit to a wall outlet. She was only down about ten percent, but as long as she was standing still, it was as good a time as any to top off her suit's power.

She froze as she heard the front door creak open. She detached the charging cord from her armpit and crept towards the foyer. Her body wasn't built for stealth, but she stepped as silently as she could. As she neared the foyer, she thought she heard the floorboards creak. She looked down and realized that had been her own foot, stepping on a spoon.

But why was there a spoon there? She hadn't seen it on her first walkthrough. She hadn't moved any utensils. It didn't make any sense. She looked up, and suddenly it was in her face. A man, a robot, an animal, she wasn't sure. It was on her before her brain had time to process what she was seeing. It knocked her to the floor with a loud clang, and sat on her chest trying to claw at her eyes.

Raven blocked its blows, looking around for anything she could use as a weapon. Still blocking with her left hand, she grabbed a metal chair from her right and put it between her and the attacker. It didn't stop it for long, but it was long enough to get a better look. It was humanoid, but small in stature, with four arms, and dressed in black from head to toe. It had four eyes peeking through its mask. Actually, no, they were more like lights or goggles.

Raven pushed the chair against the creature and scooted backward. Then she rolled to her feet and ran. She could hear it right behind her. As she passed the refrigerator, she reached out, grabbed the handle, and pulled. The door came off the fridge, and Raven spun to face her opponent, smacking it with the door and sending it flying.

She threw the door at her attacker and continued to run. This house was full of components that could be assembled into weapons – if she had more time. She ran towards her labs, grabbing anything heavy she passed and throwing it behind her. She passed a suit of medieval armor, complete with a sheathed sword on its waist. She grabbed the hilt on the way by, hoping to pull out the sword. But it was all welded together as one piece, and she pulled the entire knight off its base. So she threw the suit of armor at her pursuer, hitting it square in the chest. It only slowed it down for a second.

Raven reached her lab and hit the button to close the metal door. The creature – or whatever it was – scuttled after her on all six limbs, and nearly reached her before the door shut. She could hear the thing scratching and pounding on the door, but she was safe for the moment. This room was designed for dangerous and potentially explosive experiments. The door was nearly impenetrable.

She had to calm down and think. Her attacker had lights for eyes. That meant it was probably a robot. Except that it didn't move like a robot. It moved like a psychotic, highly-caffeinated monkey-badger with rabies. And it was focused on Raven, powering through any obstacles to get to her. Assuming it was a robot, this meant it had been programmed specifically to kill her. It wouldn't stop until it knew it had achieved this objective.

So she would have to destroy it. Except, if someone was out to kill her, wouldn't they just send another one? Maybe there was a way to make it think it had achieved its objective. Raven tried to piece together a plan, but it wasn't easy with that thing pounding on the door.

The pounding suddenly stopped. Raven was genre savvy enough to know better than to open the door. Sooner or later the robot would fall through the ceiling, or come up from the floor, or something. And probably when she least expected it. She got to work on assembling something to stop it. A lot of her equipment currently sat on the front lawn, but there were enough spare parts left to work with.

It took nearly ten minutes, and the results weren't elegant, but it was a weapon. She held a metal tube the size of a bazooka. It would fire a burst of energy strong enough to put the assassin out of commission, regardless of whether it was a robot or an animal. She hoped. The makeshift weapon had no trigger, just a hole she would have to touch with her metal fingers to complete a circuit. And it would only be good for one shot.

She considered waiting for the robot to break into the lab, but she wanted to fight on her terms. If she waited, it might catch her with her guard down. She held the weapon ready to fire, and opened the lab door. It was quiet. She stepped out and looked around. Nothing. She walked down the hall, stepping over the suit of armor, looking into every corner, every side room.

She jumped as the house's fire alarm went off. She sniffed the air. She didn't smell smoke yet, but it was a large house. She stepped through the hallways, listening for movement, trying to smell smoke, and jumping at shadows. There was a thump sound from far away, and the power went out. She waited for the emergency generator to kick in, but it didn't.

It was only midday, though, so there was still plenty of light coming in through the windows. Now she smelled smoke, and she started to make her way towards the source. She ran down one hallway, turned, and started down another when the assassin attacked again. It came from the side, bursting out of a closet and knocking her against the far wall. She tried to turn her weapon towards it, but it was too close to her now. She used her weapon like a club, trying to knock it off of her.

Once again it pulled her to the floor. She had to block her face with one hand, to keep its grabby hands from clawing at her. With her other hand, she worked the barrel of her weapon between them. Angling it slightly toward the assassin, she shoved her finger onto the contact point, and the weapon fired – sending huge shocks through them both.

The only thing that saved Raven from being electrocuted was the rubber inner lining of her suit. Unfortunately, her suit's battery had shorted out, and she was completely unable to move. The killer robot lay dormant on top of her chest, smoke rising from its joints. Raven saw flickers of flame creeping into the room. Why wasn't the fire suppression system working?

Raven's suit had a backup battery that would come online in a couple of minutes. Unfortunately, the assassin bot appeared to have one as well. She watched as its eyes went from black to a dull amber, like it was just starting to power up. Raven was in a race against time, but she couldn't do anything but lie there. She just had to hope her battery warmed up first.

The robot twitched. Its eyes got brighter. Its arms started moving, albeit weakly. With one trembling arm, it started to reach for Raven's throat.

Then Raven sat up, knocking the assassin to the floor. Her power had returned, and all systems were go. She stood over the robot, lifted her weapon, and clubbed it on the back of the head. It took two more hits to knock the robot's head off.

The flames were getting rather large now, and it was hard to breathe. She reached down to pick up the robot's head. With any luck, she could examine its software and find out who had sent it. As she carried it out the front door, she heard a beeping. She looked at the head. The eyes were rapidly flashing red.

Raven threw the head back into the house and dove for the lawn. A huge explosion shook the grounds, taking out a good portion of the house. Raven backed away from the burning wreckage. When she felt she was a safe distance away, she stood and watched it burn.

It was strange… she kept waiting for her emotions to kick in, but she felt nothing. It was her home, full of warm fuzzy memories and all that nostalgic tripe. But it was also where she had witnessed her mother's murder, and suffered through an attack so savage it left her without limbs. Still, she felt neither sadness nor relief. It was just a building to her, with no more emotional pull than the local gym or a fast food restaurant. She had no sudden desire to rush in to rescue old photo albums, nor did she feel any satisfaction from seeing this source of painful memories burn to the ground.

It was just a house. If she felt anything at all, it was a sense of closure. A chapter of her life had come to an end. The last vestiges of her father's hold on her life.

She heard sirens in the distance, and knew the fire suppression drones would arrive soon. She didn't feel like answering a lot of questions or filing paperwork today, so she walked until she reached a good spot to call an autocab, and rode back to the shuttleport. With any luck, whoever sent the assassin would think it had been successful. If not, she would cross that bridge when she came to it.

"How goes the culling?" Thresh asked as he entered Tena's office. He didn't ask how she was, he didn't even knock first. Thresh and Tena needed each other and had no illusions about being friends or family. Lovers, on occasion, but that was just for fun. Politeness was off the table.

"Thirteen confirmed kills, four probable kills, no confirmed escapes," Tena said, reading the data from her monitor.

"Good," Thresh said. "Your androids are proving most effective."

"Lifepurge 2.0 is a little buggy, but that just makes the

murders more interesting," Tena said with delight. She walked over to Thresh and stroked his chin playfully. "It's not the army of killer clones Daddy always promised me, but I'll make do."

"How many targets are left?" Thresh asked.

"That's hard to say," Tena said. "You know how dad was. A different woman every night. Every time I think I've tracked down all the little bastards, three more pop up. But as far as I can tell, none of them had any designs on joining the council. Or even knew about it. Your fears of a usurper are groundless."

Thresh punched her hard in the jaw, knocking her to the floor. "Fool. We can't take that chance."

Tena smiled, licking blood off of her lips. For her, violence was foreplay. "Oh, don't worry, I'm going to keep tracking them down and killing them," she said. "All I'm saying is that you shouldn't get so stressed about it." Rather than try to stand up, she winked and made a "come hither" motion with her finger.

"Slaying potential enemies is how I get rid of stress," Thresh said, dropping down onto one knee.

"I know another way," Tena said, pulling him the rest of the way to the floor.

What happened next was the exact opposite of making love. While "sexual intercourse" did technically occur - the appropriate organs were squished together and multiple orgasms were had by all - the event resembled a brawl more than anything remotely erotic. The pair tried to outdo each other, each attempting to prove they could tolerate the most pain, and each trying to dole out the most punishment. The contest escalated, with bodies thrown against the wall, skin slashed by fingernails, faces pummeled until blue, until it reached a crescendo of pleasure and pain.

When both parties were spent, the room looked like it had been through an earthquake. The furniture was in ruins. Blood adorned the wall, along with a few other bodily fluids. The two participants - sprawled on the floor and breathing heavily - looked like murder victims. The contest was a draw.

"Go home, Thresh," Tena said, as she got to her feet.

"Same time next month?" he asked, as he gathered up the shreds of his clothing.

"We'll see," she answered, walking out the office door. In truth, she hoped he would be dead by then. The project was nearing completion, and soon she would have no use for Threshkel's resources. She was already planning his demise, and suspected he was contemplating similar plans against her. But she wasn't worried about that. He wasn't nearly as cunning as she was; she'd see his betrayal coming from miles away.

Doctor X was calibrating the settings on another assassin bot when Tena arrived - completely nude, badly bruised all over, and bleeding from several cuts. If this had been his first day, the doctor would have immediately called the medic. Instead, he just rolled his eyes. He tried to maintain eye contact as she spoke, but he couldn't help but notice the viscous fluid dribbling down her inner thigh. *This woman has no shame*, he thought.

"Do you have the results I requested?" she asked. Her face was already returning to its normal color, and her wounds were starting to close.

"I'm going to need a little more time," the doctor replied nervously. He knew she was impatient, but he took solace in the fact that he was irreplaceable. No one on the planet knew more about gravity manipulation, and even if they did, this project was too far along for a staff change. Nobody would ever be able to decipher X's notes. If he were to disappear now, the project would have to start over.

It looked like the same thoughts were going through Tena's mind. A brief flash of anger turned into a neutral, almost bored expression. "Do not sleep until you have my results," she said flatly. "And order new furniture for my office," she added as she walked away.

X sighed. Another all-nighter. The project's completion was looming close, and he worried that he wouldn't be needed once it was finished. Tena did not like loose ends. While Tena had other projects lined up that could use X's skills, he wasn't going to bet his life on that. This lab's turnover rate was brutal, and X had witnessed a few terminations firsthand. That was the real reason the project wasn't already finished - for every two hours X put into the project, he put an hour into his exit strategy. Tonight would be no different.

But first he had secretarial duties to attend to. He knew what Tena's office probably looked like right now. Before the furniture could be ordered, a cleaning crew would have to be called. And then the crew would have to be disposed of. Tena had good reason to be paranoid - anyone who entered the lab was a potential spy, even the janitors. She couldn't risk her rivals learning what she was doing here. The project was too important.

X sighed again. He didn't like that part of the job. But might as well get started, the work wasn't going to do itself.

⁖

02.04   *Exit Strategy*

ED.02502.03.13

It was time. He had a six-hour window. Doctor X – even he called himself that now, it was no use to correct Tena – got to work erasing records.

Tena rarely went anywhere without the doctor. Whenever she went to the Mars site, she made him come along to check the progress of the cannon. She made him come to the Council meetings, even though he had to sit out in the hall. X slept on a cot in Tena's bedroom. Sometimes she even took him with her to the restroom, because she was in the middle of a lunatic rant and didn't want to interrupt her train of thought.

Even when she did leave him alone, he never felt safe. She rarely stuck to a schedule, so she could return at any time. Her erratic personality meant that even when she said she was going to be gone for two hours, she would often pop back in after twenty minutes. Either Tena just didn't trust him to be alone, or she thought of him as an emotional support pet.

X knew that the longer he stuck around, the more danger he was in. She would kill him sooner or later. Either to hide evidence, or by accident during one of her temper tantrums, or maybe even just on a whim. Either way, it was dangerous to stay in her vicinity long, and he'd already pushed his luck. Months ago he'd started concocting an exit plan in his head.

Today Tena would be gone for a minimum of six hours. Every year, on her late mother's birthday, she visited her family burial mound. It was quite possibly the only sane thing she did. The trip was nearly three hours each way. She would be making part of the journey by kipa-drawn carriage, as the Stonefolk ancestral grounds were considered a historical landmark, and hovercars were forbidden. Sometimes she even went out for drinks afterward.

Still, anything could happen with that woman, so X had to work quickly. He flew through the lab, erasing every drive on every computer. He pulled every hardcopy in the building, feeding loose papers into the incinerator. It was too late to turn back now. When Tena came back to this, she would kill him. But he wouldn't be here when she got back. If his plan worked, the lab itself wouldn't even be here.

On the roof of the tower was a device that looked like a fancy communications array. In reality, it was a prototype gravity cannon. It was much smaller and weaker than the one being built on Mars. Practically just an overpowered Levatech emitter. Barely powerful enough to pull a meteor from orbit. So far it had only been tested once, nearly two months ago. Doctor X's heart had broken that day. Tena had taken out an entire orphanage just to kill a rival. It was the moment he knew he had to get out as soon as possible.

When he'd originally designed the gravity cannon, more than two decades ago, he hadn't thought of it as a weapon. He'd pictured it saving worlds by deflecting asteroids, or fixing a moon's orbit when terraforming a planet. But the only people who had the resources to actually build one, only wanted it as a weapon. The first one had been built by space pirates, who tried to sell it to the Grunthians before the cannon mysteriously exploded. The Grunthians attempted to build a second one themselves, only for another mysterious accident to befall it. And now Tena was building one on Mars.

Once again he turned on the prototype cannon and locked onto an orbiting object. This time, instead of a chunk of space rock, he homed in on a satellite. Tena's own personal communications satellite, which she launched specifically for encrypted communication with the site on Mars.

The cannon would take fifteen minutes to warm up, and a few more to pull the satellite to the tower. Hopefully it would take out the entire building, destroying every insane project Tena had in the works. X regretted that he couldn't destroy the cannon on Mars, but he took solace in the fact that they'd never be able to build another one. Hopefully no lives would be lost when Tena's tower collapsed. There was only one other person in the tower right now, and X intended to take her with him.

Lemondrop Vermon sat in her recovery bed, much more alert than usual. Even though she was almost completely healed, Tena made sure she stayed drugged most of the time. Early on Tena had given her as few painkillers as possible, for sadistic reasons. But the healthier Lemondrop got, the more Tena had insisted she stay drugged. For the past week, Doctor X had been secretly diluting her drugs, and this morning he'd given her none at all. Then, about an hour ago, X had come in, handed her some clothing, and told her to be ready to run.

She hadn't moved much in the past couple of months, or even spent much time fully conscious. She hoped her body was up to the task. Despite being fully awake for the first time in a while, she kept wondering if she was dreaming. But she'd gotten dressed anyway, and she'd spent the last hour testing her muscles and doing stretches.

Now she heard the door unlock once again. X opened the door and said, "It's time. We have to hurry." She followed him out the door and into an elevator. The tower was one hundred stories tall, and it was crazy that most of the floors were empty. But that was completely on-brand for Tena. She wanted to overlook the entire city, but she didn't want to share. So her tower was pretty much a vertical mansion, filled with everything she'd ever wanted to own. But even she couldn't fill a hundred floors with her wants and whims, so more than half the tower went unused.

The elevator would reach the lobby in just under two minutes. Doctor X had arranged for an automated delivery truck to be waiting out front. It would take them to a safe house across town.

The elevator reached the lobby, and the doors opened. And then X's plan went out the window. Across the lobby, Tena and Thresh were entering the front door of the tower. Tena cast a confused look at the empty delivery truck outside, then turned to face the elevator. Her eyes landed on X, then Lemondrop, and her face contorted with fury.

X pounded on the "close door" button. It was time for Plan B. Tena made it halfway to the elevator before the doors shut, and she pounded on them in her rage.

"Do you think they went up or down?" Thresh asked.

"I'll go up, you go down," Tena replied. She ran for the second elevator, and Thresh took the stairs.

X and Lemondrop stepped off the elevator and into the underground parking garage. Tena had a collection of expensive hovercars, even though she detested driving. Each car had tinted windows and self-driving modes. In anticipation of Plan B, Doctor X had preprogrammed routes into all but one of them. X led Lemondrop to a 2465 Vonic X-500, a classic muscle car built for street racing.

Thresh burst out of the stairwell just in time to see sixteen cars revving up their engines and heading toward the exit ramp. Each car went in a different direction as it left the parking garage. And Thresh had no idea which one he needed to follow.

Lemondrop drove since X was too short to reach the

pedals. He watched for pursuers but didn't see any. Were they really free and clear? The more Doctor X thought about it, the more he realized Plan B probably should have been Plan A. But then he caught sight of his pursuer.

Thresh had caught up to one of the automated cars, ripped off the driver's side door, and taken over driving. He turned toward Lemondrop's car and stomped on the thruster pedal. X wondered how Thresh had known which car they were driving, but realized it probably had to do with the way Lemondrop was weaving. She was already fatigued from lethargy, and the last few minutes had been a bit much for her.

"Faster!" X shouted, and she slammed down the pedal. X had picked the fastest car in the garage, but it was hard to reach top speed on these roads. Traffic was light, but they still had to weave around or over some slower-moving cars. Thresh's car might not have been as fast, but he was a much better driver, making tighter turns and faster decisions. He gradually caught up to them.

"Should I go higher?" Lemondrop asked, pushing the car into fifth gear. From a technical standpoint, it was odd that this electric hovercar even had gears, but when the model had been manufactured thirty-seven years ago, it had been a popular feature.

"I think that would just make you easier to chase," X said. "At least down here – OOF" A hard left turn slammed X into the passenger door. "…we can try to get lost in the traffic."

"He's gaining on us!" Lemondrop shouted, as she watched Thresh loom closer in the rearview HUD.

"Head back in the direction of Tena's tower," X instructed. Lemondrop thought he was nuts, but she didn't argue.

There were a hundred floors X could be hiding on, but Tena didn't seriously believe they'd gone upstairs. She trusted Thresh to find them and do the legwork for her. She only hoped he'd bring them back alive, so she could have a little fun with them.

But no, she had a gut feeling that X had left her a surprise. As loathe as Tena was to acknowledge anyone else's intelligence, Doctor X was, in fact, a genius. There had to be more to his plan than "grab Lemondrop and run." The sooner she found his mess, the easier it would be to clean up.

She stepped off the elevator on the top floor, looking for anything out of place. She wasn't sure what she was expecting, but so far everything looked normal. Then she tried one of the computers.

Everything was gone. Lifepurge. Gravity cannon specs. Auroran physiological research. A new type of nerve gas she'd been working on. Political strategies. Inner Eye records. Her grandmother's recipe for banana hazelnut pie. The little creep had erased every bit of data on every one of her projects.

She ran to the archives room and found the backups had been destroyed as well. She checked the cloud. All erased, right down to her music collection. Tena screamed at the top of her lungs and smashed a computer screen with her fist. Then she heard a beeping and ran to the source. *What now?* she thought.

It was the control panel for the prototype cannon on the roof. The screen flashed red with a proximity alert. Tena read the screen and then immediately ran out to the balcony. She could already see the satellite plummeting toward her tower. There was no time for the elevator. She climbed over the balcony railing and jumped.

Lemondrop nearly drove into a tree when she saw the explosion. X grabbed the wheel and shouted, "Keep driving!" Behind them, two civilian cars collided, and Thresh ran into them. He got out of his car, shaking his fist with rage. Lemondrop and X zoomed past the collapsing building, too far gone for Thresh to pursue.

Thresh stared at the tower. The top twenty floors were

gone, just a flaming wreck. The rest of the building shook, shedding large chunks of styrogene and steel, which tumbled down to the ground below. And traveling down the side of the building... a tiny humanoid shape... was that... Tena?

Tena slid down the side of the tower, her stronger-than-steel fingernails leaving a groove in the wall beside her. At times she would drop a few meters, then catch herself, puncturing the tower's outer wall over and over as she made her way to the ground. Styrogene blocks fell past her, and any minute one could hit her square on, but she felt no fear. All she knew right now was anger.

She dropped the final twenty meters and rolled away from the tower. A huge cloud of dust filled the city as she ran from the collapsing structure. She spotted Thresh, and together they ran to safety.

An emergency meeting of the Council of Heirs was held later that evening. In attendance were Venus, Thresh, Tena, Vernach, Sekka, Nazdak, and newcomer Karden. The seven half-siblings needed to respond to the events of the day, find out what had really happened, and assure the public that the city wasn't in further danger.

Venus, a proud and pragmatic warrior woman, immediately got to the point. "There have been reports from all over the galaxy. Children of Vermon are being assassinated. Honestly, until this morning, I suspected Tena. But now that she's been targeted as well, I guess I owe you an apology."

"Apology accepted," Tena said with a smug look. Her arm was in a sling and she wore a few bandages, but her smaller wounds were already starting to heal. She tried not to show it, but she didn't want to be here right now. There was too much work to do. She needed to find out where Doctor X had taken Lemondrop, and every minute wasted would make it harder to find them.

Karden Vermon had only been a member for a couple of weeks, having just learned of his heritage. He was the second youngest heir present, only a couple of years older than Sekka. His usually dark skin was now pale with fear. Just what had he stumbled into? Finding out he was in line for the throne had been like winning a lottery, but now someone was killing them? He sat in silence, afraid of making himself a target.

Vernach was uncharacteristically attentive. At most meetings he seemed to be more interested in the snacks he'd brought than the subject at hand, but today's topic was life or death. "So if it isn't her, who is it?" he asked.

"I'd like to know that myself," Thresh lied. When the situation called for it, he could go from gruff brute to smooth talker like flipping a switch. "My friends, I believe that these hits came from the IGP. They've had their sights set on us for a long time. Not content with merely interfering with Inner Eye operations, they've decided to take the lazy way out and target this council."

"That's crazy," Venus said. "There's no way they'd—"

"Is it?" Tena asked, pounding her fist on the table. "Is it really so crazy? They just destroyed my home. They hired the bounty hunters that killed our father. They—"

"Now you're just making things up," Venus interrupted. "There's no reason to bel   "

"We can't just sit here and argue about it," Thresh said. "I propose we do something for once. Attack the IGP at the source. Destroy Earth, and they'll never bother us again. No one will."

Everyone but Tena stared at him wide-eyed. Even those that supported the Inner Eye thought he was over the line.

"Destroy… Earth?" Sekka asked.

"Now listen here," Vernach said. "That's a lot of heat you'd be bringing on us. We can't just—"

"It's us or them!" Tena shouted.

"You're making up an enemy to further your own agenda," Venus said.

"We… we get a lot of business from Earth," Nazdak offered meekly. "Our profits would—"

"They started it," Thresh bellowed, getting to his feet. He tried not to lose his temper during meetings, but it had been a rough day.

"Even if it was a good idea," Vernach said, "How would you even—"

"Wait," Venus said, raising her hand. She was looking past the others, to the chamber doors. The other heirs followed her line of sight, turning their heads to see.

"I have something to say," Lemondrop Vermon announced from the doorway. Doctor X stood by her side, and six armed guards accompanied them.

Tena glared at them, and X shrank behind Lemondrop. Thresh put his hand on Tena's shoulder to keep her from attacking them.

"Don't listen to her, she's delirious," Tena said.

"Welcome back, sister," Venus said, gesturing towards an empty seat. Lemondrop strode over and stood by the chair, but she did not sit down. Doctor X followed close behind, trying not to look Tena in the eye.

"This won't be easy to hear," Lemondrop said. "We have traitors in our midst. Opportunists who would slay their own family just to gain power. Ruthless criminals who have lied to our faces over and over. Tena and Thresh—"

"Now just wait a mi—" Thresh started to say.

Venus held up her hand. "Silence," she said sternly. "Lemondrop has the floor." Venus nodded to the guards, who held their weapons on the two accused.

"Two months ago," Lemondrop began, "Tena and Thresh used an experimental weapon to assassinate Cyric, with no regard for civilian casualties. The Loving Care Orphanage was destroyed along with everyone inside. Forty-seven children, gone in one violent instant. Their lives lost to

Tena's psychopathic whims, and Thresh's lust for power. Since then, they have been sending assassin droids all across the galaxy to extinguish the lives of our brothers and sisters, just so that they wouldn't have competition for the throne."

"Liar!" Tena shouted, but everyone was listening to Lemondrop.

"Everyone in this room is on their list," Lemondrop said. "Whether or not you have allied with them in the past, they have a plan for your death. And that's not all. According to Doctor Yxyllthyll here, they have also been constructing a massive weapon off planet. Doctor?"

Doctor Yxyllthyll had begged her to stay in the safe house, but she'd insisted on confronting the problem head-on. As afraid as the doctor was of facing Tena, he also felt emboldened by Lemondrop's perfect pronunciation of his real name. For the first time in years, he felt like he was among friends, and was working for the right side. So far he had been vague about the details of the gravity cannon, only saying that it was a powerful weapon and that it was being constructed on another planet. But now, with the rest of the council to protect him from Thresh and Tena, he finally felt confident enough to divulge the details.

"Thank you, Lemondrop," he said. "Yes, it's true. I've been working for Tena for quite some time. She and Thresh have been conspiring to kill the other heirs and to build a superweapon capable of destroying entire planets. I will be happy to share everything I know in exchange for leniency for my role in their crimes."

"You can't prove anything," Tena said.

"Shut up, Tena," Thresh warned.

"Actually I can prove quite a lot," Yxyllthyll said. "While it's true that the records have been destroyed, I have a perfect memory. I can give you names, dates, and coordinates that will back up all of my claims. I can even take you to the site of their superweapon."

"I'm warning you, X," Tena said, glaring at him with fire in her eyes.

"My name is Yxyllthyll," he said, glaring right back.

"I've heard enough from you two," Venus said. "Guards, take Tena and Thresh into custody. We will—"

But Thresh and Tena had an exit strategy of their own. Tena activated a device in her pocket, and all the lights went out in the building. The council chamber quickly filled with smoke, and everyone crawled on their hands and knees, coughing and looking for the exit.

When the lights finally came back on, Tena and Thresh were gone. Doctor Yxyllthyll was dead, his throat slashed, presumably by Tena's fingernails. The guards turned the palace upside down but didn't find them. They searched Thresh's residence, but it was booby-trapped. The explosion killed three officers and destroyed any evidence Thresh might have left behind.

No one could find any trace of the pair's whereabouts. As far as anyone could tell, they had left Valos. The council posted a large bounty for the capture of Tena and Thresh, but the trail was cold. There were no sightings of the duo. They'd managed to escape without leaving any flight data or warp gate records. It was as if they had simply vanished.

The council knew that a superweapon was being built somewhere, but what type of weapon? On what planet? If Cyric had been alive, Thresh's rant about destroying Earth would have given him a clue, prompting him to search Earth's nearest neighbors. While the surviving council members were clever in their own right - most of them, anyway - none of them understood Thresh the way Cyric had.

"Just look at it, Thresh. Isn't it beautiful?" Tena and Thresh stood on a long catwalk, overlooking a vast chamber carved out of Martian rock. The nearly-complete cannon was swarming with spider-like construction bots. In a month's time, it would be finished, charged, and ready to fire.

"Gorgeous," Thresh answered, just to placate her. To him, the cannon just looked like a giant metal penis, with the construction bots reminding him of pubic lice. But he didn't care about the aesthetics, just the firepower.

This site would be their home for the next month. Thresh had stayed in worse for a lot longer; he just hoped he'd be able to sleep with all the sounds of construction. The bots would need to work around the clock if they wanted the cannon ready in time. If they missed this window, it would be another twenty-six months before the planets were aligned properly for a clear shot.

Thresh imagined Earth's destruction. He wondered what it would look like. Would the cannon pull a large chunk of land off of the planet, causing the rest of the world to collapse in on itself? Would it just pull Earth out of orbit, dooming its citizens to colder temperatures and sending them careening towards other celestial bodies? Tena had offered to show him computer models, but he wanted to be surprised. He knew the devastation would be total. Beyond that, he didn't want any spoilers.

Out of the blue, Tena suddenly punched him in the face. He nearly responded by throwing her off the catwalk, but then he saw her expression and remembered her bizarre sexual urges. "Here?" he asked. "On the catwalk?"

"In front of that," Tena responded, gesturing toward the cannon.

Of course, Thresh thought. She'd probably been having similar fantasies about Earth's demise. Picturing several billion deaths was a huge turn-on for her, why wouldn't it be? And it probably didn't hurt that the cannon was a huge phallic symbol. Tena grabbed him by the collar and pulled him down to the catwalk, violently shredding his clothing with her fingernails.

Oh well, thought Thresh. There were worse ways to spend a month.

02.05   Revelation

ED.02502.03.25

The Saturn Springs Mall wasn't actually located on Saturn, but rather on one of the planet's moons. Their advertisements liked to joke, "Because if we called it the Mall of Enceladus, it just wouldn't have the same *ring* to it." They made sure to emphasize the word "ring" just in case anyone missed the punchline. Nevertheless, the mall was quite popular despite the groan-inducing ads.

The moon had been terraformed nearly a century ago, then rendered uninhabitable a few decades later after a mysterious explosion. After finally receiving the funding to fix the atmospheric generators two years ago, the moon was now in a semi-habitable state. The air was thin but breathable, and a healthy adult could probably breathe it for a good twenty minutes before becoming light-headed.

It would probably be at least another year before the oxygen levels were balanced, which was too long a wait for a site with such a great view of Saturn's rings. It was just begging for tourist credits. So in the meantime, all the buildings were constructed with retractable transparent domes and ceilings, so they could be removed once the moon was more hospitable.

So far the moon had three parks, a sports stadium, a

theater, and a dozen coffee shops. There was a theme park in the early stages of construction, but it wouldn't be open for business until well after the air was breathable. It would no doubt be the moon's biggest moneymaker once it was completed. But for now, Saturn Springs Mall was the main draw. With more than two hundred retail outlets, a food court, a bank, an arcade, and even a miniature golf course, there were plenty of activities to attract visitors.

The Bloodwind stayed in orbit, manned by Trenyn and Raven. They were working on an important project, and besides, Raven "didn't care about some stupid mall." Panther also stayed behind, as they weren't sure of the mall's pet policy. The rest of the crew took a shuttle down to do some shopping.

All of them were dressed casually. Bloodstone was in "Detanna mode," her bounty hunter armor remaining back aboard the ship. Whisper wore a long black dress with a mask and hood, making her look like she was a member of some religious order. Vik, Yna, and Dervish wore jeans and T-shirts. None of them carried any weapons – guns weren't allowed on this moon, and visitors were carefully screened.

Of course it wasn't just a shopping trip. It never was. There were rumors that an escaped criminal was hiding out as a mall employee. Hargan Leez was a master of disguise, and had designed prosthetics that could fool even the best facial recognition software. He had once robbed a bank simply by copying the appearance of the bank manager, making multiple trips in and out of the vault without anyone even blinking an eye.

He wasn't a shapeshifter, but even Dervish envied his skills. If he was here, he could be anyone, regardless of age, gender, or species.

Still, it was a beautiful mall, and there were a lot of fun things to do, so it wasn't all business. There was no reason they couldn't investigate while also having fun. It might even help their cover.

The clientèle was very diverse. Beings from all over crowded the halls and filled the stores. Whisper had initially been worried that her face covering would draw attention to herself, but there were people here literally wearing animal costumes while riding tiger-striped cows. They probably could have brought Panther along after all.

"Where do we even start?" Whisper wondered aloud.

"I want to go to the arcade," Yna answered.

"I mean to find Leez, but you go ahead," Whisper said. "We'll cover more ground if we split up anyway."

"Wait," Detanna said. "Everyone come closer. Now, you're looking for a white male, human, in his late twenties. But of course, we can't go by that. I've studied the footage from his past crimes. He's gutsy, but he's also paranoid. He touches his face a lot, presumably to make sure his prosthetics are still in place. He tries not to look towards cameras."

She made sure everyone understood, then continued. "Look for someone who doesn't want to be studied. He's probably a mall employee, but not necessarily. If he's here, he's only been here for a couple of weeks, so look for an employee who's still learning their job. Do not ask any of the store managers which employees are new. You could find yourself talking directly to Leez himself, and I don't want to tip him off."

Detanna nodded towards the mall offices. "The mall has a central employment registry. Unfortunately, we don't have the authority to look through it. Dervish, I need to you mimic one of the employees who has access, wait until they go to lunch, and browse their files. The rest of you spread out and enjoy yourselves. If you let yourself have a good time, you won't look like you're here to find someone."

Everyone nodded, and she continued. "If you do think you've spotted Leez, stare at him. Not like you recognize him, but like something is wrong with his face. Absentmindedly touch your chin, and see if he does the same. If it's him, he'll run off to check his disguise. Don't chase him, as he will have a backup plan. Just casually follow him from a distance. Memorize everything you can about his current appearance, and contact the rest of us with the details and current location. We'll meet in the food court in two hours. Got it?"

They split up, each exploring the mall in their own way. No one spotted any suspects in the first two hours. Then they all met for lunch, except for Dervish, who sent them a message saying she was currently posing as a security clerk. She showed up just as the others were finishing up their meals.

"This mall is booming," she told them. "Twelve new stores opened within the last month. I think they built an entire coffee shop since we got here. Over two hundred new employees started in the past two weeks. Here." Dervish handed a small thumb drive to Detanna.

Detanna pulled her comm out of her pocket and transferred the data to it. "Hmmm... well, I can eliminate a few of these right away..."

"A few of them stood out to me," Dervish offered, looking over Detanna's shoulder.

"Guys," Vik said urgently, and everyone looked at him. He was staring past them, and they turned their heads. The First Saturn Bank was just down the hall from the food court. There was some sort of altercation happening in the lobby. Two identical women were pointing at each other, shouting in each other's faces. Security guards were starting to move towards them when one of the women bolted.

"Let's move," Detanna said, as they all stood up. The security guards seemed confused but gave chase after a moment. The suspect turned down a side wing. Detanna was the first to reach the turn and was the only one to witness Leez's transformation. The woman's pantsuit flashed in a bright light, revealing a different outfit underneath. Detanna lost sight of him for a second as he used the gawking shoppers to his advantage.

As Detanna pushed through the crowds, she noted various discarded prosthetics on the floor. She nearly tripped over a fake boob. Leez discarded his wig as he turned down another hall. The mall's gridlike layout and crowded hallways gave him a huge advantage. As Detanna pursued, she yelled into her comm, ordering half her teammates to take a different route. With any luck, they could trap Leez between them before he managed to disappear into the crowds with yet another disguise.

But that wasn't his plan. Leez had a specific destination in mind, a place he'd scouted out and prepared well over a week ago. You couldn't sneak weapons into this mall, it was true. The weapons detectors were too good. But that didn't mean there weren't any resources already here.

The mall was still adding new stores and wings, and they stored a lot of construction equipment on site. A week ago, Leez had posed as a construction worker, and started preparing a distraction in case he needed it. Leez fled down a utility corridor marked "Employees Only." Detanna reached the corridor just in time to see him disappear through a door labeled "Electrical."

Just as Detanna reached the door, a deafening noise echoed down the hallway. Everything started shaking, and Detanna had to brace herself in the doorway to keep from falling down. She saw that Leez was already halfway up a maintenance ladder, but then her eyes were drawn to the mess he'd left behind. Leez had managed to wedge a large jackhammer between two load-bearing girders. Detanna could barely stand, and the noise was excruciating, but she had to turn off that equipment before…

…the ceiling collapsed. Whisper had just arrived at the utility corridor when the shaking started. Above her, the transparent dome cracked. People screamed and fled in random directions, trampling over each other with no clear destination in mind. The lights went out, adding to the chaos, but the shaking continued. "Stay calm, everyone!" Whisper shouted, but her contribution was lost among the screams and the hammering.

The ceiling cracked more until it finally shattered. It wasn't made of glass, but rather a super-thick plastic, but its shards were just as deadly. Whisper managed to grab two shoppers and pull them into the utility corridor, which had a much sturdier ceiling. Pieces of the dome rained down on the panicked shoppers. Finally, the shaking stopped. Emergency lights came on, shining through the dust-filled air.

An automated voice over the PA system said, "Please do not panic. There is no cause for alarm. Help is on the way. Proceed calmly toward the emergency exits." Screams of pain and fear drowned out the repeating announcement. Whisper froze for just half a second, thinking, *Follow Detanna and Leez, or help the injured?* No contest. She pushed her way through the rubble, looking for people to help.

When the ceiling fell, Vik, Yna, and Dervish had been spread far from each other. Now Vik was in top form, remembering crowd control from his IGP training. He shouted commands in such an authoritarian voice, people were compelled to follow. He helped people get to their feet and directed them toward the exits.

The collapse had only occurred in the two wings adjacent to the utility corridor. At the junctions to the other wings, walls slowly rose up from the floor, sealing them off to maintain the air quality in the undamaged areas. Security guards and EMTs guided people toward the undamaged wings.

As soon as Dervish saw the arriving EMTs, she stepped up to one and said, "I'm a shapeshifter, how can I help?" while demonstrating by wiggling several morphing fingers. They put her straight to work, slithering under rubble to guide rescue cables, locate victims, and deliver first aid supplies to people they couldn't reach yet. She also didn't need as much oxygen as humans to survive, so while some of the rescue volunteers were starting to get light-headed, Dervish was still going strong.

After maneuvering herself under one giant shard, Dervish's blood went cold. Yna lay unconscious in the rubble, bruised and covered in blood. Her arm disappeared beneath a giant shard of plastic, and Dervish couldn't pull her out. "Over here!" she shouted to the EMTs. "Please hurry!" The EMTs rushed up, one of them hauling a portable "jaws of life" device.

The small hydraulic spreader simply didn't have the power to move objects this heavy. Dervish looked around for Vik, then remembered her comm. The voice channels were too busy to make a connection, but she was able to send him a text message with her location. He showed up a few seconds later.

He had spent the last few minutes – which had seemed like hours – using his levitation abilities to lift rubble and plastic shards off of injured people. But the shard pinning Yna was much too heavy for him to lift. Even working with the EMTs, the jaws of life, and several strong bystanders, the shard could not be budged.

"She's going to die if we don't move her," an EMT said. "We're going to have to amputate that arm." There wasn't time to argue. The hall was full of dying people, and they'd already spent too much time on a single victim. Since no one else could climb far enough under the rubble to reach Yna, the task fell on Dervish to perform the amputation. The EMTs handed her an AON cutter, designed to cauterize the wound as it severed the arm.

Dervish wasn't squeamish, but having to do this to a friend made her physically ill. But she got through it, because she had to. She soon dragged Yna out to the EMTs. They strapped her onto an automated hovering stretcher. The stretcher sped off by itself, before joining a long line of automated stretchers floating in the direction of the nearest medical facilities. Dervish watched it go for a few seconds, before forcing it from her mind. There were a lot more people who needed help.

Vik got dizzy and sat down, catching the eye of an EMT. "The oxygen's getting thin. Here," he said, digging through his bag and handing Vik a face mask. It was the same kind the EMTs were wearing, and it held an hour's worth of air. Coming from down the hallway, another empty stretcher floated into position behind the EMT, to replace the one he'd just sent off. The EMT looked from Vik to the stretcher. "Do you need to quit?"

Vik shook his head. "I'll quit when the work is done." Then he stood back up and went back to looking for survivors.

Whisper was still near the utility corridor, helping anyone who wasn't beyond saving. While Alterra hadn't been in the IGP as long as Vik had, she still remembered her training, and administered first aid to anyone she could reach. When she came across a man bleeding heavily from his thigh, she didn't think twice – she took off her mask and used it as a tourniquet. Between the current chaos and her darker skin tone, it wasn't likely she would be recognized anyway.

She continued administering first aid until the EMTs outnumbered the survivors. Then she headed for the utility corridor. She was feeling lightheaded, but she had to see if Detanna was okay before she went anywhere. The door to the Electrical room had swung shut during the quake, and now the door frame was bent. She had to ram her entire body into it before it reopened.

The room was a mess. The ceiling in this section was concrete, but it had also fallen in. A maintenance ladder that had once run up the far wall, now lay across the concrete rubble. Two of the vertical steel girders were bent insanely out of shape. Leez's body was splayed face down on the detritus, probably dead. Whisper didn't really care at the moment. Her eyes were on her friend.

Detanna sat with her back against the wall. One of her legs was stuck under a concrete block, and a broken jackhammer lay across her lap. She groaned, straining her eyes to focus on Whisper as she emerged through the cloud of dust. "I think one of my ribs is bro…" Detanna started to say, then her eyes locked on Whisper's.

It was only then that Whisper remembered she was currently unmasked. Her hand went to her face, and her eyes went wide. Detanna's eyes, on the other hand, were filled with fire. Their eyes remained locked like this for several seconds, until Detanna, in her most passionless Bloodstone voice, said, "Run."

She could have. With all the confusion going on out there, it would have been easy to get lost in the crowds of injured people, sneak aboard one of the medical ships that would be arriving soon, and steal a shuttle. Eleven different escape scenarios sped through her mind. She had the skills, she was sure she could pull it off. New planet, new identity… new family.

She couldn't. She just couldn't. It was either live in isolation, or make new friends under false pretenses. Lying to Detanna all these months had been heartbreaking. She wasn't about to go through it again with someone new. Besides, she wasn't sure how bad Detanna's injuries were. If she left, would Detanna be found in time? The air was getting thin, and Detanna could have internal bleeding.

Alterra grabbed a steel bar – part of the broken jackhammer – and used it to pry the concrete block off of Detanna's leg. "I'm not kidding," Detanna said.

"I know," Alterra said. "But I have nowhere else to go. Let's get you back to the ship." Alterra helped Detanna to her feet. They each put an arm across the other's shoulders, and they limped down the corridor. As soon as the EMTs saw them, they were given oxygen masks. They tried to put Detanna on a stretcher but she refused.

Vik spotted them from across the room, waved Dervish over, and the two caught up with Alterra and Detanna. "Yna's in a bad way," he said to Detanna. He explained the situation as they headed back to the shuttle. The survivors were currently being transported to a medical ship that would soon be in orbit, because the mall's own little hospital was already filled to capacity. They could pick Yna up as soon as she was well enough.

It was a slow trip to the parking lot, with everyone taking turns supporting Detanna, who clearly didn't want any help. Along the way, Vik kept stealing glances at Alterra. The oxygen mask covered the lower half of her face, but he could still see more of her than he usually did, and something kept nagging at him.

It wasn't until they were onboard the shuttle, and she removed the oxygen mask, that Vik recognized her. "You!" he shouted, his hand reaching for a holster that wasn't currently there.

"Vik, it's been a long day, please don't make me kick your ass." Alterra was strapping Detanna into a seat, wincing as she saw the pain Detanna was in. Detanna still hadn't said a word since the electrical room.

Since the other three looked busy, Dervish sat in the pilot's seat. She set the controls to return to the Bloodwind. It was a completely automated flight.

"You killed fourteen thousand IGP officers. Some of them were my friends." Vik's face was red, and his hands were already balled into fists.

"I was framed," Alterra answered, not even looking at him. She was examining Detanna's injuries and going through the shuttle's medical supplies. Detanna just stared straight ahead, saying nothing. Alterra tried to give her an injection for the pain, but Detanna shook her head. Alterra tried to administer it anyway, but Detanna knocked it out of her hand.

"Like I've never heard that before," Vik said. "If you're

innocent, then why did you run?"

Alterra refused to debate. "I surrender, Vik. Bloodstone can do whatever she wants to with me. But first she has to survive the trip back to the Bloodwind. Do we have a medical scanner on board?"

Vik ignored that last question. "Bloodstone can have whatever pieces are left when I'm done with you," he said. "I've been wanting a piece of you for a long time." He assumed a fighting stance.

Alterra could have easily taken Vik in a fistfight, and she knew it. Vik probably knew it too. But Alterra didn't have the emotional energy for this. If Vik wanted to beat her up, she was going to stand there and let him.

He was about to throw a punch, too, when Dervish suddenly tackled him. She wrapped him up in amorphous pseudopods, holding his arms to the side. Tears streamed down her face as she screamed at him. "Shut up shut up shut up! Detanna's injured, Yna might not make it, and Whisper's going to jail! How many friends can I lose today?"

With Vik temporarily subdued, Alterra turned back to Detanna. She was now unconscious.

The shuttle docked with the Bloodwind. Raven and Trenyn were waiting for them and took Detanna straight to the medical bay. The other three also followed. While Raven scanned Detanna and prepared for surgery, Trenyn quickly examined Alterra, Vik, and Dervish, patching up any minor injuries. Then they were ordered to leave the medical bay so they wouldn't be in the way.

Vik told Alterra, "Follow me." She complied, and he led her to a detention cell. "Get in," he ordered. It still wasn't too late. Alterra could easily take out Vik, then leave in the shuttle. But she was tired. She entered the cell and sat down. She looked at her hands, shifting her skin tone back to Alterra's pale shade. It was a sign of defeat. It meant she was accepting her fate.

Vik headed for the bridge. He was about to call the IGP and set up a rendezvous point, but he hesitated. He knew they couldn't leave the area until they had Yna back. But he didn't want to hand Alterra off here, so far from Earth. Anything could happen between here and Earth. She might escape again. It was better to wait until they could deliver her personally.

Also, it felt wrong somehow to go forward without Bloodstone's permission.

Dervish sat outside Alterra's cell, hugging her knees and crying. Panther came over to comfort her.

Detanna woke up a few hours later. She had a cracked rib, and her leg was broken in two places. She'd survived worse. The first thing she said upon waking was, "I need to see Alterra." Raven and Trenyn transferred her to a hoverchair, and stood aside. Detanna went straight to the detention cells.

Alterra sat on the cot in the holding cell. It was a small room, about two square meters. Amenities included the cot she was sitting on, a sink, and a toilet.

On the other side of a clear plexiglass wall, Detanna pulled up in the hoverchair and spent a few seconds watching her. Her face wore a look that could freeze magma.

"Any word about Yna?" Alterra asked, rubbing her forehead. Her head was pounding now.

"Not yet," Detanna said neutrally.

"Look, I'm sorry," Alterra said. "I wanted to tell you from the beginning. I swear I'm innocent. Vermon set me up. He —"

"I don't want to hear it," Detanna said, standing up in a fury. She winced at the pain in her leg, but only for a second. Her icy stare was gone now, replaced with blind hatred. "I trusted you. You've been lying to me since the moment I met you. And then you seduced me. I thought we had something together. Was any of that real? Or was it just another ploy to keep me distracted?"

"But you would have—"

Detanna cut her off. "I can't believe how stupid I was. This is exactly why I used to work alone. No emotional attachments."

"But I didn't—"

"Whatever you have to say, save it for the court. My job..." Detanna paused, her voice hitching. "My job is to take you in. It's up to the courts to decide if you're guilty."

"But... they'll execute me."

Detanna paused and took a breath. Looking Alterra directly in the eyes, she said, "Maybe they should. Maybe... the universe would be a better place without you in it." Detanna looked away quickly, then half-stomped, half-limped away from the cell, leaving the hoverchair behind.

Alterra's face crumpled. She threw herself to the floor, wailing with inconsolable grief. It wasn't the looming possibility of execution – she stared death in the face nearly every day lately – but the fact that she'd lost a friend. More than a friend. She was now completely alone. No one would stand up for her at the trial, no one would come to her defense, and when the sentence was finally carried out, no one would mourn her. Maybe she could escape, but then what? She was tired of being on the run. Always wearing masks, always looking over her shoulder. No. She would stand trial, and face whatever consequences fate had in store for her. At least the reward money would bring joy to her friends.

Farther down the hall, Detanna leaned back against the wall. She wiped her eyes and tried to catch her breath. A single loud sob escaped her throat. *Pull yourself together,* she thought. *It's just a job. It's always just been a job.* She limped back to her quarters and collapsed into a chair.

An hour later, Detanna's door buzzed. She ignored it at first and continued to stare at the wall. On the third buzz, she sighed and said, "Come in."

"I believe her," Raven said, walking through the door. Detanna didn't look at her. "Destroying that station took a level of heartlessness of which few beings are capable. I refuse to believe the woman in that cell could do such a thing."

"She's been lying to us since day one," Detanna said, no trace of emotion in her voice.

"Because she had to! She wasn't in a position to trust anyone!" Raven didn't raise her voice often, and the outburst almost made Detanna jump. Almost.

"It's a con," Detanna said. "We can't trust her, it's all been a lie."

"Is that really what you believe, or what you want to believe?" Raven asked. "Is that reward so important to you that you'll send a friend to her death?"

"How dare you—" Detanna began.

"Detanna," Raven interrupted, holding up her hand. "If nothing else, please think about this. In the months we've been together, she's had dozens of opportunities to kill you. Maybe hundreds. And it would have been the rational thing to do. You've been her biggest threat this entire time. Anyone willing to kill thousands of IGP officers wouldn't think twice about eliminating a single bounty hunter."

Detanna let that sink in. It really was an odd discrepancy. As careful as Detanna was, there was no way to protect herself at all times. There probably were dozens - she refused to believe hundreds - of ways Whisper could have eliminated her. In fact, Whisper had actually saved Detanna's life a couple of times. She even came to her rescue today.

It didn't add up.

It was two days before Yna could be returned to the Bloodwind. Her left arm was gone, severed just below the shoulder. The first thing Raven said to her was, "Would you like me to make you a new one?" Few things excited Raven, but she definitely had a passion for designing artificial limbs.

"Let me think about that. I have something I need to show you, but it can wait. What's this I hear about Alterra?" Raven filled her in. "We have to have a talk with Detanna," Yna said. "Now."

The Bloodwind headed toward the warp gate that would take it to Earth. While en route, everyone on board – except Alterra – gathered for a meeting in the galley. Detanna attended as Bloodstone, fully armed and armored. Vik wore his IGP agent uniform, complete with sidearm. Their outfits sent a message – that this was official business, and emotional arguments would not be tolerated.

They sat at one side of the table, while Yna, Dervish, Raven, and Trenyn sat opposite. Panther lay on the floor behind them, nuzzling Yna's leg. "I assume," Bloodstone began, "That we're here to discuss how to split the reward money."

"She's innocent," Raven said matter-of-factly. The others on her side of the table had all agreed to let Raven be the spokesperson for Alterra's defense. Bloodstone seemed to respect her the most, and she was the least likely to lose her temper.

Vik's face was already red. "Don't you dare..." Bloodstone held up a hand, and Vik stopped talking.

"What evidence do you have to suggest that she's innocent?" Bloodstone asked. Her voice was already hard to read, but the helmet's speechbox made it even more monotone.

Raven paused. "Because she said so, and I can tell when people are lying."

Bloodstone crossed her arms. Raven could practically read her facial expression despite the helmet.

Raven continued. "It's not like we just met her yesterday.

We know her now. She feels bad when she steps on a bug. She's saved all of our lives several times. She despises crime. She..."

"...is a very good actress," Bloodstone finished. "I'll give her that. But she lied to us. And once you catch someone in a lie, it becomes that much easier to expose the rest. She's been living this false persona for so long, she probably believes it herself. But if she were innocent, she should have turned herself in."

"That would have been a death sentence," Raven said.

"The courts are fair!" Vik blurted out, but Bloodstone held up her hand again.

"The courts can make mistakes," Bloodstone admitted. "But we have video evidence. Everyone saw her threaten to destroy the space station right before she did it. How do you explain that?"

"She says it was the shapeshifter Vraxx," Raven said. "But there's dozens of ways she could have been framed."

"Such as?"

"Doctored video?" Raven offered. "Holograms? Clone? Android? We just fought a master of disguise. Don't tell me this kind of video can't be faked."

"There's no evidence for any of that," Bloodstone declared.

"Then maybe you should look for it," Raven said.

"That's not my job," Bloodstone said for what seemed like the millionth time. "My part is to bring them in. Her lawyer can look for evidence. Topic closed." Bloodstone uncrossed her arms and put her hands on the table. "Now, we need to discuss how to split the reward money. Not all of you were present when we caught her, but since we've all been working together on this for such a long time..."

"Keep my share," Raven said, standing up. "When we get to Earth, I'm out. You can use the extra credits to buy some new friends." She walked out of the room.

I'm with her, Trenyn declared, following Raven.

"Me too," said Dervish, standing.

"Same," Yna said. Dervish and Yna left the room, Panther following behind.

"More for us," Bloodstone said to Vik.

"More for you," Vik answered. "I never cared about the money. I just wanted her caught and punished."

"You don't even want a little cut?" Bloodstone asked incredulously.

"Would I like to be rich someday? Sure. But I want to earn it. This reward money comes from the deaths of my friends. It feels tainted, and I'd feel guilty every time I spent a credit. Now if you'll excuse me, I'm going to go pack." Vik started to stand up.

"You're leaving too?" Bloodstone asked.

Vik nodded. "It's time to get back to my life on Earth. Look… I want to thank you for the experience. This crew has opened my eyes in ways I never… well, let's just say I'm more open-minded than I used to be. I hope I'm a better person for it."

Bloodstone nodded, almost imperceptibly. She had bigger things on her mind than Vik's personal catharsis.

While Vik wasn't the best at reading emotions, something about Bloodstone's body language gave him pause. "Are you okay?" he asked.

Bloodstone nodded again. Vik thought he saw her shudder slightly.

"You did the right thing," Vik said. "She was a mass murderer. Who knows what she would have done next? By turning her in, we saved thousands of lives."

"I know," Bloodstone said quietly.

"Well… if you're sure you're all right," Vik said, turning toward the door. "See ya."

Bloodstone watched him leave, still lost in thought. She had never been one to seek external validation. Until she'd met this crew, she'd been a loner, believing that one should only look out for themselves. The opinions of others meant nothing to her.

Or did they? Somehow, Vik's approval was worse than no support at all. It would have been one thing if everyone disagreed with her – she was used to that – but siding with Vik made her feel dirty. If only one person was going to agree with her, she wouldn't have picked the misogynistic cop. She probably would have picked Raven. Intelligent, unemotional, someone who could push sentiment aside and delve straight to a logical conclusion.

Bloodstone shook her head. She was kidding herself. If she could only have one person on her side, Raven would have been her second choice. The first, obviously, would have been Whisper.

Back in the medbay, Raven examined Yna's severed bicep. "Do you think we should... you know..." Yna whispered in case Bloodstone had the place bugged. "Should we break her out?"

"I believe that if that woman wanted to escape, she could have. But given her spirits last time I saw her, we could blow a hole in the wall and she'd stay in her cell. She has accepted her fate. Now, what was it you wanted to show me?"

"Okay, this really freaked the doctors out. Might even be why they discharged me early. They had a lot to deal with over there." Yna took a slow, deep breath. The stump of her arm started to glow, the same way her hands glowed whenever she used her power. Sprouting from the stump, a ghostly blue arm manifested, proportionately identical to her other arm.

Raven stepped back, astounded. After her initial shock, she took out a medical scanner and examined it. "Is it solid? Can you hold things with it?"

Yna reached for a medical instrument from a nearby shelf. At first, her blue hand passed right through it. Then she concentrated and was able to pick it up. She held it for a few seconds, and then it fell through her hand and clattered on the floor.

"And it doesn't burn things?" Raven picked up the fallen instrument to see if it was hot, then remembered she couldn't feel heat with her artificial limbs. Yet. She always had upgrades in mind.

"I can make it burn if I want it to, just like before," Yna answered.

"I think I've had your condition wrong all this time," Raven said. "I always thought you were generating the energy through your skin. But maybe the real you is the energy, and you're just inhabiting this body." Raven's voice picked up speed, as it often did when she encountered something new. "I wonder what else we could cut off without hurting you. If you lost your head, would it manifest an energy body, or would the body manifest an energy head?"

"Um," Yna said. "I'm not comfortable with these questions."

"Sorry, just thinking out loud. I'm going to have to think about this for a while. Let me get some more readings, I promise not to amputate anything."

When Yna got back to her room a few minutes later, she saw Panther was stretched across her bed. She sat down next to him, comforted by his fur. Her mind was reeling.

Alterra was going to go on trial, and would most likely be found guilty. This group, who she had come to think of as her family, was breaking up. She wasn't sure where she would go from here. She hadn't even come to terms with losing a limb yet, and her entire world was changing.

She reached over and petted Panther's head, provoking a comforting purr. She knew one thing. Wherever she ended up, Panther would be with her. They were in this together. She curled up next to the big cat and fell asleep.

02.06 The Trial

ED.02502.04.10

"Your honor, we have some new evidence to present." The defending counsel had to restrain himself from sounding unprofessionally giddy. This was the sort of game-changing evidence that would get his name on the news. He would never want for work again. Meanwhile, the prosecutor sat glumly behind her desk. She had been briefed on the new evidence and knew it would have to be allowed.

"I would like to call to the stand, Bloodstone." The renowned bounty hunter, clad in the usual black flightsuit and helmet, was escorted into the courtroom and sworn in. Gasps were heard all around the room, and the judge had to call everyone to order. Confined to a transparent cubicle in one corner of the courtroom, Alterra stared wide-eyed. What was she doing here? They'd parted on such volatile terms, there's no way she'd come to Alterra's rescue.

Then a thought occurred to her. What if she's here to drive the final nail in the coffin? Bloodstone cared only for her reputation and didn't like loose ends. She was probably here to make sure Alterra got executed, so one less person would know her true identity. Alterra dreaded whatever her former friend was about to say.

Bloodstone sat down in the witness chair. "Please state

your full name for the record," the bailiff said.

The bounty hunter took a deep breath, then removed her helmet. There was no going back now. "Detanna Zephyri Taush," she said boldly.

This time it took much longer for the courtroom to calm down. Alterra's jaw hit the floor. Whispers of "Bloodstone's a woman?" and "Bloodstone's human?" filled the air.

Even the judge took a few minutes to take it all in. Here sat one of the galaxy's most mysterious celebrities, her true identity laid bare. "Bailiff? Can you confirm this woman's identity?"

"Your honor, if I may," Detanna offered. "The Bounty Hunter Registry has a record of my genetic profile in an encrypted file." It took a few minutes of inputting passwords, verifying thumbprints, and scanning retinas, but eventually they were able to confirm that Detanna was, in fact, Bloodstone.

"What brings you here today, Ms. Taush?" the defense asked cordially.

Detanna got straight to the point. "I have evidence that proves that the woman in that video is not Alterra Sarr, but a Marae shapeshifter."

More gasps were heard, order was called, and Detanna presented her evidence. She had taken the video of Alterra threatening to destroy EarthStation 1, and scrutinized every detail. Voice analysis. Mannerisms. Diction. Blink rate. But she saved the most telling of all for last. When Marae imitate humanoid faces, they tend to get the features reversed. This isn't noticeable on most faces, but Detanna's software was thorough. While Alterra didn't have any scars or birthmarks that would make mirroring obvious, no one's face is truly symmetrical.

Detanna presented a frame-by-frame report, so in-depth it would have been tedious if not for the impact it made on the case. Every frame measured her facial features by the micrometer, such as the distance from her eyes to her eyebrows, the angle of the edges of her lips, or the height of her hairline. And then there were her teeth. Marae didn't tend to copy teeth in perfect detail, and the images showed huge differences in tooth size and spacing.

Detanna was having the time of her life. There was an undeniable euphoria in being seen for who she truly was for a change. Her presentation took just over an hour. The court then adjourned for the day, so that the court's own experts could have time to analyze Detanna's data and make sure they came to the same conclusion. The judge then requested Detanna's presence in his chambers.

Before she could even sit down, the judge said, "You turned her in for the reward."

"Yes," Detanna answered.

"And then you showed up here to prove her innocence."

"Yes."

"Do you not see a conflict of interest? I find it remarkably convenient that you didn't turn in this evidence until after you collected the reward money."

"I know," Detanna admitted. "I didn't complete my analysis until after I turned her in. Just like everyone else, I assumed she was guilty. No... I think I wanted her to be guilty. I couldn't see past that reward."

The judge wasn't expecting such an honest answer from this hardened bounty hunter. He started to say something, but Detanna kept going.

"This morning I returned the reward money. I told them to donate it to the IGP Disaster Relief Fund. They need it more than I do. I considered keeping a portion of it for myself, for a... medical procedure I've been saving up for... but now's not the time. Alterra's more important. I think..."

Detanna had been staring at the floor, but now she looked into the judge's eyes. "I think I love her," Detanna finished.

The judge chuckled and shook his head. "Well shoot, what are you telling me for? She's three floors down. I'll make a call and get you a visitor's pass."

02.07 Finale

ED.02502.04.12

The verdict was delivered, and Alterra Sarr was now a free woman. Bloodstone got in touch with everyone and they agreed to meet on the Bloodwind for drinks. No masks, no disguises, for once everyone could be themselves. "I have an announcement to make," Detanna said, tapping a spoon against a champagne flute. "I want to apologize. To all of you, but mostly to Alterra. I've never been happier to admit I was wrong."

No one held a grudge, and the mood stayed light. Toasts were made, and everyone hugged everyone. At one point, Yna excused herself. Then Raven took Detanna aside and asked, "So… about that operation you were saving up for?"

"Guess I have to start over," Detanna said. "I'm sure another opportunity will arise eventually."

"You know," Raven said. "You happen to be friends with one of the best genetic biologists in the galaxy." She nodded to Trenyn across the room. "If we can get the details on this operation, and the blueprints for the machine it requires, we just might be able to replicate the procedure. It will take a while, and a good deal of money to build it, but I bet we can do an even better job than the people you were going to pay."

Detanna smiled wide, then hugged Raven hard. "Thank you."

Yna slowly walked through the ship. Something was off somewhere. She could hear noises... like indistinct voices calling her. Following her instincts, she stepped into a restroom and looked into the mirror. She saw four energy beings in the reflection. No... three beings. Her own reflection was the fourth, appearing as if her energy self was superimposed over her human form.

These creatures looked just like Yna did when she was fully transformed. Just like the things she... saw? Dreamed about? ...that time on Vortal Station.

She wasn't afraid. Whatever these things were, she felt a kinship with them. They may have even saved her life when she was floating helplessly in space. But this time, they appeared to need her help. They spoke in a language she'd never heard before, but somehow she understood every word. Then suddenly, the information came faster and faster, until her head felt like it would burst.

Back in the galley, the party was still going on. Yna came through the door, walking silently. One by one, the others stopped laughing and stared at her. She was manifesting her spectral left arm. She also had a glowing blue scar running down the left side of her face. It crossed over her left eye, which was now just a glowing white orb. "We need to go to Mars," she said. "Right now."

Mars would have been a six-hour trip, but both planets had warp gates nearby, so it only took a couple of hours. Half of that time was spent in line to use the gate. During the trip, Yna explained as much of the story as she understood.

She came from a race of energy beings called the Yllia. They lived in another dimension, an energy-filled universe they called "Yvva." Sometimes the Yllia sent explorers from Yvva into this dimension, for curiosity and research purposes. However, the Yllia could not survive very long in this dimension, so they had to bond with another creature if they wanted to stay more than a few minutes.

Rather than steal someone's life, they looked for a host that was either recently deceased or comatose with no hope of recovery. The process usually gave the host amnesia, unable to remember either of their former lives. Once the merged being had spent a few years in this dimension, they were called back to Yvva so that others could learn from their experiences.

But that's not why they had contacted Yna. There was a much more pressing matter at hand. Somewhere on Mars, someone had built a machine. A terrible, destructive weapon that could annihilate worlds. This weapon drew its energy directly from Yvva, causing devastating effects to the energy dimension.

Yna didn't know the exact location on Mars, but she felt like she might be able to detect it once they got close.

"Wait," Alterra interrupted. "Do you know what this weapon looks like?"

"Yes," Yna said. "They put an image of it in my mind."

Alterra pulled out a tablet and scrolled through her files, until she found some sketches. "Did it look like this?"

"That's it!"

"What is it?" Vik asked, leaning in closer.

"Oh, this is not good," Alterra said. "Remember that gravity cannon I destroyed a while back? The Grag Prime told me that the Inner Eye was building another one."

"I remember that," Detanna said. "I've been putting out feelers, trying to find out where it was going to be built. Never got any leads. It's been so long, I was hoping the construction had failed."

"Guess not," Yna said.

"Did you get any readings on the one you destroyed?" Raven asked Alterra. "Maybe we can program the scanner to look for a similar energy source."

"I did, but I lost them. They took all my equipment while I was there, and I had to escape in one of their ships."

"Just get me close," Yna said. "I'm sure I'll be able to sense it."

It's still a big planet. Can we narrow it down? Trenyn asked.

"Well," Detanna said, "I don't know the range on this weapon, but if they're building it on Mars, then they're probably planning to fire it at Earth." She paused to let that sink in. "So... if there's an optimal time in the orbits of both planets..."

"I see what you're saying," Raven took over. "When Earth and Mars are closest together, there will be an area of Mars that gives it a clearer shot than anywhere else. They would have done the math on this way ahead of time."

"The Yllia think it's almost complete," Yna said. "The weapon is powering up, drawing energy from Yvva."

They may just be charging it for a test fire, Trenyn added. *But they wouldn't test a weapon like this until it was almost ready to be used. It would draw too much attention, and risk them getting caught before the orbits were right.*

"Right," Raven said. "So either way, they're planning to use it soon. I'll run the math, and see if we can find an optimal location for the weapon." She headed for the bridge to use one of the computers. Trenyn followed.

"While you're doing that," Vik said, "I'll see if I can find any unusual paper trails. Suspicious construction records, land bought by fictitious companies, that sort of thing. Alterra, you know IGP databases, want to help?"

"Of course," she answered. "Should we contact the IGP?"

"Not yet, we don't have enough to go on. But if we find the weapon, we'll send them a message before we go in." Alterra nodded, and they walked off together.

Despite the imminent danger, Detanna couldn't help but smile at seeing Vik and Alterra work together. Just a couple of days ago, Vik wanted to see Alterra executed. Heck, Vik probably would have paid good money to throw the switch himself. But it wasn't just them. The entire crew had broken up, but here they were, all working together, ready to throw themselves into danger. It was oddly heartwarming.

By the time they reached Mars, they had it narrowed down to six plots of land. They started with the one Vik found the most suspicious. It had been purchased by a company that, as far as Vik could tell, had been created just to buy that piece of land. It was isolated from any nearby settlements. A construction company had been hired to build an underground structure, but the blueprints had been erased from public records. After the job was completed, the construction workers themselves had perished in an unexpected cave-in.

Actually, there wasn't much point in looking at the other sites. This had to be it. As the Bloodwind entered orbit, Yna confirmed that she felt a pull toward the planet. They looked for a place to land that wouldn't arouse suspicion. The Bloodwind would have to stay in orbit, it was just too big to land discreetly. And someone would have to stay behind in case they needed a quick getaway.

Detanna frowned. That was going to be a fight. They all had scores to settle with the Inner Eye, and none of them wanted to miss the action. Before she could even broach the subject, however, Vik begrudgingly volunteered. "The rest of you take the shuttle," he said, clearly not happy about it. "I'll stay in contact with the IGP, so they know it's not a hoax. You keep me updated with what you find down there, so I can relay the info to them."

The rest of the crew boarded the shuttle. As the ship descended, they could see what looked like the hatch to a huge missile silo. A couple of nondescript buildings sat nearby. There was no activity; the site looked dead. But Yna could feel her people calling to her. This had to be it.

There was no way to approach without being detected.

They could only hope that the owners were overconfident. If the Inner Eye didn't expect to be discovered, they might not feel the need for heavy security. But the bounty hunters made sure they were prepared for whatever they encountered.

Bloodstone wore her usual armored flightsuit, weapons strapped anywhere they would fit. She was still recovering from the injuries she'd suffered at Saturn Springs Mall, but she'd have to power through it. She wore a jointed metal cast that doubled as leg armor.

Whisper also wore her bounty hunting uniform and helmet. Raven wore an armored combat suit over her robotic body, for extra protection. Trenyn wore a similar combat suit, pockets crammed full of virtrinium blades.

Dervish couldn't wear armor without sacrificing her abilities, but she chose a durable form for combat. Hard chitinous plates formed all over her body, and sharp spikes protruded from them. She looked a bit like a human wearing an armadillo costume.

Yna also had to forgo any extra armor. She knew that once combat began, she would change fully into her energy form. Anything she was wearing would be destroyed, so there wasn't much sense in overdoing it. Panther sat by her side, also unarmored. He seemed uneasy about her current form, what with the one energy arm and the facial scar. He kept sniffing her to make sure it was really her.

As the shuttle approached the site, they scanned the environment. Everything looked like a false front, but it would have fooled anyone who wasn't already suspicious of the site. There were a few metal silos on the outskirts of the site, designed to look like food storage units, but the Bloodwind's scanners identified missile launchers within them.

There were no dunes or hills to hide the shuttle behind, so they brazenly parked next to one of the buildings. Whatever was about to happen, a quick getaway was probably more important than stealth. They stepped out of the shuttle and into the cool Martian air.

Mars had been livable for over a century, having been terraformed in the late 2300s. However, it wasn't very populated yet. There were a lot of disputes over which countries owned which land, and in the meantime, people were being careful about how much money they put into colonizing it. Nobody wanted to build a trillion-credit city only to have to pack up and move if it turned out they didn't own the land.

In the meantime, Mars was mostly being used for science experiments and storage. Some people even called the planet "Earth's attic." There were a few small settlements, but those were practically grounded space stations that could be easily relocated if necessary. None of these settlements were nearby; in fact, it looked desolate as far as the eye could see.

The squat metal building also looked desolate. There were no lights on in the windows, and no signs of movement. Bloodstone approached the metal door, looking around for security cameras. Nothing. The door was locked, but there was a control panel to the left, with an easily hackable data port. The door swooshed open, proving that the building did at least have power.

The bounty hunters entered the structure. It was set up like an office building, but there was no furniture. The empty rooms looked like they'd never been used. It was eerily quiet. "Let's see if we can find a way below ground," Bloodstone said. The search didn't take long, and they found a stairwell next to an elevator. They decided against the elevator because it might attract attention.

The first few flights of stairs were unremarkable, just a plain vertical shaft with metal walls. But then it opened up and they found themselves in an immense underground chamber. The stairs ended on a long metal walkway, part of a system of scaffolding that covered all the outer walls. From here, they had a great view, and there was a lot to take in.

Above them, they saw the same hatch they'd seen on the surface. Below it, what was obviously the gravity cannon. This metal tower dwarfed everything else in the chamber. It sat on a hydraulic platform, ready to be raised once the hatch opened. Crawling on the cannon's surface were hundreds of spider-like construction bots, making adjustments and applying finishing touches to the machine.

On the far wall, they saw a platform containing a control station. Two human-looking people stood talking to each other. Raven thought there was something familiar-looking about them, but they were too far away to see much detail.

Yna tugged at Bloodstone's elbow, then pointed urgently at the base of the gravity cannon. A metal box, about two meters square, appeared to be serving as the cannon's power station. There was a row of lights on the front of the device, presumably to indicate the charging status. Nine of the lights were green, but the highest was blinking yellow. It was almost completely charged.

"That's where they are," Yna whispered.

"I'll sneak down there and check it out," Whisper offered. She followed the scaffolding until it reached the wall. The chamber was brightly lit, so there weren't a lot of shadows for her to hide in, but she kept the cannon between her and the humanoids on the control platform.

The other hunters watched her climb down the scaffolding. When Bloodstone glanced back at the control platform, she did a double take. The humanoids were gone. "Uh oh," she said.

Suddenly, all the construction bots stopped moving. Their heads perked up like they were receiving new information. Then, in unison, they turned towards the ground and began swarming towards the base of the cannon. Towards Whisper.

"Get down there!" Bloodstone ordered. Each of the hunters found their own way down, some heading for the stairs, others climbing down access ladders. Bloodstone stayed on the high walkway, running in the direction of the control platform. If she could get there, maybe she could shut down all the bots at once.

As Whisper descended, she could hear the chit-chit-chit of hundreds of metal legs. She climbed downward until she was a few meters from the floor, then jumped to the ground. Swarms of mechanical spider bots surrounded her. They were bigger than they looked from a distance – the enormity of the gravity cannon made everything look small.

Each bot was about two meters wide, painted reflective yellow with black stripes. Each had a rectangular head with a single red eye, six mechanical legs, and a pair of arms. At the end of each arm, a metal ball featured an array of construction tools – welders, AON cutters, and so on. These machines did not appear to be designed for combat, and yet they were obviously very deadly. Especially in these numbers.

The bots stopped their advance about a meter from Whisper, holding their tools up menacingly. Above, Whisper could see the others still climbing down ladders to reach her. In the distance, she saw Bloodstone descending a stairway to the command platform. Then she heard a familiar voice.

"Look who's back!" Tena Vermon stepped around the cannon and into Whisper's view. The bots shifted aside to make a path for her as she approached. "I really was hoping to run into you again," she said in the sweetest voice she could manage. "Let's cut to the chase. I'm willing to make a deal, Alterra. I'd still very much like to make an army of assassins using Auroran DNA. That's not so much to ask, is it? All you have to do is come with me, let me extract some of your DNA, maybe help me train my up-and-coming assassins… and I'll let all of your friends live."

"So you can kill billions more? Why would I do that?" Whisper asked.

"I can get your DNA just as easily from your corpse," Tena said. "But your friends don't have to die today. If you —"

Just then Yna landed on top of Tena, having leaped down from a scaffold. Her face full of fury, Yna screamed, "Your machine is killing my people!" While grasping Tena's neck with her human hand, Yna pressed her energy hand onto Tena's face. Tena's flesh sizzled, and she howled in pain.

Then Tena yanked her attacker off of her, held her off the ground, and thrust a hand straight into Yna's chest. Her razor-sharp nails easily broke through Yna's breastbone, tearing through skin and organs like butter. Yna's eyes opened wide, her mouth frozen in mid-scream. Then Tena pulled back her hand, how holding up Yna's heart.

"YNA!" Whisper shouted. The other hunters had reached the floor and now stood frozen in shock. Tena let go of Yna's body, which landed with a thud on the floor. Her energy spirit, however, remained where it was, hovering in front of Tena.

Yna, now made of pure energy, was very disoriented. She could see her own body crumpled on the floor. The initial injury had hurt, but now she felt no pain. She studied her hands, now equally transparent and blue. Then she saw Tena, and all of her anger came back to her. She pounded on Tena's face, but her non-corporeal hands passed straight through the woman. Then Yna concentrated, focusing all of her fury into her hands.

Just as she was about to unleash her full rage, she heard voices. They were so much louder now that her body was gone. No longer distant murmurs, these were clear, distinct voices calling her name. Forgetting about Tena, Yna floated toward the power generator.

"Purge all unauthorized beings on site," Tena ordered, lamenting that it didn't sound as cool as "Kill them all" or "Wipe them out." These bots had simple A.I. and had to be given very specific commands. As waves of bots swarmed past her, she stepped aside and reached for the nearest ladder.

The bots were everywhere, and the hunters were in the fight of their lives. Raven smashed at them with her bare hands, going for their weakest points – the eyes and the joints. She soon discovered that each one was powered by a battery pack on the underside of the unit, easily removed if you could get underneath one. She relayed this information to the others as best she could, but it was loud in here.

Trenyn's blades were flying, cutting through bot after bot. After hearing Raven's advice, Trenyn used their telepathy to tell everyone else. By stepping on the flats of two of the blades, and balancing very carefully, Trenyn was able to levitate up to one of the walkways. They were a lot more help from this vantage point, where they could manipulate their blades from a distance, to assist whichever teammates needed it the most.

Dervish fought with her bare hands, and sometimes her bear hands, constantly changing shape to keep from getting overwhelmed. She stretched her arms, grabbing the underside of the walkways, pulling herself out of danger, and swinging to safer spots. She noticed the bots weren't chasing Tena, so she tried imitating her form. It worked. The bots swarmed past her as if she wasn't there. As they scuttled by, she did whatever damage she could, smashing out their eyes and such. They didn't fight back, they just kept running past her.

Panther was in a rage. Witnessing Yna's demise had put him into berserk mode. He suffered several cuts and burns but didn't even notice. His claws weren't sharp enough to cut through their armor, but he was more than strong enough to take off their heads. He pounced from bot to bot, swiping off heads and dodging their attacks.

Whisper wasn't destroying bots. It seemed futile, with there being so many of them. Instead, she went after Tena. Jumping off the back of one bot, she whipped a handrail and climbed up to the walkway.

* * *

Bloodstone studied the control panel, looking for bot access. While most of the bots were swarming her friends, a few had noticed her position and were headed her way. She didn't have much time. She tapped through menus and submenus, looking for some sort of shutdown function. *Whoever designed this menu system was extremely disorganized,* she thought.

"Get away from there!" a voice bellowed. She turned just in time to get punched in the face. Despite her helmet, it felt like getting slammed by a rhino. Her helmet's red dome shattered, and she stumbled backward against the computer. Detanna pulled off her helmet and wiped the blood from her eyes.

"Bloodstone is a woman?" Thresh said, upon seeing Detanna's face.

"Don't you watch the news?" she answered, drawing her gun. For such a huge man, Thresh was remarkably fast. He snatched the weapon from her hand and crushed it in his fist. Detanna brought her other hand up and fired two tiny concussion grenades from a device on her wrist. Thresh fell backward, and Detanna turned back to the computer. She knew she only had seconds before her opponent recovered.

It wasn't the right menu, but one of the options looked promising. Under the "Permissions" subheader, there was an option labeled "Grant Full Permissions To All Present." Just as she was about to press the option, Thresh tackled her from behind. Her finger brushed the screen, missing her target and brushing the option below it: "Revoke All Permissions From All Present." Then Thresh picked her up and slammed her into the computer, shattering the screen.

At that moment, Tena was running along a walkway, enjoying the carnage from afar. She saw Thresh wrestling with Bloodstone on the control platform. It looked like he had things under control, but she headed in that direction anyway. The cannon was almost charged, and she wanted to fire it before there were any more surprises.

Speaking of surprises, some of the bots started breaking off from the swarm and headed in her direction. *What's that about?* Tena wondered. Then she saw Whisper sprinting towards her, and readied herself for a fight.

Dervish also noticed that the bots were starting to attack her again. As she ducked out of the way of one bot's AON blade, she considered other forms. What would they not attack? She considered trying to blend in with the wall or a steel column, or even mimic a construction bot, but her non-humanoid forms had never been particularly convincing. Suddenly she had an idea. She shifted her form, and the bots immediately started ignoring her again.

Yna floated in front of the power box, studying the control panel. She could hear her kin calling to her from inside, but she wasn't sure what she needed to do. It took concentration to make her fingertips solid enough to press buttons, and with everything that was going on, she couldn't concentrate. She was also afraid that her current form would short out the control panel, potentially making things worse. There was an access hatch on the back of the power station, but it was locked. She studied the hatch and attempted to burn through the lock.

While bashing and throwing bots around, Raven saw Yna attempting to open the power station. She made a point of working her way in that direction. She saw Trenyn nearby, and she signaled to them to cover her. A flurry of Trenyn's virtrinium blades shredded the bots before her, clearing a path to the power box.

Whisper and Tena stood face-to-face on the walkway, just a few meters apart. "Last chance, Alterra," Tena offered teasingly. "I can set you up with a cushy life. Big money, no risk. We can make it happen."

"You really are insane," Whisper replied, shaking her

head.

Tena shrugged, then lunged forward. Whisper barely had time to react as Tena's nails slashed across her helmet. Before Whisper had even recovered, Tena's other hand thrust towards Whisper's side, just breaking the skin. Whisper fell backward, feigning a much bigger injury, slamming her back hard against the walkway. As Tena attempted to jump on top of her, Whisper thrust her feet forward, catching Tena in the stomach. Whisper only had seconds to catch her breath before Tena was nearly on top of her again.

This wasn't good. Whisper was used to reading body language and reacting. But Tena was simply unpredictable. Whisper had to stay on the defensive, keeping those unnaturally sharp nails away from anything vital. Whisper reached out with her whip hand and whipped one of the guardrails. Then she rolled sideways, under the guardrail, and over the edge of the walkway. Leaping forward, Tena just missed impaling her in the chest with her spiked heels.

After swinging beneath the walkway, Whisper grabbed the opposite side and started to climb back up. One of Tena's bony heels had gotten wedged in the walkway grating when she'd tried to stomp on Whisper, and she struggled to pull it out. She was still watching the wrong side of the walkway when Whisper whipped her from behind. Tena shrieked as the electrified whip wrapped around her waist, sending jolt after jolt into her body.

But it didn't stop her for long. With an unholy wail, Tena spun her entire body, simultaneously freeing her stuck foot and lashing out with her dangerous hands. With a superhumanly quick swipe, she sliced the whip in half, rendering it inoperable. Completing her spin closer to Whisper, Tena elbowed her in the ribs with one of her bony protrusions. It didn't go deep, but it was enough to send Whisper staggering.

Still recovering from the electric shock, Tena stumbled backward a few steps. Her vision was doubled, and it was hard to focus. But she was able to see a couple of construction bots climbing onto the walkway behind Whisper. Tena could hear more of their chit-chit-chit steps behind her as well. This was not a safe place to be. She looked in the direction of the control platform, but couldn't focus that far. She needed to get over there, but Whisper was in her way. Well, Whisper would have to go down.

Back on the control platform, Bloodstone was in trouble. Her opponent was built like a tank but somehow moved with unnatural speed. Without her helmet, Bloodstone couldn't use her fighting HUD, which was usually her biggest advantage. Her suit still contained several hidden weapons, but Thresh had already shrugged off some of them. Bloodstone looked at the remaining computer terminals. She had to find a way to shut down the gravity cannon, at all costs.

Bloodstone narrowly dodged one of Thresh's huge fists, but it still hit her shoulder hard enough to send her careening toward the guardrail. Instead of stopping herself, she used her forward momentum to flip over the railing, disappearing from view. Thresh followed her, jumping over the railing and landing flat-footed on the floor three flights below. He looked around, confused. He had expected to find Bloodstone, or at least her broken corpse, but instead found himself surrounded only by hostile construction bots.

He glanced upward. Bloodstone was hanging from the control platform, suspended by a thin wire. She had used a wrist grappling hook to save herself from the fall, and was now climbing back onto the platform. Bloodstone ran toward one of the remaining computer terminals, tossing a concussion grenade at an approaching bot. It would take at least thirty seconds for Thresh to climb back up here. Hopefully that would buy her enough time.

At the base of the cannon, Raven limped toward the power

station. One of her legs had been nearly severed by a bot's AON cutter, and it was emitting sparks. Luckily both arms worked, and she used them to help Yna tear the back panel off of the power box. What they saw inside surprised them both. Inside some sort of stasis field, a swirling purple mass pulsed. It looked like a nebula – no, storm clouds – no, a misshapen black hole… it kept changing form and color, cloudy tendrils undulating at its edges.

But through the cloudy exterior, they could see millions of tiny pinpricks of light. Stars. Galaxies. They were looking through a window to another universe. And this machine was somehow pulling energy from it. Glowing humanoid forms floated into view, staring back out at them. Suddenly Yna could not only hear the voices of the victims, but she could feel their pain as well. Raven could see the agony she was in, and set about finding a way to shut down the device.

Up on the walkway, Tena lunged toward her opponent, only for Whisper to catch her across the jaw with a roundhouse kick. While Tena recovered, Whisper reached into her boot, fumbling for a virtrinium knife she kept sheathed there. She didn't get to it in time, though, as Tena tackled her and pinned her to the ground. She punched and clawed at Whisper's helmet until it could barely be called a helmet anymore. Then she ripped the mask away and continued her assault on Whisper's bare face. It was all Whisper could do to block Tena's deadly hands. Whisper's own hands were getting bloodier by the second, and she could barely see for the blood in her eyes.

Tena was in full frenzy mode, ready to tear into her prey until there was nothing left but pulp. But then she saw something out of the corner of her eye. Could it be? She slowly stood up, having completely forgotten about Whisper for the moment. Was that really…

The late Lord Teykor Vermon, founder of the Inner Eye, stood before her on the walkway. "Father? Is that really you?"

"Um, yes, it is I. I have returned. To life." Lord Vermon looked very uncomfortable and struggled for words.

"But how did you survi—" Tena began, then finished her sentence with an ear-splitting scream. Whisper had plunged a knife into Tena's spine, right between two of her lower vertebrae. Blinded by rage and pain, and partially paralyzed, Tena teetered toward the railing. Whisper took this opportunity to kick her in the face, sending her toppling over the guardrail, into the swarm of construction bots below.

"Dervish? Is that you?" Whisper asked, and Lord Vermon nodded. Whisper stepped toward her, then stumbled. She was suffering from a lot of injuries. "Help me get over there," she said, pointing to the control platform. Dervish put one of Whisper's arms over her shoulder, and they made their way toward Bloodstone.

Meanwhile, Bloodstone had found the submenus she was looking for. There wasn't a self-destruct function that she could find, but she discovered the next best thing. A window popped up that said, "ARE YOU SURE? THIS ACTION CAN NOT BE UNDONE" followed by "Y/N." Thresh was almost at the top of the stairs, and three construction bots had made their way over the guardrails. Bloodstone tapped Y.

The bots stopped for a few seconds, then turned around. Thresh ran to the railing, watching in horror as all the remaining bots scuttled toward the gravity cannon. They climbed up the sides and began cutting off panels, starting at the top. Turning toward Bloodstone, Thresh yelled, "What have you done!" Behind Bloodstone, another pop-up announced, "Dismantle Mode Engaged." Seeing red, Thresh once again charged at Bloodstone.

At the base of the cannon, Yna watched as Raven worked at

disabling the power station. There were at least a dozen ways she could have destroyed the thing, but she needed to be sure she wasn't going to do more harm than good. Hundreds of bots swarmed past her, climbing up the cannon and carrying pieces back down to be recycled. No longer in danger, Trenyn and Panther joined her.

With Trenyn's help, Raven was able to stop the machine from drawing power from the portal. Yna immediately felt a rush of relief. No more pain, no more cries for help overwhelming her mind. Inside the portal, the ghostly faces no longer looked pained, and radiated an air of gratitude. Raven turned to her incorporeal friend. "Yna, can you understand me?" She wasn't able to speak in this form, at least not in a way Raven would understand, but she nodded. "I'm going to shut down the containment field now. When I do, the portal will shrink and then disappear."

Yna cocked her head, not sure where Raven was going with this. Then she understood. "I don't know how long you can survive in this dimension without a physical body," Raven said. It was true. Yna already felt like there was less of her than there had been a few minutes ago. She was dissipating.

Panther looked up at Yna, confused. He knew it was both her and yet not her, and he could tell she was conflicted. She had been his only friend at a time when both of them needed one. Yna floated over to Panther and put all her concentration into giving him a big hug. It wasn't completely solid, and the static made Panther's fur stand on end, but they both felt comfort in the gesture.

Yna looked at Raven and nodded, and they cut off the containment field. Yna gave a final wave before leaping into the shrinking portal. And then it was gone. The lights on the power station went dark.

On the control platform, Thresh lurched around in a zig-zag pattern, looking for something to hold onto. When he'd lunged at the bounty hunter earlier, Bloodstone had been ready with her AON blade, and he had charged right into it. It now protruded from Thresh's stomach, the burning hot blade boiling his guts from the inside. He tried to pull it out, but his hands were slippery with blood, and he was getting dizzy. He made his way to the stairs, trying to remember where they kept the first aid kit. His foot missed the first step, and he tumbled down all three flights.

Bloodstone rejoined Whisper and Dervish, the latter of whom had reverted to her usual female form. They got the attention of their teammates down below. It was too loud to shout and their comms weren't working here, but Trenyn's telepathy still worked and they relayed a few messages back and forth. It was a simple message anyway. It was time to leave.

The bots had nearly finished dismantling the cannon, and some had started taking apart the rest of the underground base as well. The bounty hunters needed to get up to the surface while there were still stairs to climb.

Raven's leg finally gave out as they started up the scaffolding. She lagged behind the rest of the party, dragging her dead leg behind her. Trenyn went back for her. "If we can just…" Raven started.

There's no time, Trenyn said.

She knew what they meant. She unzipped her shirt, opened the front breastplates, and Trenyn pulled her limbless body out of the artificial unit. They carried her up the stairs, catching up to the rest of the group as they all reached the surface. "Where's Yna?" Bloodstone asked as they boarded the shuttle.

"She's not coming," Raven answered. Seeing Bloodstone's expression, she added, "No, it's a good thing. I'll explain after takeoff."

Down below, Tena dragged herself across the floor. She couldn't feel anything below her waist, and she had hundreds of deep cuts all over her body. She eventually made it to a small workstation, where a computer tablet sat on a desk.

Pieces of the ceiling – both metal panels and red Martian rock – fell to the floor around her. The hard-working bots had dismantled most of the scaffolding by now, and even some of the base's load-bearing support columns. Tena pulled herself up with one arm, grabbing the tablet off the desk. Then she dragged herself under the desk and turned the tablet on.

It was difficult to operate the tablet because she kept getting blood on the screen. She scrolled past several options that might have actually helped her, such as one that would have immediately powered down all the construction bots. No, revenge was first and foremost on her mind. She scrolled straight down to the last entry, "Weapons Systems." She cackled with glee, coughed up some blood, and cackled some more.

The shuttle was halfway to the Bloodwind when Vik saw the alert. Several A.I.-guided missiles had locked onto the shuttle. Neither the shuttle nor the Bloodwind currently had any external weapons that would deter such a threat. Vik cursed, calculating his options. Then he had an idea. He pulled on a spacesuit and headed for the airlock.

The first missile hit the shuttle in the thrusters, making it careen out of control. It looked like it would slam head-on into the Bloodwind. But then it suddenly stopped, mere meters from collision.

Vik stood on the side of the Bloodwind, using his Levatech ability to keep from floating away. With one hand, he pushed and pulled the shuttle, guiding it toward the docking port. Once it was close, the ship's Levatech docking system guided it the rest of the way. With Vik's other hand, he pushed the remaining missiles away, knocking them into each other until they exploded far from the Bloodwind.

The rest of the hunters quickly disembarked from the shuttle and headed for the bridge. Bloodstone switched on the communicator. "Vik, this is Bloodstone. We're safe. Come in, and we'll get out of here."

But Tena had one more card to play. Furious that her missiles hadn't destroyed their target, she tapped one final button. Then the remainder of the ceiling completely collapsed, turning the entire facility into a tomb.

Vik slowly walked around the side of the Bloodwind, making his way toward the airlock door, when he saw it. This missile was much larger than the other ones had been, and it was headed straight for the Bloodwind. "I'll be a minute," Vik said into the communicator. "One last mess to clean up."

Vik tried to repel the missile, but it was too large for his powers to affect. He sighed, then pushed himself off of the Bloodwind, free-floating through space. He pulled himself to the missile. Upon reaching it, he laid his left palm on the missile's surface, using his attraction power to keep from floating away. The sudden jerk of being pulled by the missile dislocated his shoulder, but he managed to hold on. With his other hand, he started ripping panels off of the missile, hoping to disable it before it reached the Bloodwind.

He looked up and saw the Bloodwind looming close. This was not going to work. There was only one other thing to try. He remembered Analon Leebo, the Glorkan from Doctor Eshton's experiment group, who could teleport using his Levatech implants. Vik had spent months trying to figure out how Leebo did it, wondering if his results could be replicated. Vik had calculated how it might be done in his head, but had felt it was too dangerous to actually try it.

This was going to hurt.

Vik concentrated on all of his implants, willing space

itself to pull towards him, in order to create a singularity. He was mere seconds from hitting the Bloodwind, but he had to put that out of his mind. He pulled and pulled, tensing every muscle. He could feel his body trying to tear itself apart. He could see reality warping around him. And then... POP.

The other hunters watched on the viewscreen, and let out a collective gasp as the missile blipped out of existence. It just seemed to get sucked into itself, before collapsing into nothingness. There was no sign of Vik. They scanned the area with every sensor they had, until they finally had to admit he was gone.

The IGP arrived on the scene about an hour later. Bloodstone filed a police report, going into great detail. The IGP thanked her for destroying the gravity cannon, but would need proof of the weapon's existence before any sort of reward might be offered. The IGP started their own search and rescue to look for Vik, but to no avail. Salvage crews were called to the Mars site, but there was so much rubble that it would take weeks before anything could be found.

Once the bounty hunters were no longer needed, they left the scene, taking the slow route back to Earth. A memorial service would be held for Vik eventually, and Detanna planned to give a speech about the heroism of his final moments. In the meantime, the hunters held their own service for Yna. Even though she wasn't actually dead, they still felt a great loss at her transcendence, and everyone wanted to say a few words in her honor.

In the weeks that followed, Raven received another invitation to join the Council of Heirs on Valos. This time she accepted. With her help, the Inner Eye was dismantled. A fringe subgroup, calling themselves the True Eye, severed ties to Valos and kept some criminal operations active. However, they were nowhere near as big a threat as the Inner Eye had been. The Council of Heirs brought Valos into a new era of prosperity.

The bodies of Tena and Thresh were never found. Rumors persisted that one or the other was the secret leader of the True Eye, but there was no evidence to support these claims.

The shapeshifter Vraxx was eventually caught by an up-and-coming bounty hunter called Parzak, real name Zak Blood. But Bloodstone first knew him as Zak Lisbon, leader of the East Side Daggers.

At Vik's funeral, Raven met Zeva, the younger sister of the late Zhari Ze-Rastt. The two really hit it off. They became great friends, and for a while, they were even roommates.

Dervish and Panther made a home on Valos. Panther became good friends with Sekka Vermon, and spent many hours playing with her and her other animal friends.

Dervish had grown tired of the complications of humanoid society, and spent weeks at a time in feline form, frolicking with Panther through the golden fields and other natural wonders Valos offered. When she was ready to rejoin civilization, Dervish studied law and became an advocate for Marae rights. Her efforts had a huge effect on the Marae slave trade, and the Grunthian slavers lost many of their best customers.

Raven and Trenyn were true to their word, creating the transition machine of Detanna's dreams. Then they found ways to make the process more affordable, so trans people all over the galaxy could reap the benefits of this device. It also proved useful for regrowing lost limbs and curing other physical maladies.

Detanna and Alterra gradually shifted from bounty hunting to crime consultation. They no longer went into the field themselves, but rather used their considerable resources to gather information to assist other bounty hunters and law enforcement officers. They also ran classes to train future bounty hunters.

Occasionally, when passing a mirror, one of the former hunters caught a glimpse of a ghostly shape. A transparent blue humanoid would give them a friendly wave before disappearing.

Detanna waited until after her full transition and recovery before she finally proposed to Alterra. She wanted to be her true self at the wedding. It was a beautiful ceremony, with Detanna in a feminine cut tuxedo, and Alterra wearing a traditional Auroran wedding robe. They spent their honeymoon on a luxury train that circled the planet Hermoso - where they discovered and brought down a slave trafficking ring, but that's another story - before settling down on Valos so they could be closer to their friends.

While life was not without its challenges, each of the former hunters found complete fulfillment in their new lives. The galaxy wasn't perfect, and it never would be. But at least for some, things were better than they had been in a long time, and would only improve as time went on.

...at least for a while.

02.08   *New Blood*

ED.02508.01.15

Steady, remember what Bloodstone taught you, the young man thought. *Jump the gun and they just run.* If his first shot missed, the mission would get a lot more complicated. He watched through his scope, patiently waiting for his prey to walk into view.

The target was Tarlos "The Squid" Prozner, a multi-tentacled bank robber who recently pulled off the crime of a lifetime. Using some sort of underground AON drilling device, he had managed to detach an entire bank from its foundation. Then he had fastened Levatech disks all over the building, causing the entire structure to float into the air. After that it had been a simple matter to tow the bank away with a spaceship, taking it who-knows-where. And he had done all of it in a single night.

Of course, he hadn't done it alone. His three lackeys had done most of the work. Korbek was the muscle. He was a Grunthian, and Prozner's personal bodyguard. Altoon was the weapons expert. He was an orange-scaled Vhelran with about a dozen guns holstered around his body. Yeela was the tech expert, without whom they never could have pulled off the heist. She wore cybernetically-enhanced clothing, and always had a drone flying nearby.

From his spot on the roof, Parzak could see three of the four. Everyone but Yeela, who had stepped away a few minutes ago. The rest were just pacing around the dock, talking, occasionally taking a drag on a vape. Every time he thought he had a clear shot on Tarlos, one of the accomplices would walk in front of him.

"Move and you're dead," came a woman's voice behind him.

Parzak sighed. *Always cover your back,* he imagined Bloodstone admonishing him.

"Drop the gun, and turn around," Yeela added.

"But you said not to move," Parzak said. "Which is it?"

"You think you're funny," Yeela said. "We'll see how funny The Squid thinks you are. Now turn around."

Parzak carefully turned around and dropped his gun. Before it reached the ground, Yeela held out her arm. The gun flew into her hand, pulled by Levatech emitters in her glove. She looked over the weapon, her bionic eye automatically analyzing it. "Long-range stun disks?" She looked Parzak up and down. He wore a dark blue flightsuit with red armored plating and several pouches full of weapons and other surprises. Rather than a helmet, Parzak wore HUD goggles and a cloth mask over the lower half of his face. His unkempt hair was dyed blood red.

"I thought you were an assassin," Yeela said. "But you're just some bounty hunter." A disc-shaped drone hovered near her head, but now it moved closer to Parzak and pointed a small cannon at him. "Move a muscle and my drone will fire. Did you really think you could take all four of us alone?"

"Who hunts alone anymore?" Zak said. "That's so five years ago. Say hi to the gang!"

Yeela looked around but saw nothing. Somewhere in the distance, a cricket chirped.

"The… gang!" Zak said again.

Yeela coughed.

"Come on, guys, we worked on this…"

A glowing white arrow flew out of the darkness, skewering the drone, which fell out of the air and clattered harmlessly onto the roof. Yeela looked for the source. A humanoid-shaped cluster of shadows quickly dispersed, revealing a woman dressed in black. Wisp, the young clone of Alterra Sarr, nocked another arrow, which immediately started to glow.

But she wasn't alone. Two other bounty hunters appeared behind her, having used her shadow form as cover. To her left was Vex. This young human woman was dressed in punk clothing and had neon blue hair. In her hands, she repeatedly flipped a pair of AON daggers with glowing blue blades.

To her right was Sekka. She had white hair with pink highlights, and white eyes. Her outfit was a bit garish, with tight pink pants and a white leopard print top. A pink squirrel peeked out from her hip pouch, and a literal feather boa – that is, a live boa constrictor with tiny feathers – was draped over her shoulders. She held out her left arm, and a small flying reptile swooped out of the sky to perch on her forearm.

While Yeela was distracted by these new arrivals, Parzak scooted away from her and drew another weapon. "You're late," he told his friends.

"You said that building," Vex said, pointing toward another roof with an AON dagger.

"Sorry," Parzak said.

By this time Yeela had signaled her allies, and they were already on the way up the side of the building. Korbek easily scaled the wall with his apelike arms, Altoon floated up with a pair of Levatech boots, and their boss climbed up using his tentacles. The two sides sized each other up, weapons drawn.

Parzak spoke first. "Tarlos Prozner, you and your team are wanted for the unusually thorough robbery of the

Maple First Bank of Gazna City, Galea. Come along peacefully, and none of you will be harmed. Resist and… well, it probably won't be pretty."

"Who even are you people?" Tarlos asked.

"We're the Bloodhunters," Parzak said.

And the fight began.

02.09 *Epilogue*

ED.02734.02.13

POP.

About a meter off the ground, approximately twelve kilometers from the ruins of the Mars gravity cannon, the air rippled and pulled in on itself. The distortion only lasted a second. A man seemed to struggle with all sorts of gravitational forces as he extradited himself from the warped air. He landed on the ground with a soft thud, his clothing in tatters, his skin bruised and bleeding, his eyes crazed. He picked himself up and surveyed his surroundings, marveling at just how… "normal" things looked this side of warped space.

Where even am I? he thought. This appeared to be Mars, not far from where his crewmates had landed to destroy the cannon, but now he could see buildings off in the distance. A city? That definitely hadn't been there before. *How long was I gone?*

Doing his best to shake off the residual madness, Vik stumbled his way towards civilization.

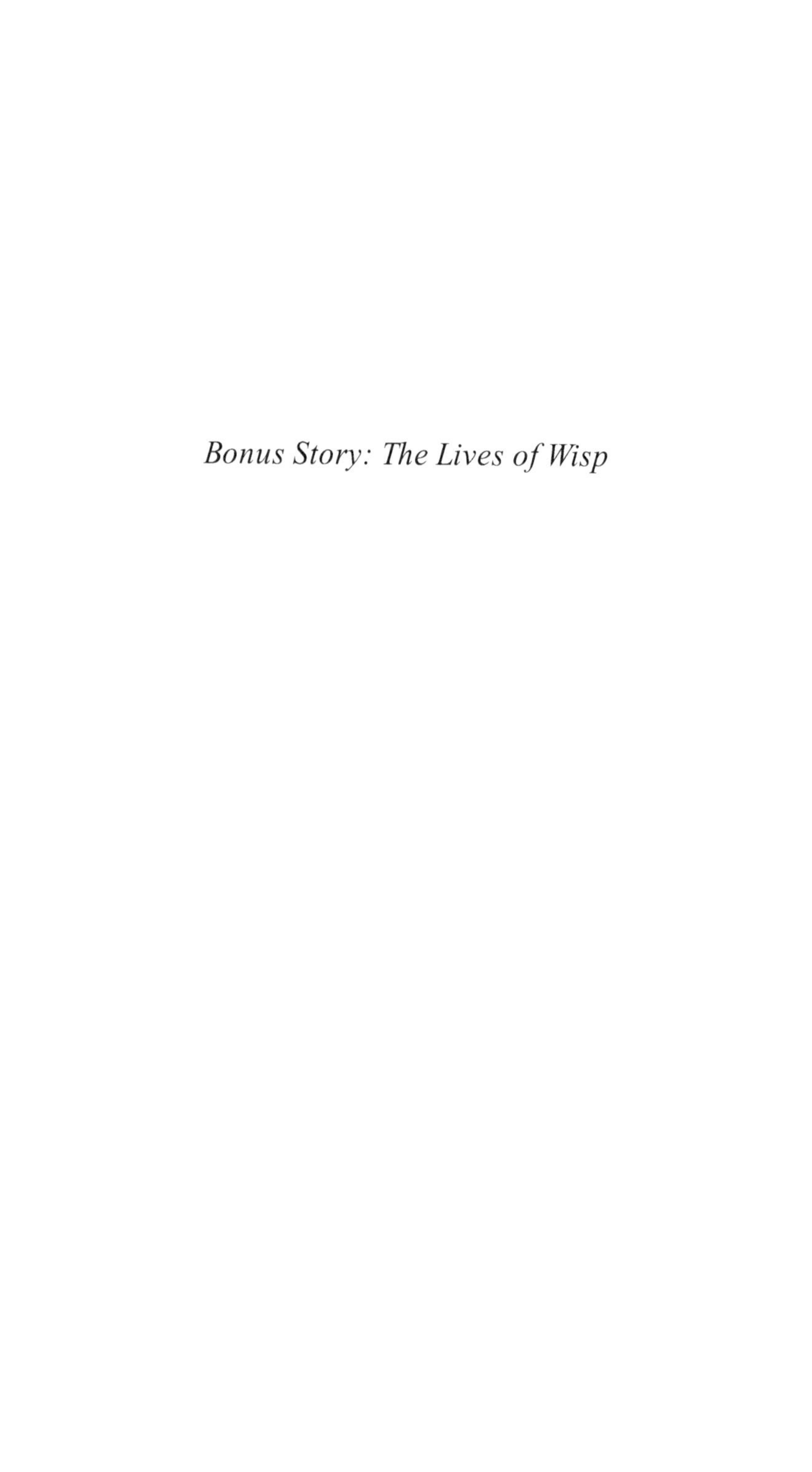

Bonus Story: The Lives of Wisp

03.00 *Another Time*

The exact year and location of our story are unknown. Only one person alive remembers these events, and for her it was so long ago, she doesn't always remember it the same way. She knows it started in medieval Europe, but after that the details get a bit fuzzy.

In telling the story, she'll use a mix of slang from multiple time periods, ranging from the fifteenth century to the twenty-fifth. She will insist certain legends are fact, claiming she fought alongside characters such as Robin Hood and the like. She tells her stories with such fervor that you may even wonder if it's the history books that are wrong.

But while the veracity of her tales may be suspect, it's still well worth your time to listen to them. She has had many lifetime's worth of adventures, and she tells them so well. Embellished or not, Wisp's stories are a feast for the ears. Presented here is the version of her origin she tells most often, though whether it's the most plausible is up for debate.

The good King Gerald of Peladon was betrayed and defeated by his own general, Garvan of Draklar. Garvan ordered the deaths of the royal family and all its supporters. He then assumed the throne and began his long reign of cruelty. Taxes were raised until the kingdom's citizens were on the brink of starvation. Those who complained were tortured and killed. Young women were taken from their homes to be subjected to the king's pleasures. King Garvan reveled in watching his people suffer.

Until finally, eleven years after Garvan's bloody takeover, a new hero appeared.

It was nearly dusk, and a small carriage rolled through the forest, led by two exhausted horses. An old man whipped the reigns, hoping to make it to town before the fog got much worse. If his passengers didn't make it to their destination on schedule, there would be hell to pay. These weren't the kind of people who liked delays, and for the amount of money they were paying, they deserved the quickest trip possible.

The driver saw a movement ahead of him. Something had darted across the trail. Probably just a deer. The forest was full of them. Still, he knew to be on his guard. It could just as easily have been a wolf, or worse. What he saw next caused him to pull the reigns hard, bringing the carriage to a quick stop. From within the carriage came the sound of tumbling cargo, followed by an outraged curse. "What the hell are you doing out there?"

"Sorry, my lord," called back the driver. "But I didn't want to run over that dead body just there." The angry nobleman, his head now halfway out the door, squinted in the direction the driver indicated. It was a body, all right. Human. But it wasn't dead, it was rising. And from among the trees, more people emerged, like the wood nymphs of legend. But these were no magical creatures; they were well-armed men dressed in the unkempt cloth of forest bandits. There looked to be at least ten, possibly twice that, wielding a variety of swords and bows.

The apparent leader of the group, a robust bald man with

a two-handed broadsword, stepped forward and demanded, "Step out of the carriage, all of you!" The elderly driver immediately complied, climbing down from his high perch. The nobleman stepped cautiously from the carriage, keeping one arm inside the vehicle. The other passenger, a woman of delicate beauty, peered out the door and also began to rise. Her husband motioned for her to stay inside.

"We don't want any trouble!" the nobleman called out, which resulted in a burst of laughter from the gang of thieves. Enraged, the nobleman pulled his other arm from the carriage, revealing his sword. "I'll cut you all limb from limb!" he shouted. He assumed a standard swordsman's stance, one that reflected all his years of breeding, education, and training. But before he could even pick his first target, an arrow struck him in the shoulder. He went down, dropping the sword in favor of clutching his wound. Behind him, another bandit held his bow drawn, ready to fire a lethal shot if the nobleman tried anything more.

The gang leader was greatly amused. "I said everyone out, that includes you as well, my lady," he said, walking around the side of the vehicle. In an almost genteel way, he offered his hand and helped the noblewoman out of the carriage. Once she was out, his gang surrounded their three captives with weapons drawn. "If you listen to me, you might get out of this with your lives. We will take everything of value. This includes your horses and your fine carriage there. I'm afraid you'll be walking home. In addition, please remove those nice garments you have on."

The nobleman, rising from his knees, glared at the leader and spat in his face. The leader responded with a hard punch to the stomach, causing the nobleman to double over. Two bandits grabbed the nobleman by the arms and proceeded to pull off his elegant clothing. Two more bandits removed the woman's exquisite dress. "Hey, boss," one of them asked, "will we be taking this fine lass with us as well?"

"No!" the nobleman cried. "Touch her and I'll kill you!"

The leader kicked him hard in the crotch. As the nobleman doubled over once again, the boss chuckled and said, "Maybe we should. She might be fun to have around. Besides, we wouldn't want to leave her in the hands of this gelding."

All three victims were now in their underclothes, their fine imported outfits neatly folded up and packed back into the carriage. The nobleman and the driver were tied up, back-to-back, and lay helpless in the mud. The lady was also bound, and two of the bandits grabbed her roughly, pulling her towards the carriage.

Before they got her inside, the leader stopped them. "One moment, gents," he said. He grabbed the noblewoman by the back of the head and pulled her in for a kiss. She bit him on the nose, then spat in his face. "You wench!" he yelled, and pulled out a dagger. He held it up to her face. "You'll show some respect or I'll..."

A gleaming black throwing star hit him in the back of the hand, and he bellowed in pain. He dropped to the ground, screaming and attempting to extract the weapon. The noblewoman seized the moment and kicked him in the side. The other bandits looked around for the attacker, but could only see trees and gloom.

And then, like a demon rising from the mists, a silhouette emerged from the fog. It was a decidedly feminine shape, a very fine figure indeed. As the details came more clearly into focus, they saw a woman dressed entirely in black, including her face. Her bright blue eyes were visible between the cloth strips that made up her mask, and a long red ponytail flowed from the back. Her boots were of expensive black leather, as were her form-fitting pants. Small sheaths housed daggers on her right boot and left thigh. Her sleeveless black shirt laced up the front, and she wore armored wrist pads onto which more throwing stars were fastened. They could see the hilt of a longsword protruding from her backpack, and in her right hand she wielded an ornate short sword, the sheath for which hung from her belt.

"Let them go," the mysterious woman said. Her voice was harsh and commanding, yet still possessed a lilting regal quality. The thieves froze. They had never seen the like. Some slowly drew their weapons but were afraid to use them. A few seconds went by, as the bandits pondered whether to fight or flee. After all, it was just a girl, but the way she had appeared had them spooked.

"Kill her!" the leader screamed, still crumpled on the ground. That broke the moment of indecision. In unison, the thieves attacked. A few arrows flew towards her first, which the woman quickly dodged. Catching one arrow in her left hand, she thrust it through the neck of the first assailant to reach her. She blocked another bandit's blade with her shortsword, then bashed him in the nose with the base of her other hand. Ducking the swing of yet another sword, she drew her longsword. She now wielded a sword in each hand and fought expertly with both. She blocked attacks from every direction, following through with attacks of her own. When not stabbing and slashing with her swords, she delivered roundhouse kicks and foot sweeps to her opponents.

Soon the large number of her opponents threatened to overwhelm her. The nobleman, still tied to his driver in the mud, strained his neck to watch the battle. From this angle, all he could see was a crowd of thieves covering their prey. The nobleman knew that she had been defeated. This was seemingly confirmed when the bandits stopped their attacks and lowered their weapons. There were only five surviving brigands, and they seemed perplexed as they scanned the heap of their dead comrades. As he watched them pick up and roll bodies out of the way, the nobleman finally realized what was happening. The thieves had lost track of the woman. Then he felt a tugging at his arm. He was being untied. He turned his head just in time to see the black-clad redhead cutting his bonds.

The thieves, finally catching on, turned and came at them.

The mysterious woman suddenly flew through the air, knocking out one thief with a jump kick to the face. Before she even landed, she cut the throats of the next two nearest bandits. The final two thieves wisely fled into the woods. The battle was finished.

Except for the leader. Clutching his wound, he rose one last time. His facial expression was that of a man who knew he was already dead. Shakily lifting his broadsword with his right arm, he swung it down heavily at the stealthy woman. Swiftly dodging the blow, she swung her short sword one final time, right across his throat. He fell again, this time for good.

By this time the nobleman had finished loosening the ropes that bound his lovely wife. As he helped her to her feet, they both looked toward their savior. "I thank you greatly," the nobleman said, "Name your reward, and it will be done."

"That's not necessary," the dark woman answered. "Justice is reward in itself."

"Well, at least let us give you a ride into town," the rich man offered.

"That too, is unnecessary," came the answer. "I have my own way home." And with that, she disappeared from view, fading into the fog like a spirit.

"But wait!" the nobleman called. "At least tell us your name!"

The voice came back, softly, over the fog. All they heard was the one word, like the sigh of a ghost. "Wisp," it said, and nothing more.

This continued for several months. Travelers were attacked in the forest, only to be rescued by this mysterious woman. Sometimes she would even venture out of the forest and foil robberies within a town's limits, but only on dark, foggy nights. Once she even rescued a family from a house fire, quickly disappearing afterward. She never accepted a reward or stayed for praise. Local legends grew and spread from town to town. Some peasants believed she was some sort of spirit, returned from the other side to help others in an attempt to save her own soul. Others believed she was a demon, despite her noble deeds. King Garvan, however, had another theory.

As usual, it was a noisy night at the old tavern. Large hairy men drank huge amounts of beer while singing obnoxious tunes. Bawdy women danced lewdly as gawking men threw coins at their feet. Dirty jokes were told, fights broke out, and gamblers accused each other of cheating. The noise died down as the doors flew open, and a young man burst into the establishment. This would not ordinarily have drawn attention in itself, but this man wasn't dressed like the pub's usual denizens. He was decked out in the finest of linens, complete with cape. In his right hand, he clutched his sword so tightly that his knuckles were white.

"I need to hire a mercenary squad!" he cried. "I've been robbed! They have my daughter! Somebody help me, please!" He shakily sat down at the bar.

Several of the bar's patrons lost interest and went back to their drinks. A couple of burly men sat down next to the gentleman. One asked, "Just how much are you willing to pay us?"

"Well... I don't have any money… they took it all. But you can have whatever you recover as long we rescue my daughter! We have to save her, I'm afraid they'll... they'll..." The gentleman took one of the patrons by the shirt and shouted into his face, "Just help me! They took her into the woods! I know the way they went!"

All listening patrons shook their heads. "You couldn't pay us enough to go tonight," one said. "Those woods are haunted. Perhaps in the morning we can gather a search party."

"But please!" the gentleman pleaded, lowering his head to

the bar. "Someone has to help me..."

"I'll help you." The voice was soft. Female. But loud enough to be heard over the noisy bar. Several people looked around, unable to tell the direction from which the sound came. Then she appeared. Stepping out of the shadows, as if she had been there, unseen, all along. Several patrons stepped back in awe and recognition. They had heard stories of this Wisp before, but she had not been sighted in this particular village.

"But you're just a..." the gentleman began. Apparently he had not heard the stories.

Wisp replied warmly, "I can do the job. And I'll do it for free."

A nearby intoxicated man nodded in agreement. "Oh yeah, lishen to her," he slurred. "If anybody can get yer daughter back, itsh her."

The gentleman looked puzzled. "I have no other choice. If you will ride with me, I will show you where they went."

An hour later they rode a single horse through the woods. Wisp sat behind the gentleman, whose name was William. Wisp held his waist tightly and asked several questions in his ear. He told her about the robbery, and how everything he had was stolen, and how none of it mattered if his daughter was dead or her innocence was lost.

Eventually they reached a clearing and stopped the horse. William dismounted and walked a few steps. Wisp followed. "Why are we stopping here?" Wisp asked. "Are they nearby?" William pointed to a set of tracks in the dirt.

"There!" he shouted. "Oh thank you, my lady, thank you," and he turned and hugged her, hard. It was so unexpected that Wisp didn't know what to do.

"What do you mean? I didn't do anythi—" And that's when she noticed the cage dropping from high above in the trees. She twisted out of William's grip but it was too late. The steel cage hit the ground and instantly latched onto a dirt-covered steel base that Wisp hadn't noticed before. Wisp and William were trapped. Or rather, Wisp was trapped. William had obviously deceived her. "Let me out of here or I'll kill you," Wisp threatened.

"Go ahead," William answered. "It is my duty to give my life for the king. My job is done."

A group of knights emerged from the forest. Two of them brandished blowguns. Wisp shouted, "Let me out of here!" She fiddled with her wrist guards, where she kept a hidden lockpick. One of the knights blew into his weapon. Wisp spun William around and the dart hit him in the neck. The knight reloaded the blowgun and both knights blew this time. Wisp tried to dodge, but there was limited room in the cage. She managed to sidestep the first dart but the second hit her in the shoulder. Within seconds, everything went black.

"Your Highness, we have her." The captain of the guard, his mannerisms as refined as that of high nobility, graciously bowed before his king.

"Take me to her," King Garvan answered, showing considerably less eloquence. The captain led the king through the castle, down a stairway, through several long halls lit by flickering torches, past several guard stations, and into the dungeon area. Both were taken aback, simultaneously surprised and angry, as they entered the final hallway. Although the rest of the prison area was well guarded, there were no guards whatsoever in this particular passage. The captain ran to Wisp's cell and saw two unconscious guards lying inside.

"My L-l-l-lord," the captain stammered, unlocking the cell door.

As the captain tended to the sleeping guards, the king examined a hidden lever behind a loose brick on the back wall of the cell. The rusty lever gave easily, showing that it had recently been used. He had been expecting this. Garvan turned and walked out of the cell without a word, leaving the captain of the guard lost in his puzzlement.

Later that night, King Garvan sat in his study, scrutinizing the historical records. The only light in the room was a candle on his desk, which cast irregular patterns across the documents. The candle's glow only penetrated the darkness enough to allow the king to read, but he slowly became aware of another presence in the room. He looked up and saw a dark feminine shape standing before him. Garvan smiled. "I know who you are," he said. "There are very few people who would know the secret passage out of that dungeon."

"You speak with a lot of confidence for a man about to die," Wisp said.

Garvan continued to smile. "Come now, can't we be civil? We can help each other, you and I."

"I will help you," Wisp replied. "Help you get to Hell." She drew her short sword and raised it above her head. She brought it down quickly, with every ounce of strength. The blade stopped half an inch from the king's head. Garvan didn't even blink, and he kept right on smiling. The blade was held against the empty air, as if it had struck a stone barrier. Wisp's eyes opened wide. She raised the blade again, brought it down, and again it stopped at the same place. She tried to force the blade downward, but it would not budge. Wisp took a step back and exclaimed, "What in Hell?"

"You can come out now, Tyverm," Garvan commanded.

From out of the shadows, a sinister-looking man coalesced. He was dressed in a black robe and had long gray hair that matched his mustache and goatee. The irises of his eyes were white. "As you command, my master," he said.

Garvan explained, "This is my sorcerer. He does little odd jobs for me, like predicting my future and placing curses on my enemies."

To this Tyverm added, "I have cast a spell of protection on the good king. Your blade can't touch him."

"So you see," Garvan added, "I have no reason to fear you. And since you can't beat me, why don't you join me? You would be well paid. I could use you."

"Oh, you'd use me all right," Wisp answered. "But I'll never join you." And with that, she took two steps backward and vanished into the darkness.

"Summon the guards—" Garvan began.

"They won't find her," the sorcerer interrupted, walking over to the open window. "She's halfway to the forest already."

In the basement of a peasant's home, a meeting was underway. The dirty room was packed with villagers, who tried to keep their voices down even though emotions were running high.

One brawny peasant spoke passionately. "I say we storm the castle now. Why wait? We'll take them by surprise before they even suspect a rebellion. We could leave this very—"

The town's blacksmith cut him off. "We can't possibly win! It'll be a slaughter! King Garvan has legions of trained soldiers! All we have is a bunch of farmers with a few swords!"

Another man, this one more dignified in his mannerisms, stepped forward. His name was Cedric, and he had once been the captain of the guard himself. But that had been years ago, before he'd been caught showing mercy to villagers who couldn't pay their taxes. Cedric now lived in hiding. With great authority he declared, "No, we can win. And we will win, because we have to. Every day Garvan rules is a day more of us die. All we have to do is prepare ourselves well. We can craft weapons; I can train you to use them."

"Suicide," the blacksmith said. "We won't even make it to

the castle before we're attacked. And once we get there, how do you propose we get in?"

"We will sneak in," answered Cedric. "And for that, we will need help."

A few hours later, a horse trotted through the forest. Cedric was at the reigns, shouting "Wisp!" at the top of his lungs. He rode on through the day, over hills and through several forests, but he had no luck. There were several times when he felt as if he was being watched, but it could have just been his imagination. He was even attacked by thieves once, but he quickly dispatched them. No shadowy woman came to his rescue. Perhaps she had been too far away to know about the attack, or maybe she just knew that he could handle the situation.

Later that night, as Cedric prepared for bed in a friend's cellar, she came to him. The cellar was very dark, and Cedric thought he was alone. Then a hushed voice came from the darkness. "Your makeshift army won't beat Garvan's forces."

Cedric, who was under a blanket on the floor, sat up and looked around the room. "Wisp?"

"I wish I could help you. But I can't lead an army to their deaths. I'm sorry."

"It won't be that way," Cedric said, still unable to see the origin of the voice. "I know that castle inside and out. My men will sneak through the forest, and into the castle through secret passages. We will come out in Garvan's bedroom, and he'll be dead before he can even sound an alarm. Then we will attack the castle from the inside out. Any guards who refuse to accept the new rule will be vanquished easily. Everyone will have the benefit of my training. They will be able to defend themselves should any problems arise."

Wisp stepped out of the shadows and said, "King Garvan has a sorcerer now. He will know you are coming."

Studying Wisp's ethereal form, Cedric said, "Well, that's where I hoped you could help us. You're good at avoiding detection. Maybe you could teach us a few tricks."

"My skills took years to learn," Wisp answered. "I believe in your cause, but I don't know of any way I can help you. I'm sorry." Then the shadows took her once again.

"Wisp? Wisp!" Cedric called, but she didn't answer. Disappointed, he went to bed.

A month later, Cedric's ragtag army made its way through the forest. They stayed off the main roads to avoid being seen. The army was over one hundred men strong, but Cedric was unsure of their chances for success. But he also knew that there was no other way to assert their independence from the evil reign of King Garvan.

They had been meandering their way through the trees for nearly an hour, and were finally within a few miles of the forest's edge. Once there, they would no longer be under the cover of trees, and they would have to wait until nightfall to cross the last field to the castle.

Cedric called his troops to a halt. The crunching sound of leaves underfoot gradually fell silent as the men complied with the order. While Cedric had trained the villagers as much as he possibly could, he still heard and saw much more than everyone else as he studied the forest ahead. One of the men standing beside Cedric started to ask what was going on, but Cedric held up his hand to silence him. "Stand very still and listen. I think there's something—"

And Cedric saw it. An arrow came straight towards his face. To Cedric, time seemed to slow down. He could see the arrow coming, and he knew that he would never make it out of the way in time. It would hit him in less than a second, and his life would be over. But then, moving at an inhuman speed, a blade came down in front of him and sliced the arrow in half, the two pieces flying harmlessly away. Time resumed to normal speed. Cedric saw Wisp to his left, sword drawn. He wanted to thank her for saving his life, but there was no time for words. The arrow was the first of many, and Cedric had an army to command. Turning to his men, he shouted, "Take cover!"

Many of Cedric's followers ducked behind trees and held up their wooden and leather shields. Some of the more cowardly men dropped their weapons and fled. Others were hit by the onslaught of arrows that now came through the trees. Crouching behind a large gnarled stump, Cedric turned to Wisp and said, "Maybe you were right. Looks like we'll be making our stand here." He glanced out from behind the stump and saw Garvan's armored soldiers filing through the trees. The preliminary barrage of arrows had abated, and now the melee would begin. Cedric drew his sword and bravely rose to meet the enemy.

For a few moments, Wisp watched Cedric battle. He was an incredible fighter, she could see that easily. He had no problem fighting four or five men simultaneously. He always seemed to know what the enemy would do next, reacting to attacks that were out of his field of vision. Of course, he had trained many of these soldiers himself, back when he had been their captain. So it wasn't surprising that he could anticipate their attacks. But knowing this did little to diminish the respect Wisp felt for this man.

Still, even if he could handle fighting five men at once, it was not five men that he faced, but hundreds. And while the majority of his men did stay and fight, they hadn't had much time to train, and they were clearly outmatched. At first Wisp didn't engage in swordplay openly, but protected others instead, dispatching enemy soldiers from behind before they could kill Cedric's men. Eventually, however, even Wisp found herself dueling like the rest.

Finally Cedric realized that this plan was doomed. "Retreat!" he called out, though at this point most of his men had already done so. As the rest of the peasants turned and ran from the forest, Garvan's soldiers lowered their weapons and turned back toward the castle. They had been ordered not to pursue the group. After this disaster, the villagers would be afraid to rebel again. No sense killing more taxpayers than necessary.

Wisp found herself in a three-way swordfight with a pair of enemy soldiers who had apparently realized she was Wisp, and was therefore worthy of a large bounty. She had two swords drawn and was doing quite well until a third soldier launched an arrow from a distance. Wisp was unable to dodge because she was too busy blocking the thrust of an enemy's sword. The arrow pierced her right forearm clean through, and pinned her arm to a tree. Wisp screamed in agony but continued to fight with her free arm.

She fought defensively, using one sword to block thrusts from two attackers. Some of their attacks got through, and she received several painful wounds. The third soldier drew his bow again. Wisp painfully tried to wrench her arm from the tree, but it was an iron arrow and it had pierced the tree too deeply. She was unable to move, and this next arrow would be lethal.

...If it had been fired. Just then the archer went down, felled by Cedric's sword. In seconds he was beside Wisp, and the rest of her attackers lay crumpled at their feet. Wisp smiled and tried to say "Thank you." It came out more like "Thad knew." The world went dark.

The world was still dark when Wisp finally awakened. She was on the floor, under a blanket. As the room came into focus, she realized that this was the cellar where she had visited Cedric. Wisp could just make out his form kneeling over her. She tried to speak but her mouth was dry. She reached out with her right hand and was rewarded with blinding pain.

"Don't try that yet," Cedric said. "Here." He lifted her head with one hand and put a cup to her lips. As she sipped, Wisp realized that she wasn't wearing her mask. She looked down and saw that she was wearing a loose-fitting robe.

Seeing her eyes widen, Cedric explained, "You were pretty hurt, Wyn. I had to dress your wounds."

Wisp sat up, and managed to ask, "You know who I am?"

Cedric nodded. "Eleven years ago, Garvan killed King Gerald and took the throne by force. He tried to kill all the members of the royal family, but princess Wynnifred escaped. She was presumed dead but no one ever found the body. You look so much like your mother."

Wisp nodded and hugged him. She wept for the first time in ten years. She finally cried herself right back to sleep.

Cedric cared for her all the next day. Wisp rested, Cedric tended to her wounds, and they spent hours in conversation. Sitting in the basement, lit by the glow of a single candle, they told each other their entire life stories.

"When I escaped the castle, I was only eight," Wisp explained. "I was rescued by one of the servants. He knew that my life would be in jeopardy no matter where he hid me. So he took me far away, to the trading ports, and we stowed away on a ship. We were discovered, and my loyal servant was killed. I was put to work, and when the ship finally docked in the Far East, I was sold into slavery. Eventually I became the property of a martial arts master. He helped me sharpen my mind as well as my body. When I was eighteen, I decided to come back here, and see if I could make a difference."

"You've been through a lot because of Garvan," Cedric said. "He must pay for his crimes. Help me defeat him, Wyn. If we can overthrow Garvan, we can put you back in your rightful place as ruler."

Wisp shook her head. "I don't care about power. And I don't care about revenge. I just don't want that man to hurt any more people."

"When you get down to it, that's the only important thing," Cedric agreed. "You saved my life yesterday. I wanted to thank you."

"You saved mine as well," Wisp replied. "So we're even. But here's your reward regardless." She kissed his lips. It was short and quick, like the kiss of a pixie, but Wisp still turned away quickly, blushing at what she had done.

"Well, if we were even then now I owe you one," Cedric said, and kissed her back. This kiss was stronger and more passionate.

They continued rewarding each other throughout the night, in increasingly greater methods. When they finally slept, the sun was already beginning to rise.

Twelve hours later, as twilight was just beginning to claim the day, Wisp and Cedric were up to their knees in sewage. They were making their way through the castle's sewer tunnels, trying to locate the secret passage that would lead them to the king's quarters.

"Once we find the king," Cedric said, "we may have to stay in hiding for quite a while. We have to wait until he's alone."

"And what then?" Wisp said, "Our weapons can't harm him, not with Tyverm's protection spell."

"I'm not sure I believe that," Cedric replied. "But even if it's true, we'll just kill the wizard first. That should break the spell."

They found their way out of the sewer system and, after another hour of quiet walking, they finally located the king's quarters. At first, they considered lying in wait in the king's bedroom. Garvan wasn't married, so they weren't likely to encounter anyone besides the king himself. But, as Wisp pointed out, the king often liked to stay up late, poring over large tomes in his study.

They continued to explore the hidden passages. The castle was a virtual maze of concealed hallways, and although both Cedric and Wisp remembered the layout, it was still a daunting task. They finally found the study just minutes before Garvan entered the room. Wisp and Cedric hid just inside the secret entrance to the room, and watched the evil king through a crack in the mortar. Garvan went to a bookshelf, selected a tome, and took it over to his desk. As he hunched over the large book, Cedric said in a hushed voice, "Now or never, Wyn."

Wisp had suggested sneaking in, but Cedric didn't know if he could be that stealthy. So they opted for the element of surprise. They threw open the passage door and burst into the room, swords drawn. Cedric pointed his sword at the king's throat while Wisp closed and locked the study's main door to prevent help from arriving. "I'll bet you didn't expect to see me again," Cedric told the king.

"Likewise, I'm sure," the king replied. Garvan's face shimmered and faded, revealing the face of the sorcerer Tyverm. The evil wizard stood and smiled, then made a quick gesture with a small, rectangular wand. Cedric was thrown across the room by invisible hands. Then Tyverm pointed his wand at the door and it flung open, breaking off the lock and knocking Wisp to the floor.

The real Garvan entered the study, his sword drawn, and followed by eight of his best soldiers. "Kill them," the king ordered. The soldiers drew their swords.

Cedric was on his feet instantly. Despite being outnumbered, he fought well and brought the first three soldiers down with just a few fluid swings of his sword. Wisp joined the fight as well, and in seconds the remaining soldiers were crumpled on the floor. Outraged, Garvan yelled, "Tyverm!" The evil wizard pointed his wand at Wisp, but she jumped out of the way. Behind where she'd been standing, an invisible force hit a bookshelf, scattering books everywhere.

While Tyverm was busy with Wisp, Cedric attacked the king. Garvan was not as good with the blade as Cedric, but Cedric's blows kept bouncing off the king's invisible shield. He tried attacking from various angles, but his strikes did nothing. Garvan was so smug that he barely put any effort into his defense. He knew Cedric would tire eventually, making it easier for Garvan to land a fatal blow.

Hoping brute force was the key, Cedric made a two-handed swing that would have cut Garvan in half if not for the spell. But the blade bounced off Garvan's barrier so forcefully that Cedric lost his grip on the sword and it scattered across the room.

Garvan grinned with confidence and raised his sword. Desperate for a weapon, Cedric grabbed the closest object he could find, a wooden chair. Garvan brought down his sword, and Cedric blocked the blow with the chair, which splintered into pieces. Then Cedric spun past Garvan, and using the chair leg as a club, he hit the king in the back.

The blow connected, surprising both of them. Reacting quickly, Cedric went on the offensive, going after every tender spot with the chair leg. It had broken in a way that left a very sharp tip, and Cedric used this to inflict several painful wounds before Garvan could regain the upper hand.

Garvan was incensed. He had a sword, his opponent had a sharp stick. It shouldn't have been a contest. But his overconfidence had led to injuries, and each injury provoked his temper, and in his rage he made more mistakes. He swung his sword angrily and clumsily, and Cedric used the opening to impale Garvan's forearm, causing him to drop the sword.

The king screamed at Tyverm, "Forget the girl, you idiot! Get Cedric!" Tyverm looked away from his opponent to see that he was too late. Cedric had Garvan at his mercy, and the chair leg moved inexorably toward the king's throat. Reacting quickly, Tyverm aimed his wand at Garvan and fired a tiny glowing ball of energy. Wisp, thinking that the spell was meant to hit Cedric, jumped into the orb's flight path. She was knocked across the room by the impact and hit the wall hard. Cedric's chair leg found its mark, impaling Garvan through the throat. The evil king gurgled for a moment, then became still.

Cedric stood over the corpse. This was a moment he had

long anticipated, and it was nowhere near as satisfying as he had hoped it would be. Wisp got to her feet and regarded Tyverm. Her weapons drawn, she said, "Your turn, wizard."

Tyverm pointed his wand at himself. He shimmered for a second and vanished.

"You think he'll be back?" Cedric asked.

"I doubt it," Wisp replied. "With Garvan gone, Tyverm has no reason to return. He'll probably go to some other kingdom and influence their evil king."

"You know what this means, Wyn," Cedric said with a smile. "It's time you received your birthright. You're going to be queen now."

Wisp shook her head. "You know that's not what I want."

"You'll be a good queen," Cedric said. "You're fair, just, and kind. And beautiful. Your children will be healthy and your family lineage will be long."

"Let's not discuss it right now," Wisp said. "There's much to do. I've got a lot to think about. And please, for now, don't tell anyone that I'm Princess Wynnifred."

"As you wish," Cedric answered. "For now."

There were no other challengers to the throne. When Garvan died, the loyalty of his troops died with him. With no heir to the Peladon throne, the people were forced to select a new king on their own. Of course they picked Cedric, it was unanimous. During the ceremony, Wisp politely disappeared.

A few days later, when King Cedric was asked to select a queen, he declined. This upset some of the citizens, who were worried about the future of the royal lineage. But everyone agreed to give the new king some time to make up his mind. A few weeks later, just one month after Cedric had been crowned, the long-absent Princess Wynnifred was discovered. She claimed to have been in hiding for the past decade, waiting for the day when Garvan was defeated.

At first, the citizens were worried. Should they de-throne Cedric and crown Wynnifred queen, along with whichever man she chose to be her king? Or should Cedric, who had already proven himself worthy, retain the title? In the end, it didn't matter. The day after the princess was discovered, Cedric and Wynnifred were wed, and everyone in the kingdom rejoiced. The kingdom was so elated that no one even questioned the fact that Wynnifred's first child was born only eight months after the queen's discovery.

Throughout her reign, Wynnifred occasionally kept her dual identity, going out at night and protecting the innocent from thieves and murderers. She taught some of her skills to her husband, and they had many grand adventures together. They were good rulers. They were fair and just, always putting the needs of the people before their own. They raised many sons and daughters, and instilled in them a strong moral code; to always treat people with dignity regardless of their social status. When King Cedric and Queen Wynnifred finally abdicated the throne to the eldest of their offspring, they had ruled for forty wonderful and prosperous years. Even after retirement, they continued to have many adventures before finally settling down. They lived happily for the rest of their lives, and they died peacefully within days of each other.

03.01 Reawakening

Approximately twelve years after the death of Queen Wynnifred of Peladon, and over a hundred miles away, Willania Porter became a woman. Willania, or "Willa" to her friends, had been raised to believe that a woman's place was in the hovel, where she could give her husband many children and care for all his needs. She wanted nothing more in life. She was never given to outrageous flights of fancy, and all her dreams and hopes revolved around the idea of serving her man.

On this day, Willa officially considered herself of childbearing age. Her stained bedsheets confirmed it. Despite her discomfort, this was the happiest day of her life. Sure, she was only twelve, and she still had straight hips and a flat bosom, and the boys her age still threw rocks at her... but she knew that this was the first day of a new era. She was a woman. And from here, it was just a matter of time before she could start a family.

When she took her sheets down to the river for washing, she paraded them around, letting the neighborhood boys see the dark red stains. The boys pointed and pretended to gag. One even threw a crab apple at her. But Willa would not be daunted; she was walking on air.

While washing her sheets in the river, she let her mind wander. She saw visions of her many, many children and their strong, caring father. She saw herself cleaning, and cooking, and mending, all without complaint. She envisioned intimate moments with her future husband. She dreamed about teaching her daughters how to clean and cook and mend for themselves, preparing them for their future husbands. She saw herself crying at a daughter's wedding, and holding her grandchildren. She saw herself dressing a small child, and she saw herself tending to a child's fever, and she saw herself slicing the throat of a thief.

"Huh?" she said out loud, and shook herself out of her daydream. Where had that thought come from? She tried to settle back into her little fantasy, tried to picture her children's faces, tried to think of some good names, and then she thought about kicking someone in the face. She saw herself - only it wasn't her - but in a way it was - and she was dressed in black, and she was engaged in a fight with a band of robbers. Except it wasn't like her other daydreams. It was more like a memory.

Shaking such thoughts out of her head, Willa finished cleaning her sheets and took them back home to dry. She didn't think about it again that day.

That night, however, was another story. All night she was afflicted with dreams about fighting villains and defending the innocent. She was older in the dreams. She looked different, and she had red hair The strangest part was, that even though she had never been interested in tomboy activities like fighting, somehow the events of the dream felt right. In some ways, she felt as if everything she was doing was perfectly natural, as if she had been doing it for years. When she woke the next morning, she was perfectly relaxed and ready for the day.

That morning she decided to go out to the nearby field and pick flowers. It was a beautiful day and she wanted to get out of the house so she wouldn't be in her father's way. He was constantly building things, and sometimes she got yelled at if she got too close to his projects. On the way to the field, she encountered Joren, a boy she liked. As usual, she teased him and told him that he was going to marry her someday. As usual, he picked up a rock and threw it at her head. But this time, instead of ducking, Willa stuck out her hand and caught the rock. In one fluid motion, she swung around and launched the rock back at the boy. It hit him square in the head, and he fell to the ground.

Willa rushed over. "I'm so sorry, I'm sorry, I didn't mean to do that, it just happened, I don't know why I did that, I don't know how I did that, I'm so sorry..."

"Get away from me!" Joren cried, and he got up and ran off. Willa noticed that he was bleeding. She couldn't understand it. She had never been able to catch or throw with any accuracy, much less with power. Obviously it had just been a lucky catch - and throw - but why did she even do it in the first place? It seemed so natural, a perfectly normal self-defense reaction.

Willa went on to the field, but somehow, picking flowers seemed pointless. After a while, she sat down in the field, reclined lazily, and watched the clouds. She started to daydream about boys and husbands and having children, but she couldn't get into her fantasies with any fervor. She decided that she must still be upset about hurting Joren. That's all. But still... being a housewife just didn't seem to hold any interest for her right now. It just seemed... mundane. She let her thoughts run off on their own for a while, just to see where they would go. After a while, she realized that she was dreaming about learning martial arts - and what are martial arts? - from an old man. But it was more than dreaming. It was remembering.

Weeks passed. More memories - if they were memories - surfaced. She gradually discovered - or rediscovered - new skills and abilities. She developed several theories about these alternate memories, but she didn't share this secret with anyone. The more she remembered, the more real the memories seemed. And it wasn't just memories and skills she was experiencing, her personality was changing as well. Many things that had once seemed important to her now seemed boring. She was developing new interests. Her father was a bit troubled by her behavior, but he didn't say anything to her.

Once, she looked in the mirror and saw a different face staring back. She blinked and looked again, and the vision was gone. But one aspect of the hallucination lingered. Her hair had begun to turn red.

Months passed. Willa, now a complete redhead, remembered more and more of this other life. Not always fighting, but some other things as well. Being treated like royalty. Formal ceremonies, grand living quarters. Servants waiting on her hand and foot, whether she wanted them to do so or not. A little research and Willa discovered that she had been born about nine months after the death of Queen Wynnifred of Peladon.

Years passed. At sixteen, she was betrothed to marry a young man named Talphus. While none of the villagers were very wealthy, Talphus came from one of the more respectable families, and any girl would have been proud to have him as a husband. But not Willa. Not anymore. And she refused. Her father finally gave her an ultimatum. Willa left home for good, and none of the villagers ever saw her again.

Not long after, reports of a mysterious being began to circulate throughout the village. This person - if it was a person - would appear during robberies and save the victims from the attack. Rumors flew, and memories soared. Some remembered old legends about a similar person. But that had been in a different kingdom, and a different time. However, this new hero did go by the same name. Wisp.

03.02   *The Cycle*

Wing's parents were amazed at their daughter's sudden progress. She had always been an above-average fighter, but now, in her thirteenth year, she showed signs of greatness. Surely the gods had been visiting her, for she had mastered fighting styles that she had never been taught. She was even teaching these new moves to her own masters, and they were having trouble keeping up with her. Wing even bore the mark of the gods: a shock of red hair that had only recently begun to grow. Red hair was rare in these lands. It was taken as a sign.

Her parents' beliefs notwithstanding, Wing knew the real reasons for these changes. The spirits of her ancestors - or somebody's ancestors, anyway - were living through her. She knew this because she could now remember things she had never done, places she had never been, sights she had never seen. She knew these new fighting styles because the ancestors had known them. But it was more than that. These spirits were not just giving her knowledge, they were becoming her. Or, more accurately, she was becoming them. They were infusing her with their soul, coalescing with her conscience. Soon they would be one being, of one mind.

However, Wing did share one belief with her parents. She was destined for greatness. Within this clan of ninja warriors, Wing would become the best of them all.

And she did. Decades later, as she lay on her deathbed, her children and their children came to her, praising her life and her accomplishments. They told her that she would soon join her ancestors. But Wing knew better. Her destiny lay with the souls of the future, not the past.

Wyndsong Parsons was drowning. She had been tried, "fairly" and "justly," and now she was being submerged in the town lake. The townsfolk claimed that her unusual skills came from an unholy union with the devil. But she knew better. She had never worshiped Satan, nor did she even believe such a creature existed. It was hard to be afraid of demons when your own neighbors had tied you to a pole and were now dunking you in the lake. Especially when her only displays of power had been used to help people.

Wyndsong knew where her skills came from. Her past lives were her source of power. Nothing sinister about it, it was just lifetime after lifetime of experience and knowledge. Still, all her abilities couldn't help her escape this time. Finally she just closed her eyes and shut out the pain. Maybe in her next life people would be more understanding.

It had not been a childhood dream to become a cop. Wendy Paxton reached this decision as a teenager, after it had "all come back to her." In each of her lifetimes, eventually there was a day when it would "all come back to her." Right around puberty, she would start getting these memories, and soon she would become herself again. She had now lived more than twenty lifetimes, in different bodies, but always with the same red hair. Her mind, while different in early youth, would finally return to her "real" personality, lifetime after lifetime. No doubt about it, she was Wynnifred, reincarnated with all her memory now intact. She was also Willa, and Wyndsong, and Willow, and Wanda, and several others, but she was mostly Wynnifred of Peladon, a.k.a. Wisp.

With each life, the remembering process became easier and faster. This time, it had taken just a few days to realize who she really was. The real trick, after sorting out the memories and suddenly gaining years of maturity overnight, was to figure out how to best use her skills in this more modern age. She always tried to find ways to help people, in whatever way she could. This time she decided to become a policewoman. It was the nineteen-sixties, and while the world was becoming more enlightened, she still wasn't as accepted as a man would be in the same position. *In my next life*, Wendy thought, *I'm just going to be a vigilante again. It's much easier if you don't have to go through legal channels all the time.*

It wasn't as if she needed a job. She had been wealthy in most of her recent lives. She had discovered ways of transferring her money from lifetime to lifetime. Once she hit the magic age of remembrance, she simply had to dig up the loot, or withdraw the savings, or whatever method she used at the time, and she would be set for life.

But she wanted a job. It gave her a sense of self-worth. And fruitful or not, Wendy had chosen her profession this time around and she was determined to go through with it. The police training had been a snap and she had graduated at the top of her class. She had even shown up the men during the fighting exercises. And yet somehow she'd been stuck with a desk job. She despised it, but as always, she swore to rise above it.

And she did. A few years later, she managed to get transferred to street patrol. And a month after that, she was shot on the job. She died on the operating table, thinking about how preferable this was to drowning.

03.03 *Titus*

July 4, 1988

A busy street in downtown Nashville, Tennessee. A red-haired woman pushed her way through the crowds. She was looking for someone, but she wasn't sure whom. She was in town for pleasure, one more city down in her ongoing goal to see as much of the world as possible. She didn't have a strict itinerary, and had just been doing touristy things when she'd done a double-take.

Out of the corner of her eye, she'd seen someone familiar. Someone she'd met before. Someone who should not be here, not in this time or place. She had to find him again, or she'd go crazy thinking about it.

She ran in the direction she thought she'd seen him go. Everyone was walking slower than her, so he couldn't have gotten far. She ran past several throngs of people, turning around to scan their faces. Nothing. She looked at the nearby shops and peeked in a couple of the windows.

A finger tapped her on the shoulder. "Wisp?"

She turned around, and her eyes widened. The man had gray hair and wore sunglasses. His facial features were unmistakable.

"You're... you're..." she said.

"We should go somewhere to talk," the man said.

* * *

They picked a restaurant and got a table. Both of their minds were racing, and neither said a word until they sat down. Hundreds of years ago, they had been mortal enemies. But neither felt the urge to attack the other today. The circumstances that had made them adversaries no longer applied.

Wisp spoke first. "You look the same, but how did you recognize me?"

"That's... difficult to explain," the man said. "Your hair is a unique shade of red, and even more unusual on a Native American woman. And you move like the Wisp I knew. But mostly, I just felt your presence."

"I feel it too," Wisp said. "Just... who are you, really?"

"You first," he said.

She told him a quick version of her story. How after she'd died, she'd been reborn over and over, each time remembering her past lives. He didn't look the least bit skeptical, as he knew his story was just as strange.

"Your turn, Tyverm," Wisp said.

"I go by Titus now," he said. "I change my name every few hundred years. I try to keep up with the times. Not a lot of Tyverms walking around these days."

"So you don't get reincarnated?" Wisp asked. "You've just had one long, continuous life?" He nodded. "Just how old are you?"

"I'm older than God," Titus said with a sly smirk.
"No, seriously."

"I am serious," he said. "Well, the son of God. By about ten years."

"You're saying you knew... Jesus?" Wisp asked, unconvinced.

"Do you believe in God?" he asked.

"I don't know. I mean, I know there's something supernatural going on in my life, but that doesn't have to mean gods."

"Well, I don't know about God, but I can tell you with one hundred percent certainty that Jesus was real. I've met him. But..." He hesitated for one too many beats.

"Well?" Wisp prompted.

"You won't believe it," Titus said.

"I last saw you several hundred years ago, but you haven't aged a day. I've been reincarnated several times since then. We lead unbelievable lives. If you actually say something that surprises me, I'll eat my left shoe."

"I think Jesus was a space alien," Titus said.

Wisp opened her mouth, closed it, then reached for her shoe.

"Ketchup?" Titus offered, holding up a red bottle.

His smile cracked her up. Laughing, she let go of her foot and buried her face in her palms. Looking up between splayed fingers, she said, "Okay, you're telling me... not only was Jesus real, not only did you meet him, but he was from outer space?"

"I told you wouldn't believe me."

"I believe you believe it," Wisp said.

"How patronizing," Titus said.

"I still want to hear this. Go ahead. Convince me."

"I was on the brink of death," Titus said. "Jesus visited me, and he healed me. But I wouldn't exactly call it spiritual. He used a device, like a television remote. It was like he was using technology he didn't understand." He paused, lost in thought.

"Go on," Wisp said.

"All these years, I never understood why I couldn't die. But the past few years, I've started hearing theories about nanotechnology, and it all makes sense. The technology isn't there yet – at least not on Earth. But other planets might have had nanotechnology for thousands of years."

"So in one breath, you're asking me to believe in Jesus and aliens."

"Five minutes ago you thought it was magic. Is this really

weirder?"

"Okay, fine," Wisp relented. "But how do you go from, 'he healed me' to 'he's an alien?' It's a bit of a leap."

"I witnessed his ascension," Titus said. "A lot of the Bible played out exactly like it says in the book, it's just described by people who didn't have the words yet. Imagine a squirrel trying to describe someone leaving in an airplane. The disciples said he was carried away by the clouds. I would have described it as more of a flying chariot, at the time. But now, after reading a lot of science fiction, I'm starting to remember it more like a little spaceship. And it was headed towards a mothership in the sky. He was headed home."

"Don't you think that sounds ridiculous?" Wisp asked.

"More ridiculous than 'magic man that lives in the clouds?' Here's my take on Christianity. These guys watch other planets. They study societies from afar. Sometimes they see a preindustrial world where the people are about to wipe themselves out. The aliens like watching populations develop, and don't want to see one end before it starts. So they send down a guy to teach them how to live in peace. These primitive people wouldn't understand the concepts of spaceships and such, but they do believe in gods and magic, so the aliens use religion to manipulate them."

Wisp nodded, started to say something, then stopped.

Titus continued. "They make up concepts like Heaven and Hell so we'll be afraid to sin. But these 'moral lessons' are really about keeping us alive. It's not 'morally wrong' to covet your neighbor's wife or to dishonor your parents, but it does prevent fights, which prevents wars, which keeps us from wiping each other out."

"But a lot of wars start over religion," Wisp said.

"Maybe we were supposed to grow out of religion as we discovered technology ourselves. Maybe we're supposed to be far enough along now that we don't need it. Maybe when they think we're ready, they'll return to Earth and tell us the truth, that the whole religion thing was made up because we needed guidance to survive the early stages of civilization."

"This really is hard to swallow," Wisp said.

"Religion is hard to swallow, if you're not taught it at an age when you think Santa Claus is real. But we know technology is real. We see it improving every day. With an infinite number of planets out there, it's perfectly rational to believe that some are inhabited. And if that's true, then of course some of them are going to be technologically ahead of us."

"Okay, okay," Wisp said. "So Jesus healed you. You found you couldn't die. I assume that's when your eyes went white. Then you became… a wizard?"

"My eyes didn't turn white until later. I'll get there. After Jesus ascended, and his disciples left, I found something Jesus had dropped. It was like a magic wand. Black, rectangular."

"The wand you used on me," Wisp said, realization dawning on her.

"It had writing on it, strange symbols that didn't mean anything to me. Curious, I kept it. I didn't touch it for years, I just kept it in my home, like a memento. It wasn't until I realized I was immortal that I looked at it again."

"How did that come about?" she asked.

"Well, it took me about thirty years to realize I wasn't aging like my friends. And then I was stabbed by a brigand. Should have been fatal, but I lived, and it healed quickly. I wasn't sure what was going on, but I decided to just live my life. Eventually I married a woman much younger than me, but she grew old before my eyes, and I outlived her."

"I'm sorry," Wisp said.

Titus paused, remembering his lost love. "I was distraught when she passed. I'd kept that wand hidden for many years, but now I dug it out and tried to decipher it. I decided that if it belonged to Jesus, then it must be divine. I held the wand to my wife's head and prayed. Nothing happened. I tried holding it in different ways, rubbing my thumb over the symbols, but there wasn't even a twitch. I buried her and got on with my life."

Wisp looked relieved. "I totally thought this was going to go into horror movie territory for a second…"

"And then I woke one night to find her in bed next to me," Titus said.

"Ah, there it is," Wisp sighed.

"She was mindless. She followed me around for days. Didn't speak, didn't eat. Just went through the motions. She sat when I sat, slept when I slept, stood and watched when I worked. At first I was overjoyed to see her alive, but soon I came to realize that this was worse than death. I took out the wand. I figured that whatever the wand did, it could undo. And I was right. I must have pressed the right combination of symbols, because she died again, and this time she did not come back."

"That's… just awful," Wisp said.

"I want you to understand that it was maybe… two hundred A.D. at this point? I was very superstitious, as most people were, and there were no such things as microchips or remote controls. To me it was a magic wand, and I didn't want to mess with forces I didn't understand. And yet, I couldn't quite bring myself to part with it."

"Understandable," Wisp said.

"As I got older, I got bolder. I'd already outlived everyone I knew, at least twice. I'd been blessed with more life than people usually got, so I figured, what do I have to lose? I started experimenting with the magic wand. I'm not proud of this, but I tested it on animals. I found that if I wounded an animal, and pointed the wand at them while holding my thumb over a specific symbol, their wounds would heal. I found another symbol that would instantly kill them. None of the animals I healed became immortal, that glitch stayed exclusive to me."

Wisp winced at the animal cruelty. She had spent many

years hunting for food, but she never left her prey in pain.

Titus ignored her expression. "Over the next few centuries, I did some very bad things. I went through phases of barbarism, and phases where I liked to be seen as a hero. I seized power, I healed the sick, I made my way into the history books a couple of times. I got bored with life, even tried to kill myself a few times, but it never took. I even tried using the device on myself, but all it did was turn my eyes white. From then on, I could control minds."

"Did you ever find out what the other symbols did?"

"A few, you've even seen them in action. One could wrap a person in a magnetic shield, making them impervious to metal weapons. Another could push or pull objects from a distance. One let me create illusions and turn invisible."

"Which setting did you use on me?" Wisp asked.

"Healing. I was aiming for the king, you understand. But I was sweating, and I either hit the wrong symbol or hit two of them at once… I don't know."

"Where's the device now?"

"Eventually it stopped working. It probably ran out of batteries, but that concept would have been beyond me at the time. Every few decades I'd go through a suicidal period. One time I tried jumping into a live volcano. I survived. The device did not."

"Okay, so your theory is that – what did you call it? Nanotechnology?"

"Yes," Titus said. "Think of swarms of microscopic robots that work together. They can heal any wound by sealing it from the inside. They can project holograms to create illusions. They pretty much grant the user godlike powers."

"So, how do I keep getting resurrected?"

Titus thought a moment. "I have a theory. When I hit you with that 'spell,' the microscopic robots bonded with you. Made you stronger. Probably made you heal faster, and kept you from getting sick. I'm sure you've lived during plagues, did you ever get infected?"

"No," she said.

"There you go. But they didn't make you superhuman. You could still die like anyone else. And whenever you did, the swarm left you and sought out a new host, carrying your consciousness with it."

"Whenever I reach that age," Wisp said, "You know, where I realize who I am, does that mean I'm killing the girl who previously inhabited the body?"

"I don't think you have anything to feel guilty about. This is your life cycle. Does it... feel like you're edging out her personality?"

"No, it's more like I'm regaining lost memories. Like I'm recovering from amnesia."

"Do you retain the girl's habits, thought patterns, things like that?"

"Yes," Wisp said. "I still love my new parents, I still like her favorite colors... for a while, anyway. I even still have her fears, but some of them start to feel silly. It feels more like growing up than taking over."

"I think you're safe," Titus said. "You're not stealing a mind, you're just adding to it. Let your conscience be clear."

"I'm not sure you're the one I should look to as a moral compass."

"Fair enough," he said.

"So, why do I always have the same initials?"

"Oh, that's because – wait, really?"

"Yes."

"Are you sure?" Titus looked puzzled.

"I'm pretty sure I know my own names, yeah."

"So every one of your lives..."

"Yes," Wisp explained. "My name always starts with a W. If I have a surname, it starts with a P. If I have a middle name, my initials are WSP. It can't be a coincidence."

"Okay... so I thought the nanites were taking over your mind upon adolescence. But obviously they're affecting your life before you're even born. Hmm... and you're always female?"

"Yes."

"Always a redhead?"

"Eventually, yes. Even when it would be incongruous with my heritage. You try being the only redhead in a superstitious town of brunettes." Wisp remembered the time she was executed for heresy.

"Maybe they infect your parents first? Then migrate into your body when you're born, lay dormant for thirteen years or so, then wake up? Maybe it has something to do with preparing the host body for your arrival... Or maybe the nanites just seek out someone with those initials. I just don't know."

"I can't believe you used technology on me without knowing what it does," Wisp said.

"Again, I wasn't aiming for you. And it was the same technology that made me immortal. I thought I'd found a way to share it with someone else. I would have done anything to keep my king alive. I would have done anything just to have a friend with whom to share immortality."

"Are you still... you know... evil?"

He sighed. "Look. I'm not the same person you fought back then. But I'll admit, there has been some back-and-forth. I wouldn't call it evil. Just... a different way of looking at the world. Every time humankind takes a step forward, it takes two steps back. Every time a good leader gains power, their reign is followed by someone who undoes all the good they did. Every time new lifesaving technology is invented, some greedy bastard appropriates it for profit. The longer I live, the more I see these patterns repeat themselves, over and over."

"But..." Wisp held up her hand.

Titus refused to be interrupted. "I have no hope for the future. I'm not saying we're all going to destroy ourselves. I believe there's enough sapient life in the universe that some form of civilization will survive any disaster. But every improvement will be unraveled, usually within a century. Every time a disenfranchised group is granted equality, they have less than a hundred years to enjoy it before a new regime robs them of their status again."

"That seems a tad pessimistic," Wisp said.

"I can no longer enjoy the little victories. Because I know they won't last. Humans disgust me more with every passing year. Wisp, I need your help."

"So you want me to..."

"Help me end it," Titus said. "I don't want to live in this universe anymore."

"Assuming I even agree, how?" Wisp asked. "You actually know a way?"

"One way or another, we're both being kept alive by nanites. I believe... well, I have a theory, anyway... that our nanites are linked. I know they have to be connected somehow, it's how I found you. And I know you felt it too, when you first ran into me today."

"I did," Wisp said. "I only saw you for half a second, but I just knew it was you. It was like I recognized you before I actually recognized you."

"I believe that our mutual existence fuels each other. Whenever you die, my nanites find you and send your consciousness to a new body. When I die, even if I die in such a way that my nanites should be disintegrated, your nanites find me and heal my corpse. But..."

Wisp continued his thought. "...if we were to die simultaneously..."

"Then there would be no nanites left to heal or resurrect either of us," Titus concluded. "Of course, we'd have to die in a way that completely wipes out the nanites, like—"

"It's a nice little theory," Wisp interrupted. "But who says I even want to die?"

"Don't you?" Titus looked incredulous.

"You call it a curse, but I haven't exactly been suffering."

"Then do it for me," he said.

"But there's so much to live for," Wisp said. "We can explore the world together, and see everything!"

"I've seen it," Titus said. "Several times. It's lost its fascination. I'm not like you. You get to experience life anew each time, in a new body. But for me, it's just one long road, and I've walked it too many times."

"But think of what the future might hold," Wisp pleaded. "New technology, space exploration..."

"Doesn't interest me. Wisp, I'm tired. You at least get a break between each of your lives. I believe that during that time, your soul rests. Not mine. My very consciousness is tired and needs to sleep. I have to find a way to die."

Wisp sighed, paused, then said, "I'm sorry, no."

Titus turned red in the face. "Why you selfish little…"

"Selfish? Because I don't want to go off and die with you?"

Titus took a couple of deep breaths. Then he lifted his sunglasses and stared hard into Wisp's eyes. She thought she saw a weird glow coming from his eyes.

"What are you doing?"

Titus sighed. "Nothing. I apologize for my outburst, it was uncalled for. But please, just… think about it for a while. When you come to a decision – whatever you decide – find me here." He pulled a pen out of his pocket and wrote something on a napkin. It wasn't a street address, it was a longitude and latitude. "Even if you disappoint me, it will be nice to see you again." As Wisp studied the napkin, Titus stood and walked away.

The small cabin stood surrounded by trees, on the summit of an isolated mountaintop, on a tiny island in the Pacific Ocean. With Wisp's resources, she probably could have hired a helicopter to fly her up there. But being the adventurous type, she rented a sailboat from the mainland, then hiked up the mountain. As she reached the peak and saw the cabin in the distance, she was charmed by the picturesque beauty of the scene before her.

It was a simple stone cabin, not much bigger than Wisp's garage back home. She wondered if Titus had built it with his own two hands. He'd certainly had time to. Did he own this island? Did he live here full-time? She doubted the cabin had electricity or plumbing, so surely he only stayed here when he wanted to get away from it all.

She didn't have to wonder if he was home. The closer she got to the building, the more she felt him. She was sure he felt her presence too. Upon reaching the door, she raised her hand to knock, but the door opened. "You came," Titus said, and gave her a hug. Wisp wasn't sure they were really that close, but she hugged him back anyway. "Please, come inside," he said.

A few minutes later, they sat at a small table, enjoying some tea. It turned out the cabin did have electricity, thanks to some solar panels in the back. It had been a month since their last meeting, and they made small talk, catching each other up, and dancing around the elephant in the room.

Finally, Titus could stand it no longer. "Well, have you decided?"

Wisp sighed. "Yes and no." Titus said nothing, just waited for her to continue. "Yes, I will be happy to die with you. But only when I'm ready. There's still a lot I want to do. There are so many lives I could live. I want to be an astronaut someday. Maybe not in this lifetime, but someday. I could..."

Titus shook his head. "So what are you talking, another century? Two? I can't stand this anymore, Wisp. I'm going crazy here."

Wisp tried to say something comforting, but her lips were going numb.

"Don't you get it? Your hesitation is going to cost lives. I told you, I've lost faith in humanity. If I have to stay in this universe much longer, I'll lose the last shred of goodwill I have left. Nothing matters anyway, so I might as well enjoy my immortality. I'll become a mass murderer. Or an evil overlord."

Wisp could no longer move her body at all. *What was in that tea?* she thought.

"Good thing I didn't leave it up to you. There are enough explosives in this cabin to vaporize us both. I didn't want it to be this way, Wisp. I wish you could have seen reason, and arrived at this by choice." He walked over to the sink, out of Wisp's view. She tried to turn her head, but she couldn't even move her eyes. She heard a cabinet door open, and the sound of something heavy being picked up.

Titus stepped back into view, holding a large plastic box with an antenna on it. There was a silver lever on the box's side. Titus leaned in toward her and kissed her on the lips. "Goodbye, my love," he said, and flipped the lever.

The explosion blew the top off of the mountain. Across the bay, people thought a volcano had erupted. The site smoked for days. No survivors were found.

Fourteen years later…

Not a hint of the cabin remained. The site was just a big pile of rubble, surrounded by trees. Wisp surveyed the area, wondering if Titus had finally found his peace. Of course, he might be completely healed by now, and on his way to becoming a villain as he'd threatened. She'd cross that bridge when she came to it.

Concluding her visit, Wisp took the time to set a bouquet of flowers on the ground, as close as possible to where she estimated the cabin had been. She closed her eyes, spent a moment in silence, and did something she had rarely done in any of her lives… She said a short prayer. For a moment, she almost thought she could still feel his presence. Finally, she walked away and climbed down the mountain.

Had she glanced behind her as she left the grounds, she might have seen a man emerge from the surrounding trees to pick up the flowers.

03.04   *Among the Stars*

ED.02347.06.19

Excerpt from the highly encrypted personal logs of Wexla Saurel Priviz, space explorer.

Thursday, 1700 hours, finds me sitting crossways in the pilot seat, legs hanging over one armrest, playing pinball on a datapad in my lap. I'm on a roll, I've got an extra ball locked and I've just achieved multi-ball. Then the unthinkable happens: triple drain, right down the center. In frustration I nearly throw the datapad across the cockpit. But I don't. Instead I calmly pause the game and adjust the cigarette in my mouth. I don't smoke. Once they discovered a way to make those healthy, fluoride cigarettes actually taste good, it seems like half the people on Earth took up the habit. But not me. Mine's not even lit, I just have it because it reminds me of my wife. It's been months since I've seen her. I hope I can go back soon.

It's hilarious, I took this job because I wanted some solitude. I've had trouble relating to humanity these days. Then, between missions, I met her. The woman with whom I wanted to spend the rest of this life. Now I only see her two months out of the year, if that.

I've been riding the warpstream for the better part of a

year. It's a dangerous way to travel, but that's how we find new habitable planets. Warp into random points in the universe, and hope you don't appear inside a star.

Okay, okay, I'm making it sound more dangerous than it really is. While the warpstream is pretty random, it specifically scans for masses of gravity when deciding where to drop you. It's designed to look for planet-sized gravity distortions, and to spit you out at a safe distance from them. So the chances of actually winding up inside a celestial body are pretty slim... but not zero.

Hopefully you find something good and place a beacon, so the next ships can home on it more easily. Eventually they build a warp gate so people can travel there safely.

My supplies are at less than half, and if I don't hit paydirt soon I might have to cryo back anyway. Whenever I find myself brooding like this, missing everything I've left behind, I invariably start humming an ancient Elton John song. He's right, it is lonely out in space. Sending out thousands of single-pilot vessels, as opposed to a small number of colossal exploration starships, was supposed to increase the odds of success. But it does have its drawbacks. Disgusted with myself - after all, no one forced me to accept this mission - I return to my game.

But only for a moment. A loud beep emits from the control panel beside me, startling me into losing my next ball. I instantly sit upright and examine the computer readout. And there it is. A solar system. I might be able to go back home sooner than expected. There is the familiar but still-jolting shudder as I drop back into realspace, and then I start scanning for habitable planets. Of course, the odds of finding a planet that's immediately habitable are virtually nil, there's always some amount of terraforming that has to be - hello, what's this? Breathable atmosphere, two-thirds water, stable weather patterns... I guess I know which one to check out first.

As the craft starts its automatic descent, I make preparations. I remove my flightsuit and pull on the body glove. Covering every inch of my body up to my chin, this thin fabric is both heat and cold resistant, and can filter out any harmful biotoxins while still allowing my skin to breathe. It even monitors my heart rate and other vital statistics. Next I put on my body armor. It's light and form-fitting, but it's strong. Built into the armor and helmet are weapons, scanning equipment, a jet propulsion system, air supply, communications, and a music player, without which I truly could not survive. I finish donning my suit just as the ship sets down. At least I know the ground's stable. The hatch opens, the ladder descends, and I climb downward. I step off the ladder-

-and into paradise. The sky is a calm shade of lavender-gray, with the occasional pink cloud coasting by. The ground is covered with reddish sand, giving way to dark clay here and there. The vegetation that surrounds me is serene and beautiful, with white-barked trees that are barely taller than I am. In the distance I can hear the twittering calls of some sort of animal. So obviously this sphere supports life. I do a bioscan. Several animals in the vicinity, none of them larger than a cat. I see one of them now. It resembles a koala, but it's only the size of a guinea pig. It scampers up to me, and I reach down and pet it. It nuzzles against my boot, making a sound similar to purring. This is beyond trusting. This is an animal that has never seen a predator in its life.

The bioscanners tell me that the air is breathable, time to put that to the test. A press of the button and my faceplate slides up into my helmet. I take a deep breath, and it's heaven. The air is clean, cleaner than I've ever breathed. Earth never had air this clean. I catch the sweet scent of some kind of flora, and my heart races. The air is cool but not cold against my skin. I walk around, leaving the purring animal behind. I keep telling myself I'm just doing my job, scouting the area and making a judgment as to the planet's habitability, but I know that I'm really just enjoying the scenery. This, right here, this is why I do this job.

I find a beach. The water is so clear I can see the bottom. An impulse hits me - completely against regulations, but I'm compelled. I scan the water, it's safe. Did I expect anything less? No toxins, no chemicals, not even dangerous aquatic lifeforms, just pure H2O. I take a quick glance around, as if there were actually a possibility of someone watching. Then I take off the body armor, followed by the body glove. I test the water with my toes. Perfect. Of course. Next thing I know, I'm in it up to my neck and having the time of my life. I swim, I splash, I float on my back. It's the most enjoyable experience I've had on this entire mission.

Eventually I do heed my responsibilities and grudgingly put my biosuit back on. I make my way back to the ship and begin to file my report.

"Solar System 31526, Sector 17, Subsection G2, 4th Planet"
"Geologic State: Stable"
"Atmosphere: Earthlike"

Right. Earthlike? This is better than Earth. Much better. I finish the report, citing detail after perfect detail, until finally my finger hovers over the send button. This is it, a successful mission, I can finally go home. I look out the viewscreen, at this incredible planet, and and think about what it will look like in ten years. Maybe it won't be so bad. Architecture these days is rather pleasing to look at, and we don't pollute the air as much as we used to. There will certainly be fewer of those interesting trees, but some will survive. And those friendly animals... Okay, so maybe they won't always be as trusting as they are right now. But they'll survive. All in all, this will be a great place for the human race to perpetuate its rapidly increasing population. A place to start over, and maybe do things right for once. So...

My finger hovers a second more, and finally I hit the erase button. I'll keep looking, but I'll remember this place. For now, maybe I'll just keep this planet to myself.

03.05   *Corton*

ED.02484.07.02

As soon as Wisp entered the room, people stared in disbelief. Their eyes pierced her like blunt razors - intended to hurt but not containing any real power. After all, Wisp didn't respect these people, and she wasn't bothered by their opinions. So what if she wasn't quite dressed for this occasion? It was too stuffy a crowd anyway. All their elegance was just a facade. None of these people knew what it was like to work for a paycheck. It was a room full of unappreciative inheritors gifted with undeserved wealth. Granted, Wisp was the wealthiest of the bunch, but she had also spent many years of her life as a pauper, so she was thankful for every credit she possessed.

But maybe she was being too critical. It was a special occasion, an exclusive party, and an elegant club. Anyone not wearing a twelve-hundred-credit outfit was going to receive stares. If Wisp had entered wearing jeans and a T-shirt, she might have been asked to leave. But in her current outfit? Likely, the only thing preventing them from hurling a volley of stones at her was their utter shock... and a lack of stones.

It didn't matter. Wisp had faced worse crowds, ones who threw actual daggers, not just mental ones. And like them or not, these people needed to hear what Wisp had to say. She stepped up onto the stage and stood behind the microphone. "Ahem," she said. Before, only the people closest to the door had seen her. Now, the entire room - three hundred people at least - stared at her, mouths open. Wisp stood there on the stage, framed by the giant window which offered a spectacular view of the beach.

Wisp was in a very vulnerable state. She wore a ripped nightgown that was too short to cover her underwear. Though the length barely mattered, as her gown was nearly transparent in this light.

Again, her clothing was trivial. As soon as they heard the news, the audience would forget all about how she was dressed. Wisp gulped, gave a half smile of apology, and said, "Ladies and gentlemen, I have something of an announcement to make. We're going to crash."

There was a collective gasp of disbelief from the audience. And why not? When a woman dressed like this addresses this sort of audience, why would she be believed? Much simpler to assume she was drunk or crazy.

Wisp continued, "I'm serious. There's been a malfunction. This ship is on a collision course with the planet." As if to accentuate her point, the window - actually a giant video screen - flickered and went out. Similar windows around the room did the same. Soon they came back on and revealed what was really going on beyond the walls of this glitzy country club. The blackness of space, dotted with bright stars, was interrupted by a blue-green ball in the center of the screen. And it was getting closer.

It was supposed to get closer. That was the destination of this space-faring yacht. It was a pleasure cruise, for the cultural elite. The destination was intended to be Golora, a world of beauty and splendor. It was to spend two weeks there, during which time its passengers would sleep on the blue sandy beaches, swim in the crystal clear waters, and make love in the warm red snow. There was to be mountain climbing, surfing, anti-gravity parasailing, hang gliding, skiing, snowboarding, bungee jumping, and whatever other sports these spoiled passengers enjoyed doing. In all likelihood, the majority of the passengers would probably just work on their tans.

However, they were approaching this planet way too fast. Once they reached orbit, they were supposed to spend an entire day circling Golora, so that the passengers could appreciate the view from space. But it looked as if they were approaching the planet at top speed, with no intention of slowing. A wave of panic began to spread through the crowd of snobs.

"Stay calm, everyone," Wisp told them. "We've got plenty of time, and there are more than enough escape ships located throughout the vessel." Immediately people started pushing and climbing over each other, trying to get out of the room. In a few seconds, the room was empty. "Well, that went well," Wisp said to the empty room.

Wisp's real name was Wrathia Skarr Penumbra. But she'd long ago given up keeping track of her birth names, and insisted people call her "Wisp" in every lifetime. She could remember every one of her lives, and she retained all the skills she had learned from them. This was why she wasn't afraid to die now. She knew that if she died, she would simply be reincarnated a few years later, and even if she didn't, she had lived enough.

In this particular lifetime, Wisp was an undercover agent for the Galactic Nations who often posed as a wealthy socialite. She was a Nithari, a species of humanoids with pale skin and pointed ears. Most Nithari were bald, and yet Wisp possessed a full head of hair in her usual shade of red. She would usually cover by saying that she was half human, because no one would have believed the truth.

For this mission, Wisp had boarded the spaceyacht Bacchus, posing as a rich tourist. There had been several yacht robberies lately, ones very similar to the one going on now. In each of these events, something had caused the passengers to evacuate, after which the entire yacht had disappeared. The reasons for evacuation differed; in the first one, the environmental systems had been shut down, causing the ship to lose life support. The next robbery involved the threat of an asteroid collision after a pleasure ship's navigation systems had mysteriously locked, the following one occurred when a cruise vessel's engines overheated and threatened to explode.

In each instance, after the passengers escaped, the ship recovered and flew off for parts unknown. Naturally their homing beacons ceased to work, and these disasters always occurred in areas of space where police monitoring was nonexistent. Also, these robberies always happened on vessels full of wealthy travelers. This meant that not only did the criminals make off with an expensive new ship, but they also had access to whatever belongings the passengers happened to leave in their rooms.

This was the fourth such robbery, and Wisp intended for it to be the last. Since the last theft, many such luxury liners had begun traveling with police escorts. While this successfully deterred more hijackings, it also prevented anyone from catching the thieves. While pursuing this investigation, Wisp made sure she only traveled the least protected cruise lines. Wisp had been to the planet Golora seven times this year, and she hadn't so much as taken in the view. Until a few hours ago, Wisp had had every indication that this was going to be another wasted trip. That was, until she had been woken in her room by someone trying to kill her in her sleep.

Of course she'd dispatched the assassin quickly, then immediately headed to the bridge. What she'd found wasn't a pretty sight. The bridge crew was dead, and the controls were locked. The ship was on a collision course with Golora.

And that's why Wisp was here now. Apparently Wisp was the only one who had turned in early; the entire complement of passengers appeared to have been in the ballroom when she had arrived. Just to be on the safe side, Wisp used the intercom to announce a general evacuation message to the entire ship. Satisfied that the people were safe, Wisp sought a good hiding spot for the next phase of her plan. This ship wasn't going to crash. Not really. And that attempted assassin couldn't have been working alone. Sooner or later, someone would show up and take control of the ship. Wisp intended to hide out and learn where their main operation was.

Problem was, they obviously knew she was here. When the assassin failed to report back, it was possible that they would abort the mission. Or at the very least, alter it. Wisp needed to know more before she could continue. She headed back to her room to interrogate her would-be killer. She had left him there, unconscious and tied up.

She returned to her cabin, only to find the assassin was gone. He couldn't have revived that quickly on his own. He must have been rescued. That complicated things. Now Wisp knew that she was not alone on this vessel. Worse, the criminals knew of her presence as well. For all intents and purposes, the mission was botched.

But she wasn't going to give up. Surely she could turn this to her advantage somehow. *Think.* They wouldn't take this vessel back to their base of operations if they knew Wisp was hiding on it. And if she evacuated, they still wouldn't go because they'd be afraid she was tracking them. But - if Wisp allowed herself to be captured, they might take her with them. And then she simply had to escape.

But... she didn't want them to know that she was getting captured on purpose. She couldn't just throw up her hands and surrender, or they would know it was what she wanted. So, Wisp made her way to the bridge, all the while acting as if she were trying to stay unseen, but intentionally failing at stealth. She entered the bridge and faced the control panel. Almost immediately she felt a gun in her back. Wisp threw her hands in the air and surrendered.

"Turn around," a voice said.

Wisp turned to face her foe. He was dark-skinned and sported several facial scars. He was dressed in black, and his skin-tight uniform revealed a muscular frame. "Who are you?" he demanded.

"I'm just a passenger," Wisp explained. "I was asleep when the alarms went off. I couldn't find the escape pods." She knew the thief would see right through this, but that was what she wanted.

"Sit down over there," the pirate said, gesturing towards a chair with his gun. That was all Wisp needed. In the half-second that the gun wasn't pointed at her, Wisp kicked it out of his hand and punched him in the face. The pirate retaliated by slamming into her stomach with his shoulder. Wisp kneed him in the chest, but the thief picked her up and threw her across the room. Wisp actually had to let herself be thrown, and she hoped it wasn't obvious. She hit the wall hard and pretended to be down for the count. She slowly opened her eyes to see that the gun was now in her face.

Soon the ship was on its way to parts unknown, staffed by a full complement of pirates. Wisp spent most of the trip tied up in the captain's room, which she shared with Corton Taush, the man who had "captured" her. He was the leader of this band of pirates, and he spent many hours interrogating her during the trip. Wisp, of course, would tell him nothing. But he never tried torture. Either he sensed that she wasn't the kind of person who would give in to torture, or he just didn't feel that it was part of his job. He kept telling her, "It will go much easier if you tell me who you're working for now. Once we arrive, my boss will be a much more difficult interrogator." Wisp responded by asking questions of her own, such as where they were going or who his boss was. Unwilling to answer Wisp's questions, he would change the subject and they'd talk about other things.

They spent a good deal of time talking. Corton was oddly genteel for a pirate, and easy to talk to. He was keen-minded, but untrusting and dedicated to his mission. He refused to untie Wisp's hands for any reason, even for a moment. He fed her by hand personally, using extra-long utensils just in case she tried to bite him. When she had to use a restroom, he would call in two armed escorts, and the three of them would watch her as she did her business. So it wasn't as if any romance was brewing.

But under the circumstances, Corton treated her quite well. He realized how unique Wisp was, even if he didn't know how she came to be. He was fascinated by her intellect, as well as her physical skills - he'd realized early on that Wisp had allowed herself to be captured. They had many common interests, and they both knew that in another time and place, they could have been friends.

The trip took several weeks. They dared not use any official warp gates, and therefore they went many days out of their way to use "no questions asked" gates. Corton interrogated Wisp less frequently, now convinced that she would never betray her government. Wisp also asked Corton fewer questions about their destination, and centered her inquiries on why he had chosen this way of life. At first he was evasive, but gradually he started to open up.

"I have kids to feed," he revealed one day, tired of eluding the question.

"You?" It wasn't that Wisp thought pirates couldn't have kids. It was more that she couldn't imagine choosing such a dangerous life when one had family to live for. Then she remembered some of her past lives and realized her own hands weren't entirely clean.

Corton nodded. "Two sons... well, a son and a daughter. It's complicated."

She looked around the cell. "We appear to have time."

"...Okay. Well, I had one son with my ex-wife and another son with my ex-girlfriend."

Wisp smirked. "Tell me these relationships weren't at the same time."

"No, the girlfriend was later," Corton said. "My first son… I went off and left him… her. She's transgender. I hate to say it, but she's part of the reason I split with my wife. There were signs when she was younger. First we ignored them, then we fought over them. Eventually we were arguing all the time, and I couldn't take it any more. So I walked out."

Wisp nodded, trying not to judge. "Go on."

"But I gave it some thought, did some research… I guess I still don't really understand it, but if this is what she needs to be happy, well, it is what it is. I tried sending her an apology, but she has me blocked. All I want is to make it up to her, and let her know it's okay to be who she is. I've been saving up, someday I'll quit pirating for good and spend some time with both my kids. If they'll have me."

Wisp smiled. "I bet they do. They might resent you at first for being absent so long, but family is important. They'll come around."

"Do you have any children?"

"Now that's complicated," Wisp said.

"We have time."

"Y…yes. I have had children. But that was lifetimes ago."

"Wow," Corton said. "You must be older than you look."

"You have no idea."

They finally arrived. It was a space station that functioned as a chopshop, with all manner of equipment for processing stolen vehicles. It orbited a mostly uninhabited planet, where a major construction project was underway.

The yacht was thoroughly searched for valuables, then stripped for parts. Wisp, now confined to a cell within the station, didn't get any visitors for several days. Her hands were no longer bound, but there was a camera on her at all times, and there really was no way out of the cell. It was just four bare walls, a plain bed, and a toilet. The air ducts were simply a bunch of tiny holes in the wall, and the door must have been half a meter thick. Twice a day, a slot in the door would open, and a plate of food would slide through. If Wisp was too close to the door when the slot opened, an electric shock would fire from a hole in the door and knock her back.

Then, a full week after their arrival, she met Corton's boss. She was doing push-ups when an electronic voice told her to stand away from the door. When the door opened, a pair of armed troopers entered first, pointing their weapons at Wisp's head. A third pirate came in and tied Wisp up. Finally, a large, pale-skinned man entered the cell. He was a full head taller than Corton and much more muscular. He was a Sethran, which was an offshoot of the human race. He had close-cropped white hair, and a large scar which extended from his right cheek down to the base of his neck. "I am Commander Gerrolk," he said. "You will tell me what I want to know, now."

Wisp was taken to another cell, stripped, and strapped to a table. An ominous-looking device was suspended over her by a mechanical arm. It featured an array of tools, including needles, electrodes, blades, and oddly-shaped spiked probing devices. The machine had obviously been built for torture, and it did its job well, as Wisp found out over the next few days. However, she did not crack.

There was no way to escape, so Wisp endured the torture, slowly gathering information of her own from her captors. They didn't seem to be worried about her finding out too much, as none of them expected her to leave this station alive. Gerrolk in particular enjoyed bragging about his operation. From him, Wisp learned that they were in the Linanani system, that these small jobs were only temporary, and that some of the pirates on this station were actually scientists. They were using the money they made to build a giant gravity cannon, capable of destroying an entire planet. Apparently it was going to take a decade or two to complete the construction of the weapon.

And then, after about two weeks of interrogation, Corton came to see her. "I've got to get you out of here," he said, as he turned off the motion sensors and released her bonds. Rubbing her wrists, Wisp sat up and asked him why he was helping her.

"Gerrolk is going to kill you tonight," he answered. "He was going to hold out for a ransom, but since he doesn't even know what agency you work for, that's not going to work. He thinks you're learning too much about our operation, and you're no longer worth the risk. The bastard can't see what a wonder you are. It would be a great tragedy if someone like you were to die." He paused, then continued, "I wouldn't even work for him if I didn't have to..."

"Thanks," Wisp answered, and she kissed him on the cheek. It just a light peck, but they both felt an odd spark. It was nothing romantic, it felt more familial than anything. For just a moment, they pondered the strange energy that seemed to hang in the air between them.

"No time," Corton finally said, gently pushing her away. He opened the door and found himself face-to-face with Gerrolk. The Commander pushed Corton back into the room. A pair of guards followed Gerrolk into the cell, and the door locked behind them. Corton and Wisp raised their hands.

"So, betrayer," Gerrolk said, pointing his gun at Corton's face, "Any last words?"

"Go screw yourself," he answered. And then Corton's head disappeared in a spray of crimson, splattering Wisp with blood.

Wisp was wide-eyed with horror. "You... you... you..." she stammered, and then launched herself at Gerrolk. She got in a couple of good hits, but in her rage, she forgot about the guards. They shot her once in the leg, again in the arm, and once more in the side. Then they pulled her off of Gerrolk and placed her back on the table, once again engaging the steel bonds.

Gerrolk got back to his feet, wiping blood off of his mouth. "Such spirit," he laughed. He grabbed the arm of the torture machine and activated several of the devices at once. Six vibrating blades and three spinning drills of various sizes now protruded from the arm. "Last chance," he said. "Who do you work for?"

Blinded by pain, Wisp could only say, "He... had children..."

Gerrolk took the arm of the machine and thrust it into Wisp's chest. As her vision dimmed, she saw the torture device removed from her gaping chest cavity, and come at her again, this time at her face. She was dead before it reached her.

Gerrolk was pleased. After fourteen years, Doctor Yxyllthyll's weapon was nearly ready, and it would be finished way ahead of schedule. He had already signed a deal with the Grunthians, and soon Gerrolk would be able to retire to a life of luxury on Valos. He stood inside the cannon's control room, monitoring system functions. All systems normal. He kept glancing at the viewscreen, anxiously awaiting the arrival of the Grunthians, who were coming to inspect the site and finalize the payment. It was silly, really; the long-range sensors would alert him to the Grunthians' approach long before he'd be able to pick them up visually. But he kept glancing at it, just the same.

Finally, the scanners bleeped, and he knew his buyers were on the way. He contacted the approaching ship, and received an automated response instructing him to prepare the landing bay for their arrival. Apparently the Grunthians weren't much for chit-chat. Gerrolk entered the control codes, and the landing bay doors opened. Gerrolk looked at the viewscreen once again, and he now saw the Grunthian trade ship, headed straight for him. At their current speed, they would land in mere minutes. Good. He hurriedly finished up some minor system tweakings, trying to make everything absolutely perfect for his clients.

The scanners bleeped again, this time more loudly. Gerrolk turned back to the screen and saw the Grunthian ship still approaching. Fast. Much too fast. And it wasn't headed for the landing bay, but rather straight at the cannon's control room itself. Gerrolk screamed and started to prep the station's weapons systems, but he knew there wouldn't be time. Suddenly the ship let loose with its six forward energy cannons and four napleen torpedo launchers. As the station exploded around him, Gerrolk didn't even bother trying to find a place to hide. There was no point. Instead, he simply stood there, wondering why the Grunthians had suddenly decided to destroy the weapon he had built for them.

Then his viewscreen flickered on, displaying the cockpit of the trade ship. Sitting in the command chair was a red-haired human girl, waving at him. Gerrolk blinked, perplexed. Even as a nearby wall exploded inward, showering him with a rain of piercing metal shards, Gerrolk thought more of this puzzle than of the pain. Finally, as he bled to death in the collapsing structure, Gerrolk's last thoughts were of how oddly-familiar that girl had looked, especially her hair...

On board the Grunthian trade ship, thirteen-year-old Wivveena Seela Pilzon - "Wisp" to her friends - took another pass at the structure, surveying the damage she had done. The site was a total loss, there was nothing that could be salvaged. As she set a course back to the nearest warp gate, Wisp thought about Corton, and how unfulfilling it was to have avenged his death. Wisp had never looked at revenge as something sweet, but as a dirty task - one sometimes necessary to balance out good and evil.

Then Wisp thought about Corton's children. She had no idea who they were or if they'd even survived childhood.

She wished she had a way to contact them, so she could let them know of their father's bravery. They had to be adults by now, and Wisp wished the best for them, whoever they were. Really, that's all she could do.

She wondered whether or not the gravity cannon would ever be rebuilt. Of course it would. The scientists who designed the weapon were probably still out there somewhere, thinking up even more destructive creations.

Finally, Wisp's thoughts turned to those of home. She had yet another childhood to finish, with parents who loved her and were probably sick with worry right now. She had told them that she was going to spend the night with a friend, but that had been two weeks ago. By now there was probably a district-wide search for her going on. She would have to come up with a good explanation as to where she'd been. But that wasn't a problem, she had time.

One way or another, she always had time.

03.06   Vermon

ED.02508.01.18

There you are, Wisp thought, as her scanners picked up the tech. The Southern hemisphere of Valos was still mostly unpopulated, and the cryotube stood out like a sore thumb. She landed her craft and approached the wreckage.

It had been six years since her most recent reawakening. Her previous life had been short but eventful. After destroying the gravity cannon in 2498, she lived another four years, only to die at seventeen in a random spaceship crash. And then she reawakened in this body in 2502, in the same year she died for once.

This body's first eleven years had actually only taken a few days, though she had experienced the years in real-time. When Wisp's memories had come flooding back into her mind, it had also triggered the realization that she was living in an artificial environment. After rescuing her clone donor and escaping Tena's space station, Wisp had spent the next few years exploring the galaxy and discovering the innate abilities of this new body.

She had visited Alterra Sarr a few times over the years. Wisp was curious about Auroran culture, and while she didn't identify with it, it was fascinating information nonetheless.

Wisp had been to Valos several times since her rebirth. On her first visit, she'd recognized it immediately. She had discovered it more than a century before when she'd worked as a space explorer. She'd deleted her logs at the time, but apparently the planet was eventually discovered anyway. It was used as a prison at first, then there was a revolt led by Teykor Vermon, and eventually the planet claimed its independence. She'd seen pictures of Vermon and, much like the planet, she'd immediately recognized him.

On her last visit to Valos, she'd felt a presence. She knew he was somewhere on this planet, and she had to find him. History said Teykor Vermon had been dead since 2500, but Wisp knew better. And there he was now, crawling out of the wreckage of a cryotube. He was still covered in burns and other wounds. He must have been torn to pieces for it to have taken this long to heal.

Eight years earlier, Lord Vermon survived the explosion of his space station by hiding in a cryotube, the type used to transport prisoners and slaves as cargo. The cryotube had ruptured in the explosion, but remained mostly intact. Vermon spent a few years in orbit around Valos, with no oxygen, in a constant state of death and regeneration. Recently the cryotube fell out of orbit, crashing into the planet. Vermon had just now recovered enough to move.

Wisp wondered if he would even have the mental capacity to communicate. The last eight years had to have been maddening. He surprised her by recognizing her right off. "H... hello, Wisp," he said, struggling to his feet. He was nude and covered in blood, but he seemed to know who he was.

There was some spare clothing in Wisp's shuttle, which she gave to him, along with some water. They sat together for a while, not speaking, while Wisp put some ointment on Vermon's wounds. She needed his head to be as clear as possible before she made her proposition. She knew this man had a capacity for great good or great evil, and she wouldn't take advantage of him without knowing where his moral compass pointed now.

As they stared into space, Wisp flipped a dagger over and over in her hands. After more than an hour of silence, Vermon spoke first. Looking at Wisp's dagger, he said, "You helped me so you could kill me?"

"I helped you so I could give you the choice," Wisp said. "Rumor has it that you're the leader of an evil criminal organization."

He nodded, stared off into space for a moment, then broke down in tears. For a moment, he was the same man she'd had lunch with in 1988.

"I fell off the wagon. More than a century ago. I hadn't seen a new version of you in so long… I thought maybe your curse had ended. But mine kept going. Centuries of watching civilizations rise and fall, people making the same mistakes over and over again… I'd had enough. I used my abilities to seize control. I started having children again, with no regard for their future or well-being. I've taken so many lives… so many… I even considered destroying Earth."

Wisp felt a twinge of guilt. He'd warned her that he might turn homicidal if he wasn't stopped. Maybe she should have supported him a few centuries ago. But then, his plan to kill them both hadn't worked anyway, so it's not like her support would have made any difference.

He wiped the tears from his eyes. "It's so good to see you again," he said, hugging her. "I've lost my way without you…"

"There, there," Wisp said hesitantly. "I know. I've been following your career. I've even cleaned up a few of your messes. But I wasn't about to approach you until I knew I could do so safely. But I'm here now, and I'm giving you the choice. Do you want to continue your immortality?"

"You mean, you can break the curse?" His face was a combination of hope and terror.

"Let's say that I can. Do you still want it broken?"

Vermon thought long and hard before replying. "No. I'm at a place in my life right now where people respect me, and I live in luxury. I've worked too hard to lose it now. I put in my years of suffering to get here, and I've earned the right to enjoy my retirement."

Wisp wasn't sure how to respond. Finally, she said, "Then disband the Inner Eye, or whatever it's called these days. Hurt no one else. Retire on your ill-gotten wealth. In a few hundred years when it starts to peter out, seek me out and I'll end your curse for you."

His previous grief was now gone. "Disband the— Do you hear yourself? The Inner Eye is my greatest triumph! The people I've hurt aren't important. Only people like us matter. People with potential!"

Wisp sighed. "I was afraid of this. Titus... or Teykor or whatever... You know I can't let you live. You're too powerful and too cruel."

"Wisp. You have to understand, we're better than them. We can make the universe a better place, both for ourselves and for them. Help me. You'll see. Just let me show y— Urgh!"

She stabbed him in the chest. It wasn't sporting, and it wasn't how she'd wanted this conversation to end, but he'd had enough chances.

Vermon scowled. "Did you really think that would stop me? I survived a space station explosion and you think a little knife is..." Then his face turned gray, and his body went slack.

In her spare time, Wisp had spent the last few lifetimes researching nanotechnology. She had constructed a knife that, once it pierced Vermon's skin, would destroy any nanites that attempted to repair the damage. All of his nanites would be drawn to the wound, only to be deactivated upon drawing near.

Wisp watched the body for several minutes. No sign of healing. No twitching, nothing. She pulled another device out of her backpack and used it to scan his corpse. No active nanites were detected. What's more, she couldn't "feel" him anymore. Her nanites and his had always shared a link, even before she knew he existed. When he slipped away, Wisp could feel the connection go slack.

Just to be sure, she burned the corpse. Then she put the remains in a body bag, packed up her ship, and flew away. Once she was in space, she launched Vermon's bones into a star. Then she returned to one of her homes. This was her favorite, back on Earth, a tiny cottage in one of the planet's few remaining forests.

Wisp pulled out the knife and stared at the blade. Now that Vermon was no longer a threat to the galaxy, she felt lighter. For years – lifetimes, even – she'd felt like she'd left the bathwater running somewhere in the universe.

She turned the knife over and over in her hands. She could relax now. She could end her own curse. And yet, this was the most powerful form she'd ever had. This body was almost supernaturally agile. She could see in the dark, alter her skin tone, absorb light and sound… and that was just at seventeen. Imagine how powerful she would be with a few more years of training. She could be a force of great good in the universe.

But could she resist the temptation to seize power, or would she end up like Vermon? Her intentions were honorable, but would they always be? Once she'd tasted power, would it be so easy to remain benevolent? She was nothing like Vermon, she knew that in her heart. But then, Vermon had been like a different person each time she'd met him. Immortality had a way of corrupting a mind. Could her own heart be so easily swayed?

She was enjoying her current life. Her time with the Bloodhunters had been fun. She didn't need the money from bounty hunting, but she liked tracking down criminals. It was honest work, and it exercised every skill she had. But it also felt like a step backward.

Now that Vermon was gone, she felt like she'd fulfilled her destiny. She'd defeated the final boss, and now she was sitting through the end credits. Would any challenge in her future lives compare? Was there a bigger threat to look forward to, or was she just going to tread water for another dozen lifetimes? And what if the universe needed her again, but she'd already chosen to die?

She spent hours staring at the knife, weighing the pros and cons, assessing her susceptibility to temptation. End the curse? One more life? Two? Keep going forever? She pondered the possibilities well into the night.

Until finally, she made her decision.

Author's Notes

I don't write novels. I write collections of short stories. My attention span is on the unpredictable side, and I'm not sure I have the concentration to write a single novel-length story.

But I do like writing, maybe a little too much. In real life, I'm painfully shy, and people who don't know me very well get the impression that I never speak. But stick a keyboard in front of me, and in twenty minutes I'll churn out a thousand-word blog on the most pointless of subjects. My friends and I send each other e-mails that feel more like book chapters, but when we meet in person, I grunt and nod my head more than I actually talk.

When I dusted off my bounty hunter stories to rework them into a novel, I realized they weren't quite long enough to make a book. I'd already written the beginning and the climax, and I wanted to fill the rest in with short stories. So I decided I would keep adding solo stories, showing off the adventures of various bounty hunters, and set them about a month apart. Once I had enough to fill a two-year timespan, I'd call it a book. The problem was, it still didn't feel long enough. I finally decided to look into just how long a novel should be.

So, according to a few internet searches, a novel has to be at least 50,000 words. Any less than that, and it's a novella, or a short story if it has fewer than 20,000 words. For a new author, they recommend your first book be between 80,000 and 110,000 words. So I looked at my own book's word count. Was it long enough to publish yet? Mine sat at around 169,000 words. Honestly, that blew my mind. It didn't feel that long. Just for fun, I compared it to a few of my favorite books by other authors, and most of them were in the 150,000 words range.

Well, I didn't write this to get rich, and I don't care if it gets a couple of bad reviews over its length. But… I have a tendency to turn down good advice, and it often leads to disaster. So after a lot of debate, I decided to break Book 1 into two parts. Note that I had already written most of Book 2 by this point, so what was originally Book 2 is now Book 3. I had to move a couple of chapters around to make it work, and write a new intro story for Book 2. So "I Know Who You Are" is the most recently written of all the stories in this book, even newer than those in the upcoming Book 3.

I'm honestly not sure if it works better this way. It might have been better to keep it one big novel and remove a few of the weaker short stories. But I'm a pack rat, and the thought of removing entire chapters makes me cringe. Besides, I really wanted the reader to understand how these characters had come to rely on each other before the climax tore the group apart again.

There is another reason for the month-long spaces between the chapters. I originally envisioned this as a comic book series, rather than a novel. Unfortunately, I can't draw worth a damn. If such a thing were ever to come to pass, I wanted plenty of room in the timeline to insert new adventures. Again, I didn't write this to become rich and famous, and I don't expect it to get made into movies. But if anyone wants to write any Bloodhunters fanfiction, comics, or other art, I would be delighted to see your work.

Xine Fury

Special Thanks

I would like to thank:

...My amazing spouse, KJ, who continues to give me the space and encouragement I need to be myself.

...Cyanimations, who created the cover.

...Kaius Coolman, who read my books with great fervor and gave me some excellent advice.

About the Author

Xine Fury is made of meat.

Also By Xine Fury

The following books by Xine Fury are also available:
    Bloodhunters v1: Bad Blood
    Bloodhunters v3: New Blood
    Geek Cutes
    Rainbow Nightmares
    Gender Rolls
    Side Quests
    Nomads of Zyden

Find them here: bit.ly/XineFury